HOUSE OF ILLUSIONS

RUBY JEAN JENSEN

HOUSE OF MIRRORS– HOUSE OF ILLUSION

"Jodi," Blane whispered, reaching back and shoving at her with his hand. "There's some—some strange clowns in here. Get out, Jodi. Run!"

She started to obey his command, but then froze, as she watched the clowns that came out of the mirrored darkness.

The cheerfulness of their costumes, the ruffles, the big, fluffy buttons, the funny stockings and shoes, all the frivolities, ended at their necks. The eyes that looked at them out of their hideous faces were slitted and blank and deadly. The clowns were coming single file, one after the other, down the corridor toward them. White-gloved hands were slowly rising, as if pulled by the strings of a puppeteer, and the fingers were curving inward like claws. Blane's elbow dug into Jodi's ribs. "Run!"

He was trying to save her, to get her out of this terrible place that was like something deep within the earth, a terrible place of dark mud and endlessness and putrid, decayed things—and death. Death in clowns' costumes ...

First printing: April, 1988 in the United States of America

Published by: Gayle J. Foster, Carrollton, Texas

Library of Congress Control Number: 9781951580315

Cover Artist: SelfPubBookCovers.com/Sarah

❀ Created with Vellum

PROLOGUE: 1927

Early morning light struggled with the shadows on the midway. The crowd was gone, the rides were still, the music from the merry-go-round had been replaced by the lonesome whine of the wind, and the sobs of the little girl as she ran, her short, stubby legs stumbling at times, almost causing her to fall.

She was following her daddy, who was still wearing his bright clown suit. She saw him go up the steps to the House of Illusions and disappear through the doorway.

With tears blinding her, with her hands catching splinters on the rough steps, she called out, "Daddy?

Daddy!"

But there was no answer. Behind, somewhere in their tent, was her mother, packing her bags to leave. And Daddy was going into the House of Illusions, where it would be so hard to find him.

She struggled up the steps, and into the shadows of the unlighted mirror house. Somewhere in the maze ahead she heard sounds that froze her tears. Her daddy wasn't alone. She almost turned away, fear driving her back out into the early dawn and down the steps again.

She stood still, in a corridor of mirrors.

Then she caught a glimpse of red. One of the colors in her daddy's clown suit, the color of his big, big clown mouth and the funny hair on the top of his head.

She fought her way forward, toward him, seeing dozens of little girls like herself in the mirrors, all running, their fat little arms out, their mouth hanging open, and tears sliding fresh out of their eyes. Then the clown was there too, somewhere separate from the little girls. His arms were up and there was something tiny glittering in the air in front of him, spinning, casting dark lights like darts in the mirrors, black lights, evil green, gray, swift and piercing.

Shattered by the fragments of the mirrors were all the colors—red, blue, green, purple, more colors the little girls hadn't learned—and now, suddenly, added to the colors was a great shadow falling over it all. It was coming down like a huge bird, wings spread, toward the colors of the clown suit and the spinning thing that hung in the air, hanging by a thread from the clown's white hand.

The glittering object fell from the hand of the clown and rolled, and the child saw it no more. Her eyes were on the clown suit, her daddy's costume, and the great black wings that were beating it down.

Her cries echoed along the hallways of the House of Illusions, absorbed, caught, and held. She saw the clown suit on the floor. Her daddy had fallen. The great black bird was gone.

The little girls ran, toward each other, into each other. But when she put her hands out she felt only the cold, slick glass.

She fought her way along the maze, through the mirrored corridors, and suddenly her daddy was there, at her feet. All the colors of his suit, and the funny, red, yarn hair of his head were lying in a strange, distorted heap.

She fell upon him, but felt only the hard floor of the mirror house.

She sat up, and picked up the clown suit.

It hung empty in her hands.

CHAPTER 1

JODI LOOKED OUT AT THE CLOUDS BELOW THE WINDOW OF THE BIG JET AND SAW the soft rainbows of colors, the gold and pink and lavender. She poked her sister, Amy, with her elbow.

"Amy, look. Did you ever see anything so pretty?" Amy didn't answer, and Jodi turned away from the window and looked at her. Amy's head was lowered into her arms. She was scrunched so low in her seat she seemed even smaller than Jodi, and Amy was eleven years old now, suddenly three years older than Jodi, although just a month ago there had been only two years difference in their ages. Jodi looked down upon Amy's dark blond hair helplessly. Amy was crying again. She hadn't wanted to leave their mother.

Jodi put her arms around Amy's shoulders and her face down to Amy's head.

"Amy, I'm here with you," she said, trying to find words to comfort Amy in her loneliness. "I'm going with you, Amy."

She could feel Amy's sobs in the small jerks of her sister's body, and Jodi sat with her arms around Amy, offering no more words.

The clouds beyond the window had changed. Suddenly the bright colors of the sun were gone, and a gray look had taken over, and then even the sky was gone as the clouds enveloped the plane.

Jodi had been filled with excitement at the prospect of going up in an airplane. Amy was afraid to. Jodi hadn't minded going to spend the summer with their dad, even though she didn't know him. But Amy hadn't wanted to. Amy wanted to stay with their mother and Erin, their mother's new husband, but the house was too small now because of the new baby, and the other little boy that Erin had brought with him.

Amy raised her head and leaned it back against the seat. Her eyes stared miserably past Jodi, as blue as the sky had been before the clouds filled it.

She said, "She doesn't want us anymore, Jodi. Now that she's got the new baby, and Erin and little Jimmy, she doesn't want us anymore."

Jodi said, "That's not the reason she's sending you to our dad, Amy. The reason is, she thought it would be good for us."

"The reason is," Amy shot back with bitterness and anger coming to the surface, "she doesn't have room for us. She's filled up her life with Erin and their babies. His and hers. She doesn't want us.

"The house is too little, that's all. When it's time to go to school again, we'll go back home."

"The house will still be too little. She'll never have room for us. Not anymore. Not now that she's rid of us."

"That's not true, Amy. Mama loves us. They'll get a bigger house."

"You're young yet, Jodi. But don't you know something? Women love the children of the men they love. Mama loves Erin now, and his little boy, and their own baby. She doesn't love our dad, and she doesn't love us."

"I don't believe that," Jodi said, though her heart tightened, catching a corner of the fear that lived with Amy.

"It's true."

Jodi stared at the seat ahead.

"Then," she finally said, "when I get married and have children, I'm going to stay in love with my first husband."

They were quiet, each staring at the seat ahead, Amy sitting two inches higher than Jodi, her legs longer but thinner, so that her shoes looked too large for her narrow ankles to hold. White anklets had wrinkled down, and she reached to straighten them and pull them up over legs that were beginning to need something done about the hair. Jodi watched her carefully fold her anklets down.

Jodi wore jeans, and her own socks were hidden. She saw Amy cast a look toward them, and she expected her sister to tell her to straighten her socks, but she didn't.

Amy sat back and closed her eyes, and Jodi twisted in her seat to look out at the clouds and think about the summer ahead and all the stuff that Amy had told her.

Jodi couldn't remember ever seeing their daddy, though Amy could, she had said. His name was Russel, and he and their mother had been divorced since Jodi was just a baby. Amy was only three the last time she saw him, but she could remember that he was tall and blond, like a Viking.

He had come from one of the northern states. Amy didn't know which one. Where his parents had a farm. Grandparents.

It seemed odd to think there were grandparents, and a dad, in this world whom she had never seen. She visualized the grandparents as old and gray-haired, yet when she thought about her friend's grandparents, the image changed. Mandy's grandma and grandpa were slim and lively and went to dances all the time. A lot more than Mandy's mom and dad did. Yet when Jodi tried to see her own grandparents in the image that Mandy's presented, something seemed all wrong.

She knew a little about her dad's looks. Not only had Amy described what she remembered, but then were some pictures, snapshots, taken a long time ago when she and Amy were little. In one of them a man was standing with his arm around their mother, and a little girl stood at his feet. In his arm was a small doll-like bundle wrapped in a blanket. Herself, she guessed. Then, in another, the man was in a creek with Amy by the hand. But only his back was toward the camera. There were a few more that had been torn down the middle.

That, she supposed, had happened when her mom and dad were mad at each other. Or perhaps, after her dad had left, her mama had torn his picture apart and thrown them into the bottom of the box.

So maybe Amy was right. Maybe when their mother tore their dad out of her heart, she displaced them too. And now that the new baby had been born she was sending them to live with their dad. Not just for the summer, but always.

IN THE NARROW bed at the end of the trailer house, Russel stretched full length. His feet touched the cool wall. His arm, around the neck of the woman at his side, had begun to ache, and he straightened it too and struck the end of the trailer with his fist. Once, twice, a dull thudding.

"Someday," he said, "I'm gonna own me a bed I can stretch out in without hitting my head on one end and curling my toes on the other."

"Ummm," Lakisha murmured, putting her mouth against his shoulder and nibbling lazily. The sun was rising high in the sky. It was almost time to get up and go out. The midway would be opening at noon. The crowd would be thin to start with, and their need for popcorn and hot dogs even

3

thinner for awhile. Then the day would drift along toward evening, and the lights would begin to glow in the sky above the carnival, and the music would penetrate the shadows, and the crowd would increase. And Russel would be busy selling hot dogs and popcorn and cotton candy. Except today he had to go to the Tulsa airport fifty miles away and pick up a couple of little girls whose names he had helped to pick out. But that was a hell of a long time ago, it seemed, and a long way from this world he lived in now.

"What the heck am I going to do with a couple of kids?" he asked the walls and the ceiling of his small trailer house. When the carnie moved, he moved too, dragging his trailer along behind his pickup while his business rode on one of the trucks. He'd been living like this all summer long, just as he had been for the past five years. It was a great life, but he hadn't planned on adding kids to it. The truth was he had almost forgotten he had the kids.

Lakisha moved, stretched her own long, supple body, and began to dress. "Do just like the rest of the people on the midway. Let them play with the other kids."

"But ... where'll I put them?"

"You got a bunk bed up front, ain't you? Put them there." She looked down at him and smiled an impish, twisted smile, then ruffled his hair with both hands, roughly. "So you're a papa, huh? Keeping things from Lakisha, huh? Don't worry. They're big kids. Eight and eleven? You don't have any problems. What if they were one and three? Then you could worry."

The trailer house trembled as she walked along the short corridor into the main part, the combined kitchen and living room. She paused at the door and threw him a kiss.

"See you later, Russ."

The door closed.

He watched it for awhile, thinking of his life with the carnie. He had drifted from state to state, job to job, always wanting something he hadn't found. And then he'd been offered the grab joint with the carnie, and nothing had ever suited him better. During the summer they traveled, him and the rest of the carnival people, and during the winter they stopped over in Florida. What a way to live.

But he hadn't figured on adding kids to his way of life.

True, there were kids here—quite a lot of them, it seemed at times—but they traveled with their families, a mom and a dad, and sometimes even a grandparent or two, old carnie people, veterans.

His time with Lakisha would be curtailed too. She was a big, beautiful, blonde dancer, one of the girls with the kootch show down at the end of the midway, one of the few sideshows left, and every night after the show she came to his trailer. There was no way he could go to hers. She roomed with three other girls and the owner of their show.

He got out of bed and squeezed into the small shower. He didn't like having to duck his head to pass through the door. That was another of the things he wanted to put behind him. Another year, and he would be able to afford one of the bigger trailers, maybe even a motor home, with plenty of space and head room. He hadn't figured on adding two kids to his life.

JODI HAD WATCHED the light disappear from the clouds as the day ended. And by the time the plane landed, the lights were on in the cities and were speckled around the countryside like fireflies. With Amy clutching her hand, they moved with the crowd into the terminal, and all the faces were faces of strangers, none of them paying any attention, all rushing past, meeting people they knew or simply going to wait for their luggage.

Jodi didn't recognize the tall man even when he came up to them and asked, "Are you Amy and Jodi?"

They nodded, and suddenly Jodi felt as bashful as Amy, as unable to speak. The man smiled down at them. He was wearing a short-sleeved shirt and blue jeans, and one of the reasons he looked so tall was he also wore cowboy boots. His hair was blond, and his cheekbones prominent. In his chin was a round little hole that looked dark with the whiskers he hadn't been able to reach. Jodi recognized, with sense of surprise, her own face in a way, with the high cheekbones and the dimple in the chin. She was blond too, her long hair tied back and held by rubber band and a ribbon.

"I'm Russel," the man said. "Sauer. I guess I'm who you're looking for."

Jodi nodded. A note pinned to her blouse carried her name, but now she felt for it and found it gone, lost somewhere in the plane or along the paths she had taken since leaving the plane. She felt Amy's fingers tighten on hers.

Russel looked uncomfortable. His gaze wandered off around the big room, as if he were looking for someone else. He loosened the string tie around his neck. Jodi, watching him, was suddenly aware how handsome he was, and a feeling of pride warmed her. She didn't know him, but she liked his looks. His shoulders were wide and straight, his neck strong. Yet he didn't look quite as tall as Amy had said he was. That was all right, though. She wondered if she were supposed to call him Dad. Somehow didn't seem to fit him.

"I reckon we'd better go get your luggage, right, girls?"

They followed him, and then stood looking at the piles of suitcases that tumbled around the mushroom thing. Watching, Jodi surmised you were supposed to grab the ones that belonged to you before they disappeared again.

She pointed at a brown one that popped up.

"Is that the one?" Russel said, and pulled it out.

There were three altogether, and he carried them all, one under his arm.

They went outside into warm air, and across a street and down another and into a parking lot. Jodi had to run half the time to keep up with Russel. He walked ahead of them without talking. Amy had not said one word since leaving the airplane.

They reached a pickup, and Russel tossed the suitcases into the open rear and then unlocked the passenger door.

Amy hesitated just briefly, then climbed up and in, and Jodi followed her.

When he turned on the switch the radio began booming country-western music, and for a long while that was all Jodi heard.

The lights of the city fell behind and they were traveling down a highway, through the night, the lights of houses flicking past.

Through the window glass Jodi could see the sky was clear, and stars seemed close enough to reach up and touch. Where are we going? She wanted to ask, but suddenly she felt as timid as Amy.

Russel turned the radio down and cleared his throat.

"Well, girls. I guess I might as well warn you. I travel with a carnival."

Jodi looked at him past Amy's head. His profile was sharply outlined against the dark window beyond. Pale light rose from the dash, making the more prominent parts of his face rosy.

"A carnival?" Jodi repeated. "A real carnival? With rides and things?"

He smiled. "Yeah. That kind. I own a grab joint. I've been traveling with this carnival for five years now. I mean, this is my sixth season. I plan to stay with it for the rest of my life."

"What's a grab joint?" Jodi asked.

"A—uh—a concession stand. Where you buy things to eat." He glanced her way. "Do you like cotton candy?"

"I don't know."

"You never ate any?" He sounded shocked. "Don't you ever go to carnivals?"

"Once. Or twice maybe. Sometimes they stop in the shopping center near our house."

Amy said, "We've gone to the amusement park."

6

"Pretty much the same. The only difference is the carnivals travel."

They rode on, the radio soft. He hadn't turned it up yet.

"What are you going to do with us?" Jodi finally asked.

"You're going to stay with me. If it doesn't work out, you can go to the farm for the rest of the summer and stay with my mom and dad, but first we'll see how it goes."

Jodi turned and looked out the window. She had been riding forever, it seemed, going from daytime on the West Coast to dark night here in the Midwest. She wasn't exactly sure where they were. She knew only that the plane had landed in Tulsa. She wanted to ask questions, but Amy's head had dropped lower and lower and was now touching her shoulder. She had stopped crying hours ago, and now she was sleeping. Jodi didn't want to disturb her.

They passed through one small town after another, and by-passed other, larger towns where the lights made red glows in the atmosphere above them. And finally they reached a town where the pickup moved along streets and out to a fairground. The lights of the carnival began to show up, and a bunch of feelings began to fight one another in Jodi's stomach. She sat up straighter, watching the lights of the Ferris wheel arching up into the sky, and her movements woke Amy.

Jodi felt an odd excitement. Now she could hear the sounds of music, a jangle of sounds, competing, as if each ride were trying to drown out the sound of the other. There was a smell too, of hay and animals and people crowded. And deep beneath the excitement came a feeling of dread, as if behind the bright lights of the midway, somewhere in the shadows into which the pickup was moving, there were things to be wary of.

Russel parked beside a trailer house, one in a long row of other trailer houses. He got out, slammed the pickup door.

Jodi and Amy followed him, neither of them wanting to take the lead. Amy pushed Jodi ahead when Russel went around the end of the trailer house and opened the door and held it for them. Jodi stepped up into a dark room, where the only light filtered in from the flickering movements of the Ferris wheel. Then Russel snapped on the overhead light, and Jodi saw a small living room and kitchen combined. He piled their luggage on the floor.

"We'll unpack tomorrow," he said. "There's a bed up there, over the couch. You climb in and sleep. I've got a boy running my joint, and I have to get on to work. See you tomorrow." He started to leave, then stopped. "Hey, I'm sorry. Have you eaten? Help yourself to whatever you can find. And the bathroom's right down there. You can't miss it. Well. That's it, I reckon. See you tomorrow."

The door closed.

They stood still. Jodi saw Amy's gaze go up to the narrow space above the couch. An edge of a pillow showed there, and a sheet and blanket. A pile of clothes had been pushed to one end.

"We have to go to bed, Jodi."

"You go first."

While Amy was in the bathroom Jodi opened the door and stepped out into the darkness. Some of the other trailers had lights on, but the ones in the row at each end of Russel's were dark. Ahead, not twenty feet away, the backs of tents hid all the excitement of the midway. Light streaked through between the tents, and skimmed overhead, making the space where Jodi stood seem as dark as a tunnel in contrast.

As her eyes adjusted to the darkness other outlines emerged. Something round and not very high, with a bumpy top, sat at the back of the tent. A trash can, Jodi guessed. And piled near it were boxes that had held something, maybe even some of the things Russel used in his grab joint. Popcorn maybe, and the candy he had said he sold.

There was a sudden movement in the dark to her right, at the end of the trailer.

Jodi stared, feeling it too close for comfort, whatever it was. She heard a faint sound, a jingle, as of a tiny bell. Then silence, and she could feel it looking at her. As she stared, she could almost see something, a combination of colors, it seemed, and a large mouth that was painted with red and outlined in white, but a mouth that curled downward, not upward in the way of a good clown.

A sudden fear gripped Jodi, a dread of what she couldn't see but could only sense was there. Something darkly apart from the sounds of people and music on the bright midway.

CHAPTER 2

WHEN THE CROWD LEFT AT MIDNIGHT, LITTER REMAINED. RUSSEL LET DOWN THE shutters on his small restaurant on wheels, paid the kid who had helped him, and locked the door. Lights were going out all around. Big lights around the midway blinked down to safety lights that were left on the rest of the night. Odors of food—of hamburgers, hot dogs, popcorn, candied apples—were drifting away, and the music had stopped. People were yawning instead of talking as they let down the flaps on the tents and drifted off toward their trailer houses. Most of the litter would remain on the ground until morning, when the cleanup crew would come out and start gathering up stuff that should have been put in the trash bins.

Russel paused to police up around his own grab joint: paper napkins that had been used to wrap hot dogs, sticks that had held cotton candy, boxes that sprinkles of popcorn still spilled from. Among all that, and trampled by hundreds of feet, were cigarette butts, wads of chewing gum—one of which he got on his shoe and had to scrape away—and other crap that he wasn't about to examine.

But he wasn't complaining. A lot of litter meant a good crowd. Well, maybe he bitched, just like the rest, but it was a good-natured bitching.

"Dirtiest damn bunch of marks we've had all season," said Johnny Bird, owner and manager of the balloon game, with a grin that said he liked it. The compartmented apron he wore bulged with coins the marks had paid to throw darts at his balloons, trying to win big teddy bears for their girls. "Yeah. Good spenders, huh?"

Russel walked down the midway, passing game tents and a few sideshows, all of them closed now. There was nothing quieter, or more desolate, than a midway without people, a midway closed for one reason or another. The bones of the big rides stuck up into the air like so many prehistoric skeletons, empty of life, no longer blazing with lights or blaring music to drown out sounds of competing rides. Like the others, he hurried away from the deserted midway as fast as he could.

Lakisha was coming down the steps of the girlie-show tent, still dressed in her costume. She always changed in the trailer she shared with the other girls and their boss, and he liked it that way. The costume she wore was one variation or another of a Hawaiian skirt and grassy bra, and underneath was a G-string about as thin as a string could get, with a little patch of velvet to cover her pubic hair—or at least part of it—and two more velvet patches to cover her nipples. In some towns she had to keep the patches on, and this was one of the towns. But even so, her strip was popular, and no wonder. She had a fantastic body—with a little help, he suspected, from a plastic surgeon. He couldn't quite be sure that nature never made boobs as great as Lakisha's, but he was suspicious. Not that it mattered a whole lot to him. She was still all flesh and warm, rich blood with a lot of passion.

They met, and she twined her arm through his and pressed against him. He could look level into her eyes. Her hair was full and thick and bleached white-blonde. Her eyelashes and eyebrows were dark, and her eyes brown, so her appearance was striking, to say the least. Her face wasn't really beautiful. Not the pretty, soft look that he had always favored. She had a strong nose and mouth, lips full, teeth big. But the total effect was of beauty. "How's it going?" she asked.

"I could hear them bastards yelling all the way down to the other end of the midway," he said. "You must have given them an extra wiggle."

She jiggled her eyebrows suggestively. "More than that. You should've come and watched. I'll give you a free pass."

"I wouldn't be able to stand it."

She sniffed his shoulder. "Ummm. You smell good. Are you going to feed me?"

"Yep." He held up the paper sack that was warm with hot dogs. "Got chili on 'em."

They passed between the tent of the girlie show and the solid sides of the House of Mirrors, and were immediately out of the midway. Even the alley between trailers and tents was several yards away, and there was nothing beyond but a grassy field and a row of dark trees beyond.

They sat in the cool grass, elbows touching, facing away from the tents of the midway toward the black trees across the field. To their left was the glow of the town, rising into the atmosphere and drifting away. It wasn't a large town, and the glow didn't amount to a lot. The sky above was dark, and the stars far away.

Lakisha bit into a hot dog and moaned her delight. He watched her with a grin on his face. He loved to watch her eat. If she ever was on a diet, he'd never heard of it.

"When you get to be fifty," he said, "you're going to weigh two hundred pounds."

She was good-natured too. He had started their relationship by teasing her, and she had seemed to like it. He surprised even himself at times, because he'd never teased anyone in his life outside of his sisters and cousins. Certainly he'd never teased his girlfriends.

"And you'll weigh two-fifty," she said. "Because I'm going to settle down and cook you three big squares a day, with plenty of dessert. Strawberry shortcakes, chocolate brownies, banana cake ... umm, now that's what I call living. Did you bring me any dessert?"

"I brought you three dogs, one with chili, one with relish and mustard, and one with everything."

"But no dessert?"

"Well, maybe a candied apple."

She laughed. "A candied apple!" She sobered. "Hey, tell me how it went."

He shrugged. "Oh, okay. I wouldn't have known them if I'd met them on the midway, though. They're a couple of cute kids. But I want them to meet you first."

"First?"

He could feel her looking at him. His eyes had adjusted to the dark and he could see the shape of her toes in her sandals, the gold straps over her feet catching a light from somewhere and the make-believe jewels there glittering like cat's-eyes. He knew what she was thinking. Marriage. She was dying to get married, for some damned reason. He kind of thought she wanted to have a baby, because she babied everything that would allow her to baby it, from Zulu the dwarf, part-owner of the whole shebang, to the carnival dogs and cats. And sometimes he thought it would be great to have her forever, but something held him back.

For one thing, he didn't know a damn thing about her. When he had asked, she had shrugged away the question. He didn't know where she came from, who her folks were, or anything. She had been with the carnival when he joined it, and she'd been with it a couple of years before that. He wasn't even sure of her age, but allowing for the seven years she had been with the carnie, she had to be at least twenty two years old. She might be thirty-two. He told himself it didn't matter. Yet it did. When she brought up marriage he felt oddly itchy.

"Well, like you said, maybe we ought to let then get acquainted with you before you go home with me," he said, looking down into the darkness of the grass between his knees. He pulled a sprig and chewed on it. It was a tough grass, like Johnson or fescue, wide-bladed, dark green, the kind that would take a lot of tramping without giving up the ghost and turning to dirt and mud.

"Oh yeah," she agreed. "I'd die if one of them came into your bedroom and caught me naked there. I've got to meet them first. When shall I be over?"

"Tomorrow? Any time before eleven. I've got to be at the joint by eleven, to set up."

"I know that. Okay. Ten-thirty?"

She finished the last bite of her last hot dog, wadded the paper, and stuffed it along with the others into the paper bag. Russel wadded the whole thing and put it into his back pocket. He looked around, and she noticed.

"Let's go over to the trees," she suggested. "This is too close to the trailers."

They walked hand in hand through the grass. A dew was beginning to rise, making the grass slightly damp. He drew her closer as they walked, his arm around her waist, his fingers playing with the round fullness of her breast. She began to snuggle nearer even as they walked, and before they reached the shadows of the trees she turned, put her arms around his neck, and kissed him, long and completely, blending lips, mouth, and tongue with his. It hit him like a laser to his groin, and he could hardly wait to get her into the shadows and down into the grass.

It was odd, he thought, how modest she could be. They had to hide in the shadows of the trees, even though the grass was high enough to conceal them from anyone except someone who might stumble across them.

And even though she was willing to sleep with him every night, and not leave his trailer sometimes until daylight—and she knew that everyone in the carnie knew she slept with him—still, it had to be proper. That is, she wouldn't blatantly live with him. She wasn't about to move in unless he married her. And now, she wasn't going to sleep with him at all until his daughters met her and approved of her. That is, not in his bed.

When they got up and dressed he was exhausted. That was the way it always was with Lakisha. She wore him out.

"I need my bed," he muttered weakly, yawning.

"Poor baby," she murmured, rubbing his head with one hand. "Want Lakisha to take you to your beddy-bye?"

"Ummm."

With her arm through his, she practically dragged him back across the field and into the alley. A dog barked once from beneath a trailer.

Lakisha said, "Shut up, Roscoe. It's only us."

The alley was dark and still. Only one trailer had a light burning, and it was in a tiny window that had to belong to a bathroom.

Lakisha whispered, "That's Jimmy's trailer. You know, the woman who runs the dice game? Her husband died, remember, and she's alone and nervous. She always leaves a light on."

Lakisha knew them all, and whether they had night-lights. It was always she who walked alone along the alley, leaving him snug in his bed. When they reached the trailer house that she shared with Bob and his girls, he stopped and kissed her cheek.

"Good night, babe."

"Hey, what do you mean? I'm taking you home."

"But... here's your trailer. I thought you weren't going to stay with me until you met the girls."

"I'm taking you to bed, just like I promised." He grinned and shrugged, and allowed her to lead him on. His strength was beginning to come back, but the desire to sleep was still there and growing. Instead of talking he yawned. Her side was warm against his, her hip bumping against him with each step, with the sensation going again to his belly and edging down into his groin again.

He put an arm around her and hugged her so close they could hardly walk. At the step up into his small trailer house he whispered to her, "They're probably sound asleep. Why don't you come on in for awhile?"

She pulled back. "Some other time. Night, sweetheart."

"Sure you don't want me to walk you back home?"

She laughed softly, and shortly. "You never do. Why start now?"

"We could walk on back to the trees again maybe."

"Horny, horny. Go to bed. Sleep it off."

She pulled away with a puckered kiss on his lips, and he went inside and stopped himself just in time from turning on the light.

He stood still in the dark room, shapes of things beginning to be just barely visible. The couch at the end of the room, the lamp hanging over it, a chair—its round back showing up from the small amount of light that came in from the night-lights around the midway. His trailer house was cluttered with stuff, so that even in the dark he could see the piles of magazines and papers on the coffee table. He'd have to clean it up, he guessed. But he'd thought that for the past several days before he'd gone to get the girls, and somehow just hadn't gotten it done.

It was as if he were alone in the trailer. He knew they were there, in the bunk above the couch at the front end of the trailer, that narrow space he had used to store extra junk before he'd had to push the junk to one end and make a bed at the other. He wondered now if he'd left enough room for their legs. They were both taller than he had expected, When he'd last seen them Amy was only three, and not very tall. And here she was—ten? Eleven? He hated to admit he wasn't really sure what year she was born in. But he guessed she might be as much as eleven. Which made Jodie eight, because she'd been just a baby when he'd last seen her.

He sighed, and went down the narrow hallway to the bathroom, unbuttoning his shirt as he went.

He couldn't hear them, but he knew they were there.

Were they asleep?

Or were they both lying there awake, staring at the ceiling right above their heads? Had they cried? Or were they glad to be here?

Naw. Hell, no. Why should they be glad to be with a dad who hadn't even remembered their ages?

LAKISHA STROLLED DOWN the shadowed alley, going back toward her own trailer. She had wanted to be alone. She couldn't think unless she was totally alone, and she seldom had the chance. It made her nervous just knowing she was going to meet a couple of little girls she hadn't even known existed until a few days ago. Two people who might become very important in her life. She hoped.

Would they like her? She reached up and touched her hair. Would they think her hair was too blond? Would they look on her with scorn because, instead of the dancer she had wanted to be, she was a stripper in a traveling carnie?

Actually, she was glad, now that she'd had time to think about it, that Russel had the girls. They were instant family, in a sense. Something she had always longed for. Family.

That is, if Russel would ever marry her.

Maybe the girls could be friends of hers, in a way that no one else ever had been. Junie, Alice, and Austria, the girls in her show, had never really become friends. There seemed to be too much rivalry among them, which had always puzzled her.

Each vied for the most applause, for the most response from the men, and although she had never told anyone, Austria and Alice were somewhat embarrassing in their rivalry, their competition, and—she hated to admit it even to herself—the way they threw their bodies around. They liked strong acts, the towns that allowed a full strip or pretended it wasn't happening. They cared only about how turned on the men got, while she—well, she preferred the softer act, the mild strip. She didn't like showing her privates to anyone but her lover, the man she hoped would become her husband.

She wanted out of this work. That was something she'd hardly ever admitted to herself either. She wanted a vine-covered cottage, a fenced yard, and a bunch of kids. That was what she wanted.

But she had never told anyone. Not Russel, especially. She felt in her heart that she should wait and let him think of those things himself.

She'd had no idea that he'd even been married before.

And here he was with two daughters, eight and eleven years old.

It was hard to believe. Russel seemed like a big, old kid himself—a hayseed, actually, like the marks that came to the carnie in the rural areas it traveled through mostly.

The girls, Jodie and Amy, were going to spend the summer with him, he said, mainly because their mother had married again and had a new baby.

Lakisha felt her heart grow sad. If Russel didn't make a home for them now, what would happen? Would it be the same thing that had happened to her? She recognized the pattern. Parents divorce, as hers had when she was too young to remember them being together. Mother remarries, filling her life with his family, his children. The older child, as she had been, is then pushed out, and shipped from relative to relative, all of them too busy for her, none of them very close—aunts, uncles, people she never really knows, people she's willing to love, but who don't want her love.

At fourteen, already five-eight and 125 pounds, Lakisha had left home, hoping to become a dancer. After a couple of men who'd tried to make a hooker out of her, she'd been given the job with the carnie.

Zulu, bless his heart, had rescued her. Though his head came no higher than her waist, he had the biggest heart she'd known in all her life. He had found her in a bar where she'd gotten a job serving drinks, after lying about her age, and had told her there was a guy in his carnie who had lost one of his dancing girls and needed another one.

So she had been with Bob and his revue ever since. Going on seven years now.

But this wasn't really what she wanted.

She loved Russel, body and soul. He was the first true love of her life, and he would be the last. She knew that.

Sometimes, such as now, with the smells of the carnival lingering in the air, with the night lights barely showing her the boundaries of the alley, she had a feeling that it wouldn't end good, this love of hers. That Russel would disappear from her life, and she would be left here, to follow in Junie's shoes —Junie, who was in her early forties now, and who was beginning to gather insults from the marks who came in to watch her dance and strip. This very night Lakisha's heart had ached for Junie when one of the marks at the back of the tent had yelled out, "Take it off! What're you trying to hide, Grandma?"

Junie had finished her act, but she had left the stage in tears, stumbling past Lakisha with her head high and pretending she wasn't blinded by the tears that had started to roll down her cheeks.

It hadn't helped that another mark had yelled, "I'll take that grandma anytime!"

Both of the others, Alice and Austria, were young. And the way they acted, the way they treated Junie, it was like they thought they'd stay young forever.

Stupid assholes.

Both of them had come on to Russel, had done everything they could to take him away from her. But Lakisha had hung in there until they'd gotten bored and stopped.

She realized she too had stopped and was just standing there, the thoughts swirling in her head, colliding, getting mixed up. Past, present, future. A future she dreaded because she was afraid it wasn't going to be what she wanted.

She had this feeling. She could feel the frown on her face as she tried to trace the feeling, trying to find what had caused it. Had it only started when she'd heard about the girls?

Russel had told her he came from a farm up north, that his parents still lived there. He had two brothers there too, on farms near their parents, and a couple of sisters—one had married a farmer and the other had married a businessman. All of them were far away from the life with the carnie. But he had never told her that he had been married. He'd just said he wasn't married, and somehow she'd thought that took in all the past too.

Was she naive or what?

She heard a whine to her left, and noticed that she was within arm's reach of the Orson's trailer. Sally and Paddy owned a game of darts, and they were the only ones who brought along their big dog. They kept him tied under the trailer most of the time.

He came out now, on his stomach, and she spent a few moments rubbing his ears and murmuring to him. His long, bushy tail swept against the trailer, making a soft thud, thud. A pale light, filtering through a tree from the midway, glinted on his round, red dome. His eyes reflected the light briefly.

"Gotta go," she murmured. "Better keep that tail still or you'll wake your folks."

She walked on, past the Orson's trailer, toward the next. She knew most of the people who traveled with the carnie. At least she knew what they looked like and what most of them did. But there were others she did not know well at all, especially some of the newer ones. They put up their tents, took care of their business, and after hours they slept. Some of them ate in the cook tent, but most of them went back to their own trailers to eat. It was like a small town all its own, a town that moved, spending a few days here, a week there. Some of the people were sociable and some kept to themselves. In the winter, when they all went back to Florida, it was the same there. Some had homes, and others parked their trailers in the wintering trailer park. She stayed with the main part of the carnival, living with Bob and the girls—especially Junie, who was Bob's girl. They weren't married.

Maybe that was the way it would be with Russel and her. They would stay together, but they wouldn't marry. She would keep dancing and stripping and he would keep running his grab joint.

That was better than nothing, and she felt somewhat relieved.

She noticed a sound behind her, a footfall, a rustle of grass at the edge of the dark alley, and an unusual fear snaked up her spine and chilled the back of her neck.

Instead of turning to look, she merely stopped again, her ears alerted, listening hard. Silence. Somewhere in the trees where she and Russel had made love a whippoorwill called and called again. Frogs in a pond trilled.

Night sounds she hadn't noticed were in the air now. Somewhere a highway carried a big truck that whined with the pulling of a hill.

But behind her was silence.

Still without looking around, but listening intently, she started to walk on, and again she heard the footfall, a soft, nearly soundless movement, a brush of material, a whisper of cloth, of grass.

She whirled suddenly. Someone was following her.

She saw in the darkness the outlines of a figure, a large, whitish glob on a head. A mouth? A clown's mouth?

"Izzy?" she asked. "Is that you, Izzy? Jade?"

She waited, staring, and the figure seemed to blend into the dark and hold there against the back of a tent not ten paces away.

She could understand Izzy or Jade being out in the alley. They were the only clowns in the carnie, and had their own sideshow. A popular show that got a lot of kids. She'd never seen their act, but she had heard it was good. Kids loved it.

They lived in a trailer too, and they had a right to walk the alley. But why didn't she get an answer?

"Izzy? Is that you?"

Silence. Then she heard another subtle brush against the tent, and the fear came through Lakisha again, like a warning from deep in her mind, the part that knew about things her conscious mind didn't know.

She turned and began to run. Her own trailer was only four trailers away. If she wanted help, all she had to do was scream, but she ran instead, her heart pounding, her breath burning her lungs.

When she reached the steps into the trailer she stopped and looked back again, but the alley was dark except for spots of lights that came between the tents and through the tree beside the House of Mirrors. Feeling suddenly safe, and slightly silly, she considered something. Whoever it was in the alley probably had wanted privacy too, just as she had. And it was someone that the dog, Roscoe, knew well. Or he would have barked.

With a long sigh, she opened the door and stepped up into the front room of the trailer.

A night-light showed her on the way along the hall to the bedroom, where she had a lower bunk in one of the four bunk beds. Someone was snoring softly.

Lakisha stepped out of her costume and tumbled into bed, pulling out from beneath her pillow the short nightgown she wore. She slipped it over her head, and then lay listening for Roscoe to bark, to let her know there was a stranger in the alley. But the night was still.

AMY LAY on her left side, her hands pressed together and under her cheek like a sandwich. Her eyes burned from her long hours of weeping. She stared now dry-eyed through the narrow window beside the bed. She was glad it was there. It helped her to feel she wasn't lying in a space she couldn't sit up in without banging her head against the ceiling. It helped control the claustrophobia she felt on the verge of getting, the panic of being in such a small, low-ceilinged place.

Through the window she could see the tops of more trailers that stretched in a curved line all along the backs of the tents. She could see the grassy space between the trailers and the tents, and the spots of light that came through from the rides and things of the carnival.

She had lain awake and watched the carnival stop all activity. She had heard the music stop, and had seen the lights go out until the midway was dim. While beside her Jodi slept, she had heard Russel come into the trailer, and she had seen the figure of someone else who wore a costume that sparkled in the glimpses of light. The woman had gone back down the alley alone, and Russel had gone to bed. She had felt the trailer tremble when he walked.

There was in her throat a huge knot of pain. She wanted to go home, and yet she was trapped here, like an animal in a cage. If she allowed herself to give in to her feelings she would start screaming and pounding with her fists on the metal above and on the long, narrow glass of the window.

She tried to swallow the knot. She had to move. With her hands out she felt for the glass, and discovered a lever at the end of the window. She pushed it, and the glass opened out. A fresh, cool breeze swept in, bringing with it a suggestion of popcorn and hot dogs, and animals somewhere, and green grass.

She sucked in the fresh air as if it were water and she were dying of thirst.

Then, with her face in the opened window, she at last felt the first stirrings of sleep.

The sound of a tiny bell brought her awake with a jolt and she stared out of the window into the darkness, where only the shapes of trailers and the peaks of tents caught the light from the carnival midway. She stared. Something had moved in the alley making a faint sound, a tiny jingle, like the bells she had worn on her shoelaces when she was still little. Like the bells she had seen on some toy clowns' suits.

Then, slowly, as she stared, she began to make out a face in the dark. It seemed to have a white mouth, a blur that was ghostly and unformed, with a suggestion of a head and the body invisible. Like a head suspended in the darkness at the side of the tent across the alley.

Though the window was between her and whatever it was, she didn't feel safe. Quietly she cranked it shut, and drew back from it, her body pushed against Jodi. Even in the darkness of her bed she felt she could still be seen.

CHAPTER 3

J ODI WOKE UP, AND FOUND HERSELF STARING AT A CEILING WITHIN REACH ABOVE her head. It was paneled with something that looked like wood boards, but was obviously plastic. She reached up and touched it, and was surprised to feel that it was slightly warm.

She turned her head to the left. Amy was beside her, her face turned onto its cheek. Her mouth was open, and she was so close Jodi could feel her breath. Beyond Amy was a long, narrow window, and through the window Jodi saw sun glinting on the top of other trailers.

Now she remembered. They had come last night to spend the summer with their dad. A thrill of anticipation rushed through her. They were in a carnival and they were going to be here all summer.

She turned onto her right side and looked through the trailer. Below her was the living room, with chairs and things, even a small television perched on a shelf. Then, connected to the living room and separated only by a table and chairs, was a tiny kitchen. Beyond the kitchen was a short hall, and in a room at the end she could see the foot of a bed and two big, bare feet almost hanging off.

She looked for the ladder down and found it, and dropped down into the living room. The couch was under a window and the overhang of the bunk bed. Their suitcases sat in the middle of the floor. She opened one, and rummaged around until she found her own clothes. She pulled out a clean shirt, then put on the jeans she had worn yesterday.

She was on her way out of the trailer when she happened to think that she hadn't even washed her face. She stopped and considered the importance of washing her face against the possibility of waking up Russel and Amy. Not waking Russel and Amy came out the winner, first in importance. She could wash her face later.

She opened the trailer door quietly and slipped out into the early morning air.

It was cool, almost chilly. Dew glistened on the grass, and dampened her shoes when she crossed the alley.

No one was awake, it seemed. Although the sun had risen enough to be a great red ball in the east, the lights were still on at the front of the tents, looking pale and washed out. No one was in the alley or, as she saw when she passed between two tents, on the midway either. The merry-go-round, just across the pathway that circled the whole carnival, with all its molded horses, was still. All the other rides down the center of the midway and at the far end were still. The tents all had their faces covered, flaps down. Only the signs were uncovered. Signs that Jodi read until she grew tired of reading.

"RIFLE RANGE, BALLOONS -Try Your Luck"
  "LOOP A LOOP."
  "DART BOARD."
  "FEED THE PIG."

Pictures were painted on the signs, some of them plain weird, like caricatures.

She walked along, going to her right, and passed a small, trailer-like conveyance with windows all around that advertised hamburgers, drinks, popcorn. She could see candy bars beyond an uncovered strip of window. Was this her dad's place? But as she walked on she saw more places to buy food, some of them in tents. She passed a smaller merry-go-round for little, tiny kids, and a ride where little cars were attached to poles. Everything looked so different from any carnival she had ever seen. But that was because it was so quiet and so empty, she knew.

She went on, faster, around the midway and back toward the other end. She passed tents, closed, and came to the big rides: the Loop-o-plane, the Ferris wheel that seemed to reach up into the clouds. She wanted to go in and sit in one of the seats, but the gate was locked and she was afraid to climb over. What if the owner saw her and got mad?

She passed on by, and came to larger tents, with platforms in the front. One of the signs above the door had printed red letters that said, "CLOWNS. The Funniest Show on Earth." Another, right beside it, said, "GIRLS. GIRLS. GIRLS. DANCING, EXOTIC, BEAUTIFUL GIRLS." And in curved lettering, "Rainbow Review."

Right next door to the Rainbow Review tent was a house, not a tent.

Jodi stopped and looked up at the sign. "HOUSE OF MIRRORS."

The midway was still empty. Papers littered part of it, although there were trash cans set back at the sides of the tents. But still no people had come, no owners, no one. Jodi guessed they wouldn't open for a long time yet.

She looked up at the wood door to the House of Mirrors and at the wooden platform, smaller than the one for the big girlie tent next door, and the steps that led up to it.

There was a railing, worn satin smooth by a lot of hands over a lot of years. Jodi's hand ran along it as she climbed the three steps. She put her hand on the door knob and turned, and to her surprise the door opened. It squeaked faintly, as if inviting her in.

She pushed it back a few inches and peered inside. A light burned in a mirrored hall, one bulb at the front, another farther back, and ... more? Or were they only reflections of the bulb by the door? She went in and closed the door behind her and stood with her back against it.

The interior had a cold feel, as if the glass were made of ice. She could see herself in the mirror on her right and again on her left, and faintly, again and again at the end of the hall, as if there were other girls standing with their backs against the doors, staring at her.

Jodi smiled, and the other girls smiled.

Jodi began to make signs with her hands, and the girls at the end of the hall copied her. Jodi laughed, and the other girls laughed too, but in silence.

The floor beneath her feet was made of boards too, just as the steps and the platform were. Boards that had been rough once, but which had now been polished by all the feet that had entered this hall and walked along it. Jodi could see the path going on down the center of the wood hall with the mirrors on the walls, like a path into a forest of glass.

She stepped away from the door, and the girls at the end did the same and came toward her.

The corridor ended, and she found herself looking at reflections of herself in four other alleys of glass, going on and on, branching off from the entry hall in pathways that were more narrow, yet seemed endless with the reflections of the mirrors. A ceiling light burned in each one, though it seemed that, as the hallway continued on into the world of mirrors, a darkness descended, a shadow coming down from the ceiling, like old, old mirrors that had developed a blight and were going bad. She stood in the circle where all the hallways joined, and saw herself reflected uncountable times, getting smaller and smaller the farther away they were, like hundreds of little girls wearing blue jeans and a fresh plaid blouse with blue, red, and green over white, a little girl with blond hair pulled back, and a face that was sober now and looked almost scared. She turned, feeling afraid now, wanting to go back out into the sunlight.

But where was the corridor she had entered through?

She took a tentative step, and then another. The little girls moved dizzyingly as she moved, and she felt as if her head were spinning, and her stomach revolving. Panic rose into her throat, a hot gall, bitter and full.

She closed her eyes.

She was only a few feet away from the door where she had entered, she reminded herself. She had been in a mirror maze before, and there was always a way out. She had to get out by herself. There was no one here to help her. And besides that, she would feel like a real fool if she had to call for help. It would be like the time when she was younger and had gone into the rolling barrel and then hadn't been able to stand up like the other kids, and had fallen and rolled and rolled and had begun to cry when the man finally stopped the barrel and let her out. And all the other kids had looked at her and been amazed that she was such a baby. They hadn't known what a baby she was until then, and worse, neither had she. She had thought she was just as big and as brave as they were. It hadn't helped a lot when the teacher, who had taken the class to the amusement park, had told her that some people's brains are more sensitive to movement than others and they become motion-sick faster.

She felt the same way now. Motion-sick.

But as she stood quietly with her eyes closed, she began to feel better. She put her hands out on both sides, and touched the cool glass of the walls. When she opened her eyes again the dizziness was gone, and was replaced by an excitement that was tinged only a little with fear.

There were enough lights on in the corridors that she could see her way along, so she went forward, and when she found a branching corridor she turned right. The hallways seemed darker now, the shadow, the blight, coming in behind the mirrors overhead and extending down the walls like water stain. Some of the corridors had no lights at all, and she was led forward only by a light coming from somewhere farther on, somewhere to the right or left.

It was no longer fun. She wanted out.

She tried to remember each turn she made, and panic rose again, threatening to overwhelm her. She made herself swallow, stop, think. She had entered and gone straight ahead, and then she had turned left into —which one?

Whirling, she looked back, but there was nothing but the endless reflections of a little girl in a world of mirrors, her eyes looking large and dark in a white face.

With her hand trailing along the mirrored walls she went forward, back the way she had come, she hoped.

Then she heard a sound, a whisper of cloth, glimpsed a movement, a flash of colors that were not her own. She stopped, heart pounding. Someone else was in the mirror maze. Whoever had opened the door maybe, and had left it unlocked behind him, or her. Or them.

She pushed against the wall, her back flat against it, her palms on the cold glass, as if it would hide her from whoever else was in the maze. The thought of calling for help, from someone who might know how to get her out into the sunlight again, only briefly brushed her mind. The fear she had been holding just beneath the surface most of the time was escalating, rising with her heartbeat. Was it the owner? Would he be mad at her for coming through the door without paying? Would he tell her dad, or would he punish her himself?

She wanted to run, but she didn't know which way to go. She stood very still instead, hoping that somehow she wouldn't be seen, although her reflection seemed to be everywhere, above, all around. The only thing that protected her was the darkness of the hallway in which she stood, and the stains that had grown behind the glass like sores.

Staring toward the movements, she realized that whoever it was stood higher than she, as if he or she were on a stairway of mirrors. She forgot herself, and strained in silence and in stillness to see that rise in elevation far down the one corridor, where it narrowed like a tunnel, as if there were a long distance to the end. Whoever it was came down, step by step, on the mirrored stairs, and she could see large, floppy shoes and ballooning pantlegs that were tucked into red and white socks showing above the shoes. Then the colors of the costume became more visible, as if in descending the stairs the person had drawn closer to her. Now she knew—a clown.

Then, as others came, she saw the mixed colors, the movements of pieces of clowns, broken by the cracks in the mirrors. The face of one became as clear as if he were coming into her own corridor. She saw a dark green face with a huge, white mouth, and long, white eyelashes drawn upward onto the forehead, and in the middle of the face a great, red nose. Ruffles circled the neck like a necklace, and the sleeves of the costume ballooned like the legs, and the hands wore white gloves.

The face was not a happy face. The mouth had a droop at each corner and white teardrops were painted on the cheeks. The eyes looked like holes, dark and fathomless.

They were not looking at her.

Another face separated from the endless reflections of colors, another face with dropping mouth and eyes like holes in a mask.

They were looking down, as if they were searching for something. They made no sound now. The silence that surrounded Jodi was almost unbearable. She longed to turn and slip quietly away, but when she moved she heard the boards beneath her feet make a faint squeaking sound, like a mouse trapped.

She stood still again, afraid to move, staring at the clowns as they moved along the corridor, their faces down. It seemed, as they drifted farther away again, that there were more than two. That there might be hundreds of them. But the reflections were deceiving, and if she hadn't seen distinctly different colors and faces she would have wondered if perhaps there was only one.

But only one was enough to paralyze her with fear.

They grew smaller as they went back into the distance, and then as suddenly as they had appeared they were gone again, and nothing was left but the reflections of the scared little girl who was standing with her back pressed so hard against the mirrored wall. In the distance the girl looked as if she had frozen in midair, her arms stiff at her sides, her hands spread, with nothing at her back, nothing at all to support her.

She waited a while longer, daring now at last to breathe. She stared at the spot where she had last seen the loud colors of the clown, but there was nothing.

She turned, and with her hands touching each wall, went forward until she came to the end. She turned right, and turned right again. The bitter taste was in her throat again. A scream of panic lay just beneath the surface.

Was it possible to get lost in a maze of mirrors and never get out?

She stopped again, and tried to breathe normally. Mama had used to get nervous, she remembered, and a lady preacher had told her to stop whatever she was doing and practice breathing exercises. Jodi could remember her mother stopping, in the middle of the kitchen, the living room, the yard, even at the store, and, lifting her chin and sucking in her stomach, take deep breaths. In, out, long, slowly.

Jodi sucked in her stomach and lifted her chest and chin and breathed out, long, slowly, and felt her rapid heartbeat slow. She took several long breaths, then she moved forward again. When she came to the end of the corridor and found herself facing four different ways to go, she pointed to each one and whispered under her breath, "Eeny, meeny, miny, mo ..."

Then she saw something glittering, like an eye blinking, an eye made of mirrors. It was on the floor of the third branch, lying in a crack of the mirrors where they joined one panel to another and both panels to the rough boards of the floor.

Jodi picked it up.

It was oblong, like a teardrop, but larger. Silk threads had been braided into a long necklace, and a web-work of silk threads held the piece of mirror. It had been cut with many sides, like a diamond, but instead of containing all colors of sparkling lights, it reflected, like the mirrors of the walls.

Jodi saw herself in it, so tiny, as if she was no more than half an inch tall.

She looked up at herself holding the pretty little necklace, and realized that, for a few moments while she was inspecting her find, she had not been afraid. In fact, she glimpsed in the mirrors a smile at the corners of her mouth, a smile that flashed on and off, like bits of sunlight through the leaves of a tree.

But she remembered where she was, and she slipped the braided thread of the necklace over her head, and let the teardrop mirror fall against her blouse.

Going forward again she forced herself to think calmly of finding a way out. The House of Mirrors was only a building with solid outside walls, she knew, and the hallways inside had to end at one of the walls eventually.

Of course she wouldn't get lost forever.

People went through the mirror maze every day.

Of course there was a way out.

But if she always turned to the right, or to the left, she might go in a continuous circle, and not find her way out until the House of Mirrors opened for business and the people started coming in.

So, if she turned right, then left, then right, she wouldn't be going in a circle, would she?

The necklace flashed tiny bits of light distractingly into the mirrors around her, and she covered it with her hand.

There was something about the reflecting images from the jewel of the necklace that made her think she saw not only the tiny little girl, but other figures, other colors. The clowns again?

With her hand covering the teardrop necklace, she continued on.

She turned a corner, and came face to face with a large, ugly head sitting on the narrow shoulders no higher than her own. It had bushy white hair and bushy eyebrows that grew almost together in a frown, and the eyes were sharp and piercing and glaring at her on a level with her own. It was an old man whose legs were hidden somewhere in the floor below. But no. It was a boy no taller than herself, wearing baggy pants and a white shirt. He had stopped as suddenly as she, as surprised as she, and was staring at her.

And she saw her first impression was right, his face was not the face of a little boy. His face was old, with wrinkles and gray, bushy eyebrows.

He made some kind of sound, a grunt, something that sounded like ooof as if he had been struck in the stomach. Then he said, "Well. Who are you?"

He was real. He wasn't another part of the reflections that were unreal, just more of something that was a continued reflection.

She felt a great relief, as if she were very tired and had collapsed onto the floor. She stood still, with her hand cupping the jewel of the necklace.

"I—I'm Jodi," she said, her voice sounding thin and faint.

"How'd you get in?"

His voice had a tinny sound, finer than a man's, and his head looked enormous for his little shoulders. He had a square chin and eyes so dark brown they were almost black. The heavy, white eyebrows made his eyes look as if they didn't belong to him.

"I—I came in through the door."

He frowned even more deeply, and raised a chubby little hand and scratched his cheek. Then suddenly he smiled.

"Jodi, you say? You must be one of Russel's kids, right?"

"Y-yes. I was just looking. I didn't hurt anything."

"Well."

"I'm sorry I came in without paying. I'll pay you my ticket."

"Oh, that's all right. Come on, this way is out."

She followed him, somewhat comforted at last by his presence. The fear of punishment was far less than the fear of being lost in the mirror maze. She wanted to ask him if anyone had ever been lost in the House of Mirrors, but couldn't find her voice again.

He walked ahead of her, and turned a corridor to the right. She was surprised to find it was the wide hall at the front of the building. Had she been that close to it all the time?

"You shouldn't go in here alone," the little man was saying. "There are a lot of branches in this old House of Mirrors. A lot more than you'll find in most mirror mazes."

"I won't do it again."

He opened the door, and Jodi saw the bright sunlight, and the rides of the midway, the tents, and some people now out wandering around.

"I'm Zulu," the little man said. "The House of Mirrors has been with this carnival long before your time, little lady, and even before your daddy's time. And you come back and go through it whenever you want to, but always let me know."

"Thank you. I'm sorry I went in without asking."

He patted her shoulder. "Naw, that's all right. I reckon I left the door unlocked behind me when I went home last night. I meant to clean up first and was too tired. Some of the people drop candy wrappers and paper bags that held their hamburgers, and all kinds of things. And I have to check it out every morning and collect the trash and sweep the floors sometimes. You run along and have a good time. You'll like spending the summer with the carnival."

He went back into the House of Mirrors and closed the door, and after standing on the platform a minute looking into the activity of the midway, Jodi went down the steps.

She had never noticed before how nice it was to be outside in sunlight and fresh air.

Her hand was still gripping the necklace she had found, and she held it out in her palm and looked at it.

Probably one of Zulu's customers had dropped it. Should she give it to him, in case the owner came back for it? Or was this a case of finders keepers?

She went back up onto the platform and stood by the door. When he was talking to her she had forgotten all about the necklace.

He might be mad if she knocked on the door and disturbed him again.

Besides, she wanted the necklace. She looked at it again, letting it lie in her palm. She counted the sides. Eight. It was larger in the middle and sloped to points at both ends.

She'd keep it awhile, she decided. She wouldn't knock on the door and make Zulu mad at her for bothering him again. She'd wait until she saw him later, and she would ask him if somebody had asked for the necklace.

Meantime, she would wear it.

She let it drop against her chest. Deep within it she could see herself, still tiny and far away. And she could see the rides along the midway, the Ferris wheel looking so tiny, tiny. And the Tilt-a-whirl. Some tiny people, no bigger than the littlest red ants, moved about, opening the flaps on tents, getting ready to open the carnival.

The sun was above the trees now, and warming the midway.

How long had she been in the wilderness of the mirrors? It had seemed a very long time.

She walked along the midway, passing tents of games, looking at the men and women who were getting things ready in their tents. Some of them smiled and spoke to her, and others were busy, paying her no attention at all.

She slipped between two tents and into the grassy alley by the trailer houses. Then she began to run. A dog barked at her, and another, with a finer voice, barked from the interior of one of the trailers. She could hear voices and smell food, bacon frying, bread baking, coffee perking. One woman sat on the steps of her trailer with a cup of coffee in her hands. Her hair was twisted up into those funny new curlers like Amy had, and she looked even funnier than Amy did, with sprigs of hair sticking out from the curlers. She wore a long robe, but her feet were bare, and her toes looked splayed out, big, with red, polished nails.

The woman watched Jodi run past, and Jodi guessed she was trying to figure out whose kid she was.

The smell of food came through the open door of Russel's trailer, and she could hear him cooking, banging pans around, clattering dishes.

She climbed the steps into the trailer and saw Amy standing at the end of the short little counter where Russel was turning bacon in a pan.

"Where've you been?" Russel asked without taking his eyes off the smoking pan of bacon.

He flipped the slices awkwardly, and Jodi wondered why he hadn't let Amy do it. She was good help in the kitchen, their mother had said lately. Now that Amy was growing up, their mother had let her do a lot of cooking.

"Out," Jodi said, meeting Amy's severe glance with reluctance. "I was just looking around," she added. "Looking at the rides and things."

Amy's eyes had captured the necklace and were staring. "Where'd you get that?"

"I found it."

Russel turned away from the burners of the tiny stove and looked at Jodi, and his eyes too found the necklace and stared a moment. The bacon in the pan began smoking worse, and with a muttered word he picked up the pan and dumped all the bacon, with grease, onto a platter. Then he picked up the platter and holding a spatula against the bacon strips, poured the grease back into the skillet. He dumped a bowl of beaten eggs into the hot pan and they sizzled and fried as he rapidly stirred. "Let me see it," Amy said, putting out her hand.

"You can look at it," Jodi said, holding the teardrop of mirrors out where Amy could see it better, "but you can't have it."

Amy touched the jewel and looked carefully at it. Jodi saw her face in it, distorted, her forehead narrow and tapered, her chin in a point, but the middle of her face wide and funny-looking. But like her own faraway image, the face was tiny, tiny, like the bud of a flower. Or the head of an insect.

"Where did you find it?" Russel asked, dumping the pan of scrambled eggs onto the platter with the bacon. He set it in the middle of the small table. "Sit down and eat. I'll pour some milk. Where did you find the necklace, Jodi?"

She had hoped she wouldn't have to tell.

"In the House of Mirrors," she said faintly, pulling the necklace back from Amy and sliding into a chair at the table.

Russel poured two glasses of milk and one cup of coffee, then grabbed the toast that leaped suddenly out of the toaster. He tossed them each a slice of toast, and put more bread into the toaster.

"What were you doing in the House of Mirrors? It's not open yet, is it?"

Jodi took a bite, but couldn't swallow right away, and when finally she was able to swallow it hurt. It hurt so much tears came involuntarily to her eyes. She was going to have to tell what she had done.

There was no way out now. She wondered what Russel looked like when he got mad. Would his eyes get narrow and sharp, the way Mama's new husband's did?

"No, it's not open," she murmured with her face down so that she couldn't see his eyes change and get mean-looking. "I mean—the door was unlocked, and so I went in. I'm sorry. I didn't see Mister Zulu when I first went in. Only when I came out. I didn't think it mattered if I went in without paying. I mean, Mister Zulu wasn't there to take my money."

Amy snorted. "What money? You don't have any money to buy tickets to anything."

Russel said, "All right. As soon as you've finished eating, take the necklace back and give it to Zulu." Jodi sat looking into her plate. She would see the little man again, distorted in the mirrors in the front corridor, his great head nearly swallowed by his shoulders, his body broadened and squashed, and his features accentuated. He hadn't been fearsome in his voice and his manner, but he had looked—frightening. She didn't want to see him again so soon. Seeing him again was even worse than having to give up her pretty necklace.

Russel sat down and began to eat, his eyes on Jodi. Then he smiled. "What's the matter, cat got your tongue? Lost your appetite?"

Jodi said, "I'm just not hungry. I already ate some." It was only a white lie, and would save her from being sick from food she couldn't eat maybe. Tonight she'd say her bedtime prayers to make up for it.

"Well, if you'd rather, you can take the necklace to India. She's Zulu's partner. Or, Zulu is her partner, I guess, since India's been with the carnie all her life, and Zulu came in with her later. So you just take the necklace up to India. She'll give it back to Zulu."

Jodi got up from the table.

Russel sat back, tipped his chair onto its two rear legs, and looked at Jodi, the amused smile still wavering at the corners of his mouth. "I bet seeing Zulu in the House of Mirrors was a surprise, huh, Jodi?"

She looked down, her head nodding slightly. Amy looked from one to the other, left out of the conversation, not understanding what Russel was amused about.

"That'll teach you to go into places you're not invited in, eh?"

Jodi nodded again.

Russel put his chair legs back onto the floor and began eating again. "Go down the alley toward the end of the midway," he said, motioning with his fork, "and you'll find India's trailer near the end, not far from the rear of the House of Mirrors. It's one of the biggest trailers on the alley. Just knock on her door."

Jodi went out the door and down the step to the ground and stood looking the long distance to the other end of the alley. The tents curved to her right, and the trailers lined along the alley curved too. She couldn't see the board walls of the House of Mirrors, but she could see the end of a long trailer that looked like it might be larger than Russel's, or the ones on either side of it.

People were in the alley now. She could hear the voices of kids somewhere, kids that must belong with the carnie, because the rides hadn't started yet, the carnival wasn't open to the public.

She went forward gingerly, feeling as if she had stolen something and was facing the humiliation of taking it back. She never had, in all her life, been subjected to a disgrace like that, but one of her friends had, and she had suffered right with her. And it was only a broken toy that was at the edge of a yard. Even she had thought it had been abandoned, but when Sharon had found it and taken it home, she'd been sent right back with it.

Now Jodi was being sent back with something, and she didn't have Sharon at her side to help her.

She saw people sitting at the ends of their trailers in lawn chairs. Men, women, having coffee and rolls. They watched her as she passed, as if they knew she was new in camp and was already in disgrace. She kept her head down so she wouldn't have to speak to them.

Others sat on their steps, just watching her go by.

A little dog came out yipping, tail wagging, and sniffed at her heels, and a lady said, "Spider! Get your ass back here." The dog ran back to her, and they both went up into a small trailer that was no larger than Russel's. Inside a man's bass voice boomed something about the damned dog, and the woman told him to shut up. Jodi went on, her head lowered.

She passed a boy who stopped and stared at her. She could see from the corner of her eye that he was about Amy's size, and he had hair as white as any gray hair she had ever seen, only on him it was just a natural light blond. Or someone had bleached it. Here, she felt, she wouldn't be surprised if that were so. The people seemed so mixed, so different from the ones she had known on her street at home, so different from the small amount of family she had known. They were kind of exciting, in a way, and kind of scary in another way, and she would be very glad when she had gotten through with this torture of giving the necklace to India.

She rounded the corner and came abruptly to the gray boards of the House of Mirrors. It stood off the ground about eighteen inches, supported by blocks. The grass beneath it was long and green, not trampled like the grass of the alley and the midway. It looked as if the House were sitting on top of the grass, not bending it at all, just floating there, like a house of magic.

Jodi looked at the trailer behind it, and saw that it was long. There was another trailer farther on that she could see now that was also long. Both had closed doors and curtained windows. No one sat on the steps at either trailer, or wandered about outside as they did near so many of the other trailers. There was no sign of life here, and Jodi was feeling more afraid than ever.

Why hadn't she asked if Amy could come with her?

But Amy wasn't brave. Amy was more of a scaredy-cat than she was, ordinarily.

Jodi removed the long necklace from around her neck and cupped the pendant in her hand. She saw the reflection of her face, distorted as Amy's had been and looking far, far away. And then suddenly another image began to move deep within the tiny, angled mirrors, something that was a mere speck in the background behind her own ugly face. A spot of color, two colors, three. Red. Green. Purple. And then black. And the white, outlined mouth of a clown as it came nearer and grew larger, like something unfolding, rising out of its cocoon. From a speck of color it became an eighth of an inch tall, and then a quarter of an inch, and then there were two of them, coming behind her.

She whirled, her heart stopped, her skin cold as death.

She whirled and looked, toward the passageway between the House of Mirrors and the tent next door. She looked down the alley. Everywhere behind her she looked, but there was no one—nothing but the grass and the trailers and the walls of the tents and the gray boards of the House of Mirrors.

CHAPTER 4

WITH THE NECKLACE IN HER HAND, JODI LET THE PENDANT FALL. IT DANGLED AT the bottom of the braided silk chain, swinging. For the first time she looked at it with fear. She suddenly didn't want it anymore. She wished she hadn't picked it up. It wasn't hers. She should have left it where it was, and told Zulu about it. Maybe this necklace was the thing those clowns in the House of Mirrors had been looking for.

She looked up at the nearest trailer. Her shoulders trembled, the way they always did when she was so scared she could hardly move. Her voice trembled too when she was faced with doing something horrible, like standing up in front of the class and giving a book report, or telling what she had done during the summer.

Only this was worse.

She swallowed her reluctance and made her decision. She would go to the nearest door and hope it was the right one.

She had to stand on the step to knock on the door. The sound was tinny and weak, like a limb blown by the wind pecking a wall. She doubled her fist to try again when suddenly the door opened out toward her. She stepped back and down, forced off the step. That put her in a position where she was looking up, and the woman that filled the door looked as huge as a house.

She wore a bright wrap that reached to her feet, a silken robe with splashes of colors as brilliant as the clowns' suits. Her hair was black with white streaks and pulled back into a big knot at the back of her neck. Her

35

face was olive-skinned, with black, shining eyes and full lips. There was a black spot in the middle of her forehead, a patch of some kind. She wore several strands of necklaces, all colorful beads. Jodi stared up at her, transfixed, speechless.

"Well, good morning," the huge woman said, and smiled. Her voice was soft and mellow. "You must be new here. Are you one of Russel's youngsters by any chance?"

Jodi nodded. "He—he—he sent me to see India."

"I'm India. Come on in. What's your name?" She reached down to help Jodi up the steps, and Jodi saw rings on all her fingers. Her fingernails were long and polished in a dark red, and looked like spikes at the ends of her long, sausage-like fingers.

"Jo-Jodi. Jodi Sauer."

Jodi entered a room with wall hangings and fringed sofas and lamps. And then she saw at the end of the room, standing in shadows, a row of clowns with bright costumes and terrible, frightening faces, so that even the smile on the clown nearest her looked more like a horrible sneer, his eyes black holes in a bulging face, the white-circled mouth looking as if it would open to show long, pointed teeth for tearing into living flesh.

Jodi drew back toward the open door, her heart thudding wildly, her knees almost giving way. But then India was laughing, a big, deep laugh that made the front of her long robe tremble.

"Ah, you see my children, my clowns, eh? Don't jump so. They're only costumes. They won't eat you."

The door shut behind Jodi, and the room was suddenly almost dark, the white mouth of the nearest clown like a pale light in the gloom. Beyond him the other clowns looked down, or sideways, and one head was tipped back so that the very real but horrible mask of the face seemed to peer steadily at the ceiling. Some noses were long and drooping, chins pointed. Lumps like growths covered the face of one, and the eyes were slanted and cruel. Jodi had never seen clowns with faces like these. They were masks more suited for Halloween horror costumes than for clowns.

"Sit down, dear. I wasn't expecting company so early, but my people are always welcome. Are you going to stay with us all summer?"

The sofa made faint squeaking and groaning sounds as India sank into the middle of it. The clowns were lined against the wall across from her, so that she could see them all the time, and Jodi wondered how she could stand to look at them.

Jodi sat on the edge of a chair that matched the sofa, except it had a silk throw of quilted patterns that was different from the one on the sofa. It looked rich. The whole crowded room looked rich and colorful with tapestries and lamps with tassels and several different rugs overlapping on the floor.

"Yes, ma'am. My dad sent me to—to—" She couldn't talk for looking at the clowns. It was like having them alive and ready to move, and she felt uncomfortable that they were at her back. She kept looking over her shoulder, unable to pull her eyes away.

"You like my clowns, eh?" India said. "I have made every one of them. Every stitch. They're my children."

"Your children?"

"Yes, my children. Of course not in the sense that you're your papa's child. They are only costumes, but I have made each and every stitch that went into them. You see, many years ago when I was even younger than you, my little one, I had a papa who was a clown. And he made his own costumes, and painted his own face. So, all these years, I have used my spare time to make costumes. No one else has created any part of these, except of course whoever wove the cloth."

"Even the faces?" Jodi asked.

India laughed, and the sofa made noises again, little squeaks and groans as if the weight upon it might break it down.

"No, no. I must admit I had them made. I drew the pictures and gave them to a company that makes masks. And some I found in stores that sell Halloween masks. My children had to have faces, didn't they?"

"Yes, ma'am. I guess so."

"Of course I could have gotten plain Halloween masks, but they weren't right for my children. And I could have gotten pretty faces, I suppose, but they weren't right either. Did you ever see a clown with a pretty face?"

"No."

"No, of course not. A clown can have a funny face. And a clown can have a grotesque face. Well, my clowns have grotesque faces."

"Why?" Jodi asked, forgetting that she had felt scared. Now she was more curious than scared.

India pursed her lips, and they looked puffy, red, and moist. Her black eyebrows came together, making a small ditch between. Then she laughed.

"Perhaps they're naughty children. You have a sister, don't you, Jodi?"

"Yes, ma'am. Amy's her name. She's older than I am. Eleven."

"That must be very nice for you. I didn't have any sisters or brothers either. I always thought it would be nice to have someone to play with all the time."

"We don't play much."

"Don't play?" India sounded shocked. "Why on earth not?"

"Amy's too old. She works most of the time." India stared at Jodi, as if reading something there that Jodi hadn't intended. Their mother wasn't really mean to Amy, it was just that she'd needed help, and Amy was the oldest. And besides ... Amy liked to be around the house.

Jodi added, "She likes to work."

"Hmm. I didn't know Russel had children until only a few days ago. Well, I'm sure both of you will enjoy being with the carnival."

Jodi looked back at the clowns. She had hardly ever been so uncomfortable. "Do do they have names?" She couldn't bring herself to call them children.

"As a matter of fact, they do. I named each as I made him. The one by the door is Joey. Very much like your own name, right? But I called him Joey because there are Joey clowns. Then the others are Dizzy, Sawdust, Hazy, Bozo, Rube, and Scarecrow."

"They're funny names," Jodi said. "But they—they're kinda scary-looking."

India rose, and the sofa made its groans again, almost like sighs of relief. When she walked across the floor the trailer shook, even more than Russel's had, though it was a lot larger than Russel's.

One of her ringed hands picked up a limp arm of a clown, the one she'd called Joey. There was a white glove at the end of the arm, like a hand with no bones.

"Yes, but not really. Even grotesque clowns are funny in a way. It can be funny when a scary clown pops out from between the tents and the corner of the House of Mirrors, ready to grab you. Young people liked to be scared a little. Don't you?"

Jodi twisted uncomfortably. "I don't know. I guess so. Sometimes."

"A grotesque clown can make you feel glad to be back in the real world."

India put her fingers up and touched the cruel face of the mask, the horrible sneer, the mouth that held the suggestion of needle-sharp teeth hidden there. Then she came back and sat down on the sofa, sinking into it almost to the floor. She spread her hands palm down beside her, and the jewels in her rings caught the light at the curtained window, what little there was, and made it into miniscule points of fire, of green, red, gold.

Jodi squirmed, and suddenly remembered why she had come to see

India. For a while the clowns had made her forget, but as they stared at her she remembered, and she could feel its sharp point cutting into the flesh of her palm. It was almost like the clowns could see it in her hand, had seen it, were looking at it, bringing it back to her attention.

She held it out. The mirrored pendant swung freely from the necklace, rotating, casting tiny flashes of light around the room.

Frowning fiercely, India leaned forward. The look on her face was for a moment almost as frightening as the clowns' faces. Her eyes narrowed, as if she were squinting to see better what Jodi held. "What is it?"

"A necklace," Jodi said. "Russel told me to bring it and give it to you."

Jodi got up and stood at India's heavy knees, spread wide in her full-length robe. As Jodi looked at the woman's face it began losing its color. The makeup on her eyes and mouth stood out like the makeup on the clowns. She stared in horror at the rotating pendant encased in its thin web of silk. "Where did you get that?"

Jodi stepped back away from the woman.

"I—I found it in the House of Mirrors."

India's eyes raised to hers, and her voice was only a harsh whisper. "What were you doing in there?"

Jodi dropped her gaze so she wouldn't have to look into another pair of accusing eyes this morning.

"The door wasn't locked, so I just went in. I'm sorry. I won't do it again, I promise."

"Where?"

Jodi looked up without answering. She didn't know what India meant.

The soft and mellow voice was suddenly so harsh it made Jodi tremble. "Exactly where did you find it?"

"It was in a crack, between two mirrors and the floor. It just looked like part of the mirrors at first. Then I thought it was a diamond, because it sparkled."

She held it out to the woman again, but India drew back and turned her face away, twisting features repelled, as if Jodi were holding out a snake to her.

"Throw it away. Take it out to the trash can and drop it in and let it go forever."

"But the trash truck grinds things up."

"Yes, yes, let them grind it up! Quickly now, go!"

Jodi moved toward the door, the necklace still dangling from her fingers.

Pinpoints of light flashed over India's face, and she ducked as if they were slivers of poison coming at her.

The woman rose abruptly, the couch readjusting to its original size. The trailer shook as if the earth were quaking as India went with Jodi to the door.

"I'll go with you," she said, her heavy hand with all its rings touching the back of Jodi's neck almost as if she were holding Jodi by the collar. "I'll go with you to see that you mind me and put it in the trash can."

"But—but—"

"It's a bad thing, Jodi," India said, her voice less of a menace now. She sounded very tired suddenly, weary, as if she could no longer bear life the way it was for her. "It's a very bad thing, this that you have found."

"But—"

"I know what you're thinking. You're thinking, if no one wants it, why can't you have it? You must promise me that you'll throw it in the trash. And to be sure you're not tempted to break your promise, I'll go with you."

Jodi held the necklace out at arm's length now, but still she could see her own image in it, the size of an ant, and behind her the image of India, and the clowns again were there, far in the background, and they were the clowns that were hidden behind the walls of the trailer. How could that be?

Maybe the necklace was bad, in some way, the way the clowns were scary. Maybe India knew.

The big hand touched Jodi's shoulder and urged her along. They passed two trailer houses where India spoke to one man and the boy Jodi had seen earlier.

"Blane," India said, "you'll have to show Jodi around the carnival. She's new here. She's Russel's daughter."

"Okay," he said, and fell into step with them. "What're you doing?"

"Just getting rid of some trash, nothing for you to concern yourself with, my boy. Run along now and go down to see Jodi later and show her around. Russel will be working, and too busy to look out after her."

"Okay," Blane said, and whirled off, swinging a yo-yo from his fingers. It whistled in the air, faintly, as it rose up the string and swept downward again. He began whistling too, disjointed notes that made no tune, like the birds in the trees.

India took Jodi's arm and helped her reach high enough to drop the talisman over the side of the dumpster. Jodi turned her head and saw that Amy, standing on the step of Russel's trailer, was watching her.

. . .

Zulu hated the three steps up to the House of Mirrors. He'd been climbing them since he was a boy of fifteen, almost fifty-five years, and they'd never been easy, built as they were for big people. But they were getting harder now, and his knees hurt for hours after he had to go up and clean out the House. Instead of getting more tolerant, he was getting cranky. It was something he tried to hide, though. People wouldn't want to buy tickets from a cranky dwarf, even to go into the House of Mirrors.

He paused on the second step and looked up. The little girl had caused the extra work. How had she gotten in? The door had been locked when he'd come to clean up, just as it always was, right? Even if he had said differently to make her feel less scared? He'd put the key in the lock and turned and pushed the door open, and then, less than ten feet in, he'd met the scared kid. Had he forgotten to lock the door last night after all?

Could be. It was a tough day yesterday.

Already he was looking forward to winter, and summer had barely started.

He climbed another step, having to stretch his short legs more than nature intended. Every day when he climbed these steps he thought back to his childhood, when he'd kept expecting to grow and hadn't. He'd had to pretend not to care about all the "short" jokes while he'd watched friends shoot up and become tall. By the time he was twelve he knew something had happened to his hormones and he was an outcast in his family. He had two brothers who were more than six feet tall, and he had average-sized parents. His baby sister, four years his junior, grew up and was looking down at him by the time he was fifteen.

He couldn't stand it any longer.

Then one day the carnie had come to town, and he'd gone to see the freaks—something that didn't exist anymore. There'd been a fat lady and a fat man and—something that was rare, even in those days—a fat kid. There had also been a whole group of little people, but they were midgets, perfectly formed, looking like perpetual children, not just mismatched like himself with dwarfed legs and arms and no neck. However, they'd been kind to him, with a different kindness than his family showed. This wasn't just a tolerance, but an acceptance.

And on that day he had met India, a beautiful girl of thirteen, and he had fallen in love. All these years, his love had ached in his heart, something he'd never dared express. He could only serve her, in any way he could, in any way she wished. They were growing old together, and so had become the only old-timers with the carnie, the originals. When she'd offered him a partnership, years ago, he'd grabbed at the chance, because it meant staying near India.

She had never married, and neither had he.

She was owner of the House of Mirrors, but she had never wanted anyone but him to operate it.

Strange old House, it was. Weird sometimes, the way parts of it kept turning dark. But India wouldn't allow him to have it fixed. There was something there for India. He didn't know what exactly.

"Hey, mister," a young voice said.

Zulu looked over the old board banister and saw a faintly familiar face. A few freckles, a little peeling where he had sunburned, hair falling down over his forehead in the way of fourteen-year-old boys, he stood looking expectantly at Zulu, half scared, but hoping. Zulu remembered how it was. He had felt the same way the day he had approached the boss and asked for a job. They showed up regularly, kids did, wanting to travel with the carnie. Usually he sent them on their way. But today his knees hurt, and the broom seemed heavier than usual, and the kid, the little girl, had given him a surprise and made his heart pound harder than usual. It caused him a weakness that was beginning to make him wonder if something was going wrong with his heart.

"Yeah?" Zulu said to the kid, who was getting pale between his freckles. "You want a job?"

The kid looked surprised, and almost like he was ready to run. He'd been spooked anyway, probably, by Zulu's looks, and to have his mind read by the little, weird guy was almost too much. Still, he had courage. He didn't run.

"H-How'd you know?"

Zulu grinned at him, and a nervous smile jerked for a brief flash at the edges of the boy's mouth. He still didn't know whether to run.

"Because I was just standing here wishing I had me a kid to sweep out the House of Mirrors. You want the job? It'll take you about an hour, and I'll pay you minimum wage."

"Uh—yes, sir. Thanks."

"Think you can handle a mirror maze? Ever been in one?"

"Sure. No problem."

"Hokay. Come on up. The broom's right here and there's a dustpan and wastebasket inside the door."

Zulu went back down the step to the ground.

"I'll be back in an hour," he told the boy. "Mind you sweep it good, and if you find any trash, put it in the can here at the corner of the House. You might carry the little basket along to put trash in if you need to. There's always things like gum wrappers and wadded napkins. People are careless, always have been, always will be."

"Okay. Thanks."

"Lights are on. Some lights are always on, in there."

India wants it that way, he thought to himself, carrying on the conversation in his mind. That was another of the mysteries of India and the House of Mirrors. Don't ever turn out the lights, Zulu, she had told him many times.

"I'll be back in an hour," he told the kid again. "Just wait for me here on the porch." He paused. "Hey, kid."

"Yes, sir?"

"Maybe you'd better not go too far away from the stripe on the floor. It leads back to the square room in the center. If you follow it you won't get lost." The boy hesitated, as if he weren't certain now he wanted the job after all.

But then he said, "Okay. I won't get lost."

THE KID ENTERED the House of Mirrors as gingerly as he had entered the carnival area. He hadn't attempted to come through the gates, though he had come close enough to see they were closed. Actually, the gates were there, with short fences angling away on either side, to remind people they had to pay a dollar a head, unless they were twelve years old or younger. But otherwise the carnival was wide open. The field it was located in was not fenced. On one side was a block of woods, on another a street, on still another a farm. The farm curved around two sides.

He knew because he had spent a couple of hours circling the carnival, giving it enough distance that no one would see him.

He didn't know the town. He had come in on a truck, a hitchhiker from a hundred miles away. His mom and the son-of-a-bitch she had married last year probably hadn't even missed him yet. And when they did, they'd probably be glad he was gone.

He still had sore places on his back from the last beating the old man had given him.

"Call him Dad," she had said. "After all, he takes better care of you than your own dad does."

Maybe.

To hell with them all.

43

He picked up the broom and went into the corridor. It was the first House of Mirrors he had ever been in, and he almost dropped the broom and ran. Who the hell were these guys? Skinny little freaks with messed up hair and peeling noses. His free fist had doubled instinctively, and his feet dug in, ready to support an attack.

Then he saw, and he felt like a dozen fools, and no wonder, for a dozen reflections told him he was just that ... a fool.

He took a long breath and looked down at the floor. It was made of wide boards, and the edges looked raw, as if they had never even been sanded, while the center was worn so much it seemed to slant slightly inward, like a ditch, or a path through a weird woodland made of glass.

He began to sweep vigorously, then realized he was sweeping in the wrong direction. He'd have to go to the back of the building and sweep forward.

With the broom pointing forward like a rifle, he went down the hallway. It seemed wider than it was, with the mirrors showing him distances and spaces that weren't there. At his sides walked rows upon rows of other kids just like him. And it gave him a damned weird feeling.

He came to an end in the main corridor and saw more branches than he could count. But were they real? He put out his hand and touched a mirrored wall. He reached to the right, and saw the boys in the mirrors reaching too, and the reflections went on and on and became smaller, and he knew it was not an illusion but another corridor.

For a moment he felt dizzy and sick, too many reflections, too many different ways to go. Then he discovered if he looked down at the floor it was easier.

It was then he saw the white stripe. It was gray now and going straight on down the mirrored aisle, and nearly stamped out in places, but this must be the stripe the little guy told him about.

Okay, if he followed it, he would probably come to the end of the House of Mirrors, and he could sweep his way back. Or what was it the dwarf had said? The room in the center?

What room?

He walked slowly, going along the aisle of the stripe, bypassing other corridors.

But he was going in circles, it seemed, because the stripe kept turning left, and other corridors went off to the right or straight on back. If he only swept down the line, the little guy would fire him on the spot.

He needed a job.

He began to sweep vigorously, every time he saw a piece of paper or a little hunk of dirt that had fallen off some good old boy's boots. People came in here wearing all kinds of crap on their feet, it looked like.

Oh, well. It was a job he had wanted, and it was a job he was going to get.

He'd clean the place so well the little colonel would not only give him a job, he might give him a partnership.

INDIA STOOD in the alley long after the little girl had reached the trailer down the way and had gone inside with the other, older girl.

That was a case of the younger being the prettier, as it so often seemed to be—a cruel touch of nature. As if in giving birth the first time, the mother was just learning how the job was done, and on her second try she perfected the creation.

Fate could be cruel.

And Mother Nature the most cruel of all.

She remembered the girls' names, just as she remembered most of the names of the other people who traveled with her carnival. Jodi and Amy Sauer. Russel had told her about them, surprising her, surprising even himself, it seemed.

"Why Russel," she had said to him, "why have you never mentioned them before?"

He had been with the carnival five years, and although she didn't visit with him a lot, she did make a point of trying to know as much as she could about the carnie people.

Still, she recognized their need, in some cases, not only to be anonymous, but practically invisible. Some of them, she suspected, were running from the law, or from something or someone. But as long as they behaved them-selves, and did their jobs, she let them alone.

She went back toward her own trailer, a frown on her face, forgetting to speak to Isabelle on her step until she was spoken to.

"Got some new children in the alley, I see," Isabelle said.

"Yes. Russel's."

"I didn't know he had any. Of course, these days people have kids all over the place, don't they?"

India paused, but wished she could go on. Her head was beginning to ache. Isabelle still traveled with the carnie even though she didn't keep her fortune-telling booth open a lot of the time.

"Well," India said, "the families are smaller, aren't they? Fifteen or twenty children weren't unusual a century ago."

"Ah, but folks tended their own."

"I expect Russel will tend his."

India started on, her headache spreading to the back of her neck. She needed to sit down and rub her neck.

"No, he won't."

India stopped. "What?"

"I can see evil in the wind. Can't you smell it? Something bad is going to happen to those children."

India closed her eyes. An image of the necklace flashed unwanted into her darkened vision, a liquid drop of mirrors, falling, falling, lengthening as it fell, touching the ground and sizzling like acid on the skin. And from it something was rising ... something large and dark and winged.

"I must go," she said quickly, opening her eyes, seeing the alley with the backs of the canvas tents and the fronts of the trailers. People sat or moved, as in slow motion. Those who were passing by into the entrances to the midway nodded at her, and she was grateful they didn't speak.

"What's the matter?" Isabelle asked. "Anything I can do for you?"

"No, thanks." Just shut up. Don't be telling me the bad things, the ... India swallowed, and the pain receded for a blessed moment. She stopped.

What had Isabelle meant?

Isabelle was always talking, though. It was almost as if she had made up stories about people's palms for so long that she was beginning to believe she really could tell the future.

She climbed the steps into her trailer and closed the door.

Inside it was cool and shadowed, the curtains closing out most of the light and all of the eyes that walked past. She was alone with her children.

She sank back into her favorite position on the sofa and stared at her children, the clown costumes aligned against the wall.

Foreboding lay like a black cloud within the room. In her first glance at the clown masks it seemed even they had turned against her, and their fathomless eyes held cruel intentions, promises of death as horrible as ...

As what?

For a moment a memory had almost surfaced, but it was gone again, like a bad dream that left only the dark and ragged edges in the mind.

It had something to do with the necklace the child had brought to her.

She closed her eyes again, and searched her mind for the answer, but there was only darkness behind her lids now, with specks of light like the slivers thrown by the jewel when first the girl had held it out to swing from her hand.

India took a long breath and loosened the sash that held the front of her caftan against her stomach. A tight belt made her nervous sometimes lately. Somebody had said—probably Isabelle—that it was a sign of ulcers. But it was probably too much stomach that it was a sign of.

Maybe if she dieted ... ?

But no. What pleasure did she have beyond her cake and pie?

She got up and went into the bedroom.

It was hung with silk tapestries, and the lamp shades were like the shades on the living room lamps, very old, with tassels that dated back to the twenties or earlier. Even when the silk cover had shredded, she'd had the tassles removed and resewn onto the new shades. Some people might think her crazy, the way she held to the things of the past.

In the corner hung a happy clown suit, but her eyes saddened when she touched it. The fabric had faded over the years, but the mask she had added to it smiled just as her papa had smiled with his great, wide, painted-on mouth, and the big, red nose looked just like the nose he had worn. Tiny bells on the sleeves and legs jingled faintly, like the voices of elves singing. Or wailing.

Her papa's suit. The papa she couldn't really remember.

The comfort she had always derived in seeing and touching the suit was missing now, and again, even with her eyes staring at the red, blue, green of the suit, she saw the long, honey-mirror droplet of the necklace jewel.

She turned quickly away, and went to look at the tapestries on the wall.

One of them had pictures of horses prancing around a ring, with a pretty young girl standing with a foot on one and the other foot poised for a ballet leap.

She had always dreamed that the girl was she, but of course it never had been.

The tapestry was old, given to her by her adopted mother, just as everything she owned was given to her by that mother and that father.

She couldn't remember another life with anyone else, not in actuality, though sometimes she seemed to remember. Her mother—the woman who had reared her—had said her papa was a clown, a good clown.

And it was as though she knew.

And he was in her dreams.

But there was someone else in her dreams, someone she couldn't quite see, and it frightened her. Even now, it frightened her.

47

She fingered the empty old suit of her papa. Her mother had told her it was the suit he had made, her papa, the suit he had worn all the days of his life with the carnie.

It was her sole connection to the parents she couldn't remember.

Sometimes it helped if she lay back and closed her eyes and let her memory wander.

Somewhere back there she remembered them, the two people who had been her life before her adoptive parents took over.

She knew they had traveled with the carnival. That her papa was the bozo clown of the carnival, the clown that went around handing out goodies to the children and doing antics that made them laugh.

And then her memory was wiped out by a sudden, black cloud, and was no more.

The frustration started instead, and gave her strange, heated headaches, as if her brain were struggling too hard to climb that hill of memory. Or as if something within her conscious mind were holding back from knowing.

And then the little girl had come with the necklace.

India felt the darkness steal over her.

The drowsiness was coming, pushing aside her conscious thoughts, opening doors she had forgotten.

She lay still.

Somewhere in the front of the house, it seemed, she heard movement. A shuffling of large shoes, a brushing of material as one bloomer leg brushed against the other.

But of course that was impossible.

There was no one in her trailer house but the clowns.

CHAPTER 5

RUSSEL TIPPED HIS CHAIR ONTO ITS TWO BACK LEGS AND LOOKED AT JODI WHEN she came in the door. There was a half-grin of amusement on his face. Bangs, unintended, fell down across the side of his forehead much as they did on Jodi's, but while his blue eyes were amused, hers were not. And that only made him smile wider. She was a pretty cute kid, he thought to himself. Not a whiner. He was beginning to like her.

"Well, did you get the job done?"

She only stared at him, her small face as serious and sober as a face could get. He detected just a bit of embarrassed anger there, he felt, and his old urge to tease rose like a giggle in his throat.

"Met you another character, eh, little gal? What'd India do, take you by the seat of the pants and the nape of the neck and toss you into the dumpster too? You look kinda frazzled."

"No," Jodi said shortly, her pretty little mouth puckering with aggravation. He loved it.

"She just upended you and shook it off your neck, eh?"

"She made me throw it away, that's all."

"I know that. I saw her with you, walking you down the alley."

"Why did she want you to throw it away?" Amy asked. "It was a pretty necklace."

"She said it was a bad necklace."

"How can a necklace be bad?" Amy asked.

"I don't know, it just can. It had things in it."

"You mean like bugs?"

Russel said, "The reason she wanted you to throw it away isn't important. India knows what she's doing."

He righted his chair, and looked at his older daughter. She was going around the tiny front room picking up magazines and papers, and putting trash, obvious trash, in the wastebasket. All in silence.

"Say, you're a regular little hen, aren't you, Amy?" He grinned at her.

She glanced at him, paused as if she didn't know how to answer, then went on making the room look neat.

Jodi was just standing there, and Russel looked at her again. What was he supposed to do now? See to it they ate, had clean clothes, and stuff like that, he supposed.

"Did you comb your hair this morning, Jodi?" He didn't have to put curlers in it for her, he hoped. It was long and straight and very pale. Pretty.

She shrugged, her gaze working its way over the table with the dirty dishes piled in the center.

"Well, you better go on and use the bathroom while it's empty. I'll gather up the dishes and put them in the sink. Then ... don't girls wash dishes? Are you girls old enough to wash dishes?"

"Oh, sure," Amy said.

"She even cooks," Jodi said with an emphasis on "cooks" as she disappeared into the bathroom.

Russel picked up the insinuation in a hurry. She had gotten even with him for teasing her.

"Better than me, huh? Think you could eat more if Amy did the cooking, Jodi? Tell you what, you come on down to the grab joint at noon and I'll show you some real cooking."

Amy had gathered a small wastebasket full of trash, and she stood in the open doorway of the trailer looking back at him.

"Is it all right if I take this to the dumpster?"

He shrugged. "Far as I'm concerned." Then he remembered, and added, "But don't run off. We've got a visitor coming around ten-thirty."

"I'm only going to the dumpster," Amy murmured, and went out of sight off the steps.

AMY WALKED SLOWLY, glancing around with curiosity, and trying not to be obvious about it. She saw a man naked except for his under shorts, sitting in an old lawn chair at the end of his trailer. The seat of the webbed chair was almost touching the ground, and his hairy legs were bent, his heels propped against the metal bar at the end of the lounge chair. His chest was as hairy as a gorilla's, and he looked as if he hadn't shaved in several days. Near him was a woman in a cotton wrapper, her hair in curlers. She was yawning, her mouth wide open. Amy tried not to look at them as she passed within ten feet. Another man, dressed, coming down the alley, paused and began a conversation with the couple about weather and marks.

Amy gathered that marks had something to do with the people who came to the carnival. Whatever they were, they had money to spend.

She went on, feeling as if she had stumbled into a very strange world on another planet. A little fear edged into her curiosity, making her shoulders feel cold and exposed. She could almost feel the eyes of the people watching her go by, though when she stole a glance at them they were paying her no attention.

When she reached the dumpster she turned and looked back at Russel's trailer, but the doorway was empty, and there was no face at the window.

She had to stretch tall to look down into the dumpster, and she was afraid the necklace would be buried, or on the bottom too far away for her to reach, but almost as if it were meant to be rescued it lay like a black teardrop diamond, reflecting the dark sides of the interior of the dumpster, on a pile of trash just over the edge.

Amy looked around again, but no one seemed to be watching her.

She carefully dumped the contents of her wastebasket to one side of the necklace, then she upended the basket on the ground and stood on it. She reached in, and the tips of her fingers just barely grazed the black mirror glass of the necklace bead. She climbed, using her knee against the cold side of the dumpster, and felt a grimy slickness, as if something gross had spilled down the sides. But she hung on, and climbed higher, reaching.

If someone should ask, she would say she had dropped it accidentally.

She suddenly remembered the huge woman in the long robe who had brought Jodi here and remained with her while Jodi reached up and dropped the necklace over the side. She would be angry if Amy took the necklace out again, after making Jodi throw it away. But why? Was she just a cranky person who didn't want Jodi to keep something she had found? As Russel said, the reasons didn't matter. Amy wanted the necklace. She had wanted it the moment she saw it. Other people could call it a talisman, whatever that was, but to Amy it was a precious jewel, a pretty necklace. Amy looked and didn't see the big woman. She had gone back down the alley toward her own trailer.

Amy almost fell, her knee sliding on the metal side. She gripped the top of the dumpster and pulled herself up again and reached over, and this time her fingers caught the braided silk thread of the necklace. She gripped it, her heart pounding now as if she had been running a long way. She pulled it out of the stinking trash dumpster, slid down to the ground, and with her back to the alley and the trailers, held the tiny glowing mirrors in her hands, cupped like a bird, hidden from the world.

Why had India wanted it thrown away?

It was so pretty, so precious. Sixteen tiny triangles were set together to form a teardrop pendant. It almost glowed, as if it were lighted from within. It was as if she could see pictures in it, of light bulbs and ... a tiny stairway? And other colors now that the light was better. When she opened her palms a little, as if to let a small bird breathe, the colors appeared. She could see her own face, tiny, among the colors. The colors were moving—reflecting something behind her?

She closed her hand over it, and turned. A man and a woman were walking by, talking to each other, not looking at her. But her jewel must have picked up the colors of their clothes, even though for a moment there she had thought she saw a tiny clown. But there was no clown in the alley.

She bowed her head and slipped the necklace around her neck, and then carefully she tucked the jewel into her blouse so that it lay cool and sharp-edged against her skin, hidden, protected.

She wasn't really stealing it, she assured herself as she picked up the wastebasket and looked carefully at Russel's trailer to see if he had watched after all.

It wasn't really stealing because it had already been thrown away.

She glanced down to see if the jewel revealed itself in some way through her blouse, but there was no indication that it was there.

No one stood in the doorway of Russel's trailer, or looked out the window, and she carried the wastebasket back into the living room and put it out of sight at the far end of the sofa. Then, listening to Russel in his bedroom whistling some tuneless notes, she began to wash dishes.

THE KID HAD HALF a basket of gum wrappers, messy wads of slick papers with red stuff and yellow stuff that probably had come from hamburgers and hot dogs, bits of relish still clinging. Crappy people, he said to himself each time he picked up a wadded paper that had been dropped against a mirrored wall. Crappy people. Messy people. Why the heck were they bringing their food in here to eat? Why didn't they eat it outside?

Once he saw a long, red smear on the mirror and it set him back a half-dozen years in growth. He thought sure as hell it was blood. He stared at it, his back against the opposite wall, while other boys who looked exactly like him—with a broom in one hand, a dustpan in the other, and the little choco-late-brown wastebasket on the floor at their sides—looked too, their eyes big and scared at the thought of smeared blood on the mirror wall.

But then he knew it was just like the smelly, slick paper with the yellow and red. It was catsup, that was all.

So he tugged his ragged old handkerchief out of his hip pocket, put a wad of spit on it, and rubbed on the mirror until most of the red crap was gone.

Then, sweeping as he went, he continued on down the corridor.

He was getting confused. The only way he could stand to do the cleaning up at all was to make sure he kept his eyes on the floor. But still, he could see the other guys moving along, like so many robots, sweeping, bending, emptying, picking up, and sweeping some more.

The ugly little guy had told him he could clean it up in an hour, but it already seemed as if he had spent half his lifetime in here.

Had he been in this corridor? Hell, who could say? The only way he could tell was by how much trash was still there.

He looked, and looked again. He knew it was another passageway, because there was a sharp corner. But the mirrors looked strange. As if black stuff like mold had grown in behind them. Also, the doorway was narrow, so narrow it was almost impossible to squeeze through.

Not many fat men ever got into this part of the house, he'd bet.

And there didn't seem to be much trash, but ...

What was that? Cobwebs?

He almost backed up, and then he decided that maybe he should go ahead and squeeze in and sweep here too. After all, the little guy didn't know it yet, but he had a permanent helper. He intended to do such a damn good job, the dwarf couldn't live without him.

He needed a place to stay. A job. And this was it.

Maybe later, when he proved he was a good, dependable worker, the dwarf would give him other jobs.

He was the boss, the guy had said, when he told him to go to Zulu, down at the House of Mirrors. That was the guy you had to see if you wanted a job with the carnie.

So all right. He'd clean this place till it shone. He'd even see if he could wipe the black stuff off the mirrors.

Though, as he peered closer, it looked like it was growing in the back, and there was no way he could clean it.

Something dark and winged peeled away from the top of the mirrored panels and whished past his head. It was there, and it was gone, and all he had time to do was duck.

He peered around, frowning, no longer looking at the ugly reflection of other frowning faces. His eyes followed the dark line of ceiling, of mirror against something that looked like black glass. What the hell, were bats getting in and roosting somewhere?

But whatever it was had been bigger than any bat he'd ever seen.

Still, he couldn't really say. It was there, and it was gone. But it had dropped down from the ceiling, or out from behind the black parts of the mirrors, he couldn't tell which. And only bats roosted clinging to a ceiling. Though Lord only knew what might roost behind the mirrors.

He put his broom handle up and tapped the top of the mirror lightly, careful not to break it, and got a hollow sound in return.

He dropped the broom to the floor, and used his hands to feel for a door-way, something invisible in the dark glass, for there was an empty sound in the wall, as if there were nothing behind it.

The sound rose faintly from farther on down the dark corridor, a soft whirring ... the wings again? The blackness of the mirrors seemed to be moving, changing, like water sliding behind glass, old, black water, and now he could hear the sound all around him, and decided it wasn't wings this time, but the sound of something sliding against the glass.

He turned, looking for the way out, his skin cold and going colder, while all around him the black stuff was covering the last of the mirrors and the light in the ceiling was fading.

He ran, and struck a mirrored wall, so dark now he couldn't see his own reflection. And behind him the sound of wings came again, distinctly, beating the stale air, whooshing through the narrow corridor toward him.

He put his face against the cold, dark mirror and tried to scream, but the sound of his voice was swallowed and absorbed, just as the light in the ceiling was absorbed and he was left in total darkness.

• • •

ZULU SAT in the old chair in his office, leaning back, his hands behind his head. Good idea, having his House of Mirrors cleaned by somebody else. It gave him free time he didn't quite know what to do with except just sit back and relax like a rich man. A man at leisure. A carnie man who was just sitting on his ass in the Florida sunshine and wintering over.

He looked at his watch. The hour was almost up.

He rose from the chair, went down the steps from his small, cluttered office and around to the opposite alley. With his hands clasped behind his back he looked and listened.

The noises had started. People were setting up, opening tents, unlocking gates to rides. The merry-go-round played a short tune—to make sure it was working good today, he guessed.

Cars passed on the street beyond, probably driving slower than usual, looking toward the gates, the rides sticking up into the sky, the peaks of tents with mysterious innards.

Zulu nodded at Lakisha, almost not recognizing her. She was wearing a dress, and she looked damned good in it. She might have been a good-looking young housewife going to the market.

"Hey, do you look sharp," he said. "Going shopping?"

"No." She stopped, acting fidgety. She touched the belt at her waist, then she touched her hair. She glanced down at her skirt and her shoes, a pair of sandals with straps and low heels. "Do you really think I look all right?"

"Gorgeous. Why? What's going on?"

"Russel's kids. His two girls. Amy and Jodi. I'm going to meet them this morning." She glanced at her watch. "Supposed to be there at ten-thirty. Do you think I'm too early?"

"Russel's got two kids?" Zulu inquired, "I didn't even know he had a wife. What's the matter with my memory lately? Not that damned Alka-Seltzer disease I hope." He reached up and rubbed his head. "I think I caught me that disease."

She looked confused, then she said, "Alz-what-ever?"

"Yeah, that one. Had this guy, this roughneck, that called it the Alka-Seltzer disease, and every time I think of it I forget what its real name is. But I think I got it."

Lakisha smiled, and then laughed. "Zulu, you know as well as I do that you ain't got it. There's nothing wrong with you. There's no saner person around here than you. Got yourself a dose of meanness maybe, that's all."

He smiled at her. It was good to see her relax, kids or no kids. "Why are you so nervous about meeting Russel's kids? I already met the little one this morning. She's eight or nine and pretty as a rose. But I know for a fact she doesn't bite. She doesn't even have thorns."

Lakisha drew a long breath. "Still ... I gotta go meet them."

He reached out and patted her arm. "Don't you worry, they'll love you."

"Do you think I'm going too early? He said to be there at ten-thirty."

"Then why don't you just cross on over to the cook tent and have you a cup of coffee for ten minutes or so? Then you'll feel more like going."

"Will you go with me?"

He hesitated. "I was thinking I'd drop by India's, to see how she is. Then I got to get back to the House, to see if a kid I hired to clean it up did the job or not. And by then it'll be time to open the door."

She waved her hand just a little and started on, but she had changed her path and was cutting through toward the cook tent on the other side of the midway. "See you later then, Zulu."

He watched her go between the walls of two tents and out of sight. He felt a little guilty for sending her on alone when she was in need of a little encouragement, but he wanted, needed, to see India, and Lakisha would find plenty of encouragement at the cook tent. Several of the guys would be there for a late breakfast and a last cup of coffee.

He went on toward India's trailer, and knocked on the closed door.

Her steps were dull sounds within the trailer, coming nearer, speeding his heart the way her approach always had. The door opened.

She made him feel miniscule, especially when he stood on the ground and she stood a couple of feet higher in her trailer house. But of course he was miniscule compared to her. She was a marvel of a woman, always had been. None of that little-bitty skinniness, but a full-figured woman even when she was a girl, with a good waistline and full bust and hips. She had long, sturdy legs, and he had been sorry when she'd started wearing the long muumuus that covered her legs to the tops of her satin slippers.

"Good morning, India." He touched the back of his hand to his forehead just as he always did when he greeted India. It was his salute to her, his tipping of an invisible hat.

"Come in," she said, though not with a smile this morning.

He detected the sadness instantly, and climbed the steps as she turned back into her shadowed living room. The steps seemed higher than usual and he tried not to groan out loud with the misery in his joints. He was glad she wasn't looking when he had to grip the door and pull himself up.

She sat down on the sofa, and he sat in a chair across the coffee table from her, so he could see every expression in her wonderful face.

"What is it, India?"

"I had a visitor this morning, Zulu. A little girl. Jodi. I understand she had been in the House of Mirrors."

"Ah. Is she going around telling on herself?"

"She was sent here. By her papa. She had found something in the House and he told her to bring it to me. I guess he thought some of the people had dropped it, but it was something I saw when I was a very small child, only five years old. It was lost then, not recently."

"Something you lost?" he asked, trying to make sense of her words. Trying also to tie it in with the look on her face. How could finding something in the House be so bad?

She shook her head.

"It was a talisman, Zulu. Talismans can carry bad omens, Zulu, and this one belonged to Raoell, the magician, the first owner of the House. That was back when it was called the House of Illusions."

He had started to frown. Her eyes seemed to be looking everywhere but at him. They looked at the wall behind him, where he knew her clown suits stood on their pedestals, and they looked at the door he had left open to let some light into the dark room. He thought she was going to get up and close the door, but she didn't.

She had never talked to him about the House of Mirrors before, and he had never asked. Though always he had known there was something she wasn't telling him, some attachment, emotional perhaps—built of fear, he could see now—and he'd understood why she had always left the care of it to him. But he still did not understand why she always made sure he changed nothing.

"This Raoell ..." he encouraged. "I don't believe I've ever heard of him."

"No, he was—gone, long before you joined us, Zulu. But this talisman the little girl found belonged to him. I can remember seeing him wearing it all the time. It was part of his costume. Or maybe it was part of him. He was an illusionist, and it was his talisman."

"Talisman? What do these things look like? It must not have been very big or I would have seen it, as many hundreds of times as I have cleaned out the House. And the little girl didn't show it to me."

"No, it's not big. It's no bigger than the end of my little finger. And it hung on a necklace made of threads, I believe. Silk threads probably."

"So it's like a locket or something."

"Yes, only this one didn't open. At least, not that I know of. I would never touch it."

Only a necklace, with a pendant hanging on it, and India was so upset?

"This magician, India. You say the House was his."

"He created the House, Zulu. It was his own creation."

"Hmmm. He must have been a crazy man. It would take a crazy man to think up so many mazes in a building no larger than the House. I always thought that. Or a genius."

"Or someone who was not a man at all, but something else."

"Something else?"

"Part devil maybe. I don't know, Zulu. I was only five when he disappeared."

"Only five. Don't you reckon that might explain why you felt afraid of this talisman thing? If you haven't seen it since then? And what happened at that time, India?"

She had turned pale, it seemed to him, her marvelous, dark, Gypsy-looking skin appearing placid and doughy, and he could have bitten his tongue—too late. He had always been so careful not to refer to her past, for the rumor around the carnie back when he joined it, when some of the old-timers were still with it, was that India's mother had been murdered by her father, years ago when she was hardly more than a baby. She had then been taken in by the owners of the carnival, some people named Owens. They had reared her as their own.

He was ready to tell her he was sorry he had asked, when she seemed to make up her mind about something and the color eased back into her face. Some of the uneasiness appeared to leave too, and she leaned back more comfortably against the cushions that were so soft they billowed around her.

"You know, Zulu, I had forgotten so many things. It was like I could remember—behind a curtain in my mind. But the sight of the necklace—terrified me, and I didn't know why exactly. Then I woke up from a nap knowing, my memory about this man as sharp and clear—for the most part —as if I had never forgotten after all."

"Some things are better not remembered."

She seemed not to hear him. "On the old House of Illusions there was a bigger platform at the front. He used to have little shows there, to get the marks into his House for the big show. Clown shows, Zulu. They were clowns. Terrible clowns, grotesque clowns."

Zulu waited, watching her, worrying about her. Was her heart good these days? He knew she'd had some trouble. He knew she was supposed to walk a certain distance each day. Was it good for her to be thinking of things that worried her?

She was looking past him at the clowns, her gaze just skimming his head. "I wonder," she mused almost to herself, "if what I have done in making my children, in copying the clowns in my dreams—if I have inadvertently copied Raoell's clowns? Because they were horrible, I remember that. They had faces that were very bad on one side, and then they would turn and the faces would be funny and smiling. These tricks—what folks thought were tricks—were one of his secrets, Zulu. Just as his House of Illusions was a secret. And all the things that happened in his show."

She had paused, and Zulu felt he should say something, though she probably wouldn't hear him, she was so immersed in the past.

"No wonder he was such a terrifying figure to you, India."

She said, "My papa was a clown too, you know."

He hadn't known, but he didn't say so. Perhaps he had heard, years ago, but he had forgotten. He had heard about the murder, and it had stuck in his mind because murder was such a terrible thing. India's mother had been young, and her life taken. But he had never asked anyone about it.

"My papa was a good clown. He was hired by the Owenses, the people who kept me after my parents were—gone. The kind people who gave me a home. My papa was the Bozo of the midway, hired just to go around the midway to make children laugh. He was the good clown. The clowns in Raoell's show ... they were clowns with changing faces."

"A child sees things differently."

"I can remember standing there on the ground with my mother, in the crowd that had gathered in front of the House of Illusions, and watching those clowns. I can remember them clearly now all of a sudden, Zulu, and I don't think a child's memory is any more distorted than an adult's."

Zulu opened his mouth to make a reply, but she didn't give him a chance.

"I don't remember how many clowns there were—dozens, it seemed. But I can remember them turning their heads around, completely around. They would show one face, then turn around and there would be an entirely different face, a horrible face."

"A bunch of fast-change artists," Zulu offered.

"No, there wasn't time. He was a magician, Zulu, he was more than an illusionist, I think now. He was evil."

Zulu opened his mouth to speak, some ounce of wisdom that he hoped would help rid India of the devils that lived in her mind, put there by the eyes of an impressionable five-year-old. But again she didn't give him a chance, even if he could have thought of something. She wanted an audience for her thoughts, that was all. She needed him to listen.

"My memory seems confined to standing in the crowd and watching those clowns. And Raoell, with the necklace always on the front of his silk shirt."

Zulu shifted positions. Other people's furniture was uncomfortable for him. His feet never reached the floor. But the discomfort in his legs was nothing compared to the uneasiness in his heart, his concern for India. Why was she dwelling on this if it disturbed her so? And he could see in her eyes that it did.

Could it have anything to do with the murder of her mother?

He wondered where her father was. Had he died in prison? Or had he ever been tried for the murder? He wished now he had asked someone long ago, someone who might know more about this thing that ate at India.

"He always wore black," India said. "He seemed—and this, I admit, might be the distorted memory of a child—but he seemed ten feet tall. I can remember seeing him on that platform, with those horrible clowns, tall, in black. He wore a black cape too, and he would spread his arms and look like a big black bird."

"Typical magician costume."

"I remember crying, and my mother picking me up."

"Why were you watching in the first place?"

"I don't know." India frowned. "There are other things I can't remember, Zulu. But on another day I remember following my papa into the House of Illusions, although I had always been afraid to go in. And I saw him fighting with a great, black bird, over the necklace that belonged to Raoell. But I realize it must have been Raoell's cape that made him look like a bird. The necklace was in his hand, and the big bird was beating Papa down to the floor. My Papa was hanging on to the necklace, though, as if it were very significant." She paused, frowned thoughtfully. "Maybe it was the necklace that enabled Raoell to be human, Zulu. Maybe Raoell was not human at all."

He started to object again. This was going too far. If India talked this way to people other than him, they would think she was losing her mind. It wasn't good that she thought these things. But again, she didn't give him a chance to speak.

"Maybe when the necklace was lost—maybe that's why Raoell was never seen again either. For on that day, Zulu, my papa disappeared. I saw him, somewhere in the reflections of the mirrors, and I saw the great black bird with the heavy wings beating him down—I have convinced myself that it was only Raoell's cape I saw, but now, on remembering, I'm sure I was right the first time. It was a bird, not a real bird, you understand, but another of

Raoell's illusions or tricks or—creations. Yes, creations. Or, perhaps it was Raoell, without his talisman. Anyway, I managed to get to Papa, and all there was ..." She paused, staring in horror past Zulu. " ...was his suit, empty. Papa was gone."

"He got out of the House somehow, India."

"No. He didn't, Zulu."

"But—"

"No. And I carried his suit with me back to my parents' tent, and I was crying, and afraid, and it was then I found my mother, lying just as the suit had lain, all crumpled and twisted. I just stood there screaming."

He stared at her now, waiting, caught up in her own experiences. But still he was puzzled about her keeping the old House of Mirrors. Why hadn't she had it destroyed when it became hers?

"She had been murdered, Zulu, and they said my papa did it, but I know he didn't. He couldn't have. She had broken bones. How could an ordinary man break human bones? But the police didn't know who else to blame."

"You never saw him again? Your daddy?"

"No. Nor was Raoell ever seen again. And all these years, Zulu, I've been trying to understand what happened, and I still don't know. But it seems to me that the talisman—was in some way Raoell. And now it has been found. What's going to happen, Zulu?"

"Nothing," he said emphatically. "It hasn't changed a thing, India, this thing, this talisman. All these years it was in the House, so now it is not in the House anymore, but that doesn't mean it changes anything."

She shook her head. "I have this terrible feeling. It's like having Raoell appear again."

He looked at her, wishing he could work the magic of ridding her memory of these things.

He scratched his cheek, and then his head. "You threw it away, you said. You saw the little girl throw it away?"

"Yes, and the trash men will pick it up, and grind it to bits. But now I'm wondering, Zulu, if that's the wrong thing to do. What if Raoell seeks revenge, Zulu? Perhaps we should get it out of the trash bin and—put it back in the House. Should we? While it was there, Raoell ..."

She didn't finish whatever it was she was thinking. Zulu squirmed uneasily. He didn't like India to be this way. He was afraid for her.

"Perhaps I should get it out and use my hammer on it," he said.

"Oh no. I think that's the wrong thing to do."

"India," he said severely, "this Raoell, he disappeared how many years ago?"

"More than sixty now, Zulu."

"Well, stop thinking of him as being something other than a mere man. He sounds like a genius of some sort, and that's all. He might have been responsible for your mother's death and your father's disappearance and decided he had better skip the country."

India said, "You know, Zulu, I hadn't thought of it before, but those clowns of Raoell's, they never showed up again either."

He stared at her again, wondering if her memory were right. "You're saying that on the day your mother was killed, a dozen other people just flat out disappeared and were never seen again?"

"That's right."

She looked at him. Her eyes were so dark they looked black, and her black hair, touched with streaks of white, pulled back in gentle waves from her forehead, made her eyes look all the darker. They seemed to snap at him, demanding that he believe.

Now he knew.

"That's why you never wanted one panel of the House of Mirrors changed. Because your papa was in that house when he disappeared."

She nodded slowly.

An antique clock, on a shelf, struck eleven. Zulu jumped.

"Good Lord, I had told that kid I'd be back in an hour, and here it is almost two hours."

Get out of here, common sense told him. Let India get on with her day and get this stuff out of her mind. He'd find that damned talisman later, before the trash men came, and do something about it.

She walked with him to the door.

"Isn't it time you got out for your walk, India?" he asked. "Remember what the doctor said. And the folks around the midway will be expecting you. In another hour we open, and there'll be too many marks out for you to walk the midway."

"You're right. I'll come along for a ways."

In the alley, just before he separated from her, he said, "I'll get the talisman, India. I'll get it. We'll put it back, if that's what you want. Perhaps in some of the corridors that are closed off."

Then he wished he hadn't said anything at all, for the look came back into her eyes, the dread, the worry—and worse, a kind of fear he had never seen there before.

CHAPTER 6

THE BOY WAS NOT SITTING ON THE STEPS, AS ZULU HAD EXPECTED, NOR WAS HE on the platform. Zulu went into the entrance of the House of Mirrors, and heard the silence and stopped, remembering the things India had told him. He felt a caution he had not felt before, as if he should walk lightly lest he be heard. And seen.

He saw that a bit of sweeping had been done here in the entrance, but there was a gum wrapper and a piece of string that looked like it once had belonged to a balloon. So the kid hadn't swept that part yet. Was he still working?

"Hey!" Zulu called, and his voice echoed from beyond, something that caused him to frown. He had never noticed an echo in the House before. Of course, he had never yelled here before either, but the House had daily, or almost daily, been filled with screaming youngsters. Echoes would hardly be heard, though, in all that racket.

Zulu started to close the door behind him, as he always had, but on second thought pushed it wide open. He recognized a nervousness that was new to him, and a reluctance to go further into the House.

The mirrors had always bothered him. Of all his jobs with the carnie, cleaning out the House of Mirrors was the one he hated most, because of all the reflections. He didn't like looking at himself that much.

When he walked along, with no mirrors near him, he thought of himself as any man might think of himself. He was there, he existed, and most of the time he felt good about his world.

But when he saw himself, not once, but dozens of times, he was overwhelmed by the ugliness of the little man. "Little man" sounded too kind for what he saw. Stunted, dwarfed, hideous. He could see it in the faces of the children, especially, when they first glimpsed him. Their eyes always got big, and they grabbed onto their mother, or dad, or whoever was in charge of them, and in a loud whisper they said, "Mama! Look at the funny man!" Only they didn't mean ha-ha funny. Sometimes they used other words, but he preferred funny, because it was the kindest.

However, to compensate, after their initial shock, they looked on him with kind eyes. Probably because he reminded them of the dwarfs who lived with Snow White.

The door had eased shut behind him, and when the latch clicked, he jumped and whirled. He opened the door swiftly, and looked for something to prop it back.

It was then he noticed the little wastebasket that he kept by the door was gone.

The broom was gone too.

If the kid had left, wouldn't he have put the broom and basket back here by the door? If he had gone to look the midway over, he wouldn't have carried the broom around with him, for crissakes.

"Hey, kid," Zulu yelled again, and heard a faint heykidheykidheykid drift away to silence.

He left the door, easing its way shut again, and made himself walk down the corridor to look for the kid.

Trying not to see the ugly little men in all directions away from him, Zulu went to the end of the corridor and turned right. This corridor dead-ended, and the kid was not there. He backtracked and chose the next corridor. It went on, as he remembered, and curved left, joining other corridors, some of which dead-ended and some of which branched. Although he had been taking care of the House since he was less than twenty years old, he had never really figured it all out. When it was taken down and moved, it was taken in large sections, each of which fit onto the platform of an old truck bed that was probably twenty feet long. All in all there were six sections of the house, and each section was numbered, so that the workmen would know where to put it when the House went back on its blocks again. And Zulu knew that some of the corridors had been closed off—sometimes with board walls or panels and sometimes with new pieces of mirror—but he didn't know exactly where they were when the House was put together.

There were too many turns and twists and a center maze that could drive a person mad if they didn't have other people along to help them get out.

Maybe that was what had happened. The kid was lost.

"Hey, kid!"

He wished he had asked the boy's name.

The echo came back, even more complete and louder, heykid heykid hey ...

He turned a corner and came into a section of the mirrors that was turning dark. The upper parts were looking stained, as if rainwater had run down behind them. He stood looking up, thinking he'd have to have the roof checked. But he'd had the roof checked before, and even replaced, and still the dark stains were spreading. Slowly spreading.

Then he saw something on the floor, against the wall.

It was the broom.

He picked it up and took a few steps forward to the turn in the corridor. As he had feared, the wastebasket was there, just around the corner. The shadows here in this part of the corridor were as complete as if there were no light. The dark stains of the mirrors seemed to absorb what little light the forty-watt bulb gave out.

The kid was gone.

Zulu picked up the basket and broom and made his way toward the entrance, taking a wrong turn twice and ending up at a dead end, and thinking to himself that if he ever got out he'd never go back in again.

It didn't have to be swept out every day anyway. It never had been, truth to tell. He swept the front entrance every day, but sometimes he let weeks go by before he tried to find his way back to the more hidden corridors—and, of course, every time it was dismantled all easily available trash was cleaned out.

It was the stuff that worried India that was worrying him too today, he told himself as he walked as far as he could with all the other little men walking with him.

The seven dwarves, each carrying a broom and a wastebasket instead of picks.

The seven dwarves hurrying for the entrance to the dark mine, hurrying to sunlight and safety.

What had happened to the kid?

Of course something had scared him—and why not? Being alone in a corridor deep within the House of Mirrors would be enough to scare anyone. He had dropped the broom and basket and said to hell with it, probably, and took off for unknown places.

But, Zulu knew as he at last came to the front entrance and went out into the day, he would not tell India about this.

AMY WALKED SLOWLY ALONG, her hands clasped behind her back. They were still soft and puckered from washing so many dishes, which included not only the breakfast dishes, but a bunch more that Russel had stuck back in places under the sink.

Russel. Would she ever be able to call him Dad? Or Daddy? It seemed almost funny. He was like a total stranger, not a dad. More like an uncle or something, if anything.

"Hi there," a soft voice said, and Amy looked around.

People were passing, going from trailers to the narrow passages between tents, going toward the midway. Some of them were coming back. Others walked the alley as she was walking the alley, just strolling along. She looked for the person who had spoken to her, and saw a tall, blonde lady smiling down. But it was not the smile of an adult patronizing a kid, it was more like the bashful smile of another kid who wanted to be friends.

"Hi," Amy said.

"I'll bet you're Amy," the tall girl said. "Russel's oldest daughter?"

Amy nodded.

The young woman put out her hand and clasped Amy's and shook it so hard that Amy felt as if her elbow were going to rattle.

"I'm Lakisha. I'm a little late. I was supposed to be at Russel's house at ten-thirty."

"That's all right," Amy said. "He's waiting for you, I think. He told me not to go far away. He's sitting in there with his feet on the coffee table and drinking a beer. Says he's got to go to work, but he's just sitting there."

"You sound like you don't approve."

"Well, I just cleaned up his coffee table."

Lakisha laughed. "Then I don't blame you. Why didn't you tell him to at least take off his shoes?"

Amy smiled. "He's kind of messy, isn't he?"

"Most men are, I think. What bothers us doesn't bother them."

They entered the trailer house, Lakisha motioning Amy to go ahead. Jodi was sitting on the floor with her knees spread, her feet together, the way she always sat, watching the little black and white TV part of the time and otherwise looking at a magazine that was open on the floor between her legs. Russel, leaning back on the couch, sitting more on his backbone than on his rear, had pushed aside the centerpiece Amy had arranged on the coffee table and had put an empty beer can in its place. He was holding a fresh can. It was sweating, halfway down, where the cold beer was. Amy wanted to scold him, to yell at him the way her mama yelled at her when she didn't do things right, but he looked at her with a grin and raised one eyebrow and she weakened.

"Well, well," he said. "A visitor. Jodi, sit up and meet Lakisha. I guess Amy's already met her, eh, Amy? Anyway, girls, have some proper introductions here. Lakisha, these are my almost grown-up daughters, Jodi Lynn and Amy Louise, known as Jodi and Amy. And girls, this is my very good friend, Lakisha ... Lakisha ... Did it ever dawn on you, love, that you keep secrets from me? I don't even know your last name."

Lakisha said, "My real name is Judith Marie Schneider. But people in the carnie don't use names like that. So I just renamed myself. No, to be really truthful, Zulu did it. He said Lakisha sounded exotic." Lakisha sat down on the couch beside Russel, and he obliged by sliding his legs over a couple of inches.

"Want a beer?" he asked her.

She gave him a quick, little frown, intended only for him, not his daughters.

Jodi had gotten to her feet, and she stood looking at Lakisha. Amy wanted to jolt her with an elbow, to remind her she was being nosy and rude, but to stick her elbow in Jodi's ribs right in front of company didn't seem a good idea either. So she stood by, a little back from the others, and watched and listened in silence.

Jodi asked, "Do you work with the carnival?"

"Yes." Lakisha glanced sideways at Russel. "I'm a dancer."

"A dancer!" Jodi exclaimed. "Is that your tent down there by the House of Mirrors that says girls, girls, girls? And it says something about exotic dancers too. Is that you?"

"Well, me and some others. There are four of us."

Lakisha blushed faintly, and Amy saw it, and gathered instantly that something about her work embarrassed her. Amy turned away, reluctant to watch another's distress. She wanted to make Jodi shut up, but she didn't know how at the moment without making everything worse. She put her hand to her blouse, between the tiny swell of new breasts, and felt the angled sides of the pretty pendant, and wished she could pull it out and let it hang free where everyone could see it. What would Lakisha think of it?

Then she heard her name.

"You'll have to get Amy to help you in your joint, Russel. I'll bet she'd be good."

"I ought to. With two windows to tend it gets a little hectic at times. But I'm afraid she's not tall enough to reach the window."

"Oh, bull. Of course she is."

Amy turned, went back to stand nearer the end of the couch where Russel sat. She had been looking forward to a long, aimless summer, but this sounded interesting. She liked to work. She was used to work. Their mama had made her work, while Jodi was sent to play with Jimmy to keep him out of the street, so that now she didn't really know what to do with spare time.

"Could I? Could I please, Russel?"

"Russel," Lakisha repeated. "What is this? Don't you make your kids call you Dad?"

Russel shrugged. "Doesn't seem to matter. Actually, I think this is the first time either one of them has called me anything, and I can think of a lot worse names, can't you, babe?" He reached over and hit Lakisha on the shoulder. "Even you have called me worse names than that."

Amy stood waiting, afraid they weren't going to remember what was being said about her helping out in the grab joint. It was just like it had been with her mother and Erin, when he'd started living with them. The two acted as if they were alone in the world, and never heard anything she said or Jodi said. Mama never talked to either of them anymore. Only to tell her to go wash dishes or cook dinner—or to tell Jodi to take Erin's little boy, Jimmy, out and play, and be sure to watch him for he's only two and inclined to wander into the street.

But instead of ignoring Amy, Lakisha looked up, measured her height with her gaze going from head to toe. She said, "She's tall enough."

"She likes to work," Jodi offered. "She had to work all the time at home, and she liked it."

"How in the hell could a girl like to work all the time?" Russel asked, a serious look covering his face like a dark veil thrown suddenly over him. "Why was she made to work all the time?"

Jodi shrugged and turned away. Their mother was being attacked.

"She didn't have any friends anyway," Jodi said. "There wasn't anyone for her to play with."

Russel sat forward, taking his feet off the coffee table, and putting the can of beer down where his feet had been. "Well, no damn wonder. How could she make friends when her mother made a maid out of her? Why didn't you let me know that, Amy?"

Jodi said, "We didn't know where you were."

Russel said nothing. He looked slowly sideways, at Lakisha, and Lakisha gave him a tight, artificial smile that said more than a thousand words.

Russel shrugged. "I guess I had that one coming."

Amy said quickly, before Jodi did something that would lose them even this home, such as it was, "I really do like to work. I like to stay busy. Could I please help you in your—your—"

"Grab joint," Jodi said.

But even though Amy had heard Russel call it that, it didn't seem a very flattering thing to call it. But it wasn't a cafe or restaurant. And what else was there?

But Russel was nodding, the half-grin back on his face, all seriousness gone again. "Right, Jodi knows what it is. Well, Amy, if you really want to give it a try, we'll see. And if you turn out to be a good hot-dog maker, and a cotton-candy maker, and a peddler as well, I'll pay you a regular wage."

"Ought to give her a partnership," Lakisha said.

"Might do that. Why, we might even start a chain of grab joints, and just scatter them all around, eh, Amy?"

She returned his smile, and a sensation new to her rose to engulf her. It was a warmth maybe even a thrill. Even though she knew he had only been kidding, it was good to have him include her in his plans.

She would work hard, she planned in silence, to make herself the best help he'd ever had. And suddenly she was looking forward to the summer, to working side by side with this handsome guy who was her dad.

She put her hand to her chest and pressed the necklace beneath her blouse. Already it had brought her luck. It was her lucky charm. She had known the moment she saw it that she must have it, that somehow she must talk Jodi out of it, or buy it from her or something, even though she didn't have any money, because she knew that it would change the course of her life.

And so it had.

The midway was filled with people, the rides were going, the music was blaring out from each ride, overlapping. Smells of popcorn were floating in the air with all the other smells. And among it all Jodi wandered, hardly able to see through the hordes of teenagers who pushed her aside as if they didn't see her.

She had gone with Russel and Amy to Russel's grab joint, and Russel had shown Amy how to make a hot dog with different dressings. They had given one with sauerkraut to Jodi, with a can of pop, and Jodi had taken it to one of the picnic benches and eaten her lunch. That was just before the midway opened. Then, straight up at twelve o'clock, the gates had been spread and the people had started coming in. The music had started and the empty rides had begun to whirl.

Now they were full.

Jodi wandered down toward the tent shows, the girlie tent, the House of Mirrors.

She stood looking up at Zulu on his porch. He was yelling.

"We need a crowd here. Not one person, not even two or three dare go into the biggest mirror maze on the face of the earth, or they'll never come out again. We need a crowd, a big crowd. Come on, folks, protect one another. Only a crowd of people can enter this old mirror maze."

They were collecting, gathering at the ticket booth, laughing, nudging one another, giving the ticket woman their money in exchange for tickets.

"Need at least a dozen," Zulu yelled. "It takes that many for protection. And mind, the owner is not responsible, you enter at your own risk! Come on, one more!"

He saw Jodi and seemed to pause, his piercing eyes holding her for a moment as if she were a helpless butterfly. She backed up. Even if she had the money she didn't want to go in again, not so soon anyway.

"Last chance!" Zulu yelled.

Another pair rushed past her, bought their tickets, and climbed the steps. Zulu went back up onto the platform by the door, walking as if his legs were stiff, putting one hand on a knee and caressing it briefly. The last person entered the entrance to the House of Mirrors, and Zulu shut the door.

To others who had gathered around the steps he cried out, "Thirty minutes, folks, each tour lasts thirty minutes. Come back then and be the first in, the leader through the wild mirror maze, the biggest and most terrifying wilderness of mirrors on earth!"

"Sssst. Sssst."

It sounded close, and Jodi looked behind her. Someone was trying to get her attention, or was it some other sound she was hearing?

She moved over toward the longer platform in front of the girlie tent.

It was empty now, but she could hear the beat of music inside, something slow and sultry, and she figured that Lakisha was dancing.

"Sssst, hey, kid."

Jodi looked around, but still saw no one who might be talking to her.

She started on down the midway. Zulu was still on his porch, and she pretended she didn't know he was there, because she felt as if he were watching her.

"Sssst. Hey, your name Jodi?"

She looked down, and to her surprise there was a face looking out at her from beneath the corner of the House of Mirrors. He was totally surrounded by tall grass, so that only his face was peeking out.

It was the boy she had met earlier when she was with India. What had India called him?

He stuck a hand out and wiggled the fingers at her.

"Come here," he said in the loud whisper, and withdrew.

Jodi was left staring down into the grass under the corner of the house where he had been. Then suddenly he was standing beside the house, his back against the wall, and motioning wildly to her.

She went into the narrow space between the tent of dancing girls and the solid walls of the House of Mirrors. Suddenly now his name came back to her. Blane.

As soon as she was within reach he grabbed her arm and pulled her into the narrow alley between the two walls.

"You're not supposed to be on the midway during working hours," he said ominously.

She frowned. "Why not?"

He shrugged. "I don't know. That's just one of the rules. Carnie kids stay off the midway during working hours. Except on very special occasions."

"What special occasion?"

He looked off over her head. "Ah ... birthdays, things like that. Sometimes carnie kids get some tickets and then they can go on the midway, but otherwise you have to stay off. It's for the marks, see."

"Marks? What's marks?"

"Them." He pointed impatiently at the people streaming past their narrow alley. "The people, dumbo."

"Why are they called marks?"

"Well, they ... hell, I don't know. Why do you ask so many questions? Just listen to me and you'll be all right. India told me to show you around and that's what I'm here for. To show you around. To show you the ropes, okay? To let you know what you can and you can't do, okay?"

Jodi shrugged. "Russel didn't tell me I couldn't be on the midway."

"Maybe he didn't know. He didn't have any kids until yesterday."

71

Jodi couldn't argue with that one, because she had hardly known she'd had a dad until about then too.

"Come on," Blane said. "Since this is your first day, I'll treat you to a show."

"You got money? Is this a special occasion?" Blane put his mouth close to her ear. He had to bend in order to make that effort.

"This is a special treat, but it's just between you and me, see? If you give away my secret, I'll just let you go and get in trouble, like you were on the way to doing just now. Didn't you see Zulu glaring at you? In another five minutes he'd have had your ass."

"What?"

"What I mean is, he'd have told you where to get off, see, and he'd have sent you to the trailer and told you to stop hanging around the midway when marks are out in force, that's what. He's the big boss, outside of India, and since she doesn't work on the midway, that kind of makes him the big, big boss. So you gotta mind Zulu. And he don't want carnie kids on the midway during working hours, have you got that straight?"

"I guess so. I mean, yes. I won't go unless it's a special occasion."

Blane straightened up. "All right. Glad we settled that. Now, this treat here. Promise you'll never tell a soul."

"Promise."

"Well, do it right, dumbo. Cross your heart."

"And hope to die?" Jodi crossed her heart.

"Okay, come on. Now remember, not a word. If you tell, we'll never get to do it again."

"I won't tell." She was beginning to tingle with anticipation. What kind of forbidden fruit was Blane about to pick? She decided he wasn't going to be such a spoilsport after all.

He took her hand, and then dropped it as if it were a hot potato. He motioned instead.

"Follow me. Do what I do."

He hunkered over and went skimming along at the side of the tent. Jodi followed, bent low.

They went around the back of the tent, where Blane dropped even lower, as if to hide from people who no longer were in the alley between tents and trailers. They passed beneath a tree and Blane paused at the corner of the tent and looked in both directions—right toward the trailers, and left down the narrow space between two tents. Then he dropped to his stomach and started belly-crawling through the grass to the rear of the other tent. Jodi followed, on her belly, right at his heels.

Blane sat up against the next tent and looked to see if Jodi were there.

He put his fingers to his lips. "Shhh! Follow me." He lifted a corner of the tent, and Jodi saw a slit there, a short one, that looked as if it had been deliberately made. He crawled under.

Jodi followed, her heart beginning to pound, because she knew that this definitely was forbidden fruit, even more forbidden than she had anticipated.

She found herself in the dark. Somewhere above were voices, two men, arguing with each other.

"Hey," said one. "What're you doing? What do you think you're doing?"

"Hold still," said the other. "How do you think you're ever going to get well if you don't hold still?" There was a moment of silence, then a burst of laughter from a crowd, voices of children mixed with a few adults. And Jodi guessed they were at a show that kids liked. But it was so dark.

Jodi sat up and saw a multitude of stars as she cracked the top of her head against something solid.

Blane's hand grabbed her arm, and his voice hissed in her ear.

"What're you trying to do, knock the platform down? Keep your head down, and follow me."

He hung to her arm, and she could feel him pulling. She began to crawl again, through grass that tickled her nose and made her sneeze. But she caught it with one hand, so that it was only a muffled woof. Still, she felt Blane's hand squeeze her arm disapprovingly.

He pulled, and she crawled, and he pulled again. Then suddenly they were in only semi-dark, and able to sit up, and Jodi saw the legs of chairs, and of people. With Blane, she sat in the dark corner of the tent with her back against the tent wall.

On the platform at the back of the tent, where they had crawled under, were two clowns.

Jodi felt a jolt of fear course through her.

The clowns from the House of Mirrors! Those strange, silent clowns who had come and gone so mysteriously. Those two clowns who had seemed to be looking for something.

Jodi sank back against the warm wall of the tent, feeling they knew who she was and where she sat and how she had entered.

CHAPTER 7

ONE OF THE CLOWNS HELD A PITCHER OF CLEAR GLASS THROUGH WHICH A PURPLE liquid was visible. He was holding it over the other's head. And then he was pouring, right into the top of the second clown's head.

Jodi stared. And in staring she sat straighter, looking more closely at the two clowns. They were different from the other clowns, she realized with a slow relief rising in her like the comfort of ice cream. These clowns had happy faces, with big, turned-up mouths and round, red noses. They weren't the clowns from the House of Mirrors after all.

As she watched, the clown who sat on the chair bent his elbow, and the purple stuff began running out again, going in at his head and coming out his elbow, and Jodi yelped with laughter, rising up onto her knees so that she could see better.

"Just what I figured," the clown with the empty pitcher said. "Your problem is all in your head."

Jodi forgot where she was as the clowns' antics continued. She had risen to her feet so that she could have a better view, and beside her Blane stood too, hollering in her ear with laughter, helping to fill the tent with sound.

When the act came to a climax with one clown chasing the other around the stage, Blane took Jodi's arm and pulled her down and back beneath the dark stage.

Behind her Jodi could hear the people rising and leaving the tent, and the footsteps of the two clowns on the stage as they prepared for the next show.

When they crawled out into the light and sat in grass beside the tent, Blane said, "That's Izzy and Jade."

"They're good clowns, huh?" Jodi asked.

Blane stared at her. "Huh? Sure. Whata'ya mean?"

Jodi shrugged. Suddenly it seemed that it would be all right to tell him, to share her experience with someone.

"I saw some clowns in the House of Mirrors this morning when I went in all by myself. They had ugly faces, with frowns and mouths that looked like this." She put her fingers in each corner of her mouth and pulled it down. Blane, watching her closely, frowned too, unconsciously mirroring the face she was making. "One of them had a costume that was patches, like old quilts. I saw one almost like it in India's trailer. The faces were—ugly faces. Who were they?"

"There's no clowns here but Izzy and Jade."

"I saw two in the House of Mirrors."

"How'd you get into the House of Mirrors?"

"I walked in."

"Through the door?"

"Sure, through the door. What did you think?"

Blane shrugged. "I know a way in. Not through the door."

"You do?"

"Sure. I know ways into everything. I'll take you in there sometime."

"Well ..." Jodi wasn't sure she wanted to go in. There was the matter of the clowns. "They were looking for something, I think."

"Who was?"

"The clowns."

"What were they looking for?"

"I don't know."

Blane looked past her toward the House of Mirrors. The rear wall was visible beyond the tent next door. But from the tent came a series of long whistles and a few shouts, and Blane's attention was diverted. His face took on a crafty look.

"Hey, you wanta see a real show?"

"What?"

"Come this way, and I'll show you. But make sure you don't stand up or anything like that, because kids are not allowed in here."

"Maybe we shouldn't go in then."

"Oh, come on. Don't be chicken."

He led her through an elaborate pathway, through tall grass where an almost invisible path had been made, around the corner of the tent, and to a pole near the front. Then, peeking out from behind a trash can to make sure they weren't being seen from the midway, Blane lifted the skirt of the tent a bare four inches and wriggled under. The tent skirt lowered behind him, then his hand appeared and motioned to her to follow. With misgivings, Jodi slid through.

This was the tent with the sultry music, the tent that said "GIRLS GIRLS GIRLS" at the front. This was where Russel's girlfriend, Lakisha, danced. If he found out she had sneaked in to watch Lakisha's show, there was no telling what they'd do to her.

She was sorry she had come. Even before she sat up in the darkness beside Blane, she was sorry.

Instead of children in this tent, there were men. Although metal folding chairs stood in rows, just as they had in the other tent, the men were almost all on their feet. The sounds and yells nearly drowned out the music.

Jodi couldn't see a thing but the legs of the men.

Blane tugged at her shirt collar, pulling her forward.

She followed the leader, on her hands and knees between the legs and feet of the men and the wall of the tent. Then suddenly she was in the edge of lights of different colors, rose, blue, green, revolving like spotlights over the rough boards of the stage, and she was looking up at a pair of long, bare legs.

No, not quite bare. The lady wore black lace stockings, attached way up high to a narrow garter belt that went around her waist. Below the garter belt was a thin little pair of black bikini panties with lace and sequins.

Jodi stole a glance at the woman's face, and was relieved to see it was not Lakisha. But whoever it was wasn't really dancing. She was jutting her rear end out toward the men, turning and twisting, and as Jodi stared she reached up and undid her bra, and it came off and her bare breasts were revealed. The men went wild, whistling and screaming for more, and Jodi stared in disbelief. Then the girl unfastened her garter belt and threw it aside, and began to peel off her stockings. When she slipped her fingers beneath her thin black bikini panties Jodi hid her face.

She sat squatting at the edge of the platform, with her face in her hands, listening to the thunder of applause and the beat of the music, and wished she were anywhere else in the world.

Then, without looking at the lady again, afraid she'd see her without any clothes at all, she crawled blindly back away from the stage, staying against the wall of the tent. When she opened her eyes and saw that she was in the dark again she wriggled beneath the tent and out into the untrampled grass.

There she sat blinking in the light.

Was that what Lakisha did too?

Take off her clothes in front of all those men?

She hoped Russel never found out.

"Hey!" a voice hissed at her shoulder.

She jumped, and almost wet her pants.

But then she saw it was only Blane. She doubled one fist and hit him.

"Why'd you do that?" she cried.

"Why'd I do what? Why'd you leave? That was only the first one. Her name is Austria. Some looker, huh?"

Jodi shrugged, picking up Blane's habit. "I don't know," she said. "I didn't see her face very good in those lights."

"Well, I didn't mean her face, dumbo."

"I liked the clown show best."

"Don't you want to go back in and watch the rest of the show?"

"The—uh—no," Jodi said. "What happens if they catch you?"

"I've never been caught."

"Why don't we get something to eat," Jodi said, more to change the subject than because she was hungry. "Would they care if we went onto the midway to get us something to eat? My dad would give us something."

"Not unless you got money."

"My dad?"

"Well, I'd have to have money."

"Not if you're my company."

"Hey, you don't know much about business, do you?" He stood up and began walking toward the alley behind the tents, a blade of grass in his mouth. He chewed intently. Then he said, "Come on. We can go to the cook tent. They might have something."

"What's a cook tent?"

"That's where the carnie people eat mostly. All of us can eat there."

"Okay."

The cook tent, Jodi found, had no sides, only a roof. There were long tables with benches around three sides, and on the tables were bottles of catsup, plastic squirt containers of mustard, salt and pepper shakers, and containers of paper napkins. At a stove on the fourth side a man with a white apron and cap was working.

A few people sat at the tables, drinking coffee or soft drinks. One of them was eating a sandwich and reading a newspaper.

Blane slid his legs over a bench, and Jodi did as he did, and sat with her arms on the plastic-covered table, as if they were in a cafe waiting for service. The cook looked over his shoulder at them. "You kids are a little early, ain't you? Dinner ain't ready."

"This here is Russel's girl. Her name is Jodi. Could we have something anyway?"

"I don't know. I'm not in the business of feeding strays."

Blane poked Jodi with his elbow and said out of the corner of his mouth, "That means he likes you."

The big man, who looked like a barrel with apron, with a wide, red face beneath his crooked cap, opened the door of a white refrigerator, poured two glasses of milk, and then reached beneath the table near the stove and pulled out a handful of cookies.

"So you're Russel's kid, huh?" he said as he put the milk and cookies down in front of them. "You even look like him, you know that? Only on you it's pretty cute."

"There's another one too," Blane said. "Another girl. I don't know her name."

"Amy," Jodi supplied. "She's already working for Russel."

"You call him Russel?" the cook asked. "What you oughta call him is Papa. What's the matter with you kids today, you got no respect for your papa? Call him Papa, little one, and he'll love you forever. And you tell him to come on over and eat dinner with us sometime. He'll ruin his health eating them hot dogs of his'n."

The cook patted her on top of the head and then went back to his stove and his work.

Jodi considered calling Russel Papa, and she almost laughed out loud. Somehow, it was almost as funny as the clowns' act.

His real name was Robert Browning Zulumonsque. But it was a name he used only when he had to file his income tax report, or when he had to talk to the police or had other business in a town where the carnie parked. At the age of sixteen he had taken the advice of an old carnie veteran and shortened his name to Zulu.

He called in one of the roustabouts to take over at the House of Mirrors while he did that thing for India. This would be one of the best times, when

78

everybody was busy at work, when the day was going good, edging on toward evening, when the lights would start showing up and the crowd would increase.

At this time of day very few people were around the trailers or in the alley. He probably wouldn't have any audience other than a dog or cat, or some of the kids.

First of all, he had to have something to stand on. He took a stepladder from one of the trucks and placed it at the side of the dumpster. Then with a stick, a broken broom handle, he leaned over and began to rummage through the trash.

It took only a minute to see what a hopeless job it was. The dumpster was almost full, and the fumes that rose from it suggested there were such things as rotting potatoes dumped in with less odorous but more revolting items such as a plastic bag of used condoms.

He got down from the stepladder and looked around, and was relieved that no one had come to watch him, not even a cat or dog. The alley was fairly quiet, the racket of the carnival muted and deflected by the tents. Flies buzzed over the dumpster—the most noticeable sound. As if it were a hot summer day, insects had taken over here at the dumpster.

He folded the stepladder and carried it back to the truck, then went to his office and looked up the number of the local trash people.

"Say," he told the girl on the phone, "this is Zulumonsque at the carnival, and I need one of your guys to come out here and empty the trash bin. A member of the carnival has lost a valuable jewel in the trash. Could you help us? I've tried to find it myself, but it needs to be emptied."

"The trash pickup is due there this afternoon. They should be getting there at any time."

Zulu nodded and hung up the phone, and only later realized he hadn't said a word in response.

The day seemed to be getting off to a strange start in several different ways. First, there was the girl in the House finding some little thing that had been lost for almost sixty years. And then the kid had come to clean up, and evidently walked off without finishing his job or waiting for his pay, and India had told him things he'd never heard before. Then, without realizing he was going to, he had changed his hawking of the show. What had he meant by suggesting that a whole crowd had to go in together or they might disappear forever? It had been a pretty good idea. He could tell by the looks on the marks' faces that they liked the idea of danger in the House of Mirrors. A new adventure, an exciting possibility of danger. But why had he done it? It had slipped out. Probably some mental thing caused by what India had told him. Or the odd disappearance of the boy.

He went out to stroll the alley, and when the trash truck eased in a few minutes later, he was waiting.

He stood by while the trash was slowly dumped into the compactor and the two men helpfully sifted and separated and looked.

Zulu shook his head in agreement with them. If there were a jewel there, it had somehow slipped through.

When the truck pulled out Zulu saw that India had come out to stand on the steps of her trailer, and he went to her, feeling like a failure. This was the only thing she had ever asked him to do that he hadn't been able to do.

"Sorry, India," he said, looking up at her. "It just wasn't there. Or it had slipped into something else, and went into the truck without us seeing it."

She drew a long sigh. "Perhaps that is just as well."

The sun was beginning to lower, with the shadows growing long in the alley. India hugged her arms against her chest for warmth.

"You go back in," Zulu said. "And I'd better get back to the House. I've left it with Johnston long enough."

She nodded, and he walked away.

He looked back just before he went through the narrow alley between the old gray board walls of the mirror maze and the tent of the kootch show, and saw that India was still on the steps, gazing thoughtfully, sadly, toward the trash bin that was now empty.

EVERY TIME AMY thought of the jewel between her breasts a strange feeling came over her. She had cheated, in a way. She had—almost stolen. Anyway, she had taken without asking permission. It was like forbidden fruit, this jewel that lay like a hot coal against her skin.

She put up a hand often and pressed it, feeling its points dig gently into her skin.

Most of the time she didn't think of it. She hadn't been so occupied in all her life. In this work there was hardly any time to think, but when she did get a chance to think about it, she knew she loved it.

She kind of loved Russel too. She liked seeing him with his funny little apron, making change at the little window on the left, while he let her sell from the window on the right.

During a lull he had shown her how to wind cotton candy on a stick until it was big and full and pink. And he had shown her all the different dressings that went on the hot dogs. She had also learned how much popcorn to put into the popper, and how much of the other stuff that was already mixed —the melted butter, or whatever it was. The smells swirled around her, and the excitement didn't lessen even as the day wore on and her legs began to feel like sticks.

The lights began to show up, and suddenly, it seemed, the sun was gone and the bright, varied lights had taken over.

The crowd increased. They were lined up now at the windows part of the time, and the requests from the teenagers became as varied as the lights and the music.

"I want kraut and mustard and catsup on mine," said a tall boy with red, unruly hair and a sunburned face.

Another sunburned face peered over his shoulder. "I'll take the same, and can you add a little whipped cream to that, sugar?"

Amy said seriously. "We don't have any whipped cream."

The two boys hollered and laughed and slapped each other on the shoulders, and one said to the other, "You're confusing the little girl, Jacobs. Get on outta here."

So finally Amy knew they were kidding.

Still, she hadn't learned much when another teen-aged boy asked for chili and relish and onions and peanuts and bananas on his hot dog. She finally realized the boys had found her a source of amusement, and were daring each other to ask for crazy things.

She didn't know whether she was glad or sorry to be sent home at nine o'clock.

"Go on," Russel said. "Go to bed, Amy. Stop in at the cook tent first for your dinner, get some vegetables and milk."

"But who's going to help you?"

"I'll just close one of the windows, that's all, if it gets too wild. Run along now."

She was tired, she found, as she left the small trailer grab joint and walked toward the alley. Her legs were like rubber, almost uncontrollable, but she would never tell Russel. If she did, he might think she couldn't do the work, and she loved working with him. Even the big boys hadn't offset the pleasure of feeling close to Russel.

The alley seemed dark and deserted, after the bright noise of the midway. Even though the separation was only a few steps, a few feet from one to the other, the feeling was a world apart.

She stood still on the edge of the darkness, seeing the bright streaks of light from the midway lying like gold bars upon the black grass in the alley and making the darkness seem all the darker.

She felt confused, not even sure where Russel's trailer was or which one it was. She remembered that he had told her to go to the cook tent for dinner, for vegetables and milk, but she didn't know where it was. Nor was she hungry. She was only tired.

To her left the alley curved toward the darkness of a distant street, and to her right it curved again, following the line of tents. A few of the trailers had lights burning in the windows, but most of them were dark.

The jewel burned against her chest, and she put her hand on it. It was her lucky charm. It would protect her. She wouldn't be afraid. Nothing could hurt her. These things she told herself while she stood in the edge of the dark looking into it, feeling her heart begin to thud heavily and panic race over her chest and back like burning ice. She wanted to turn back, go to Russel and hover by him, waiting until he could walk with her through the darkness. Yet she knew her fear was illogical. The trailer was only a few yards away. It was only her imagination that dark figures hulked in the alley waiting for her, watching her with red and evil eyes.

Her hand clutched the jewel, and its edges poked into her palm. Her eyes searched right and left down the dark alley, seeing the streaks of light from the midway like fences—no help, no comfort.

Then suddenly the trailer house directly across from her, with muted lights at the windows, blared into sound. Voices shouted, then quickly were lowered. At first she thought it was real, that strange people in the trailer were shouting at one another. Then she recognized it for what it was. Someone had turned on a television, and the volume was too high. It sounded like something Jodi would do. She was always turning the volume too high, as if afraid she would miss something. Then Mama would call to her to turn it down.

Without looking right or left into the endless yards of black tunnel with its bright fences of light that only made the dark more treacherous, Amy crossed to the steps of the trailer. Close now, she recognized it—the double white stripe down the sides, the dumpy shape. She opened the door.

Jodi was sitting on the floor in her pajamas, looking up at the TV, her hair still damp from the shower. She looked wide-eyed at Amy, as if she were nervous from being alone so much.

"Why didn't you have the door locked?" Amy said, to cover her own nervousness. Her hand fluttered toward her chest to feel the comfort of her jewel, but fell away quickly before Jodi became suspicious.

"Why didn't you come to get something to eat?" Amy asked again, before Jodi could answer her first question. "Where have you been all afternoon and evening?"

"Just around. And besides, kids can't go onto the midway during business hours."

"Who said!"

"Blane said." Jodi turned her attention back to the TV. "And we ate at the cook tent."

The cook tent. That was where Russel had told Amy to go to eat vegetables. She paused outside the bathroom door. "Where is the cook tent?"

Jodi leaned her head back on her upraised arms, using the couch as a back support. She motioned with her elbow. "It's around on the other side of the midway. Over by Zulu's office and the big truck that runs all the time to supply electricity. Did you know ..." She sat up, and looked at Amy. "Did you know the carnie even has its own generator? And makes its own electricity? It's got a truck with an engine on the back that runs all the time, over on the other side of the midway. Some of the people live in trailers on that side too. The maintenance men and the roustabouts who do the work to keep things running, and pack up and move and stuff like that."

"How'd you know?"

Jodi settled back against the couch, her eyes on the television. "Blane told me. India told him to show me around, and he did."

Amy remembered her pajamas, and went to climb the ladder and reach back under her pillow. She was a little hungry now, but more tired and sleepy. When she went into the shower, she was careful to lock the door so that Jodi wouldn't enter and see the necklace around her neck. For she kept it on even while she bathed.

Amy climbed into bed a few minutes later, going up the ladder at the end of the couch. She had to work on her hands and knees to make the bed. Although she had spread it up this morning, she had done it quickly, and now she smoothed the sheets and straightened the blanket. There was not room for her to sit without bending slightly, but her earlier feeling of claustrophobia was missing. She was too tired to feel much of anything, except a leftover glow from working with Russel all day. "Dad," she whispered to see how it felt on her lips. Then, "Daddy." He was great. She had loved seeing him move about the tiny grab joint, slapping hot dogs together and dressing them and wrapping them in their slick paper. He worked so fast it was like one hand did one thing while the other hand did another, and all the time he was ready to laugh and talk with the marks at the window.

Only he didn't call them marks when he whispered to Amy. "Customers," he had said. "They're our customers. But if you're talking to one of the old carnie veterans, they're marks. Okay? But all we do is feed, we don't fleece. Only don't tell anyone I told you so, or we might get run out of carnie town."

So they had a secret, and Amy stretched out in bed not minding the cramped space. She was looking forward to tomorrow.

"Aren't you going to watch TV with me, Amy?" Jodi asked.

"No, not tonight. Maybe not all summer, Jodi."

"Are you real tired, Amy?"

She almost said no, but instead she sighed and murmured, "Yes."

"Was he hard to work for, Amy?"

"Russel? No. He was real nice. Good night, Jodi. Hadn't you better shut it off and come to bed?"

"In a minute."

Amy slept, and woke feeling smothered. The TV was still on, so she knew she hadn't been sleeping very long. Only a few minutes maybe. She saw she had forgotten to open the window, so she cranked it up, and the cool night air rushed in. So did the noises of the carnival, all the different music from all the different rides, and the pitchmen hawking their shows, and the screams of the kids on the rides and in some of the shows. The air seemed layered with the smells of hot dogs and popcorn and candied apples, not mixing with the night air, but slipping in between it. And like the smells, coming and going, the sounds blared and faded, drifted away one moment and stung her ears the next.

She lay down, satisfied with her surroundings. She closed her eyes and almost slept again, then suddenly her eyes flew open and she was staring down into the alley, a sense of something fearsome so near, somewhere in the dark below her window.

The shadows seemed all the more intense in comparison with the bright lights of the midway, so that although she stared into the darkness below, at first she saw nothing.

Then she glimpsed a movement, so subtle, so obviously trying not to be seen that Amy strained against the opening of the window trying to make it out. The figure—the animal, whatever it was—at the same time made her want to pull back and close the window, as if it could rise to the top of the trailer and slip through the narrow space that was open.

As she watched, something moved farther away, and in staring she began to make out outlines and small splashes of white. She frowned intently, watching, hardly breathing, while in the trailer's front room below her the TV droned on steadily, and light from the kitchen spilled into the bunk bed, leaving her only partly in shadows.

She wanted to hiss back at Jodi to turn out the light, but she didn't.

Now she could see there were at least three figures moving around outside the trailer. Not at the trailer next door, but this one.

Then suddenly Jodi turned off the television, and the kitchen's bright light went out. Amy could hear Jodi go into the bathroom. The only light she had left on was in the hallway, and it did not reach into the bunk bed to touch Amy. Now she could see better, with less contrast between the dark in the alley and the dark in Amy's part of the bunk bed.

She held her breath.

Clowns.

Three, maybe four.

She could see they were clowns only by their costumes. One of them had a costume patterned with small, white diamonds, and they glowed in the dark, now that Amy could see better, almost as if they were phosphorescent. The figures all looked about the same size, just ordinary clowns, not midgets or children, and probably not women. And they seemed to be working together, in complete silence, with their heads down.

As if they were searching the ground for something, right below her window now.

She drew back slightly, a strange cold fear covering her skin, a fear that one of them would look up and see her.

They moved in closer to the trailer, so that she could see only the white ruffle around the neck of one and the costume billowing out behind as he stooped. Then, as if guided by a silent signal, they moved slowly around the end of the trailer and toward the door, the only door in the trailer house except for one small emergency exit at the rear, by Russel's bed.

Amy quietly lowered her window and locked it, and then she crawled to Jodi's side of the bed, where she could look down into the front room and see the door.

Had she locked it when she came in?

No, she hadn't.

Had Jodi locked it when she turned off the TV?

No, she wouldn't have. She would leave it open for Russel.

Amy stared, and felt the clowns were going to enter, as silently as they were searching the ground outside ...

Searching the ground in the dark.

Fear as bitter as gall came up into her throat, and she wanted to get out of bed and lock the door, but she couldn't move.

Jodi came out of the bathroom, leaving the door open to the noise of the toilet flushing. Amy slapped her fingers against her mouth to shush her, to warn her not to speak.

Jodi stopped and stared at Amy in the semi-dark of the living room.

"What's wrong?" Jodi asked.

"Shhh. There's someone—some clowns—outside the door. Lock it."

Jodi turned and looked at the door, then looked back up at Amy.

"Maybe it's Izzy and Jade," Jodi said, and before Amy could stop her, she had snapped on the light above the door and opened it and was looking out.

No one was there. Amy could see through the doorway and into the lighted area covered by the door light.

"Shut it, Jodi!" Amy cried, and Jodi shut the door and looked up at Amy quizzically.

"It's all right, Amy. No one's out there. They must have gone on." As she climbed into the bunk she said thoughtfully, "But why would Izzy and Jade be out here? They've still got shows going on."

Amy had never heard of Izzy and Jade before, but Jodi's attitude, her usual calmness, comforted Amy and she lay back on her side of the bed. "Who's Izzy and Jade?"

"They're two clowns with a show for kids. They're really funny. You ought to see them sometime, Amy."

"When did you see them?" Amy asked.

Jodi said nothing.

"Jodi?" Amy prodded. Jodi was pretending to be asleep, and Amy knew she had done something she wasn't supposed to do. She thought of maybe telling Russel, and then she remembered the jewel she wore. She felt for it, closed it into the protection of her hand, and turned her back to Jodi. With her face against the glass, with Jodi behind her for security, she almost instantly went to sleep.

She woke again, the clowns moving through her memory, so that she wasn't sure she'd had a dream or if she had sensed they were there again. She peered through the window, and saw that all the big lights, the high lights, of the midway were out. The noise had stopped.

She wanted to open her window, but she was afraid to.

Then she heard the whisper of voices, and saw Russel and Lakisha coming between two of the tents from the midway. Feeling safe at last, Amy cranked open her window and lay with her face in the cool night wind.

She slept again, knowing Russel was close.

"ALL RIGHT, you've met them, come on in," Russel whispered, his mouth against the hair by her ear.

Lakisha wasn't quite yielding to him tonight. Although her arms were around his neck, her kisses had been somewhat shallow and teasing, not what he needed, and she seemed to be holding her body back a bit.

They stood in the shadows of the alley, within reach of the walls of his trailer. For some reason she had finished earlier than he tonight, and when he'd closed up his little grab joint, there she was waiting for him.

She hadn't even wanted food—and now she was playing coy.

"No," she whispered in return, "I couldn't."

"They're asleep."

"How do you know?"

"I can feel it," he murmured, nibbling the lobe of her ear and working around her neck to her throat, where he pretended to be a vampire, with growls and slurps.

Giggling, she pushed him away, and now that she had him at arm's length, holding hands only, he knew she was serious.

It worried him.

In gaining daughters, had he lost his lover?

"Hey, babe," he whispered yearningly, trying to see her face in the black of the night. There was a faint, oval blur in front of him, haloed by a soft cloud that was lighter than the dark, but he couldn't see her enough to gain comfort from it. What was the expression on her face?

"Listen," she said. "Russel, I can't go in there yet. I only met them a few hours ago. They don't know me. What would they think of me just coming in there and going to bed with you?"

"It's all right—they're asleep."

"But I'm not sure about that. It would bother me."

He was tired. More tired than he had been in a long time. He longed for the tall grass and the shelter of the trees where they had been last night, but he was too tired to go that far. He looked around the end of the trailer.

There was a field of the same tall grass, with a tree now and then, big, dark shadows in the field. Stars in the sky yielded a little light, and the town shed a glow into the sky, as always, but those lights seemed only to enhance the darkness. They'd never be seen.

"Come around here then," he suggested, tugging on her hands.

To his surprise she jerked her hands away.

"No!" she said, as if he had insulted her.

He tried to see her face, but it was only a ghostly blur. He drew back, thinking it was just as good maybe that he couldn't see her expression.

"What'd I do?" he cried, his palms turned up between them. "I only thought—"

"No," she hissed in his face. "That's the trouble, Russ, you don't think about anything or anybody but yourself! All you want is to get your tail wrung dry, and you don't think about anybody else's feelings! Good night, Russel."

"Hey ..."

He felt like a fool. He hadn't been dressed down like that since he was a teenager, or younger, and then not like that.

He saw her moving off through the darkness, down the alley, and he took a couple of tentative steps toward her.

He stopped and stared at the blur of her quickly retreating figure.

"Lakisha?"

She went on, without another word, and the darkness swallowed her, and she became part of it, her footsteps part of the earth with its sounds of wind blowing the grass, the soft whispers of things moving, on the ground, in the ground, from tree to tree in the air. While on the other side of the muted lights of the midway the steady throb of the generators went on and on.

Russel shook his head, climbed the steps to his trailer, and entered the front room. A light had been left on in the hallway, but the living area was shadowed and quiet.

He went down the hall unbuttoning his shirt and yawning.

Tomorrow he'd have to settle something with Lakisha. They'd have a long talk, if he could manage the time.

LAKISHA STUMBLED along with tears in her eyes. Why had she yelled at Russel? Well, not really yelled, but ... she had never told him such horrible things before, and she had never even known she thought them. She was only hurt that he would let time drag on and on, and then, instead of asking her to marry him, only want her to come into his bed to satisfy his—his perpetual hard-on. Of course, she wouldn't change that, not permanently, for anything. She loved him the way he was. Even his selfishness was just another facet of his personality. He was big and good-looking and easy-going and he needed a woman, and she wanted it to be her. So why had she acted like a shrew?

She stopped and looked back, undecided. She wanted to go back and be with him. There was, after all, a door to his bedroom.

But if she went back, they'd be starting another habit. She'd be going every night to his trailer just as she had for several years now.

If she held off, maybe he would see how much he needed her, and would decide to marry her.

She turned slowly on toward the trailer she shared with the other girls and the boss, her tears dried by the cool wind. From far away came the throb of the generators, so soft and such a natural part of the sounds around the carnival that she usually didn't notice them at all. The silence of the closed rides and the empty midway enhanced the sounds near her, and she suddenly sensed she was being followed.

With her heart in her throat, and a flicker of hope, she stopped again and called softly, "Russel?"

There was no answer.

She stood still, picking out shapes in the dark alley, uneasiness beginning to chill her skin. She could see the square bulk of the dumpster, and beyond it the outlines of a tent. She wasn't sure which tent it was—the clown tent? Izzy and Jade's place?

Something was standing at the corner, she realized as she stared. She could see splotches of white in a costume, and the suggestion of a white mouth on a clown's face.

It was like last night, she remembered, something she had forgotten until now. She tried to muster an ounce of anger, but it fell flat.

"Is that you, Izzy?" No answer. "Jade?"

She took a few steps backward, and the figure pulled away from the corner of the tent and moved with her, coming out into the middle of the alley. Now she could see it was a clown, with small, white diamond prints on the costume and a large, white-painted mouth only blurs of light in the darkness.

She brushed her hand against her cheek, perplexed, trembling with a fear she couldn't control. Were there clowns other than Izzy and Jade? She distinctly remembered their costumes and their painted faces, and neither of them had a white mouth. Both had big red mouths that turned up in grins that covered most of their faces. One of them wore a pointed bald piece on the top of his head, and the other had a bushy rag mop for hair. Their costumes were polka dots.

This clown was someone she had never seen before.

"Who—who's there?" she asked, her voice quavering weakly.

No answer. The clown stood not ten paces away from her, directly in the middle of the alley. Just stood there. But she had a feeling that if she moved, the clown would move. What did he want with her?

She turned her face and looked toward the trailer she shared with the others. It was maybe fifty feet away. She couldn't see, she could only guess. But here, within reach, was another trailer, its windows dark. But at least it was there. She could reach it in a few steps.

Something else occurred to her. The dog, Roscoe, hadn't barked. That meant whoever it was that wore the clown costume was not a stranger.

She decided she would just go on, as if she weren't getting more terrified by the minute. She would calmly walk on down the alley to her own trailer and go in, just as she always did.

She turned and took two steps and stopped suddenly, her heart exploding in surprise. Two more clowns had stepped out from behind the walls of the House of Mirrors, and now stood like the one behind her, and she knew what they were doing.

They were blocking her way.

In silence they stood, their faces toward her, and this time she could see quite clearly from the splash of light that came between the wall of the tent and the wall of the House of Mirrors.

They wore grotesque faces—masks, possibly—with white mouths that curled down, and holes of eyes slanted downward at the outer corners. One of the faces had a long, pointed nose curved like a hook down toward the chin, and the chin itself was pointed and long. Around the neck was a white ruffle, and recognition struggled in her memory for a moment, a white light as unsteady as a wriggling worm, and was gone again.

She had seen the clown costumes before. But where?

And then it didn't matter.

She whirled, to pass the one clown behind her, to go back to Russel, to scream for him to come and help her.

She stopped again, abruptly. Another clown had come from somewhere to help block her way, so that now there were four.

The white blurs from the costumes and the faces were like fragmented ghosts in the dark. Wind blew the branches of the tree at the back of the House of Mirrors, rattling the leaves, and the generators throbbed.

Lakisha made a sudden dash for the door of the nearest trailer, and saw from the corners of her eyes the swift movements of the clowns as they closed in on her. White-gloved hands caught her arms and jerked her backward off her feet, and another gloved hand covered her mouth, cutting off the scream that rose instinctively to her throat.

She could hear her own groans as she was dragged away from the step of the trailer, and her terrified eyes, looking up, saw the horrible faces of the clowns that bent over her.

The swollen white mouths with their ugly droops, and the dark holes of the eyes in the masks lowered to her own face. One of them had white streaks drawn down from the sloping corners of the eyes to the jawline, like scars.

She clutched at a costume, and felt the material, the heavy cotton with the white diamonds, like patches, and just as she began to lose consciousness it seemed she remembered where she had seen the costume, but it didn't matter anymore.

CHAPTER 8

INDIA WOKE SUDDENLY AND LAY TENSE, LISTENING.

The room was dark. She had never been one for night-lights, for any light at all when she slept. Her curtains were closed, blinds drawn.

She was not ordinarily a light sleeper. She slept deeply, when she slept at all, with bad dreams occasionally waking her.

But the sound she had heard was real, not of a dream, and India's body was stiff with anxiety and tension as she listened. With her breath held, she slowly sat up in her bed, trying not to rustle the sheet.

Someone was in her trailer house, moving around. She felt no unsteadiness, as from a heavy step, but she could hear subtle movements, of cloth against cloth.

She got out of bed and moved slowly into the hall and stood listening again.

Whatever it was seemed not to have heard her. It was still moving about like a mouse, with sounds not much louder.

Whoever it was had entered her living room, and was there now, among her treasures.

She went quietly down the hall to the living room, reached around the corner and snapped on the light switch.

India began to frown, her eyes searching the living room from the sofa on her left to the door on her right. The door was still closed, and even the lock was the way she had left it.

The costumes hung on their pedestal supports against the wall at the other end, but ...

She stared at them.

The one she had named Joey was not in place. It was hanging crooked on the support.

As if someone had tried to remove it, and had left it twisted.

But no one was in the room now. No one was under any of the tables or hiding behind any of the costumes.

She straightened Joey, arranging the shoulders just right along the heavy bar of the hanger, and pushing the rod that held the hanger back farther against the wall.

To make sure her lock had not been tampered with, she examined it, to see that it was exactly the way she had left it when she went to bed.

Something boomed out behind her, and she jumped and whirled before she realized it was the clock on the shelf striking the hour of three.

It was the darkest part of the night, the witching hour, and someone had been in her living room. Yet how had they managed to enter and leave without unlocking the door?

Or was her imagination going wild?

Had she left Joey crooked on his hanger?

No, she was sure she hadn't. She would never do that.

Light bloomed softly from the tasseled lamps on the end tables, and she left them on.

She went into the kitchen and turned the light on there.

No one was hiding.

She checked the small bathroom, even the square tub behind the curtains. No one.

Perhaps it had been a dream after all, a continuation of the nightmares that had plagued her since she was five years old.

And now that the talisman had been found, and then lost again in the trash bin, an uneasiness lived with her all the time, day and night, in light or dark.

She went back to her bedroom and turned on the light.

Her papa's clown suit stood in the corner on a hanger with a rod going down to the round metal base, just like the suits in the front room.

She took it off the hanger and put it on. It fit her as well as it had her papa in his young days, the legs ballooning over the striped stockings. She adjusted the mask over her head, and looked at herself in the mirror.

She saw a happy, laughing face, big mouth turned up. Laughing silently.

While inside there was no laughter.

She pulled the old white gloves over her hands. They had lost their bright whiteness over the years, and the material on the tips of the fingers was worn almost through.

Comfortable in her disguise she left her trailer, and wandered through the dark alley. In this way she had watched the folks in the carnival for many years. The bells on the suit jingled faintly as she moved along the alley, and at times now she paused, conscious of the sound of the bells.

People slept. They all slept, it seemed. The whole world slept except her. All her life since she was a child, she would wake with the nightmares in which clowns moved through her dreams, going from the happy face of her papa to the other, terrible faces. And she would wake around three o'clock in the morning, and not be able to go back to sleep. During the winter in Florida, when the carnival was usually in its winter silence, she sewed at night. From three to five, every night. Then, when the carnival went on the road again, she put on her papa's suit and wandered about, feeling safe in the suit, feeling somehow invisible in the dark. The dogs never barked at her. If they acted as if they might, all she had to do was speak softly to them. Sometimes she saw lights on in a trailer, indicating another sleepless person. But usually the trailers were dark. Sometimes too she could hear the most amusing noises, raucous snores that sounded as if the sleeper were in a tin can, the sound magnified.

Paddy Orson, a big, hairy man who weighed close to 300 pounds and stood well over six feet tall, was one of the snorers. But another, which surprised her, was Zulu.

She always went by his trailer just to feel secure, even though it was parked on the other side of the midway, near the generators. To know he was there made her feel good.

He was all the family she had left.

Once, she had gone to a doctor and taken pills that made her sleep heavily. The dreams had stopped. But she had begun to feel heavy and depressed in her mind, and decided after a few months that the pills and the sleep weren't worth it.

She stood in the alley, just out of a streak of light that fell between the walls of two tents. The wind was blowing at a steady gait, a prairie wind, going from the gulf to Canada with nothing to stop it, and the wires that were strung around the midway and which held the bulbs that remained on all night were swinging, swinging, with a musical squeaking in different pitches, and the light that threw the golden streak across the alley swayed with the wind. It grew lighter and then dimmer on the grass, reaching and receding. Sometimes the light touched her floppy shoes with the two little bells on the pointed toes.

There was something in the air that made her feel that she was not alone in the alley this dark night, that somewhere behind her something watched, seeing in the dark with ease, watching her every movement.

If she turned suddenly, would she see it?

Her hair stirred on the back of her neck as if it were exposed to the wind.

The wind blew constantly here on this flat land. Even the trees leaned permanently with the wind. And it reached into her costume and stirred the hair on her arms and legs and brought it up in ancient warning. She turned slowly, scarcely moving, her eyes searching through the mask for things that didn't belong in the alley, for shadows at ends of trailers that were not part of the trailer. The darkness seemed darker than usual, the shadows sunk into the blackness that surrounded the trailers.

There were no stars showing now, and the glow of lights above the town was absorbed and swallowed by a moving hover of clouds. As India turned she saw a sliver of light flash through dark clouds in the west, and after several seconds of listening heard the faint rumble of thunder.

The air was electric with warning as she finished her slow turn and looked back down the alley behind her. The lights across the grass, dwindling to shadows and then dissolving into the complete dark, wavered and danced as the wire blew. An edge of a tent came loose from its stake and flapped in the wind suddenly, and somewhere nearby in a trailer someone coughed, choked, coughed again, and grew still. Metal squeaked faintly as wind pushed at the trailers, rocking the smaller ones.

Somewhere over toward the town a dog began barking, and in the countryside a cow bawled, over and over again, far away, the sounds so faint they were like night birds calling to one another.

And in the alley India moved slowly forward, the jingle of the bells on her toes lost even to her own ears beneath the rising demands of the winds that seemed now to be coming from several different directions.

The lightning was closer, and the thunder steadier, but still the alley was dark, split only by the faint, wavering streaks of midway light, not yet illuminated by the lightning.

It was going to storm. On the prairie storms could be vicious, she knew from past experience. Although they were close enough to the hills to have some protection, the wind could still batter them.

She almost fell over something in the alley. Something on the ground, unseen in the dark at her feet. With her arms out for balance she steadied herself and, looking down, she saw something pale, like exposed flesh, and she wished she had brought her flashlight.

She nudged it with her toe, and found it softly yielding. It moved with her foot and then lay still again.

Fear, lying barely dormant within her, surged suddenly forward, almost like vomit. Her heart began to race, and her mouth grew dry. She stepped back, her eyes straining to make out the shape and failing. Whatever—whoever it was—was lying still. Too still.

Had someone fallen drunk in the alley?

That had happened in the past. Always they were men, and once a woman, from a nearby town who had simply wandered off the midway and lain down to sleep it off. But the fear that was turning to absolute terror told her that that was not the case this time.

Standing a few feet away, she tried to think of what to do. She could go back for her flashlight, or she could go after Zulu and have him bring his flashlight. Or she could knock on the nearest trailer and ask them to turn on their door lights so she could see who lay in the alley, because she was sure, almost sure, it was human. Now she seemed to be finding an outline in the dark—an arm, a leg perhaps.

Swallowing the bitter fear in her throat, licking her lips to try to add moisture, she bent and touched gingerly, feeling for the pale appendage that lay at an angle away from the dark bulk of the body, and her fingers seemed to touch other fingers.

She jerked off her glove and reached out with her bare hand, felt the hand of the other person, and knew instantly that it was young and female. The nails were long and tapered and very smooth, obviously polished. The arm was bare and limp. Too limp. And too cold.

India squatted and stared into the dark above the body, looking on down the alley to where it curved. The trailer she saw was longer than the ones on each side of it, and suddenly she knew who was here on the ground.

Lakisha.

As always she had been going from Russel's trailer to her own, the long one she shared with Bob and his girls. She had been going home, alone, as always, and—something had stopped her.

India sat forward on her knees, removed her other glove, and felt for the girl's face, to confirm her suspicions. The flesh had a coolness that was not natural, though it seemed as she touched the bare midriff that a warmth lingered.

"Lakisha!" India whispered frantically. She found the girl's tapered chin, and grasped it, and found it loose and broken, the chin coming away from the rest of her face, connected only by the skin.

With an involuntary cry, India drew back.

She sat staring like a blind person, feeling thwarted by the dark, unwilling to reach out again. Into her memory came a sudden flash of the day she had returned to her tent to find her mama on the floor. Her face had been broken too, blood still trickling from her nose and mouth.

She couldn't touch Lakisha again, if this actually were Lakisha. It might be one of the other girls, but whoever it was still wore her dancing costume. India's fingers had touched the tassels that rested on the midriff below the bra. But now she could see the pale glow of hair lighter than the grass, and Lakisha was the only one of the girls with blond hair. Bob liked his girls all to have different-colored hair, so Alice was a redhead, Sally had black hair, and Junie had rich brown hair.

Why was she thinking these things?

Here on the ground lay a young woman who, she was afraid, had died the same way her own mama had died.

India got to her feet, and turned quickly toward the lights of the midway. She went between the walls of the tent of the clowns, Izzy and Jade, and Bob's revue of girls, and into the light of the midway. She crossed by the inner tents, with their games and their flaps down now for the rest of the night, and on past the kiddie rides and through the tents on the other side. The generators chugged away on a nearby truck bed. She turned left.

A night-light burned over Zulu's door. A beacon in the night to anyone who needed help.

She could hear his snores before she reached his trailer, but it was not the comfort tonight that it should have been. This was one thing Zulu might not be able to put back together.

She knocked on his door, but the wind carried away the sound. When she knocked again she realized she no longer wore her gloves, nor even had them with her. Had she dropped them along the way, or were they back with the battered body on the other side of the midway?

She pounded harder on the door, and then she tried the knob. The door opened, and she stepped up into the living room that was also Zulu's office.

The snores stopped abruptly;

"Yeah, who is it?" Zulu's voice called out.

India said, "It's me, Zulu. India. Can you come in here, please?"

"Sure, sure, just a minute. Turn on the light, India, sit down."

India felt for the switch at the door and flicked it on. A ceiling light came on and illuminated the small room brightly. Over to her right was his desk, with the filing cabinets behind it, all cluttered with papers he had filed in his own way. To her left was his chair and his small TV. There was a leather couch against the wall opposite the door, with a pillow at one end, indicating that sometimes he stretched out there to rest, watch TV, or read. An unlighted swag lamp hung from the ceiling at the head of the old brown couch.

Zulu came through the doorway on her left, dressed in shirt and trousers as if he were ready to go to work. His great mat of gray hair stood on end, making his head seem even larger. With one stubby-fingered hand he tried to comb the hair into place, but succeeded only in creating an untidy pompadour.

"You didn't have your door locked," India scolded, forgetting that she wore the clown suit and mask. "You could be robbed and killed, Zulu."

"No." He was staring at her in surprise. "Nobody enters but that I hear. I'm a light sleeper."

The expression on his face reminded her of her costume, and she slipped her fingers under the full head mask and wriggled it off. Her hair was in no better shape than his, she could feel. Though it was braided for night, the braid had come loose halfway down like a horse's tail. She flipped it over her shoulder out of her way.

"What time is it?" Zulu asked, looking for his clock on the desk and finding it under a pile of papers. "Almost four o'clock? What's wrong, India?"

She began to feel extremely weak in the legs, but supported herself only by holding to a chair until the weakness passed.

"Someone—I think it's Lakisha—is hurt. She's in the alley, over near her trailer. We need a light."

Zulu hesitated only a moment, a pause in which he frowned at India, as if trying to assimilate what she had said. He didn't ask her why she was wearing the clown suit, and she was glad. She didn't feel like trying to explain something as personal and as old as her late-night habits. Not yet.

He took a large electric Spotliter down from its nook on the wall and led the way out. Though his legs were short, he could walk almost too fast for India. At a half run he hurried now, around the alley at the end of the midway, flashing the light on and off dizzyingly, while India hurried to keep up. They passed trailers at the end, these occupied more by temporary hired help than by regular carnie people. They reached and passed the long trailer owned by Bob, and shared by his girls. Zulu slowed, and turned the light on and left it on, arching the beam ahead into the well-trod grass of the alley.

It touched the body on the ground, the bright beads of the skimpy costume, the pale, bleached hair.

India walked at Zulu's side as they approached the girl.

She hadn't moved, that India could tell, and what hope she'd had began to dwindle away the closer she came.

Zulu shined the light down upon the girl.

Her face was turned to its right cheek, and nearby was one of the white gloves of India's costume. Blood from Lakisha's nose and mouth had puddled darkly in the grass, and one finger of the glove had soaked it up like a blotter.

"What's that?" Zulu asked, his voice sounding hoarser than usual.

"I dropped it," India said. "My gloves. When I found her—I hit her with my toe—I bent down, and I took off my gloves so I could feel—so I could determine—in the dark—what it was—"

Zulu pointed the light at her trailer, on down the alley. "India, why don't you go home now? I'll do what I can here."

"No," she said firmly. "I'm staying with you. Is she dead, Zulu?"

He bent down, propping the light on the ground. He moved one arm of the girl and it yielded in a crooked and limp sprawl. After a few moments he sat back on his heels.

"She's dead," he said softly. "But she's only now getting cold. I guess she's not been dead very long." The sky was suddenly threaded with bright veins of lightning, like blood rushing through a giant's body. Thunder rippled behind it. The light from the sky moved eerily over the alley, glowing on the metal roofs of the trailers.

Zulu stood up. "She's been murdered, India. She needs to be covered. She's dead. Her arms are broken, her face is broken. She looks like she's been run over by a bulldozer."

He took hold of India's arm and led her around the body and toward her trailer.

"You get me a sheet and I'll put it over her. I'll get your gloves and bring them back to your place, and then we'll talk. But while I'm doing these things, you brew yourself a strong cup of tea."

"Broken—just like my mother," India said. "I knew something terrible was going to happen, Zulu, I just knew it."

"Come on, get me the sheet," Zulu said again. "Brew the tea. If not for yourself, then for me. I'll be back soon."

Zulu led her into the trailer, and waited while she brought him a sheet.

"Brew that tea," he said fiercely as he went out the door again.

She set to work, trying not to drop and break anything, her hands shaking hard now.

She remembered she was wearing her papa's suit, and she went to her bedroom and removed it. She looked around for the mask, but it was gone too.

She had dropped it somewhere? She had taken it off in Zulu's office, she recalled, but after that, what had she done with it?

Carnie people liked to handle their own deaths. If someone died during the summer, though, the carnie had to call in a local doctor and go through a rigamarole of red tape in order to ship the body home.

She didn't want the police.

But what could they do?

She carefully arranged the clown suit on its hanger, but it looked eerily unfinished without its head mask.

She returned to her small kitchen and finished making the tea, and then she took the pot with two cups, sugar, and cream on a tray into the living room.

Hours passed, it seemed, before Zulu knocked once on the door and entered. He was carrying the gloves, one of them dark with blood, and the limp mask.

"I think you should throw these away," he said, as he rolled the two gloves into a knot. "The police are going to ask too many questions about them."

"I found her, I touched her, that was all. I dropped them beside her."

"But why were you wearing the clown suit? They will ask why you were wearing the gloves, at three-thirty in the morning."

She frowned. "I heard someone," she said. "I had forgotten. Finding Lakisha made me forget. But I woke, hearing someone in my living room. And I came in here and found that one of my children had been—moved." She pointed at the clown suit on the right. "It was not where I had left it."

Zulu stared at the suit, at the others standing at attention in a row, and back at India.

"I know you didn't kill her, India. I know that. But the police will ask you too many questions. You heard someone, you say."

"Yes, but no one was here. And so to use my papa's clown suit as a disguise, I dressed in it and went out to look around. Someone had been prowling around, Zulu. I heard them in my own living room."

"So you went out to look around alone. You should never do that, India. You should call me."

She didn't tell him she had been going out alone all these many years, dressed in her papa's clown suit.

"What must we do now, Zulu?"

"We have to call the police, India. We have no choice."

He went to the door and looked back. The outside communications system was in his office.

"Keep the tea hot, India. I'll be back in a few minutes."

As the door shut behind him the first large drops of rain fell.

In India's mind she saw the pale body of Lakisha lying twisted and broken, the sheet now plastering to her body with the rain, the blood on the ground thinning and becoming watery and cold.

Her mother's murderer walked the midway once more.

CHAPTER 9

Cold, wet raindrops blew in on Amy's face through the open window, and she woke and reached for the lever to close the glass that reached the full length of the bunk. Heavy winds made the trailer feel as if it had turned into a cradle. The old lullaby verse came to her mind, and she sang it mentally as she tugged on the window lever. When the wind blows, the cradle will rock; when the bough breaks, the cradle will fall, and down ...

Lightning illuminated the area in a ghostly, greenish light. She could see the arch of the Ferris wheel above even the tall tree with limbs tossing like the limbs of a drunken scarecrow. She could see the tops of the tents, and the bony reach of other rides, seats swinging and rocking in the wind. She caught a glimpse of the alley, winding away past the back of tents and the House of Mirrors.

And it seemed, as the lightning stopped and left a total blackness, that she had seen figures in the alley.

Then, like spots before her eyes, a residue of the lightning, she saw the flash of lights down the alley, and dark figures with dark, shining skin.

Amy hunched at the long, narrow window, with the lever in her hand, and her face pressed into the blowing rain. She stared. The cold of the rain and the wind swept the full length of her body, but even as she closed the window the cold remained. Jodi, sleeping, had curled into a ball at Amy's back, pressing closer for warmth.

But the alley held Amy's attention. Water running down the pane of the window now blurred the scene, and she eased it open again so that she could see. The sprinkles of raindrops that blew in upon her face were as cold and stinging as slivers of ice, but at least her vision was not so obscured.

Someone was in the alley with a light. It seemed to be flashing on and off, and then she saw that it was merely pointing in different directions on the ground.

Somewhere beneath one of the trailers a dog began to bark. His voice sounded muffled by the wind and rain.

A light came on at a trailer's door, and threw a circle of visibility out onto the alley. Now Amy could see that more than one person was in the alley, and they were wearing black raincoats and hats. Their flashlights danced around the edges of the pool of yellow light thrown by the porch light of the trailer, and suddenly added to it was a circling of blue lights, flashing round and round, coming from the street, easing past the trailer from which Amy watched, going on down behind the trucks, cars, and pickups that were parked behind the trailers, and stopping.

The blue lights revolved, like eerie lightning that had dropped to the ground.

Amy shivered.

More people in rain slickers and carrying flashlights moved into the alley and surrounded something on the ground.

The dog that had been barking hushed, as if he had been scolded.

More trailer lights, near the thing in the alley, came on, and the figures in black milled about, like witches at a gathering on a dark and rainy night.

With a terrible dread in her heart Amy closed the window again and fastened it tightly. Now the rain blurred the scene, and she saw only the flash of lights, of blue and white, whirling on and on until she fell asleep again, too tired to stay awake.

She dreamed of weird lights, and among them not the figures in black, but clowns, milling about with their bodies bent, their heads down, looking for something they had lost.

AMY WAS STILL SLEEPING when Jodi woke, curled up like a pup in its bed, with all the covers gathered round her, and squeezed into a bundle in her arms. Jodi climbed half-asleep down the ladder and headed for the bathroom. While she was in there she washed her face too, so she wouldn't go back to sleep, because she didn't want to miss anything of the exciting days at the carnival. Only when she came out of the bathroom did she notice that things were different today.

The trailer door stood open, and somewhere out of sight stood a group of people who were talking, words spoken low. Jodi did not recognize a voice until Russel said something. She listened, caught more the tones of the voices than any word, most of which were too low to understand.

She hopscotched over to her suitcase and pulled out a clean shirt and hurriedly dressed in her jeans. In the bunk bed above Amy whimpered in her sleep as if she were trying to cry. She was having a bad dream, Jodi knew, and was torn between climbing the ladder and waking Amy from her dream and hurrying on out to see why Russel was standing in the alley talking to people so early in the day. When Amy grew quiet again, Jodi rushed through the door and leaped over the step to the ground.

She stopped.

The grass was wet with rain that had fallen during the night, and the sky was filled with broken clouds. Sunshine streaked through, and a rainbow hung in the west.

But the alley seemed to be filled with little groups of people, just standing around, looking at the ground or down the alley, their faces strained and serious.

It took only a glimpse to tell Jodi that something terrible had happened.

Russel was standing with a small group a few feet away, his head down, chin almost pressing into his chest. His hands were in his pockets. The five other people who stood with him all seemed to be looking on down the alley.

"Hey, ssst."

She recognized the sound instantly, but once again she couldn't see him. She looked under the trailer, and into the narrow alley between two tents on the other side of the alley. She looked with suspicion at the tall grass, though it looked as if it had been so plastered down with rain it couldn't conceal a chipmunk.

"Ssst. Ssssst, Jodi, here."

It was behind her and she turned and looked again, peering into the narrow alley that glistened with drops of rain still clinging to every blade of grass and to the canvas walls of the tents.

Then she saw a movement of fingers motioning, and at last she spotted Blane's head—just a hump on the top of a garbage can, it seemed.

She crossed the alley to the narrow space between the tents, and found

Blane hunkered behind the can. She stooped out of sight of the big people in the alley, on a level with Blane.

"Do you know what happened last night?" he whispered excitedly, his eyes round and nearly popping out of his head. His hair looked as if he had been out in the rain, and was wetly clinging to one side of his forehead, yet the very top was dry, and stood up in spikes. His clothes were damp, and Jodi understood the wetness came from his surreptitious crawling around in the grass, eavesdropping. But even as part of her disapproved, she was eager to hear.

"No, what?"

"Lakisha, the dancer, was murdered."

Jodi stared at him, her face almost touching his.

"Murdered?" she only whispered the word.

Blane nodded, shook his head up and down so vigorously he looked as if he would rattle his brains.

He got hold of her wrist and pulled her after him into the midway, where they stood at the front of a tent, out of the wet grass.

"The police were there, all around. Did you see them?" He didn't give her a chance to answer. "They took pictures and everything, and the rain was pouring down. They took pictures in the rain, and the coroner came and looked at her."

"You were there?" Jodi whispered.

Blane nodded again. "I woke up. The lights of the police cars woke me. I watched out the window, and then at daylight I went outside. The rain stopped. I thought you'd never wake up and come out."

Jodi looked back toward the alley, but saw nothing. The tent beside her blocked the view. In her mind's eye she saw Russel, standing with his head so low.

"Lakisha was Russel's girlfriend," Jodi said.

"I know. The police talked to him."

"They did?"

"Yeah, the police talked to just about everybody. Then an ambulance came and took the body away."

"Lakisha?" Jodi didn't like hearing him call Lakisha "the body."

"Well, her body. Lakisha is dead."

"Who killed her?"

"They don't know."

They went back to the alley and stood around for a long time. The sun rose higher into the sky and turned warm. Jodi saw Amy come outside, and then go back into the trailer. Russel too went back into the trailer. Zulu came down the alley and talked to different groups, and the groups began to disperse.

When Zulu approached, Blane went to stand in front of him.

"Zulu, are we opening today?" he asked.

Zulu waved his chubby hand in dismissal, as if to brush Blane out of his way. "I don't know yet. Run along and keep busy, Blane." He glanced at Jodi. "Show the little girl around. Keep out of the way." Blane bounced to one side as Zulu went on by, no taller than Blane himself, his big head of white hair standing in all directions, as if it hadn't been combed since a strong wind had tossed it about.

ZULU CLIMBED the steps into Russel's trailer. With his hand on the door he pulled himself up and in. This was the hundredth trailer he'd had to enter this morning, it seemed, all of them higher than the last.

Russel was sitting on the couch with his head in his hands. Not far away, standing, was the child Amy, whom Zulu had seen yesterday working her little hands to the bone in Russel's grab joint and looking as if she would have flown to the moon for her father if he had asked. She was a birdlike little creature, too thin, as if there were nothing to her but a bony skeleton under her skin and in her loose shirt and jeans. She wasn't quite as pretty as the younger girl, Jodi, but you never knew how she might turn out. Sometimes beauty crept through in odd and unexpected places, just as ugliness could grow too, like fungus sticking its head out of every crack, every damp, dark place.

"How're you doing, Russel?" Zulu asked.

Russel raised his head. He looked as if he'd been crying, but his eyes were dry now.

"Oh, Zulu. Didn't hear you come in. Sit down, make yourself comfortable. Can we get you something?"

"No." Zulu pulled a kitchen chair out from the table and hiked himself up onto it. "We won't necessarily be opening today," he said. "But neither can we move on like we were supposed to tonight after the show. The police want us to stay around an indeterminate time, they said. I've come to see what you think about going on with business as usual—or do you think we should stay closed, at least while the police detain us?"

Russel took a long breath. "I don't know. Why make the carnie people just hang around? They'd rather be working, I know. I would. I don't see that it would matter to Lakisha. What about her family? Is anyone going to claim her body?"

"Yes, some folks have been notified. She has a mother living in ..." Zulu dug into his pocket for a piece of paper that had a name and address written on it. "Next of kin was her mother, who lives in Rochester, New York, or Minnesota. Yeah. Minnesota. The police talked to her, the mother, and she just said to ship the body on home, that she couldn't afford to come down here."

Russel nodded. "I guess I didn't have any legal rights. I threw that chance away. If I had kept her with me, this wouldn't have happened. If I had gone with her, walked her home ..."

"Both of you might have been killed," Zulu said. He stood up. "Then we'll go ahead and open. Like you say, it's better for the people to be busy. Even if there's no crowd, it's better for the people to get ready for business, to open and close."

Zulu scratched his cheek. "I have to get back to my office and call the next town and tell them I don't know when we'll get there."

He went out of the trailer with almost as much trouble as it took getting in. Russel had stood up behind him and followed him out, his eyes looking drained of life. But at least now he had something to do, Zulu figured. Instead of sitting around worrying about what he should have done to keep Lakisha alive, he was going to open his grab joint.

Maybe the crowd would come anyway. At least this first day after the murder, before the news spread. As Russel had said, Lakisha would want the work to go on.

"I GUESS they're going to open up after all," Blane said, looking past Jodi.

Jodi hurriedly crawled out from under the fence that surrounded the Loop-o-plane. She had felt they were treading on thin ice when they went in, even if they hadn't really tried to get into the seats of the planes.

Now she saw the people moving onto the midway, men and women who were working in silence to raise tent flaps, and unlock gates of rides. Down toward the end of the midway the music of the merry-go-round spurted up and the horses began to move.

"I didn't think Zulu would open up," Blane said. "I remember last year an old carnie guy died, and we stayed closed to honor him for a day."

"Was he murdered too?"

"No, he had a heart attack. Nobody's ever been murdered before. It was someone from town who did it, bound to be. Nobody here would do anything like that. Listen, follow me. I know someplace we can go even when the marks are in the midway."

"Where?"

"Follow me."

Blane ran toward the end of the midway, past the Ferris wheel and the Bubble Bounce, and on past the Humpty Dumpty ride. Jodi cast a longing glance at the rides, but the owners were coming now, opening gates, opening doors of ticket booths. And she didn't have the money for a ride on any one of them. Even if carnie kids were allowed on the midway.

She followed Blane, leaping over heavy ropes of cables as he did, going off the midway beside the Bubble Bounce, and out toward the back alley where dozens of big carnival trucks were parked. Somewhere off to her right Jodi could hear the sounds of the generators that kept on and on even when people died.

Blane was running close to the backs of the rides at the end of the midway now, and slowing. Jodi caught up, breathless. He pressed against the back of a building that was not made of canvas, and she realized it was the House of Mirrors.

He looked in both directions, like a spy.

"Okay," he whispered. "Promise you'll never tell."

"And cross my heart," Jodi whispered back, making the cross over her chest.

Blane dropped to his belly and crawled out of sight beneath the House of Mirrors, and with only slight misgivings, Jodi followed him.

The grass was dry beneath the floor, and so tall that Jodi felt as if she were in a jungle. Blane made a path for her through the grass, a virgin path, never crawled before.

When he sat up, his head barely touched the boards of the floor above.

Jodi sat up beside him, eyeing the boards in the meager light for signs of spiders and creepy-crawlies, creatures that might drop down the back of her shirt collar and sting or bite.

Blane could see her cringing and began to smile. "What're you, afraid of a little bug?"

She hadn't wanted him to know. Now he'd be throwing things at her, like boys did, and even if the things they threw were made of plastic they'd scare her and make her yell, which was what the boys liked. So they'd just throw more stuff more often. It was things like that which had made her not like boys very much.

"No," she said shortly, and tried to look comfortable and at ease. "Let's get going, wherever we're going. We didn't come under here just to sit in the grass, did we?"

The House of Mirrors was less disturbing to her than being beneath its floor where the bugs were.

"Okay. Don't tell."

"I already told you I wouldn't."

"Then follow me."

He got down on his hands and knees and battled through the grass again,, and then he was rising, straight up into the floor above.

It was darker here, and Jodi had to use her hands to feel for the hole into which Blane had disappeared. Gingerly, afraid she would put her fingers on a fat spider, or something else that would wiggle and crawl beneath her touch, she found the hole in the floor.

It was a tight squeeze, but when she managed to reach her arms through she felt Blane get hold of her and pull.

Then she was standing in a narrow corridor that was barely lighted from somewhere beyond. Mirrors reflected her and Blane, standing almost chest to chest in the narrow space, but the reflection was dark, stained, almost invisible.

When Jodi spoke, it was with a soft whisper, and even then she felt she had been detected by someone or something in the dark, mirrored walls.

"Where are we?" she asked.

"In the House of Mirrors," Blane said.

"I mean—what part?"

Blane shrugged. "I don't know. I only know where the hole is, that's all. Except I know that this part is closed off, and marks never come in here."

Jodi frowned, looking up at the ceiling and the webs that clung to the edges of the boards and swung down against the dark mirrors. Even here, then, she was not safe from the spiders.

"Why is it closed off?" she asked, still whispering.

Blane shrugged. "I don't know." He was answering her now in whispers, his eyes still big and searching the ceiling, the walls. "Weird, huh?"

"Yes."

"Want to look around?"

Now Jodi shrugged. She was not going to be chicken, but already she was willing to go back down through the hole and out. She looked down, to be sure the hole was still there. It looked as if someone with a heavy step had broken through at one time and the floor had never been repaired. The broken edge of the board was jagged, and the hole extended to one of the boards that ran crosswise beneath the building.

"Why are the lights on in here if it's never opened?" Jodi asked, because she could see that a bulb was burning somewhere and the light fell more brightly at a certain point in the mirrors, as if shining past a wall into another hallway. The reflection, so confusing, looked as if a dozen corridors were somewhere ahead with brighter lights, an offering of darkness lifted.

"I don't know. It's just a crazy house, that's all. Coming or not?"

Yet Blane hesitated, as if he half hoped she'd say no and lead the way back down through the hole.

"What if the murderer is in here?" Jodi asked in her muted whisper.

Blane was silent. He looked on toward the lighter part of the mirrors, and back into the more shadowed areas.

"I hadn't thought about that," he admitted. Then he looked at the hole through which they had come and said, "A murderer couldn't come through there. The police said the killer musta been a big guy, because of the way she looked. They said it took a lot of strength to break her up like that."

"They told you that?" Jodi asked in awe, thinking Blane must be a lot more important than most kids.

"They didn't tell me, dumbo." Blane sneered in his usual derision. "I just happened to hear what they said, that's all. They were talking to my dad, see. They knocked on the trailer door because our trailer was one of the closest ones to where she was killed." Blane's eyes widened again for an instant. "And I didn't even hear a thing. Not until the police were already there. But they came and asked my folks, see."

"Are your folks carnie people?"

"Sure, what do you think? I'd be here by myself?"

"What do they do?"

"They're concessionaires," Blane said importantly and with his shoulders lifted he led the way on down the corridor. "They own a lot of things. Games and things. I'll show you sometime."

Jody could see his reflections, looking as if he were walking past murky waters, black water in a swamp. Other figures seemed to be reflected beyond him, like shadows of tree trunks rising naked in this strange world they had entered.

"Blane", she said, keeping her voice low, her anxiety coming through enough to stop him.

Blane looked back at her, but she was looking beyond him, at the reflections in the dark mirrors, at figures moving in that eerie world behind.

. . .

INDIA SAT ON HER SOFA, feeling cold as ice. When the knock came on the door, she called out for the visitor to enter, but her only movement was to pull up the shawl and cover her arms with it. She looked at her clowns, her children, for comfort, but the comfort they usually gave was missing. She felt as if she were immersed in an unending nightmare. She knew she was awake, but even her children today looked as if they would turn on her, their faces no longer familiar.

Two men dressed in suits entered. They were vaguely familiar, but India had seen so many of the police, in uniform and otherwise, that she couldn't be sure she had seen these two before.

"Miss—uh—India Xerxes?"

They even got the pronunciation right, so India surmised they were the two she had talked to earlier, or that Zulu had told them her name.

"Yes. Sit down, gentlemen."

"We'd like to ask you a few questions again, ma'am, if you don't mind."

India nodded her head.

One of the young men was looking at the clowns as if he hadn't seen them before. She felt obliged to explain.

"They're my own creations," now wondering if they really were or if they were copies of the clowns that had been in Raoell's show. Yet she remembered only two clowns—still, her dreams, her nightmares, had picked up more, until she had these seven. "I've spent my lifetime making clown costumes, and searching stores until I found masks that—fit them." Masks that were like the ones in her nightmares, she thought.

"Ma'am, you say you went out to walk the mid-way at three-thirty?"

"The alley," she corrected. "That isn't unusual for me. Almost all my life I have slept through the early hours of the night, then awakened between two and five. Sometimes I sit and sew on my clown costumes, and sometimes I go out and walk around in the alleys between the tents and the trailers."

"So you didn't go out because you'd heard anything?"

"No."

She hadn't told them about hearing someone in her living room. They would have thought she was just an old woman who was getting paranoid, she supposed, because she would have had to tell them her inside lock was just as she had left it. No one, she realized, could have gone out her door and left the lock turned.

"So you heard no sounds out of the ordinary?"

"No, I didn't."

"What time do you think you woke up?"

"Just a very few minutes before I went out. Around three-thirty. I took time only to get dressed." Nor did she tell them she had dressed in her papa's clown suit. It had nothing to do with the murder of the poor dancing girl.

"Could you tell us again what happened? What you saw and heard? Sometimes people have heard or seen something that is a direct clue without realizing it. I apologize for making you go through this again, Miss—"

"Yes. Well. I went out to walk the alley. I didn't take a light with me. I never did. Only when I do the big dog that belongs to the Orsons barks, and then I do take a small flashlight."

"But last night the dog did not bark?"

"No, not that I heard."

"Could he have barked and awakened you? Without your realizing it?"

"No, I don't think so." It had been the subtle movements in her living room that had awakened her, but that had nothing to do with the murder. However, if she said the dog barked, they might assume a stranger had come in from outside and done the killing. And wouldn't that be better for the carnival? They had to move on, to keep their commitments. It was their business, their livelihood.

So she said, "Perhaps the dog did wake me. At any rate, when I did go out he was not barking." That, at least, was true. She felt only a slight twinge of guilt at trying to throw the blame for the murder somewhere else.

She had not told them about her mother. But she knew in her heart that whatever it was that had killed her mother was the one—the thing—that had killed Lakisha.

And she knew too the police would not find the killer.

She was beginning to feel that would be up to her. Somehow, she had access to the answers, if anyone in the world did. And it was up to her to find them.

CHAPTER 10

"Come back, Blane," Jodi whispered, and he took a step backward toward her even as he protested.

"What are you, chicken?" His sneer flickered and failed.

Jodi didn't argue with him. There was something about the mirrors, the movements back in them, as if the water were oozing and changing, as if the trees that stood naked in this unreal swampland were beginning to move too, that made her too scared to go farther. It didn't matter if Blane called her chicken, just so she got out, and he came with her.

The moment she saw he was coming back, she lowered herself through the hole in the floor and wriggled down into the grass beneath the House of Mirrors. The bugs that might lurk beneath the floor had lost their ability to worry her a lot.

She moved over and made way for Blane.

He squeezed through and sat beside her.

"You chickened out." His sneer had returned, dampered by a grin of superiority.

"Didn't you see that?" she asked.

"What?"

"Something—I don't know what it was. But it didn't look like any plain old mirrors to me. It was like a world in a science-fiction show. I could see things moving besides your own reflection. Like tree trunks, moving, coming in closer to you, and ugly black and brown water moving around."

"Really?" he cried, low-voiced.

She was afraid suddenly she was making it so interesting, instead of scary as it had seemed to her, that he would want to go back in and see for himself.

She began crawling away.

"I gotta go," she said.

"You gotta go where?"

"To help my dad maybe. I have to go see if he needs me."

It was an excuse she hadn't thought of before, and she felt rather proud of herself. "See you later."

When she was out from beneath the House of Mirrors she looked back, to make sure Blane hadn't gone back in alone. If he had gone back, she would have too, but in relief she saw he too was crawling out. With a skip and a hop she slipped into high gear and ran down the alley.

RUSSEL DROPPED THINGS. He dropped a whole hot dog once, complete with lots of chili dressing, and he had to clean it up and make another chili dog for the kid who was waiting. His fingers felt numb, his hands clumsy, and his eyelids kept burning. Only the customers at the windows kept him from breaking down.

He had kicked himself as far as he could, and it hadn't changed the facts. He still felt the disbelief he had felt early this morning when he'd gone out to see what all the commotion was about and Zulu had come to him and told him Lakisha was dead in the alley.

Russel had tried to go to her, but Zulu had held him back. He'd never known until then that Zulu was so strong. When Russel had realized that Zulu was trying to hold him for his own good, he'd stopped trying to get to the body on the ground.

He'd seen only that she was there, among all the lights, in the rain.

He'd had only glimpses of her, and then he'd turned away.

They had assured him she was dead. He had wanted to see for himself, because he couldn't believe it, but Zulu had told him not to go.

Only then had it dawned on him that the death was caused by an unknown killer.

Still, he couldn't really believe it. Why would anyone want to kill Lakisha?

The only answer seemed to be because she happened to get in the way.

In the way of whom?

There had been more than one, some of the people suggested. It had taken more than one strong man to break her face and her arms and body the way they had been broken. "It was like she had been run over," he had heard someone say, "except her skin was not damaged enough for that. But maybe that was it anyway—some vehicle drove down the alley."

It made no sense. Most of the talk was speculation among the carnie people who had stood around in the alley watching the best they could through the rain and the dark. Only the police and the coroner and medical guys and other people who had some business there were allowed within several feet of where the body lay.

It didn't make sense.

Why Lakisha?

If he had told her he really was thinking about marrying her, she might have stayed. She was right, he was selfish and self-centered and thought of no one but himself.

He looked out the small, open window of the grab joint and saw a pretty little face that looked at first glance only remotely familiar. Then, with a jolt to his consciousness, he saw it was Jodi.

He mustered a smile for her.

"Hi, sweetheart, are you hungry?"

"I was wondering if you wanted me to help you too? I can make change and count. And I could learn to make stuff."

"Sure you could, babe, but right now we don't have enough room in here for another person. Why don't you just take this ..." He reached into the cash drawer and got a handful of change. "And go on some of the rides."

Jodi's face brightened, as if he had handed her the keys to the carnival. "Could I? Could I really?"

"Yes. And when dark comes, you get yourself into the trailer and lock the door, hear?"

"Yes, I will."

She ran a few feet away, pushing past the line of customers that was gathering near the joint. Then she looked back and called, "Thanks, Dad!"

Dad.

Russel had almost forgotten how it felt to be called Dad. He hadn't heard the title, in connection with himself, since another life—another world, it seemed—when a little tot called Amy had called him Daddy.

He looked at Amy, working at the other window, getting tall now, her dark blond hair pulled back and held by a band over her head, and it occurred to him that she hadn't called him anything.

But then, what the hell, he hadn't earned that either, just as he hadn't earned the right to keep Lakisha.

THE CROWD GREW HEAVIER, but Amy didn't feel so confused. It was getting easier all the time to listen to the stupid things teenaged boys wanted on their hot dogs, and then to smile at them and do the best she could to make it just like they wanted. So when one of them, one of the very same faces that had given her so much grief last night, now asked for chili, relish, peanuts, and whipped cream, she put the peanuts on top of the rest and then, to make it look like whipped cream, added a glob of mayonnaise. The kid who took it looked at it with a puzzled lack of comment while the three boys with him yelled with laughter. The joke was on him now.

The teasing subsided somewhat, but not enough for Amy to get bored. She was beginning to like the teasing. It was attention that wasn't unkind after all.

"Amy," Russel said, long after the night-lights had come on and the rides were whirling. "Would you like to take a break and have some fun?"

"I'm okay," she said.

"Why don't you go over to the cook tent and eat some vegetables?"

"Can't I just stay here?"

"You need some vegetables, don't you?"

"I could eat an apple," she offered, her heart tugging painfully at the unhappy look on his face. She had been almost too busy to look at him until now, and she wanted to please him, but to go over to a cook tent she had never been to scared her. "I don't want to go alone."

"Well, I'll take you tomorrow at noon before we open then. You've got to have better food than you can get here. Listen, Amy, you keep the windows covered while I go get someone to walk you to the trailer, okay?"

"I know the way," she said.

"I know you do, but I don't want you crossing the alley alone."

"Do I have to go so early?"

"Jodi's alone there, and I don't like it. Makes me uneasy."

He removed his little white apron, stained now with splashes of mustard, catsup, and chili like a surrealistic canvas, and wadded it and stuck it down into the plastic bag that held the dirty linen. He ran his fingers through his hair.

"Be back in a minute, Amy."

"Hey," a voice at the window behind her said. "You wanna sell me a bag of popcorn?"

She turned eagerly, but her glance swept on toward the alley, the dark places behind the tent of the balloon game—where several young guys were throwing darts at balloons that seemed to move out of the way just before the dart hit the wall behind them—and a flash of movement and color caught her eye.

They were there again, the clowns, moving in the dark. She caught a glimpse of a white ruffle and a horrible face with a painted white mouth that curved downward like a half-moon, the drooping ends going into a long, pointed chin. And for just a moment it seemed the deep eyes of the face looked directly at her.

She almost dropped the bag of popcorn, and she had to watch what she was doing long enough to give it to the customer. When she looked again toward the dark alley she saw nothing.

She put her hand on the precious jewel that hung on her chest, to be sure it was still there.

Russel came back into the little joint, leaving the door open. Beyond it stood a man who looked like a wrestler. He wore a sleeveless shirt, his brown arms bulging. His shoulders were strong, his neck short and wide. His brown hair was in a crewcut.

"Hi, Amy," he said. "You need a bodyguard, that's me."

Russel said, "Amy, this is Ken. He works for Zulu. He'll see you to the trailer."

Amy hesitated. She wasn't tired yet. She wanted to stay. "Couldn't I wait until you go?"

"Jodi's alone," he said. "Aren't you tired?"

"No. Not tonight."

"Well, after we move on to another place, we'll see. But here ... I'd rather you went home."

Amy understood. It was the murder of Lakisha that made him afraid for Jodi.

Russel said as she went obediently out the door, "Lock the trailer house door, Amy, and don't open it for anyone but me, or Zulu, or India. Make sure you don't."

"Okay."

The big man smiled down at Amy. "Ready?"

She nodded.

They crossed the midway, dodging the teenagers who wandered around laughing in groups. During the afternoon a lot of older people had come, and young mothers with children. Then, in the evening, dads had come with mothers and children. But now, as the night grew on, the crowd had changed again. There were very few small children or old people. This was a noisier crowd, and Amy liked it. But she liked the little kids too. And all the others. She didn't want to go to the trailer. But she remembered what Russel had said—when the carnie moved to a new location, maybe she could work until quitting time.

The lights were on in the trailer, and Ken knocked on the door. Amy stood at his side, looking in both directions along the alley. The dark, with the light streaks from the midway, had an eerie look that made her glad Ken was with her.

The door opened and Jodi looked out.

"There you are, kid," Ken said. "Go on in and lock the door. I'll wait here a minute."

"Thank you," Amy managed, her tongue feeling thick with shyness. One of the most miserable situations for her was to have to face and speak to an adult, especially one she didn't know very well. She had always let Jodi talk for her whenever possible. She hated being the way she was, and as she stepped up into the trailer and pulled the door shut, she put her free hand on her good-luck charm. It would change things for her. It would change her ... make her grow up beautiful and self-confident, with a lot of friends and everything.

Now she had hopes, and she went to bed with a daydream in her mind, moving hopefully like an interrupted movie. The good-luck charm, her pretty jewel, would make her beautiful and self-confident like the girls on TV and those she saw with the boys on the midway. She had something to look forward to, after all.

INDIA SLEPT HEAVILY, lying flat on her back in her comfortable bed, her mouth open. At times she stirred restlessly, and became aware that she was not sleeping well. She had wanted to stay up, to keep watch in her living room, but exhaustion had forced her to bed. She would sleep a few minutes and then get up, refreshed, for the night's vigil.

She had left the light on in the front room, to discourage anyone from entering, or perhaps to scare away the ghosts of the darkness. And it was the light perhaps, shining just a bit down the hall past the bathroom and into the open door of her bedroom, that kept her from sleeping restfully.

She dreamed of seeing Zulu bend over something on the ground, and the feeling that rose from it, like a vapor foul-smelling and evil, choked her awake.

She made a motion to turn over, and then realized she was being stared at. She was not alone in her room.

Even with the light for protection, someone had entered, and was now standing in the shadows at the foot of her bed.

Her eyes flew open, as she dug her elbows into her soft bed to push herself forward. Half sitting, she looked into the face of Rube with his witch's face, the long, pointed nose curling monstrously down almost to the pointed chin, the mouth a cruel slit, the eyes black holes of nothing, slanted and evil.

The clown was standing near the corner of her bed, its back toward the light that dwindled in from the living room. He was bent forward, as if to grab her leg, his arms hanging forward, the white gloves like dull-glowing lights on the ends of the empty arms.

India screamed, a hushed, choked sound, pushed to silence by one fist against her mouth.

Then she realized that someone had played a horrible joke on her.

She told herself that a joke was all it was, that Rube could not have moved on his own. Regardless of her beliefs—what she thought were her beliefs about the killings, about Raoell's powers and the mystery of the House of Mirrors—she did not believe that Rube had moved without help.

Still, her hand shook almost uncontrollably when she reached for her bedside light, and when she got out of bed she got out on the side away from Rube.

When she went around the foot of the bed she saw the stand behind the clown costume.

Someone had moved it, stand and all, from the living room to her bedroom, to scare her.

Why?

She moved the clown back to the living room and put it in its place, and straightened the costume on the hanger. But as she worked with it she was aware of a feeling of terrible uneasiness, and her fingers kept shaking as if palsied, making it almost impossible to make the costume look normally placed.

When she went to the couch to sit down, she saw that it was crooked on its hanger, and so was Joey, just as he had been the night before.

She looked from one to the other. From Rube with his witch face, the long, pointed nose, the pointed chin, the thin slit of mouth, the empty eyes, to Joey at the other end with the large, white mouth, curled down, and again the empty eyes. Empty eyes in all of them, yet in every one of the seven she could see them staring, staring at her. None of the faces were happy clown faces. Only the oldest clown, the first, the one she had called Lazy, had a round face, with round, red spots on his cheeks, and a red mouth that was supposed to be smiling. But even his face, cherub round, seemed ugly and evil tonight, and reminded her suddenly of the happy side of the faces of Raoell's clowns.

The memory came sharp and clear, as if she were small and helpless and looking up at the happy side of the clowns on the platform. Happy only because they smiled. But then the faces turned around and became terrible, angry and fierce and frightening rather than sad. The teardrops painted on their cheeks looked like blood rather than tears, and the pull-down of their mouths was not the kind that made a child's heart cry with them, but made her pull back as if they were saying in silence, I'm coming to get you, and I'm going to kill you in terrible ways.

How could she have been so stupid and gullible as to think these clowns were her own creations? They had been in her dreams, and she had thought they were her own original designs. And all the while she had been dreaming of Raoell's clowns. She had been creating what he had created before her.

Yet she had seven. From seven dreams.

Had Raoell presented seven different clowns on his platform show over the years?

She remembered the door suddenly.

It was locked just as she had left it when she'd gone to bed at nine o'clock, the deadbolt secure. She rose from the sofa and went deliberately to check it, not leaving a chance that she might be seeing wrong from across the room.

But it was locked.

When she walked slowly back to the sofa she was aware of the empty eyes of the clowns. And when she sat down and faced them she felt a chill move over her body.

She was afraid of them now.

They're only empty clown suits, she reminded herself. Only empty clown suits

She did not intend to sleep. She would sit here all night long. There was a possibility that someone had figured out a way to unlock her door and play these horrible tricks on her, and then lock it again after they left.

Magicians were capable of almost anything sometimes.

She knew of no magician with the carnival, except ... Raoell. But she must not think of that. She must not. Not tonight, when she was alone with the clowns.

INDIA SAT helpless in her place on the sofa, hearing the movements in the room. The light had dimmed, or her eyes had lost their sight, so that it was as if she lived in a twilight world. The furniture she remembered being part of her living room had changed, and there was little of it, a few tables, some straight chairs—where had the straight chairs come from? She hadn't seen straight chairs like these since she was a child living in a tent. Her attention was drawn away from the furniture and her surroundings, which seemed to have no boundaries in her limited vision. The movements—she remembered. Someone was moving about in her living room. She tried to see through the gloomy light, and to her horror the clowns were coming alive, as if they were real after all, and they were coming toward her ... toward her ...

She woke, choking, strangling. She cleared her throat and sat forward on the sofa.

She must have fallen asleep. She had not planned to sleep more on this night. Her bedtime hours had passed, and she had kept vigilant. Of what she wasn't exactly sure, she only knew it had something to do with her living room. The movements here last night had not been part of a dream, nor had the removal of one clown to her bedroom a few hours ago.

The light was not dim, as in her dream. A lamp at the end of the couch burned just as it had since sundown, and the ceiling light in the kitchen was still on.

Her heart was still trying to get its breath from her crazy dream. Why was she beginning to feel afraid of her own clowns, her children? She had always loved them so much, each stitch sewn into their clothing stitches of love. And now, since the talisman had been found, her nervousness was making her afraid. Bad things had happened, putting purpose behind her dread. An innocent girl had been killed. Innocent? There were no guilty ones. Who, then, had deserved death? No one. Yet her dread had been there, brought alive by the talisman, as if she knew someone would die, again, as her mother had died. Or disappear, as her papa had?

And now her fear had a focus. Her clowns. Her children. Would she have to sell her children?

Give them away perhaps, but never could she sell them.

But to think of giving them away was like giving up all her hope, all her life.

She sat forward suddenly, staring.

Some of the costumes were gone.

Joey at the end was gone, and Rube and Hazy—every other one was gone, leaving a gap between the ones that remained. The faces on Bozo and Lazy stared with their sightless eyes at her, their hideous faces looking cruel and evil suddenly, and laughing at her in crazy, silent ways, as if a terrible joke had been played on her.

She pushed herself up from the sofa, staring. How could she have sat there while someone came in and stole three of her children—her clowns?

Jerking her caftan skirt out of her way, she went to the door and stopped, a tight fear pulling at her skin. The door was still locked. No one could have locked it from outside. It was a deadbolt, to be opened and closed only by someone on the inside of the room.

Just like last night, and earlier tonight, someone had entered and left without leaving the lock undone.

She whirled, looking back toward the darkened end of the trailer.

That meant, with the deadbolt still in place, that whoever had stolen her clowns had an accomplice. And someone was still in the trailer.

Feeling as if she were lost in a continuing nightmare, fighting off the panic of helplessness, she went back through the trailer, covering every hiding place, turning on lights as she went and leaving them on. She even opened cupboards that no one larger than a child could have gotten into.

In her bedroom she stood, trying to think. Her papa's costume was on its hanger, and no one was hiding in her house. Was her lock malfunctioning?

She supposed it was possible.

In some way, the lock was not a detriment to whoever was entering and leaving her trailer.

It would not have stopped Raoell.

Whoever, or whatever it was, had something to do with her clowns.

She began to dress.

She was going out into the alleys to look for her clowns, and when she found them, she knew, she would find Lakisha's killers.

. . .

ZULU HAD WATCHED the closing of the midway. Lights were shut off, leaving on only the night-lights strung on wires from tent to tent around the midway. Rides had stopped, music stilled. Shutters were closed and tent flaps lowered. Zulu walked slowly around the midway, watching the people streaming out, watching the carnie people closing up behind them.

When the last of the people had gone to the trailers he wandered behind them, seeing with satisfaction each trailer door that closed behind each person. They knew to lock their doors, he hoped.

As he walked the alley he saw that no one was taking a last puff of a cigarette on a trailer step, not tonight. Each grim face had gone quickly from the light of the midway to the light of private trailers.

The night had gone from noisy to quiet, all in a matter of minutes.

He circled the alleys on both sides of the midway once, and then started around again. It occurred to him that he might not be indestructible himself, and he went back to his trailer and strapped on a potentially wicked hunting knife that a carnie veteran named Mayo had given him and which he had never used—what fool would want to hunt animals with a knife, for crissakes? But tonight it made him feel safer. There was a time when he had practiced knife-throwing, back when he was young, so it wasn't exactly something that he couldn't handle.

In the dark he went out to circle the alleys once more, suddenly unsure of himself now that the lights, the music, the marks, and the carnie people were all gone. The night seemed darker than it used to seem, and as he walked, trying to keep his movements soundless, he contemplated stringing new lights up along the alleys.

It was one way to add to the security of the people, to help keep them safe. Some of them wouldn't like it. They didn't want the world lighted outside their homes all the time. They wanted to sleep in the dark. But it was one way to help secure the area.

He had rounded the end of the midway and was getting away from the drone of the generators. The night seemed to take on an eerie silence that made him want to look over his shoulder all the time.

He had a flashlight with him, but he kept it dark. He stopped, listening to the sounds in the night. A truck pulled a heavy load on a highway somewhere far away, its voice reaching the fairgrounds with no more pizzazz than the buzz of an insect. Yet beneath the distant sounds of other worlds, it seemed he could almost hear something, that he should hear something that was happening now—a step in the grass perhaps, or a figure sliding against the outside of a wall.

Zulu stepped swiftly to the left and flattened himself against the nearest wall. He realized it was the House of Mirrors, and a strange, snake-like chill went up and down his backbone. His narrowed eyes tried to see through the dark, to pick out the outlines of the other figure he knew was also in the alley. He could detect furtive movements as someone—something moved slowly toward him in the dark night. Beneath his determination to be the victor was a feeling that the other could see him, knew where he was, and was coming for him.

He unsheathed the long hunting knife, and held it ready in his hand. He angled it to throw. He could still hit a target dead center, if he could see it. But his eyes failed to find the outlines of the other.

He stood ready.

INDIA STOPPED, listening, in the deepest shadows between tent and trailers. She had heard movements in the grass, and she listened hard, to make out the directions of the sounds. She would like to pull her head mask off, to uncover her ears, but she didn't want to lose her disguise. In her hand tonight was a flashlight, but she held it pointed at the ground, turned off. It might be useful as a weapon, if need be. Otherwise, she never used a light when she made her witching-hour rounds of the alley.

She heard an intake of breath, so near it seemed she could feel the reactive warmth of it through her mask. Someone was standing very near her. She jerked back, and at the same time caught a glimpse of light, just a mere flash, on a bright, flashing object.

"Who's there?" a gruff voice demanded, and a light came on, flooding her. She saw the bright object fully now, a knife that looked as long as a saber, and in the rear arc of the light she saw Zulu's white hair and lined, rough face.

She almost fainted. Then she reached out, and saw that his arm was drawing back in warning, the knife ready to defend himself. He didn't recognize her.

"Zulu," she said.

And the moment he heard her voice the knife wavered, his eyes blinked, and the heavy eyebrows raised just a bit.

"India?"

She pulled off the mask. "Turn the light off me, Zulu, please."

"India, what in the living hell are you doing out here in that garb?"

He pointed the beam of the light downward, and then shut it off entirely, and the dark descended, thicker and blacker than ever.

"Zulu—three of my clowns have been stolen."

"Stolen? Why didn't you call me? What are you doing, coming out here when there's a thief as well as a murderer?"

He had sheathed his knife again and now took her by the arm and was leading her to her trailer as if she were a recalcitrant child.

"Whoever took my clown suits is the killer, Zulu. It must be Raoell."

There was the slightest hesitation before he answered, and she knew he didn't believe her.

"Raoell's been gone for sixty years and more. You said so. He was probably as old as thirty, maybe more, back then. It's not Raoell, India. But you're going to be one of the victims if you don't stay..." He paused just slightly and said, "Stolen? When? Sometime when you were out of your house?"

"No. While I sat right there, Zulu. I was going to sit up and keep watch tonight, but I fell asleep on the sofa. And when I woke, three of my costumes were gone. Someone had taken them. While I slept, Zulu."

"Hadn't you locked your door?"

"Yes, my door was locked."

They had reached the door of her trailer, and to make sure of the step Zulu turned his light on again. He went up first, and reached his hand back for the key. India gave it to him and he unlocked the door, reached in, and looked carefully around.

Soft lights from the curtained windows of the trailer made small patches of gold along the front of the trailer, but none of the light seemed to affect the darkness of the alley.

India looked behind her, feeling a presence she hadn't seen. With the suddenly heavy mask limp in her hand she searched the darkness toward the tents, the thick black just behind the tents, separated from the streak of light that angled in from the midway. The wind was coming up again, making the electric cords sway, and the lights moved on the grass as if they were playing some kind of game, each competing with the next, racing forward, jumping back.

She felt blinded as she turned, the light of her trailer behind her now as Zulu pushed the front door open. She could hear him walking about in the trailer, searching through it for—what? The thief? The killer? A blotch of white became visible to India's eyes, and with a jolt of recognition she knew it was Joey's suit, with the ruffle around his neck, the white of the material looking pale gray in the darkness.

She stared, stepping away from the light that poured out the trailer-house door, going sideways to a darker area so that she could see. Had the thief brought Joey back and somehow propped him against the wall of the tent, or was someone wearing his suit?

She wanted to speak, but a terrible fear suddenly made her incapable of speech. She could see the clown more clearly now, the white mouth, the slanted, dark holes of the eyes, the white gloves. It was standing motionless at the corner of the tent, but as she stared it moved, stepping away from the tent and, it seemed, toward her.

Then a definite step beyond her, on her right, at the end of her trailer brought her whirling. Suddenly the other two were there. She could see Rube's terrible face, with the lumps in the skin and the cruel pull of his mouth. He was bent forward slightly, his long arms reaching out, the white gloves like pale lights of their own making. Beside him, a bit farther out in the alley, was the third clown. They were moving together now, coming toward her.

She turned and tried desperately to gain access to her trailer, but the hands of the clowns jerked her back.

She felt herself falling backwards helplessly, feeling tangled in the too-ample material of her papa's clown suit. She tried to scream, and managed a croaking cry before one of the gloved hands closed over her mouth.

She had to turn and fight. There was no other choice. She was a big woman, and fairly strong, though she had gone soft in recent years. Still, she could fight when now her life was the object.

She twisted in their hands, even as they pulled her along the ground and around the end of her trailer. With her legs drawn up she kicked out, but felt no solid body. She reached with her hands, ungloved, and grasped the costume nearest her, and her hand sunk into it, and through, and there was nothing, nothing within the material of the clown suit.

CHAPTER 11

"THERE'S NOBODY HERE, INDIA," ZULU SAID, GOING BACK INTO THE LIVING ROOM
of the trailer. He stopped, looking with surprise at the emptiness, for any
room without India was empty.

He went to the open door and flicked on the outer door light, wondering.
Had he not turned it on when he opened the door? And why hadn't he? And
India, where was she? He had entered her house first, to check to see if
someone had entered again, someone with a key, because how else could an
intruder come in and steal her clown costumes? And she had been right
behind him. Hadn't she?

With a coldness spreading in his chest, he went out the door, jumping
from the step to the ground. The door was back, wide open against the
outside of the trailer, and light from the door, and from the door light on the
exterior wall, shined out in a wide circle, reaching to the rear of the tent of
the dart game on the midway.

India stood nowhere within the light.

He turned on his own flashlight and shot the beam beyond the circle of
light in both directions.

"India!" he called frantically, beginning to run, his short legs too slow for
the reach of his mind, for his need to find her. "India!"

A light came on next door, and Monty looked out. He was a young
concessionaire, in terms of the carnie, since he had been with them only ten
or so years. He traveled with his wife Dale and their two small children. His

tanned faced peered out at Zulu. He was buttoning a shirt as he came down the steps.

Zulu shined his light full into Monty's face, then dropped it away.

"I can't find India," Zulu cried. "Get a light, Monty, get everyone you can find and get out here!"

"Yeah!" Monty turned back into his trailer, zipping his pants, stuffing his shirt into the pants. "I'll be right there."

Lights beyond blared out, and the alley looked narrower and less dangerous. The Clarks, husband and wife, came out, both of them in robes.

Zulu waved his light briefly at Estes Clark, a veteran of the carnies, although he had brought his rides and added them to this one only a few years ago.

"Help me find India," he demanded. "She was here and then she—just disappeared."

He went into the spaces between the end of India's trailer and the one next door. The grass was high and damp, and Zulu shined his light ahead and to each side in desperation.

Lights began blinking on in trailers, in a chain effect, one after the other, and voices grew in the background, in the light, behind Zulu as he waded waist deep through the thick, green, wet grass, his flashlight beam darting ahead of him and in an arc from left to right searching, searching for a sign of India. He began to call her name intermittently, in growing desperation. A great knot had swelled in his chest and moved into his throat and dimmed his eyes, so that he had to keep blinking in order to keep the film from his eyes, to keep from being blinded with the fear and the pain. Where was she? He remembered how she had stumbled across the body of Lakisha, and in wordless prayer knew he must not stumble upon his dear India. He couldn't live without India.

No one in the world knew that but him.

LAKISHA WAS TEASING RUSSEL, in a way she never had. She would run from him into a milky haze beneath the trees, and stand there with her gossamer skirts floating around her, and motion him near, promising him ecstasies unknown in his life. And then, as he moved to reach her, she would disappear.

Russel woke, sweating but cold, tossing in his bed, the sheets wrinkled and twisted beneath him, the blanket gone. With reality a cold dash in his face, he sat up and, in the straggling light that was coming and going through the window, tried to find his blanket.

Lakisha was dead, but the dream had been so real.

It wasn't possible that Lakisha could be gone.

He threw aside his sheet after his legs became tangled in it and felt the end of the blanket. He tugged up on it, and then sat still, waking more fully, looking at the light that flashed through his bedroom window and onto the wall. The voices were like an afterthought, picked up gradually from the sounds in the night, not close enough really to disturb.

Russel got up and pulled on his jeans, stuffing the top of his pajamas into the rough fabric, pulling the zipper, all automatically. His thought was they have caught the bastard that killed Lakisha. And he wanted to be there, to take one fatal punch at him if he had the power, to shoot the bastard in the gut if he had a gun, to hang him to the closest tree if he had a rope. If Johnny Law weren't right outside the door to take the creep to jail and to trial—and to a long series of messing around and doing nothing, because of the "rights" of the killer, of course—and then letting him out on parole instead of frying the son of a bitch.

Russel turned on his own porch light and went outside. Men were moving around, through the alley, which now was pretty well lighted from the trailers, and back into the field of grass beyond the trailers and the cars and trucks that were parked there, lined up as carefully behind the trailers as the trailers were lined behind the tents. Near the doors of the trailers stood a few women, and the faces that were toward Russel were wide-eyed and pale.

AMY WATCHED the figures through the window, the pane cranked up so that her face was in the cool air of the night. Fireflies danced out over the grass in the field, dimmed now by the larger lights that danced about as erratically as the lights of the tiny fireflies.

Russel had awakened her as he went out, and she had opened her eyes to see the men moving about, to hear them talking, the mutters clouds of sound like buzzing insects. Sometimes there was a shout.

She scooted down in bed so that she could see farther back into the field. Men were out there, with flashlights, and as she watched and wondered, Russel came back into the trailer and got his own flashlight and went out again. Amy didn't call out to him. Jodi was sleeping still, coiled in a knot halfway down the bed on her side. The noises, the lights, had not awakened Jodi, and it was important to Amy that she continue to sleep.

Amy wanted to be alone. There was something there, on the edge of the darkness, that kept drawing her eyes, as if her mind knew a figure stood there watching the activity of the carnie people—and she was the only one who knew.

She stared, pulling farther up into the bed, looking down the alley past the trailers with blazing door lights. Down there, where the alley curved, the trailers were not lighted, and it was there, in the darkness beneath a tall tree, at the back of—the mirror house? She wasn't sure. She had not been that far down the alley. But there, wherever it was, stood the figure, or figures, that she felt she should see.

Quietly she slipped out of bed, climbing around Jodi and letting herself to the floor. Without taking time to dress, she rolled her pajama legs up so that anyone catching a glimpse of her would think she was wearing shorts.

She slipped as quietly out of the trailer as she had slipped out of bed, and stood in the light of the door for only a brief pause as she looked around. No one was watching her. The small group of women two trailers down was looking beyond, out between two trailers into the field, and the alley had emptied so there was nothing now except the little cluster of women.

Amy ran across the alley to the tents. The light was here too, but she was alone. She went down the narrow passageway between two tents, the path she always took to go to Russel's grab joint.

The midway seemed totally deserted, and Amy stopped, fear closing in on her back like a silent ghost, turning her cold and frightened. She almost went back, yet stopped, and stood without moving at all.

Lights strung around the midway shone down upon the littered ground, but shadows lay heavily among the rides in the center of the midway and among those games with tent faces shuttered or otherwise closed. For an instant it seemed that she could hear sounds and movements from the otherwise silent rides, voices murmuring, drowned beneath the throb of something that must be the generators Jodi had told her about. It was a weird sound, a thrum, thrum, thrum, like a huge heartbeat, going on and on.

Keeping close to the tent fronts on the left of the midway, Amy went toward the end. Wind slapped her occasionally as she passed the narrow passages between the tents, as if, in finding a way through, it delighted in playing unfair games. It swung the cord the lights hung on, and there was a sound growing as she neared the end of the midway, a squeaking sound that was replacing the throbbing generators—metallic squeaks and creaks as wind moved the seats on the tall Ferris wheel and pushed the electric cords that held the light bulbs.

She stopped, looking up at the tall tree she had seen from her window. It was behind a building, not a tent, and she looked at the sign on the front. "House of Mirrors. Largest Mirror Maze in the World."

Amy pressed her hand against her necklace, remembering suddenly. This was where Jodi had found it.

The door was closed. A solid, wood door. In front of the door was a small platform, and leading up to it were steps, with a banister on one side. On the ground was a ticket booth, like the ticket booths at almost every ride and tent show.

Amy stood in the light and looked down the narrow space between the House of Mirrors and the tent beside it. It was there, in the deep shadows, that the figure stood. So far away from her trailer window. How could she have seen it from so far?

Yet she knew it was there, and with her hand clutching the jewel on her chest, she moved slowly into the darkness.

ZULU CIRCLED BACK, He had gone almost to the fence on the far side of the field, and he could see the lights of the other men working areas to his left and right. He was beginning to run, to jerk about as frantically as an insect confused and undirected by senses no longer dependable. He returned, throwing the light beam around.

Then he stood still, breathing shallowing, and told himself this was no good. This was not helping India. He had called her name until he was hoarse, and now he stood quietly, saying nothing. He closed his eyes and tried to go back to the beginning. To the moment he had lost her.

He had gone into her trailer, to check it out, to make sure it was safe for her to enter. He had thought she was behind him. He knew now that was exactly what he had thought, and why he had not been anxious at leaving her outside. In his mind he had pictured her standing safely in her front room while he searched every closet and dark corner in the rest of her house —in her small kitchen, her bathroom, her bedroom.

But she hadn't entered the trailer.

Where had she gone?

Could she have gone toward the midway, instead of into the field?

And why, dear India, why?

The other thought was just below his most conscious thoughts, the fact that she was like Lakisha now, caught by this—this monstrous thing that—broke bones as if they were twigs.

Sounds rose from one point behind. Excited cries, yells from one man to another. And then, "Zulu! Hey, Zulu!"

And this was it, he knew, as he turned and stumbled back about halfway across the field, to where a small cluster of men had gathered with their lights.

It was almost directly in his own path. But somehow he had missed seeing her.

He saw her head twisted sideways, her tongue protruding as if she had been choked. But the rest of her large body was covered by the loose suit of the clown costume, her papa's costume, gathers at the throat, wrists, and ankles making the costume look loose and empty, and oddly flat—and Zulu remembered India at the age of five, picking up her papa's clown suit, this very suit, and finding it empty. And he, as he bent to her, was afraid to touch it, for fear there would be nothing inside, that he too would find it empty, with only her poor head lying here, taken somehow from her body.

He turned away, his head down, blinded again, and now with pain in his eyes that burned like the fires of hell.

Someone put a hand on his shoulder and squeezed, and by that guidance led him away.

"You can't help her, Zulu," Russel said, his hand warm on Zulu's shoulder.

Zulu felt a terrible rage rising inside him. He wanted to lift his fists to the sky and thunder his feelings at the creator of life and death. This could not have happened to India. Not his India.

"She can't be dead!" he screamed at Russel and the others who stood around with their lights pointed at India, as if she were on stage in a play. "Get your goddamned lights off her! Get them off, damn you, damn you all to hell and back, leave her alone! She can't be dead, oh my God she can't be dead." His voice dwindled to a moan.

The lights moved aimlessly, touching the grass, arching toward the sky. The grass gleamed as the lights swept over it, the dewdrops sparkling like black diamonds, and in the grass lay India, his India, and the dewdrops were teardrops, cried from his dry eyes, his weeping heart.

Russel persisted, turning Zulu away from the sight of India lying so aimlessly twisted in the grass as if it had become her permanent bed.

"Hey, man," Russel said, "I know how you're feeling. Come on now, you've got things to do."

"We can do it," a familiar voice said. But Zulu couldn't quite place it— Eddie or Jack or maybe—maybe—

"Yeah, we'll call whoever has to be called. Police, I guess."

Russel said, "Zulu will probably want to do it."

Yes, Russel was right. There were a lot of things he had to do. India had no relatives, unlike himself. Though he hadn't been home in a long while and had almost lost touch with his brothers and sisters, they were there, as next of kin. But India had no one but him, and the carnie people, and it was up to them to see that she had a decent burial.

But first there had to be a doctor to see that she was all right. To help her, maybe, to not be dead.

His hope hit bottom, and he glimpsed the black waters of hell.

No, India was dead. He had seen the death in her eyes.

He tipped his head back and opened his mouth, his hands knotted into fists at his sides, and he screamed and screamed at the sky, but there was no sound from his throat. The scream began and ended in the depths of his soul, of his heart, of the part of him that made him love.

AMY SLIPPED SILENTLY DOWN the shadowed passage between the House of Mirrors and the tent next to it, her heart racing in fear, yet something urging her on, as if her destiny were inextricably bound up with it.

Near the end of the building she stood still, breathing shallowly through her open mouth, trying to be as silent as the shadows in which she stood.

She could see a dark bulk of something at the end of the house beneath the shadows of the tree. But it was too short to be a human, unless that human were standing in a low crouch. She stared at it until its outlines became more clear and she realized it was not a person, nor an animal, but a mere trash can. One of many that were scattered along the alley and the midway. Ordinary metal, sometimes plastic, trash cans.

She moved closer to it and then, using it as a shield, stood as near as she could get without touching it. Unpleasant odors rose from its uncovered top, and she could hear faint rattlings within it that sounded like fingers probing, but common sense told her it was only insects moving about in the paper-wrapped garbage.

She looked down the alley.

Lights on the nearby trailers had not come on yet, as if the owners were too far removed from the activity that had awakened her to have been disturbed by it. Three trailers down from where she stood a front door stood open and light blazed out. The light beside the door was on too, a yellow bug light that cast a weird glow into the whiter light from inside.

India's trailer?

It was larger than most of the others, and she thought it was India's trailer, although she had never been as close to it as she now stood.

She swallowed and turned her head slowly, looking along the alley, and from the corner of her eyes caught a brief flash of movement and color.

She stared.

Something was separating from the shadows, and moving as silently as dark and light. Then she saw it was more than one.

She froze, terror pressing her into the shadows between the trash can and the corner of the House of Mirrors.

As if they had been part of the darkness, three clowns peeled away into the vague light at this end of the alley and moved soundlessly past her.

Their faces were not the faces of clowns she had seen. Clowns she had loved and laughed at. These were the faces of terrible things, of empty eyes and cruel mouths, of witches and warlocks, of ghouls that rise from the graves of hell.

Without breathing she watched them go by.

They went to the open door of India's trailer and climbed the steps.

The door remained open.

Amy waited, but they didn't return.

CHAPTER 12

RUSSEL STAYED WITH ZULU UNTIL HE COULD SIGNAL KEN OVER. THEN HE WENT back to stand around in the alley with a bunch of the others as they waited for the police and the ambulance with the medics to arrive. Zulu came back after a while, just as the first police car drove in again, using almost the same tracks as it had used last night.

Was it only last night?

It seemed a month ago, and yet the pain in his heart burned like a red-hot coal, a harsh, raw pain, a bloody, bleeding pain. He knew how Zulu was feeling, he thought as he stared at his toes. The confusion, the feeling of reality mixed with fantasy, as if this couldn't be happening.

But maybe he didn't know how Zulu felt. His love for Lakisha hadn't lived as long as Zulu's adoration for India. And his love had been consummated, and it wasn't likely that Zulu had ever put his hands on India.

The whole carnival knew of Zulu's attachment to India. It was in his eyes, in his actions. He was her slave.

What was he going to do without her?

ZULU STARED at the House of Mirrors.

The sun had risen now, and the streaks of sunlight turned the gray boards a different color, lightened them, made them less like old boards unpainted.

He walked the midway with his hands clutched in a knot behind his back. But now he stopped and stared through narrowed eyes at the old House.

The mirrors were in there, facing one another, in all angles and degrees, some of them distorting in shape, making a figure look fat and short or tall and stringy thin. And it was in there, among those mirrors, that the beginning was.

India had told him.

He was the only person in the world she had told.

The police had come last night, and the doctor and coroner, and police photographers had taken pictures from all angles, and meantime they had let her lie on the cold ground, her body twisted, her tongue protruding, her eyes staring and oblivious to the light.

"What's going on here?" one of the main guys from the police force in the small town had asked Zulu.

Zulu had shaken his head, in silence. Since his last attempt to speak had failed, he had stopped trying.

"Two in a row? Looks like the same kind of death to me. She's got broken bones, anybody can see that."

Zulu had cleared his throat. His voice had sounded hoarse, and had felt scratchy in his throat. "You tell me," he'd said, the anger rising again, but the hopeless rage rising too. "I'd like to get my hands on the bastards that did it, I can tell you that. I can't tell you anything else. She was there behind me, and then she was gone."

"You wouldn't happen to have any gorillas around here in cages that I haven't seen, would you?"

"No. The last gorilla we had died of old age a few years ago. We called him Jim, and he wouldn't have hurt a bug. That wasn't done by an animal. Not the kind that's covered in fur. The bare-assed animal maybe, some dirty bastards ..." He'd stopped, remembering what India had told him about her mother.

She had died with broken bones, a crushed body.

They had gone around looking for clues, the guys from the police force, and then they were joined by the Sheriff's Department and the Highway Patrol. They were looking, Zulu heard through the grapevine, for tire tracks, because the state of the body suggested that it might have been run over again and again.

The police were still around, everywhere it seemed, even though, near dawn, the ambulance had taken India's body away.

They were sending it away for autopsy, and when Zulu asked when it would be released, they told him they didn't know for sure. A few days maybe, or a week, or two.

Meantime, they said, they didn't know if the carnival should open for business.

But Zulu had seen them talking together, and he knew they took one thing into consideration: the dead people were carnie people, not locals.

So Zulu went to them again, and said, "Look, these people are used to working, and India would want the carnival to go on. We've got to get to another town less than a hundred miles away. We were supposed to be there today."

"Exactly where is this place you're going?"

"Over the hills east. A town called ..." Zulu pulled a small notebook out of his pocket. "Heber Springs."

"Never heard of it."

"Yeah, I know it," the detective's companion said. "It's still in the state, right?"

"Yes." Zulu tucked the notebook back into his pocket. He was all for the police questioning the people with the carnie, keeping an eye on them, but they were looking for a killer who was strong as a gorilla, and Zulu was only looking to see if any of them had heard or seen anything.

"Maybe," the first detective answered belatedly. "We'll see."

The policemen turned their backs to Zulu and talked among themselves, and in the gist of conversation that drifted his way Zulu caught the idea that they would just as soon get rid of the carnival, the people, and the trouble that was being dumped into their laps.

"We'll let you know later," one of the guys said.

Zulu looked up at them without feeling his usual sense of inferiority and intimidation. The police always kind of patrolled the carnival, no matter where they were, as if carnie people were not to be trusted. And he had always been a bit leery of them. As the patch, the fixer between cops and carnie, he'd always gone ahead of the carnival and fixed with the city or county police the kind of shows they would let alone. The gambling shows were allowed in some towns and not in others. And the kootch shows were not allowed some places, and in others he could fix it so that the girls were free to show their privates if they wanted to. Most of them usually wanted to, it drew a better crowd. Lakisha had been one who refused to do that strong a show.

Lakisha had never done anything to warrant being murdered.

Neither had India, his lovely India.

Maybe India was right, he thought, and realized he was staring at the walls of the House of Mirrors. And he realized also why he felt so desperate to move on. He wanted to tear that old House apart and give it a good looking over. India had never let him do much with it, but this time he would take it apart, panel by panel, and he would damn well see if there were anything inside it that was suspicious.

"Hey," he said to one of the tall, handsome policemen. Several of them stood near him, most in uniform, but a few in suits and a couple in blue jeans and western shirts. All of them were tall and handsome, even the gray-haired guy that was probably in his early sixties. He was tall and well-built and wore a badge that said, "CHIEF." The gun holsters of all the lawmen were in plain sight, even on the suited guys, who had their coats open so that their black weapons showed.

Several of the men looked down at Zulu.

"You don't happen to have any missing-boy reports along, do you?" Zulu inquired.

Now he had the attention of several, all faces turned his way, the conversation stopping.

"Why?"

Zulu rubbed one hand through his hair and down his cheek. How much should he reveal? Mightn't he just be causing more problems for his people?

"There was this kid," he finally said. "Came by and asked me for a job. I gave him a broom and a dustpan ..." Carefully he avoided looking at the House of Mirrors. That was his project. He wasn't going to allow the law to tear it apart. "I gave him a broom and told him to go to work, and come to me when he was through and I'd pay him minimum wage. Well, he didn't show up again."

"What made you think he was missing?" the chief asked.

"You get to know these runaways," Zulu said. "I was one myself once."

"What did he look like?"

"He was about fourteen, and had—uh—I think he had reddish hair. A few freckles. Just an ordinary kid. Slim. Average height."

"Anything else?" The chief had begun to take notes. The wind rustled the pages of his notebook and he used one thumb to hold it still so he could write. "A name?"

"No name. The runaways don't give us names."

"The names you use here aren't real names anyway, are they?" the chief asked with a touch of anger sliding into his voice.

"Well, yeah, when we do business we use our real names. I mean, when we do business with the government. But with each other and the marks—I mean, the customers—they don't want real names. What's the point? They are not interested in names."

"Marks?" the chief asked, looking into Zulu's eyes. Zulu shrugged, sorry he had let that slip. "Marks, people."

"By marks you mean customers that you take to the cleaners, right?"

Zulu paused, thought carefully. He had to be careful not to make these people mad at him, or they might put a lock and key on the whole operation and manage to find cell accommodations for him and his crew of roughies. He knew his roughies, men who were single and a little wild sometimes, were not especially liked by the police in any area, so he had to be careful.

"They come to take us too, you know," Zulu said. "Every guy who puts down a quarter to play a game thinks he's going to win. We do our best by our customers. We couldn't live without them, and we all know it."

The chief nodded his head and his mouth curved up on one side in a wry twist, an imitation smile of sorts. "Back to this kid. What happened to him?"

"I don't know. That's why I was wondering if he was listed as missing."

"He didn't show up for his money?"

"No," Zulu had to admit, and his eyes cut toward the House of Mirrors without meaning to. He looked quickly away. If they asked where the kid had cleaned, what would he say? He hoped for crissakes they didn't ask.

"Where did you put him to work?"

Zulu looked around. Then he said, "He was sweeping platforms and steps and places like that."

"Who else might have seen him?"

"Can't tell you that. He just came asking for work, I gave it to him, and he never showed up again."

One of the younger men laughed. "Sounds to me like he didn't want to work after all. Maybe he was one of the country kids who just decided to go on back to his creek and go fishing."

Several of the men laughed, and conversation started again.

Zulu was glad. That seemed to end it. But he had the information he wanted. The kid was not reported missing, so maybe he did decide he'd had enough of the mirror maze and just wanted out of there.

"About us moving on to our next town, sir," Zulu broached.

The chief was still making notes in his little book, and the wind still ripped at the page, trying to pull it out of the chief's hands. The big man didn't answer him.

Zulu waited.

His old anger was gone. The hurt of being looked down upon, and the rage it generated, had dissipated long ago. For the most part. It still surfaced at unexpected times, but now it was not important. India was all that mattered, and she was gone, leaving behind only a few beliefs, and the new fears and the old. Leaving him a legacy.

He waited.

The chief finally folded his notebook and put it back into his pocket. He looked up, his eyes moving along the trailers in the alley. Most of his men had moved on, going on with their jobs. They were questioning the carnie people, trying to find some clue that would tie one of them into the murders so that none of the local people need get involved.

But Zulu knew they would find nothing.

"Just a minute, Mr. Zulu." He started to reach for his notes again, to check on Zulu's name.

"That's enough," Zulu said. "That's what I'm called by everyone."

The chief nodded. I'll get back to you sometime before the day ends. Where can I find you?"

Zulu scratched his cheek nervously. "Just around."

"You've got an office on the other side of the midway, don't you?"

"Yes. I'll be around."

"Well, sir, you had better be. And you had better see to it that all your men stay here too, until we have satisfied ourselves about this investigation. I can't believe that two women can be killed in two consecutive nights and the only person who heard anything is one of the dead women. It's hard for me to swallow the fact that you were with this India lady just minutes before she died and you don't know a goddamned thing about it. She just walked away from you while you were in her house and went back into the field and got herself run over by a truck or something that didn't leave tire tracks? What the hell is going on here, man?"

"Sir, I wish I knew." He could be nice, though he raged and boiled inside. He had learned to be nice to those in authority. "I wish I knew."

"Well, Mr. Zulu, I wish I knew too. But not one of your people, even the ones in the trailers closest to the dead women, heard a thing. They didn't see a thing out of the ordinary. In the case of the young woman, I was thinking in terms of a guy who got turned on by that damned kootch show and decided to do her in when he found her out walking alone. But that's not the case with India."

"That was not the case with Lakisha either," Zulu said.

"And how do you know that?"

Zulu shook his head. "I don't know, I guess. It's just never happened before."

The chief snorted out a short and mirthless laugh. "Yeah, well, that kind of thing seldom happens more than once, especially to the same person."

"That's not exactly what I meant," Zulu said, letting a little of his rage slip through. But only a little. He wanted to move this carnie, and the only way he was going to move it was with the permission of the police.

"I know," the chief said, in a kinder tone. "But you do know, Zulu, that you've got a killer here somewhere, don't you?"

"Why here? I mean, couldn't it be somebody, some maniac, just sort of passing through your area? We get some creeps sometimes."

"Sure, could be. But there's nothing to tie in anyone. We've looked into the nearby trailer parks, and all places along the river where campers come. We've checked and checked, and there's no reason to suspect any of the local people, or the visitors to the area. So I have to conclude it's one of your own men. You've got a few muscles with you, as you well know."

"Yeah, true, but not one of them would have had any reason to kill either Lakisha or India."

"How about lust? The death of Lakisha was because she wouldn't give in to his sexual advances, to put it politely, and so he got mad and broke her up. Then India caught on to him, so he took her."

Zulu shook his head. "I was talking to India just before she—went away, and she said nothing to me about suspecting anyone."

"Okay. I know. This is the same story we keep getting. I'm beginning to believe you."

"None of us know what's going on."

"And yet I have these feelings, Zulu, coming from you, that you got your suspicions. What are they?" Zulu looked up at him in surprise. What was with this chief? Telepathy?

"Surprised I caught on to you, huh?" the chief said, almost as if he were joshing. "I can see it in your face, Zulu. It's the same deadpan that men get when they know something they're not telling. And now you've got me wondering if we've got a third murder."

"A third?"

"Still surprised, huh? The kid, Zulu. You told me about him yourself. Where is he?"

Zulu expelled the air he'd been holding in. He'd thought that subject was closed, the chief assuming the kid had split. He shook his head.

"I don't know nothin', Chief, and that's the honest-to-God truth."

"All right, if you say so."

The tall man went walking off down the alley. "I'll let you know a little later about the move."

Zulu stood still, watching him go. He reached a couple of the detectives and stopped and began talking to them. The guy in the jeans and western shirt looked directly at Zulu.

Zulu turned away, going out of the alley and into the midway.

A few of the owners were straggling around the midway, looking as if they were sheep out of their pasture, their shepherd gone. They walked with hands in pockets, strolled aimlessly, waiting. Zulu felt a tug of sympathy. India would not want it this way.

She would want the carnival to keep running.

RUSSEL PULLED the two empty suitcases out of the top of the closet and began pulling the girls' clothes off hangers and out of drawers, tossing the clothes into the open bags.

Jodi came to stand near him with her hands on her hips. He saw her out of the corner of his eyes, and his heart contracted. She looked so cute standing there, as if she were overseeing his job. He didn't want to lose these two little girls he had so recently found. The love he had discovered too late for Lakisha had opened him up, it seemed, split him wide with emotions he'd never had before. He loved these kids too much to lose them, but he'd at least know they were alive somewhere in the world if he sent them away.

"Just what do you think you're doing?" Jodi demanded.

He could see Amy too from the corner of his vision. She was by the couch. She had been making the place neat, as usual, and now she just stood there in silence. Then she sat down.

"I'm sending you home," he said.

"Home? To our mom? But Russel, she doesn't want us."

"Nonsense. Get that idea out of your head." But something sickening turned over in the vicinity of his stomach. Could it be true?

"She doesn't. She wouldn't have sent us to you if she had. She's got other people now, Russel."

"What happened to 'Dad'?" he asked her, slowing the tossing down of clothes.

Jodi drew a long breath, clearly audible to Russel. "If you're trying to get rid of us so soon, I just figured you didn't want me to call you Dad."

Russel reached over and pulled Jodi into his arms. He buried his face against her small, hard chest and shut his eyes tight against the burning threat of tears.

He remembered Amy, and held out one arm to her, and as if she had run to get to him, she was there suddenly, larger than Jodi, softer. He was almost strangled in warm and loving arms.

"Girls," he said when he could speak, his head pressed tightly between the two of them. "Jodi, Amy, you're my daughters, and I love both of you more than you'll ever know—more than I knew myself. And that's why I want you out of here. Two people have been murdered in two nights, and I don't want you in this."

"The police won't let us leave anyway," Jodi said with satisfaction as he released them.

"They'll let two little girls go," Russel said.

Amy said, "Please, Dad, I don't want to leave. I like to work in the grab joint with you."

"I'm not going," Jodi said firmly, walking across the small living room to look out the open door. "They're still here. The cops. They're talking to the people next door now. I suppose they'll come here next."

"Yeah, we're supposed to hang close to our trailers. How about my folks' farm then, kids? For the rest of the month anyway. Maybe by that time this mess will be straightened out and the killer caught."

"Farm? No," Jodi said. "Not me. I want to stay with the carnival forever."

Amy sat on the couch again, but this time with a lifted chin as if by some magic she had suddenly gained confidence. "Me too. I'm not leaving you." He couldn't help the feeling he derived from their refusal to leave. The thought of sending them away had left him feeling lonely as hell, and just knowing they were with him fed something within him that he hadn't even known was there. Lakisha's death had done something to him.

"Well, then here's what we're going to do. As soon as it gets dark, Jodi has to come to the grab joint and stay with Amy and me, and get her a cushion or something and get back in a corner if she can find one, or she can stay with one of the ladies—"

"Why can't I work too?"

"We've only got two windows, and it's crowded." Amy said, "You can't cook."

"I can make change, Amy, you know I can."

"We'll figure something out."

143

He began to take the clothes out of the suitcases again. Amy came and took over the job and he got up to make another cup of coffee.

"You're going to have to quit that caffeine," Jodi said. "Too much caffeine makes people nervous. I expect that's what's wrong with you."

"And the trouble with a brat like you," Russel said with a grin, "is you wouldn't know danger if it walked beside you. That's why I'd like to ship you to my mom at least, if you don't want to go to yours. I don't want you wandering around alone, Jodi," he said seriously.

"But I don't. Blane is with me all the time. We play together. We even go to the cook tent and eat together. Zulu told him to watch out after me and show me around. Blane told me carnie kids aren't allowed on the midway during business hours."

"Oh yeah? I kind of wondered why I never saw any of them around."

The open doorway was suddenly filled with a couple of men. One of them was the guy in jeans and western shirt. Now he had a western hat tipped back on his head. He was slim and good-looking in a windblown, suntanned way. He looked like he might have some Indian blood in him, probably. He was taller than most of the Southwestern Indians.

"Can we come in?" he asked with a grin, looking at Amy and Jodi as if he were their old friend. Without waiting for an invitation he took one long step up into the trailer.

Behind him came someone from the Sheriff's Department, in uniform.

"We're detectives Joe Small and Kevin Andrews. We'd like to ask some questions, please."

"Sure," Russel said. "Want coffee?"

They agreed to coffee as they sat down, and Russel made two more cups of instant in the microwave. He gave it to them black. Real men drank black coffee, and they both looked like real men. Even if they had been inclined toward sugar and cream, Russel didn't have any of the latter to offer.

"How're you, young ladies?" the ladies' man was asking, smiling at the girls. They had sat down side by side on the end of the couch, and both looked dazed by the friendliness of this handsome guy who still wore his cowboy hat.

"Fine," they both agreed.

Amy put her hand up to her chest and pressed, as if she were feeling her own heartbeat. Russel had noticed that habit of Amy's, and considered it an unconscious, nervous reaction to stress. She often paused and pressed her hand to her heart. Now she dropped her hand quickly as if suddenly aware of what she had done. She glanced at Russel, then back at Joe, the cowboy Indian cop.

"You're Amy and Jodi, aren't you?"

"Yes," Jodi said. "How did you know?"

She looked as pleased and surprised as if this young guy had turned out to be a god after all. Russel could almost see both of his daughters falling in love.

"I asked around. I saw you in the door, Jodi, and I asked your neighbor who that pretty little girl is." Jodi was tongue-tied for a change. She flushed a pretty pink and leaned back on the couch as if to half hide behind Amy.

Joe suddenly turned serious. His smile disappeared. "I need to ask a bunch of questions, and I'm sorry about it, but I need some history and some idea of what you were doing last night at about three A.M. Your name?"

"Russel Sauer. Age thirty-two. I worked in my grab joint until closing time, and then I came and went to bed. Amy, who's eleven, worked with me. I sent her home to bed with orders to lock the door earlier. Both of the kids were in bed asleep when I got here. I checked to make sure they were all right. I asked one of the guys that works for Zulu to keep an eye on the trailer until I got off work, and he did."

"Ken?" Joe said, as if he knew more about last night's activities than Russel did.

"Yes."

"Well, then what?"

"I woke up, hearing noises outside. I went out, and found the search on for India. I joined it."

"And you?" Joe asked the girls.

Jodi said, "I was asleep. I didn't wake up until this morning. I didn't know India was dead." Her mouth began to tremble, the lower lip jerking the way it used to when she was only a baby. The memory came back to Russel suddenly, and he stood up.

"The little girls sure as hell didn't have anything to do with those murders," he said.

"Oh yeah, I know that. I'm not trying to scare them. But you understand that one murder is bad enough. In that case we could say this young gorgeous gal turned some creep on by her act in the show, and he came after her, and broke her to pieces for it. But when the same thing happens the next night to an elderly woman who's dressed in a clown suit—"

Joe looked suddenly at Amy, and Russel glanced toward her too, trying to see what expression had crossed Amy's face to get Joe's attention so fast.

Amy looked startled, maybe scared.

"She—she was wearing a clown suit?"

"Yes." Joe waited, but Amy said nothing more. She had ducked her head and once again, a quick touch, put her hand to her chest. She dropped it again almost instantly, as if she were conscious of her gesture and embarrassed by it.

"Why does that surprise you, Amy?" Joe said with gentleness. "Have you seen her in the suit before, or something?"

Amy shook her head.

"Did you see her last night?"

Amy shook her head again and twisted uncomfortably on the couch. The self-confidence she had gotten for a few minutes was gone again. She was a bashful kid and Russel felt sorry for her.

"She was asleep when I got home from the grab joint," he said again, pointedly. "And she was asleep when I went out this morning."

The guy from the Sheriff's Department asked, "Where does she sleep?"

Russel gave a nod of his head toward the bunk above the couch. "Up there."

Both men stood up and looked into the bunk, and Russel had a sudden yearning to shove both of them in and close the door on them. He turned instead to make another cup of microwave coffee. He didn't offer them more. He saw they each had almost a cup full.

"There's a long window on the other side of the bunk," the sheriff's detective said. "Runs the length of the bed?"

"Yeah," Russel agreed. "Helps to let in some air."

"So," Joe said, sitting down again, and finally taking a drink of his coffee. He set the cup on the coffee table. "So, Amy, do you sleep on the back, against the window?"

She nodded silently, and then said in a faint, squeaky voice, "Yes."

"Did you see anybody last night out there that was dressed in a clown suit or something like that? Or the night before?"

Amy shook her head. She looked up, from face to face among the men, including Russel, then she shook her head even more firmly. As if some of her new confidence were leaking back, she said, "I was asleep."

Joe gave up. "All right. Nobody saw anything or heard anything out of the ordinary. You're all sound sleepers here. Even the dogs. Not one of them growled or barked at anyone either night, not that anyone heard, or reported, anyway. So that leads us to assume the killer is one of you carnie people. Someone the dogs were familiar with."

Russel said, "They're used to strangers walking around. Marks—customers—very often leave the midway and go into the alleys. Especially teenage kids looking for someplace to make out. The dogs get used to people wandering around."

"Yet I've been told that one of them in particular seems to know that, after closing hours, a stranger on the alley is fair game. His name is Roscoe, right? And he lives nights under his owner's trailer and he barks at strangers. But he hasn't barked at anyone at all in the past two nights. So, like I said before, whoever killed those two women was not a stranger to Roscoe. And probably not to you." The two men got up. Joe's smile was gone. At the door he looked back. "Thanks for the coffee. Listen, I'd be especially careful if I were you folks."

"Yeah, sure."

After they were gone, Russel sat in silence for a few minutes, staring with a deep frown out the door.

The girls were so quiet on the couch he had almost forgotten they were there. He was back to his last evening with Lakisha, when she had refused to come into his bedroom. He could see her again walking off down the alley, going from the streaks of light that fell between the tents to the spots of darkness. The spots of darkness were wide, too wide, but he had turned away and gone in to bed, never dreaming that in one of those places of darkness danger lay waiting for her. Why Lakisha?

Why India?

Had India known something, as the police were suggesting, that made her a target for the killer?

When Zulu appeared suddenly in the doorway, Russel jumped, and coffee sloshed out of his cup and onto the leg of his jeans. It burned like hell and brought him back to the moment.

He stood up, pulled the hot, wet jeans away from his leg, and muttered a couple of favorite cuss words under his breath.

Zulu pulled himself up into the living room. He looked as if he hadn't slept for a month. His eyes were puffy and red, and his face sagged more than usual. His hair had been combed a dozen different directions by his hands, over and over, and his clothes, never well-fitting, looked as if they would fall off the next step he took.

He hoisted himself up onto one of the kitchen chairs.

"Got another cup of that, Russ?"

"Sure, Zulu. How you doin'?"

147

Russel mixed the coffee and set the cup into the microwave and stood waiting until it was ready.

"Well, we can't open for business here, but we're released."

"Released?" Russel took the cup out of the oven and placed it on a napkin in front of Zulu. He pushed over a plate that still held three doughnuts, and Zulu took one.

"Yeah. We can move on. I put the guys to work knocking down and loading up. We'll be ready to move by mid-afternoon maybe."

"Okay. Good. How come they let us go?"

"Well, for one thing, we're not going out of state." Zulu dunked his doughnut into the coffee and took a bite. Coffee dribbled down his chin and he wiped it off with the back of his hand. "But the main reason, I think, is they want to get rid of us."

"Huh!" Russel snorted. "Well, no love lost. I'll be damned glad to get out of this spot too."

"Yeah. India would have wanted us to move on."

Russel said nothing for a minute. He watched Zulu empty his cup and get up to leave. Then he said, "Zulu, you'd better go get some sleep."

"No," Zulu said as he struggled down to the step. "No, I gotta go see to the tearing down of my House of Mirrors."

CHAPTER 13

"Dad, can I go watch? Please, Dad, can I?" Jodi cried, jiggling up and down excitedly in front of him. "I'd really like to see them take the mirror maze apart! Please, Dad?" Now she was almost whining.

Russel looked at his daughters. Even Amy was perking up now.

"Well, I guess it'd be safe enough. Just stay back out of the way and—"

Jodi was running out the door before he had finished.

"Hey," he yelled, "wait up there, Jodi! I wasn't through talking to you!"

Jodi came back to the door and looked in, dancing on one foot.

"I think Amy should go with you."

"No," Jodi yelled. "I don't need Amy. She doesn't want to go."

Russel looked at Amy, and saw she was still sitting on the couch. She had one hand pressed to her chest again, but this time she seemed to be squeezing a wrinkle into her blouse. She dropped her hand almost guiltily.

"It's okay," she said, getting up. "I don't mind. I'll come with you, Jodi."

"I don't need you!" Jodi yelled. "Blane will be there, and so will Zulu."

"Lots of people will be there," Russel said. "Well, do what you want to do, girls, but do not go off by yourselves, and don't go off with any one person, I don't give a damn who he is. You hear?"

They nodded, and Jodi was gone again. Russel felt as if she hadn't heard him at all. He explained to Amy, "I have to go get the grab joint ready for moving. Have to kind of tie things down."

"I'll help."

"In this case, sweetheart, I don't need help. Why don't you just hang around here, or go on down and keep an eye on Jodi? Another time I'll show you how to arrange the inside of the grab joint for moving."

"Okay."

He stood in the doorway and watched her go. She hadn't been reluctant, and he suspected she too had an itch to see the mirror maze come down.

He felt uneasy when both girls were out of sight. Grabbing one, or even both, of them would be easy for the killer, or killers. Had he really thought they'd be safe? In the daylight, so many people around should make them safe, but would it? Just because the killer had confined his murdering to nights didn't mean he would keep it that way.

Russel took out after the girls. He went through the path between two tents just as Shilo, the owner of both, removed the stake from the front left corner of the tent on Russel's right. The tent fell with a swoosh, making Russel's heart leap and pound, and the skin on his arms feel as if it were being pulled up by the roots.

"Hey," Shilo said, grinning, as he stood back with the stake in one hand and a tent rope in the other.

"Didn't see you there. Did it give you a start?"

"Somewhat," Russel admitted. Shilo was several inches shorter than Russel, with black hair the texture of a horse's mane, but his shoulders were as developed as if he were seven feet tall. He'd shown up with his games and joined the carnie two years ago, but Russel didn't know a thing about him. If he had more names than Shilo, Russel had never heard them.

"Saw your daughters go by. Looking for them?" Russel saw Amy, her red plaid blouse prominent. She was moving on around a cart that was being pulled by one of Zulu's younger workers.

And running on was Jodi, her slim little legs looking suddenly long, as if she had grown several inches in the few days she had been here.

"They'll be all right," Shilo said as if he had read Russel's mind. "Lots of folks around who know them. Folks are watchin' each other these days, like you never know, right?"

"Yeah—right."

"But they'll be all right. They're just babies." Shilo went to another stake and began prying it out of the ground.

He was right, Russel decided. The girls were safe. Zulu was here, and Ken, and dozens of others he'd known a long time.

He turned on down toward his grab joint and began preparing it for the move.

. . .

JODI WANTED to see every piece of that House of Mirrors. She wanted to see what kinds of worlds existed in it. She had even had bad dreams about the dark and shadowed places in the mirrors that she had seen beyond Blane, that swamp-like place with the strange, scary trees that moved.

She ran down the midway, dodging past workers who were taking down their tents and boxing up stuffed animals and cheap toys of all kinds. She almost stopped to watch some of the rides come down, but knew if she stood around too long she might miss something at the House of Mirrors.

She ran on, almost getting backed into by a guy on a small tractor with a lift on it. She could see him cussing, mouthing words she couldn't hear, as she ran on around him.

She stopped.

The tent next door to the House of Mirrors was already flat on the ground. Men were carrying the platforms of both the tent and the House of Mirrors over to the long bed of a big truck, and as she watched she almost ran again, because the whole corner of the House began to move, to be pulled away from the rest. A crack began and widened and the mirrors reflected the light and movements on the midway like animal eyes gleaming at night.

Jodi went to the safest place she could spot, the tree at the rear corner of the House. By climbing onto the trash can there and teetering on its edge, she managed to reach and climb onto the lowest limb. She eased out monkey-like onto the limb that reached over the roof of the House, and flattened herself lengthwise, on her belly.

Hanging on, her arms around the limb, she watched.

A big truck backed into the open spot where the tent had stood, and another tractor chugged in and put a lift beneath part of the floor of the House. It lifted, and the corner section of the House came free, and light glinted on exposed mirrors as that section was eased onto the truck bed and put in place. Men on the bed shouted at one another and at the driver of the tractor, and helped by hand to guide the first section of the House of Mirrors to a safe, solid placement.

Jodi gaped, trying to see clearly past the leaves on the tree. She released one arm from the limb beneath her, and pushed away a leafy limb that was in her line of view.

She saw a roofline, chopped off, and a wall that ended with an open, narrow corridor. But that was all. The mirror wall that was revealed was as clear as mirror could be. There were no shadows in that front part, no black stain.

Jodi settled back and watched the tractor pick up another section and go through the same process of placing it carefully on the truck bed, behind the first section. Once again the men were yelling at one another and guiding and pointing and seeing to it the section was placed precisely where it had been placed lots of times before, Jodi figured.

She settled more comfortably on the limb to watch the rest of the procedure of moving "The World's Biggest Mirror Maze," as the sign out front read.

ZULU LOOKED into each section as it was taken from the rest, but the corridors left intact were intimidating, especially now that there was no lighting. Though he walked into a few of the corridors, peering, trying to see something that made him feel he would find the answer to India's death if only he would open his eyes, the darkness pushed him out.

He thought of getting his flashlight, but the guys would think him nuts if he insisted on going through the corridors before the sections were loaded onto the tracks.

One of them asked, "Looking for something, Zulu?"

"Oh, no," Zulu said, drawing back, jumping down to the ground. "Can't see much with no lights anyway. I was just checking it out."

"Glad I don't have to. I only went in one of these once when I was a kid, and it made me so dizzy I got sick. I don't mind taking it apart and helping load it up, but I don't aim to check it out on the inside."

Zulu only nodded an answer and walked on, around toward the corners at the rear that were still on their blocks.

The noises of the midway were almost deafening. The roar of trucks as they pulled into place to load the rides and tents, and the chug of tractors as they moved in among the trucks, hung in the air like swarms of insects.

Zulu angled around, trying to stay out of the paths of dozens of different vehicles and of workers, roughies, roustabouts, working with no shirts in the warm sun, their muscles bulging under the loads they lifted and the stakes they pulled.

Zulu went around the truck that was being loaded with the House of Mirrors. The first truck was loaded, and it groaned away, moving out into the alley that had fast been broken down and become a road to let the trucks go by. But he wanted to see the loading of the rear of the House especially. It was the back left corner of the House that had first gone bad and had been blocked off, and this would be an opportunity to see if the blight had spread into the center of the maze, because it would be opened up in the disassembling. First the front left section had gone, and then the center front, and behind that on the long truck bed the right front corner section.

The new truck that had pulled in would take the back parts, and would open up the center. Another truck then would pick up the three sections of the center, which included the square room with the distorted mirrors, the crazy mirrors that did the final work of sweeping away any sense of reality a person might have left by the time he got there.

"You got quite a show here," a voice said somewhere up in the air behind Zulu.

Zulu twisted and looked up. It was the chief again, with that odd half grin on his face that could be just his naturally friendly grin or a display of derision.

Zulu was not in the mood to analyze. Looking up made his neck ache, and he didn't want to be disturbed now. He watched the tractor with the lift move to the left side center and begin slipping the forks beneath the floor. Other men on the ground watched carefully, there to see no damage was done to the floor, that the section of House didn't tilt, that it was lifted off its support as gently as a baby being put to bed. Large clasps beneath the floor that held the House securely together, and on the walls outside, were undone, releasing that section from its companions. The mirrors flashed a reflection of sun and midway rides and sky as the section slid and moved, and the reflections of men, trucks, and tractors went into fast forward as the section was turned.

"I'll be damned," the chief said. "That's quite an operation, taking that big thing apart and then putting it back together somewhere else to make it look like it grew there. Quite an operation."

Zulu nodded.

"You got a lot of men working at this job of moving your carnival. Is that all they do?"

"No. Not all."

The chief was here for a purpose, Zulu decided, and it was going to interfere with his examination of his House. Well, maybe when they set it up again he'd have another chance, if he couldn't get rid of the chief in time. So far, the House had looked just like it always did when it was taken apart. But it was the left rear corner that most interested him. The part that was closed off and bad. He was thinking in his mind that he might open some of the sections and see what changes had come about. Maybe there—maybe—might be the answer to India's death.

Zulu decided suddenly it might be better if he talked to the chief and satisfied whatever problem had brought him here again.

"No, the guys keep the places cleaned up. There's a lot of littering done, and the machinery needs care, and stuff like that."

"Where do these guys live?"

"Didn't you question them?"

"Yes, but this is just curiosity on my part. I don't have my notes with me, and a lot of the questioning was done by other departments. It's all in a file. I hope I'm not bothering you, Mr. Zulumonsque."

Zulu's heart softened just a bit toward the chief. It tended to soften anytime any person made a point of remembering his sometimes difficult name.

Zulu shook his head. "We're just loading up, Chief, and I don't do much but see that everything goes where it belongs. But these men and boys have been working here long enough they don't really need an overseer."

"But if they do need one, that's you."

"That's right."

"You're the owner, I understand?"

"Well, I was in partnership with India. She was the original owner, inherited it from the people who raised her. Then when I joined the carnie I took over the management of several of her amusements arid concessions, and it was so much for her to handle that she offered me a partnership. I was only about twenty years old at the time.

"Good deal for you, right?"

"Yes, of course."

"So all these trucks and tractors belong to you?"

"And India."

"India is dead."

Without change of voice, of tone, of inflection, the chief threw that bucket of ice at Zulu. For a moment he had forgotten. In the discussion of the carnie, it had been like any other time they were packing up to move on. He consciously and subconsciously saw India in her trailer, getting it ready to move, while he was out here seeing to the loading of the rides and especially the House, on the dozens of eighteen-wheeler flatbeds that carried the carnie from place to place.

"A lot of money is tied up here, right, Mr. Zulumonsque?"

"Yes, I guess so."

"And who inherits her share? Was the partnership equal? She owned half?"

"No, it was not just half. It was three fourths," Zulu said, a numbness beginning to cover the raw pain of his sorrow. The chief was needling him, he knew now. That act of friendliness had a flaw in it, just like the old mirror maze.

"Who did you say inherits?"

"I didn't say," Zulu said. "But I do."

"That's very interesting, Zulu. So now you might say you're worth— what? How many trucks have you got? A field full. And how many of these rides belong to the carnival itself—three fourths of them?"

"Some are owned individually, and those owners have their own trucks to haul them on. About half the rides are owned privately, but the kiddie rides were something that India loved and oversaw herself until recently, when she kind of left it up to me. But the people who run them just work for us. Then some of the concessions are India's—"

"Yours now."

"Yes, I guess." He wished the chief would stop. He didn't want it that way, couldn't he see that? Was he crazy enough to think he, Zulu, might have killed his own India for these material things? The rage he felt he should feel was missing. Only a weariness remained, a sadness that anyone would think that.

"How strong are you, Zulu?"

"I'm not strong."

"Your muscle men, though. You could have hired a couple of them to do that job for you, right? You could offer them a lot of money, and still be a millionaire, right, Zulu?"

Zulu rubbed his cheek and ran his fingers through his hair. Forgive them, they know not what they do.

"If everything was sold, I suppose so. But India wouldn't want the carnie disposed of. It was her life."

"Not anymore."

"Chief, isn't what you're doing called police harassment?"

The chief put on his twisted smile. "Just asking a few questions, Mr. Zulumonsque. You do want the murders solved, don't you?"

"Of course I do. But I don't think you're ever going to solve them."

"What?"

"I don't think so."

"Why not?"

"Because ..." He shouldn't do this, Zulu thought even as he did it. He wasn't sure India would approve. But he was going to throw the chief a curve.

"Because," Zulu said, "these were not the first and second murders of the same—what do you call it—M.O.—like you policemen are thinking."

"Modus operandi," the chief supplied automatically. "And what the hell are you talking about?"

"There was another one, back in 1927. The same thing. Broken bones. The woman had been crushed like a tractor with a roller had gone over her."

The chief was staring down at the top of Zulu's head. He could feel it.

The chief said softly and dangerously, "I was just going to suggest that maybe one of the tractors got loose and accidentally ran over those ladies. The only reason I didn't was because of the lack of skin contusions. But maybe the skin wasn't cut or damaged because of other reasons. Maybe it just didn't show up. I was going to suggest maybe you got a tractor with smooth tires, just for this purpose, and you killed the girl first to throw us off, but the real target was the lady with the money. The money you'll inherit now."

"You got the autopsy reports back?" Zulu asked, trying to ignore the rest. It was expected they would look at him first.

"No. I could see that much for myself. Now, tell me about this other death. Where was it, where can I get the records on it, and how do you know about it? Are you B.S.'ing me? No? Then is it possible that you might have had something to do with that murder? How old are you, Zulu?"

"I didn't do it, no. That was before I joined the carnie. Actually, I was only about seven or eight years old at the time. India was hardly more than a baby. She was five."

"Who told you about it?"

"India told me. Just—just yesterday, I guess. It seems a long time ago, but —no—day before yesterday, I guess. Just recently."

"After all these years, she told you? You never knew before? And who was murdered and why?"

"It was India's mother. India found her in their tent, just like—just like— India now, and Lakisha. But what she told me made me think the killing was the same. And India thought it was done by the same person."

"Oh yeah? And who was that?" The chief pulled a note pad out of his pocket and began to scribble notes hastily. "How old would he be now? At least eighty. What the hell. A strong eighty. Maybe he was the strongman of the circus."

Zulu ignored the sarcasm. He supposed the chief couldn't help it. He was a frustrated man, like Zulu himself, wanting a killer who appeared out of the night like—like the creatures from a magician's hat.

"She thought the killing was done by Raoell, a magician, a guy who used to own the House of Mirrors. He was a great illusionist, India said, but she also felt he was more than that."

"What?"

"I think India thought the man wasn't real."

"Wasn't real? What does that mean?"

"I think she thought he was some form of creature that only managed to take the form of a man when he was wearing some talisman he had made out of the mirrors, a necklace type of thing that he always wore."

"A talisman? Are you putting me on, Zulumonsque?"

"No, I'm only telling you what India thought."

"This magician—Raoell what?"

"Just Raoell. If he had another name, India didn't mention it."

"What happened to him?"

"He lost the talisman, and was never seen again. The House of Mirrors became the property of the people who adopted India, and then it became her property."

"Okay, stop trying to be funny. So he lost his talisman—whatever, and disappeared. Back up. Go back to the murder."

"Of India's mother?"

"What was her name? Even if it did happen back in '27, I ought to be able to check it out."

"I don't know her name."

"What about India's father?"

"He disappeared at that time too. I'm not putting you on, Chief."

"Ran off. Guilty, probably."

"That was the assumption," Zulu said. "Oh yes, the last name might have been Xerxes. I'm not sure. I don't think that was the name of the people who raised India like their own. It might not have been a legal adoption, but they didn't have other children, so they left everything to India. Including the House of Mirrors."

"Which had belonged to the magician. Who disappeared."

"Right." Zulu scratched his head and gazed with bewildered eyes at the House as another portion of it was slid slowly away. "That's one of the worst mazes in the world, Chief. It must have been made by a magician that was, as India thought, something not human. Or the man was an insane genius. I wouldn't want to go very far back in it alone. A man could go insane. To try to make it easier for people to get out of the center room, which is square and has mirrors that distort, I drew a painted line back to the front door, the simplest way to get out. The only way I could do it was laying a string on my way in. I've had mixed feelings about that maze all my life. I don't mind the front few corridors, but when you get back in there, on the other side of the central square especially, you're in a place where you could go mad."

For a change the chief said nothing. With his notebook in his hand he walked over a few feet where he could get a better look into the narrow pathways of mirrored walls and hallways and corridors. Light reflected off them like hundreds of suns glinting in his face, making him squint. In the passages that led back into the interiors, places that never saw sunlight, darkness took over like a black veil or curtain dropped across the entries.

The chief stepped back beside Zulu.

"The mother dies when India is only five years old, and the daddy disappears. And the magician?" Now he sounded serious, as if he had decided to believe. "Disappeared, you say."

"Disappeared too, hasn't been seen since. India said."

"Am I right in suspecting some kind of triangle there?"

"I think so. India's mama was getting ready to run off with the magician."

"So that's why she was killed? The old man himself, the dad, did the killing and then skipped."

"Chief, she was in her tent. She hadn't been run over by a tractor gone wild. Do you really think one man could have killed those women?"

The chief said nothing,

Zulu was watching the House section. The guys tied it securely on the bed of the truck, and the tractor, putt-putting along, its noise almost drowned beneath more and louder noises, eased over to take up the middle section, where the center mirrors were.

"Would you like to step up into the center before they move it, Chief?"

"Sure, thanks."

Zulu held up his hand at the tractor handler and the other men who'd jumped down from the truck and were ready to move this fifth section.

The chief put out a hand to help Zulu up onto the floor, but Zulu ignored it and climbed by using his own hands as a kind of pole vault, and boosted himself up. The chief waited until Zulu went ahead of him into the narrow, mirrored passageway that grew dark almost instantly.

"Have you got a lighter, Chief?" Zulu asked. "Me, I never smoked. Was afraid it might stunt my growth."

The chief didn't laugh. He pulled out a lighter and snapped it on.

"I don't smoke either now," he said. "Finally got smart. But I carry the lighter around because it does come in handy."

The tiny flicker became a dozen flickers in the shadowed mirrors, a dozen large fireflies leading on into the center of the House of Mirrors.

"I can't help but think this must have been that nutty magician's favorite room," Zulu said as he went around the corner into the central room.

It was about twelve by fifteen, and the distortions were enough to make a person feel all reality had been left in another world. He began to feel dizzy and disoriented almost instantly, and made himself look at the floor for stability as he moved farther into the room so the chief could come behind him.

"Good God!" the chief exclaimed, holding the feeble light up.

Ripples of mirrors picked up the light and the white face of the chief, and the gray hair of both men, and made of them creatures disembodied in a black but endless world. Curved mirrors that made the figures look as if they were pulled taffy stood beside mirrors that squeezed them down to almost nothing on the floor, tiny, tubby things that couldn't possibly belong to the human race.

"I didn't know mirror mazes had this sort of thing in the middle," the chief said. "The only one I ever went in sure didn't. No wonder the lady thought this magician owner was something beyond man. Let's get out of here. I think I've seen enough."

But when Zulu went back to the passage on the right, to the passage he was sure would lead out, he found he had left the light behind. Darkness hovered in the passage on his right with only a suggestion that daylight was only a dozen feet away. He looked down for his painted strip on the floor, a faint white line. It wasn't there."

"Chief?"

Zulu went back, his heart beginning to thunder with anxiety.

"Chief—"

To his relief the Chief of Police was still standing in the center of the crazy room, looking up at the ceiling. Zulu looked up. The ceiling here was of mirrors too, and seemed to rise to a point, and the mirrors that made up the ceiling were so many and so varied that their reflections seemed to run off into worlds that hadn't been explored yet. For just a moment there seemed to be a stairway rising up, up.

"I thought I saw a stairway," the chief said, his voice almost child-like in its bewilderment. "Is there a stairway in this place?"

"No," Zulu said emphatically. "The ceiling does rise in the center here, to make room for this mirrored dome. But there's no room for a stairway."

"I could swear I saw one." The chief moved about, twisting his head, looking up, searching for what he had lost. "I was following you out when I looked up and saw this long glass stairway going up, and the craziest thing was there were clowns on it. Two or three, or more. I couldn't tell, there were so many reflections. And one of them had a big, black bird on his shoulder. Like a vulture. But I saw them, and then I moved my head to get a better look, and the stairway, with the clowns, disappeared. Now I can't find it again."

"The man was an illusionist, remember," Zulu said, but an icy chill was covering his back, belying the calmness of his answer. "He made this place to make you see things you don't really see. I guess I ought to just close it up and donate it to science to study."

The chief lowered his head and rubbed the back of his neck to help get rid of the strain caused from looking up. "Funny damned thing," he said. "I don't think I like it in here. But I know what I saw."

"This is the way out," Zulu said, at last finding the faded white stripe, and was glad the chief didn't stop to try to find the illusory stairway again. But the part about the clowns was what had given Zulu cold chills, and even when he was out in the sunlight again he still felt cold and filled with a strange new dread.

He didn't like the House of Mirrors either. It seemed to be changing, getting worse, getting—in some way—more dangerous, more subject to illusions that could pull the unsuspecting into madness.

CHAPTER 14

THERE WAS NO SAFE PLACE TO WALK, AMY DECIDED AS SHE LOOKED FOR A WAY out of danger. Everywhere were trucks, tractors, men loading. Even some of the larger, stronger women, dressed so like men that at first Amy thought they were men, were helping pull tents down, fold them, put them on trucks. Some of the smaller women too, Amy saw, worked with their own tents, right alongside their men.

Amy looked for Jodi and saw her nowhere. She found a fairly empty spot beside a tree finally, and watched the loading of the last three parts of the House of Mirrors. The rear parts, when they were separated from the rest, were covered on the open sides with large strips of canvas. The little dwarf, with the big, shaggy head, went around down among all the large men and motioned this way or that, and then he climbed up on one of the trucks and inspected the moorings, Amy guessed, the things that were to hold the pieces of the House in place.

Amy frowned intently, staring, trying to see into the house parts.

She had a feeling about it, a scary feeling, yet she felt drawn to it in a way that made her afraid she would start walking toward it suddenly and not be able to stop.

She turned her back when the feeling became too strong, put her face down, and covered it with her hands. Then she remembered her lucky charm, the pieces of mirror that Jodi had found in the House, and she pulled her blouse out and looked down.

Tiny reflections of something moved within the mirrored surfaces of the pendant, and she squinted, peering, trying to make it out. Then she saw it was the reflections of the House being moved, parts of it being taken onto the truck, everything reduced in size to miniscule beings and parts, and Amy stared, fascinated.

Then it occurred to her that it was impossible for the jewel to pick up those reflections.

Her back was toward the truck, and the jewel was beneath her blouse and against her skin, in the shadows created there. But the sixteen tiny pieces of mirror in the pendant reflected all that was going on behind her as if she didn't exist to block the view.

She watched, horrified, yet fascinated, unable to pull her eyes away.

As she looked into the pendant the clowns appeared, walking in single file one after the other.

They were coming down the alley toward her.

She saw the tree in the mirrors, and herself standing at the base of the tree, no larger than a tiny doll, and she saw the trash can nearby.

The clowns kept coming, three, four, coming into view from the edge of the mirror, then five, six—

"Hey, Amy."

Amy screamed. A quick, frightened squeal that was drowned beneath all the racket.

She dropped her blouse against her necklace and slapped her hand to her chest.

She looked up.

The alley held the people who belonged there, going back and forth from the midway to the trailers. Several small children were still playing near one of the trailers, where a temporary play area had been set up. A woman was gathering toys off the ground and putting them into a box.

There were no clowns.

"Why'd you scream?" Jodi asked, and dropped out of the tree and to the ground right beside Amy. She squealed again, turning to face Jodi, slapping her hand over her mouth.

Jodi had a wide grin on her face. It delighted her and usually Amy didn't mind, but this time she felt angry.

"Where were you? I'm going to tell Russel on you, Jodi."

"I was only up in the tree watching, just like you were watching from down here."

Amy turned her back to Jodi, wondering how much Jodi had seen. Had she seen the necklace? Amy decided she had better be nice.

"I didn't know where you were. I've been looking all over for you, Jodi. I was getting worried."

"I climbed the tree so I could watch them load that House. The tents and things, that's no big deal. Anybody could load a tent. But that House, I wanted to see how they did it, and do you know what, Amy? They take it apart and load it in pieces!"

Amy could see the excitement in Jodi's face, and hear the excitement in her voice, and it told her that Jodi hadn't seen her at all until the moment before she jumped down off the tree limb.

"Hey, Jodi," came another voice, and Blane came out from under a truck bed. "Hey, where you been. I been looking all over for you. Did you see them load that Ferris wheel? That's really something. They're still loading if you want to go see."

"Sure, sure."

Amy watched them run off, going down the alley and out of sight.

Instead of following them as she first intended, Amy turned the other way and went back toward Russel's trailer.

She stopped for a few minutes to play with the small children. But their mother was gathering up things now to pack away, and the mother of the two she was sitting for came and took hers. Amy walked with her as far as her own trailer, mostly in silence.

She went into the front room.

It had grown warm, the sun beating hard on the metal roof. She left the door open for the wind that seemed to blow constantly. But it blew shut again and she left it.

She needed to be busy, and she knew that things had to be put away so they wouldn't fall when the trailer was in motion. She wrapped the toaster cord around it and stuck it below, and put dishes away as securely as she could.

She wanted to look at her necklace, but she was afraid to.

What if the scene were still there? The clowns—where were they going—to the House of Mirrors? The broken puzzle of the House of Mirrors? She had been so scared. As if they were coming after her.

She remembered their faces. Horrible. There was no laughter on the faces of those clowns.

The door opened, and Amy dropped a cup on the floor. It rolled without breaking and she was picking it up when Russel stepped up into the front room. "Getting ready to move on, Amy?"

"Yes. I didn't know how to put the dishes away, so I was just setting them flat."

"That's all you can do. With luck we won't hit any rough spots. Our dishes are plastic anyway, and that's the best kind for this life. The few glass things we have—just make sure they're flat, like you said."

"Should I wrap them in towels?"

"No, that's not necessary."

Russel went around checking things out. He lowered and latched the doors over the bunk bed and closed and latched the windows.

"Well, Amy, are you ready?"

"Are we leaving now?" Amy cried in alarm. "I have to get Jodi."

"We wouldn't leave without Jodi. She's outside. She and Blane came and watched the grab joint being loaded onto its truck bed. Come on." He snapped shut a couple of the little doors.

Amy stood back, watching.

"Let's move," Russel said, and stepped out of the trailer to wait for her.

Amy stood in the alley, which was suddenly no longer an alley, while Russel locked the trailer-house door. All up and down the area of the alley pickups and cars were pulling away, trailers attached to their rears. The alley had disappeared. The tents were gone. All signs of the carnival, the small town it had created, were gone.

Moving away in a long line were the trucks.

Amy saw the familiar little grab joint. It was sitting on a long, flat truck bed with several \ \ \ \other small concessions that didn't break down as the tents and the House of Mirrors did. She recognized a popcorn stand that had sat several yards away from the grab joint when they were in place, and a cotton-candy stand. These were competitors, yet now they all rode together.

Amy asked, "Is that your truck the grab joint is on?"

"No, that belongs to the carnival. To Zulu."

Amy got into the pickup and slid over for Jodi.

Russel started the pickup and pulled it into the line with the other carnie people, and drove out the grassy road and onto the street. Speed picked up only slightly as they drove along in the procession, heading east, leaving the sun behind them.

Russel turned on the radio and country rock began to bounce.

Russel thrummed his fingers to the beat for a couple of times and then, with a long, deep breath, he stopped. A moment later he reached down and turned off the radio.

Amy wondered if he had thought of Lakisha, and India, and it had made him sad.

She put her hand to her chest, and felt the pointed sides of the pendant.

Her good-luck charm?

She wasn't sure anymore.

JODI RODE with her head out the window, like the dog in the pickup ahead. The wind felt good. It wasn't so hot that the air conditioner had to be on, and she was glad of that. There were few things she hated more.

She sat back for a minute to say what was on her mind. "Nothing I hate more than to ride in a car with the windows closed."

"You and me both, babe," Russel said, reaching over Amy's shoulder and messing up Jodi's hair.

She grinned at him, and put her head back out the window. The wind smoothed her hair back into place again, blowing it tightly back against her skull.

The countryside became more rolling. Trees increased in numbers until at times it looked like nothing but trees lived in this green land.

Behind them the sun lowered, and the rays angled across the road.

They reached another town that looked about the size of the one they had left around noon, and pulled into a fairgrounds. This one had more trees and some hills in the background, and a thick line of trees on one side that suggested a stream of water.

"Is that a creek?" Jodi asked.

"Sure is," Russel said.

"Can I go see it?"

"Maybe later."

Once again a town was being created where before there were only grassy fields, and in this case surrounded on three sides by a fence, the boundary lines of the fairgrounds. But it was a large area, and the center looked as if another carnival had been there not long ago, or it had been used to race cars or horses, because there was a long, oval bare spot, about twenty feet wide.

As Jodi suspected, the trucks with the rides, with the joints and the tents and the House of Mirrors, pulled into that area and began to set up.

Russel pulled his pickup into place behind the pickup in front, so that when the next alley was created it was exactly the same as the one they had left except for the trees. Here, there were shade trees scattered, and instead of there being one big tree behind the House of Mirrors, there were trees shading some of the trailers.

Jodi stood in the newly created alley and looked around, her hands on her hips. The sun was going down now. They had come about ninety miles, Russel had said, and they would be setting up tonight.

Amazing, Jodi thought. Just amazing.

All in one day they had changed their home place, and yet it looked almost exactly the same, except that someone had placed more trees in different places.

But then she remembered the creek and she went in search of Blane.

As if Blane had had the same idea, she almost ran into him behind the spot where the girlie-show tent was being erected.

"Wanna go see the creek?" Blane yelled above the noises of setting up the carnival. Trucks were backing into the center section. Some tents had already been pulled up and were looking strong and solid.

Then Jodi saw House of Mirrors trucks backing into place to unload.

"No," she said. "Let's watch the House of Mirrors being put back together."

"Aw, what for? They do it just the same as they always do. They'll put one corner here, another there, stuff like that."

"But how do they know which piece goes where?"

"They know, dumbo. Each one's got its own spot and won't fit anywhere else. Besides, they're marked. The guys know."

"It's just like a great big puzzle, isn't it?"

"Yeah, sort of." Blane twisted, scratched his rear, and looked toward the creek. "Hey, come on. Let's check out that stream of water."

"Okay."

They ran, racing, through the spotted trees and toward the thick grove by the water.

They came into a shady, cool area where the ground was smooth except for debris that looked still damp, as if floods had only recently drifted away.

The creek was wider than it had looked, and had a gravel bottom, with water as clear as Seven-Up in a glass. Jodi and Blane stood on a gravel bar and looked across to the other side.

The water looked deeper there, and as they watched, two boys wearing swim trunks came suddenly out of the trees and dived into the water.

Voices upstream were shouting and calling to each other. From around the bend in the creek came the shouts of children.

"Hey, this is great," Blane said. "We can go swimming."

"I can't."

Blane frowned viciously at her. "Why the hell not? What are you, a spoil-sport or what?"

"I don't have a bathing suit."

"Oh," Blane said contritely. "Well, I've got an extra one. You can borrow it."

"A boy's pair of trunks? Are you crazy? What will I wear up here?" Jodi put her hands over her nipples.

Blane looked.

"You don't need anything up there," he said in contempt. "What do you think you are?"

"Well, I'm not a boy! Girls don't wear just bottoms!"

"Okay, then you can borrow my mom's suit."

"What?"

Blane dug her with his elbow, and Jodi noticed that the two big boys had come over from the swimming hole and were not ten feet away. They looked to be about fourteen or fifteen. At least three years older than Blane, and lots bigger. Jodi realized she was trying to figure out their chances against these two guys if push came to shove and fight.

She could fight too, and that might surprise them.

"You two with the carnival?" asked the taller of the two, a boy with black hair, brown eyes, and full lips.

He was good-looking, Jodi saw, and her heart did a little dance; but he looked dangerous too. She stared at him.

"Yeah," Blane said. "So what?"

The big kid shrugged. "Just thought we'd tell you that the best swimming hole around here is over there by the bank, but it's kind of deep. We measured it, and it's twelve feet, so if you don't swim too good, better places are down around the bend. Littler kids swim there."

"I can swim," Blane said. "I don't know about her."

Jodi said nothing. She was still staring at the tall, handsome boy, and she was surprised that he had turned out to be so nice.

"Well." The boys turned away. "We'll be around if you need help. Just yell. Our houses are back on the other side of the trees and we hang out here a lot."

As they walked away Blane yelled, "Are you coming to the carnival?"

"Sure. When will it open?"

"Tomorrow at noon."

The boys waved farewell.

Jodi stood with the water washing gently against her toes and watched the boys start swimming again. Then a couple of girls, with cute suits on great bodies, came out of the trees and joined the two boys.

The sun had gone so far down the whole creek looked shadowed and was darkening fast, the water looking colder and deeper.

"We better go, Blane."

"Yeah."

They walked together back into the field. The sun had gone down now, leaving only a big red streak in the west. Lights were blinking on over at the fairgrounds. A couple of rides already stuck up into the air.

"For awhile there," Blane said, "I thought they were going to beat up on us."

"Yeah, me too."

"That's the way some kids treat carnie people, did you know that?"

"No, I didn't know that. Why carnie people? I just thought those boys were going to run us off their creek, that was all."

"Well, some folks, some towns, don't like carnie people."

"Why?"

"Well, heck, how do I know why? They think we're dirty, I guess."

"We're not dirty."

"I know that. But they don't, I guess."

"Let's run. It's getting dark."

"Okay, bet you this good-luck charm that I can beat you."

"What good-luck charm?"

"This." Blane opened his hand wider, put it over near Jodi's chin.

On his damp, open palm lay a silver star.

"Really? You'd give that away?"

"Sure." He put it back into his pocket. "But you gotta win first."

"Okay, let's go."

Blane counted to three, and they ran.

Jodi put all she had into running, but by the time she was thirty yards from the long line of trailers with the cars and pickup trucks parked beside them, Blane was reaching them, and he slid to a stop and looked back at her.

Jodi slid to a breathless stop beside him.

Blane was laughing.

"See, you ain't half the guy you thought you were."

Jodi had no breath for answering. She walked past him, into the alley and through the passageway between two tents onto the midway.

Rides were back in place, most of them still being erected.

But there was Russel's grab joint, just like always, sitting like a colorful little metallic toadstool, and beside it, resting now beneath a large umbrella that streaked its colorful wings over a picnic table, were Russel and Amy.

Jodi went toward them, leaving Blane with his silver good-luck charm.

AMY WANTED to look at her pendant again, and she thought of it with a mixture of trepidation and eagerness. She hadn't imagined she had seen the clowns, so there must be something remarkable about her treasure. It was a treasure indeed that could see things mortal eyes couldn't have seen.

But it was a long time before she was alone.

Night came and the lights were strung around the midway and turned on. Lights on the high-rising rides were tested, and looked beautiful and exciting in the night, and the music soared up for a few minutes, sometimes here and sometimes far down the other end of the midway. Kids of the carnie, the little ones, got to try the little rides—the toddler-sized motorcycles held steady to metal circling rods, boats, merry-go-rounds on a small scale over on the far side of the midway with most of the other kiddie rides —and there was almost as much laughter as when the carnival was open.

Russel popped corn, but they went to the cook tent for supper and ate beans and wieners and cornbread muffins. For dessert they ate cake. Amy thought it was the best cake she had ever tasted, even though it was plain yellow with a simple chocolate frosting.

Not until she was in the shower at eleven o'clock did she have a chance to look at her pendant.

She stood in the tiny bathroom and looked at herself in the mirror. She wore nothing but the pendant, and it lay on her chest sparkling like a diamond, picking up the one light in the bathroom and throwing it back hundreds of times, it seemed.

She looked at it through the medicine-chest mirror, and saw only the lights.

She wanted to see it closer, to pull it up into her hand so that she could look into it, but she was just a little bit afraid. She was excited too, wondering what she would see. Would she see Jodi and Russel in the front room? Jodi was probably climbing the ladder to bed, because she had already had her bath. And Russel was watching TV. The Carson Show, she thought.

Her fingers touched and fondled the pendant, and it felt almost hot to her touch, as if it were alive with something that agitated and stirred inside. Like blood?

She drew it up at last and looked into it, her breath held, her mouth open so she could breathe more comfortably when she expelled her breath in a long, soft sigh.

There were moving figures in the mirrors.

She turned so the light would shine better into it, because she couldn't see what the figures were. The odd, terrible clowns again? With the colorful suits but terrible faces? No ...

She began to frown.

The tiny figures were men, and some of them were in uniform. Among them she recognized the face of the cowboy detective who had come to their house back at the other fairgrounds.

They were looking at something on the ground.

Then suddenly the scene changed. It was night, and there was only one figure on the ground.

At first Amy thought it was one of the clowns, then she saw that it was India, dressed in a clown's suit. Her head looked as if it were disembodied and just lying there, not very well placed. Her eyes stared without moving, directly at Amy, and her tongue protruded and hung slightly to one side as if she had been choked to death.

Amy cried out in horror, then slapped both hands over her mouth, praying Russel hadn't heard her.

The pendant had fallen back against her chest, and hung still, but even in the mirror she could see the tiny clown on the ground, with India's head laid grotesquely beside it. Then she saw the images change, rapidly, like a VCR TV show being fast-forwarded. Scenes were flitting past, but she couldn't see what they were. At last they stopped. And one tiny scene was in the pendant.

Very slowly Amy picked it up again, watching herself in the mirror. For a moment she cupped the pendant in her palm, then she opened her hand and looked down.

The tiny figure in the mirrors of the pendant showed a little girl, all twisted and broken, like the body of a doll that someone had destroyed.

With fear edging icy, knife-like waves down over her, Amy looked more closely at the face of the dead child.

Jodi.

CHAPTER 15

Zulu went through India's trailer, walking slowly, checking it out the way she would have done after a move to another spot, another fairgrounds. Sometimes they hit rough roads and things were tossed around, even though the truck that had pulled India's trailer was big and heavy and had a steady pull.

India's car was right behind the trailer, where it was always parked. He had driven it himself, not trusting it to one of the boys, as he liked to call them.

They had looked at him as if he were crazy. Moving India's trailer and car as if she were still alive? Driving India's car? Him? His own car was especially equipped for a dwarf, but he had sent it on one of the trucks. And he had managed to drive India's Buick, with cushions, with the seat adjusted to the maximum, and by peering over the top of the hood like a ten-year-old kid.

Sometimes he hated himself.

Why couldn't he be like other men?

Yet now it seemed the most unimportant thing in the world. India was gone, and in her silent house he knew that most of himself was gone too. He would live only to see to the destruction of her killer, whoever he was or whatever it was.

Her clothes were still neatly on hangers.

The clowns in the front room were where they belonged, so far as he remembered.

Zulu readjusted the one on the right onto his frame. What had she called him? Joey?

Here he was treating them as if they were real, just as she had done.

But maybe she would want him to.

"All right, guys," he said. "Behave yourselves."

He rubbed his cheek and looked at them. Hideous faces, great costumes. But they had been India's passion in life.

He remembered what she had said about the clowns being copies of her dreams, and near the end she had wondered if they really were Raoell's creation rather than hers, if her dreams were memories of clowns she had seen in his acts.

If that were so ...

Zulu stared at them, and became uncomfortable and uneasy, as if there might be something here he wasn't seeing.

He shook his head. He turned off the lights and went out of the trailer and locked the door behind him.

He crossed the midway to his own trailer, the midway lights his only companions.

JODI COULD HEAR SOMEONE CRYING, and she woke and lay listening. At first there was silence in the dark trailer, then she heard the sob again, and Amy began stirring restlessly, her head going from side to side, her hands reaching as if her wrists were tied to the bed. She was sobbing, a soft, low, choked sound, dreaming, gasping in the throes of a nightmare that turned Jodi cold with fear.

It scared her to hear someone in a nightmare. Once, when she had stayed all night with a little girl whose mother had what they called problems, that mother had screamed with a nightmare, on and on, and everyone had run to her room to try to wake her. It was a long time before the woman woke. And ever since, when someone moaned or cried out in sleep, Jodi got cold chills.

"Amy," she said, keeping her voice low so that she wouldn't scare her worse and send her over the edge, the way her friend had said could happen. What edge Jodi didn't know, but it must be the edge of hell, it sounded so terrible.

"Amy," she repeated, shaking Amy, trying to see her face in the dark.

Amy continued to cry in her sleep, her head tossing from side to side.

A faint light from the midway glowed for an instant on Amy's face, and Jodi saw her eyes half-open. She drew back, unnerved. But Amy was crying harder, trying to scream, and Jodi was afraid she might go over the edge in her dream.

Jodi leaned over her as far as the low roof of the bunk would allow, and began repeating her name. "Amy, Amy, Amy, wake up, you're having a bad dream, wake up, Amy, Amy... ."

Amy grew still suddenly and stared upward. The light was there again, as if a tree limb, moving in the night breeze, allowed the light through at certain times.

Suddenly Amy threw her arms around Jodi and hugged her tightly, almost smothering her.

"Oh Jodi! I'm so glad ... so glad ... to see you, Jodi."

"Hey, let me go."

Jodi pulled away to her own side of the bed.

"Did I wake you up? I'm sorry."

"That's okay, just don't do that again, will you? You might go over the edge."

"What?"

"Nothing, go back to sleep."

Jodi turned her back to Amy, rested her head on her hands, and closed her eyes. She heard Amy turn over too, away from her.

The next thing Jodi knew it was morning and Amy was climbing out of bed over her. Sun was shining in the little window by the bunk, and birds outside in the trees were yelling their hearts out.

Jodi felt good. It was going to be a great day.

She lay still, on her right side, her hands under her cheek, and watched Russel cook breakfast. She smiled. Though Amy could cook without making such a mess, Russel seemed to like to fry that bacon and those eggs, splattering grease, making smoke. It was the way he cooked breakfast, and Jodi was beginning to like burned bacon.

Amy came out of the bathroom dressed in shorts and a yellow pullover that was sleeveless. She went silently to the table and began to set it for three. Jodi climbed down from the bunk.

"Hey, Amy, what was your nightmare last night? It must have been a really bad one."

"I didn't have a nightmare," Amy said, her face turned away from Jodi the way it always was when she didn't want to admit to something.

"Hey, you did too! And you know you did."

173

"I did not."

"Fighting already?" Russel asked. "And we haven't even had breakfast."

"Well," Jodi cried indignantly, "she woke me up with her nightmare, and now she says she didn't have one!"

"So?" Amy snapped, turning to glare at her. Yet there was a thin white line around her mouth, and she looked scared, for some reason that Jodi couldn't figure.

"Maybe she doesn't remember it," Russel said, flopping the bacon over onto its platter and dumping the bowl of eggs into the smoking pan.

"Oh, she remembers all right," Jodi said, her morning mood ruined, which made her all the madder. Why was Amy acting like this? "She talked to me! Last night, after her nightmare. She was even glad to see me."

"I didn't have a nightmare," Amy said stubbornly.

"Oh, piss," Jodi said under her breath, the worst, absolutely nastiest word she could think of at the time.

"What?" Russel asked.

"Nothing."

Jodi went into the bathroom and washed her face and sat on the stool for a little while. She could hear the sounds of breakfast continuing in the kitchen-living room, but she didn't hurry. When she dressed she wore shorts and a shirt like Amy's, only in blue rather than yellow. Their mom always bought their clothes pretty much alike, and usually Jodi didn't mind, but today she was feeling some hatred toward Amy. Why was she acting like this? Lying and all? Sometimes Amy told little lies, but usually it was only to keep out of trouble.

What trouble was she in that made her lie about the nightmare?

Jodi didn't say anything more about Amy's dream. She ate and drank her milk and then asked to be excused.

Russel said, "Sure. Just don't go very far away. Don't be going down to the creek yet, okay? I want to take a look at it first."

"When will you?"

"Soon. Maybe sometime this morning."

Amy was acting odd, Jodi saw as she eased nearer to the door. She was sitting very straight in her chair and staring at Russel.

"Can I just go play with Blane then?"

"You're not going to let her, are you?" Amy asked. "Shouldn't she stay with us?"

"Why do I have to stay with you?" Jodi demanded. Amy didn't look at Jodi or answer her. She was still sitting like a board and staring at Russel, her eyes demanding that he listen to her. She wanted Jodi to stay with her, for some obscure reason.

Russel glanced sideways at Jodi. "Your sister wants your company, Jodi, you should be glad. Besides, maybe you could help her with the dishes while I go get the grab joint ready for business."

Jodi slumped against the door frame, then she thought of something.

"Is Amy going to work in the grab joint with you today?"

"If she wants to. I hope she does, I don't know what I'd do without her now."

Amy's chin lowered and she looked down at her plate. From Jodi's viewpoint it looked like Amy was trying to see down inside her blouse for a moment, as if she had a bug crawling there. She pressed her hand against her blouse front, then dropped it into her lap.

"What about Jodi?" Amy said, but without her former belligerence. "Can she stay with us?"

Russel leaned back, tilting his chair onto its two back legs. He looked steadily at Amy, figuring her out. "You're worried about Jodi, aren't you, Amy?"

Jodi spun around on her heel and moaned. "Oh, no! Why? When people get worried all the fun is gone. I'm not going to get hurt. Blane goes with me. He sees after me."

"Blane is not very big or old," Russel said. "He probably doesn't have enough sense to take care of himself properly. I can see Amy's point, Jodi. You have to remember two people have been murdered."

"Not here! That was back in that other town."

Russel said, "Yes, you're right there." He let his chair down and stirred his coffee, just an action to keep his hand busy while his mind thought up something that would keep her from having any fun, Jodi supposed.

"Please, Dad, I won't get hurt. I just go around with Blane, that's all. I promise I won't even go to the creek. I promise. And I won't go out into the field. I'll stay where people are."

Russel said, "We can't put her in a cage, Amy. We have to trust to the good Lord that she'll be safe, don't we? And there's no room for her in the grab joint, and it wouldn't be much fun for a little kid like her, would it?"

"I guess not," Amy said.

Jodi straightened. "Can I go then?" she asked eagerly.

"Sure, go on. But be careful. And check back with Amy, Jodi, every hour or so. Maybe that will make her feel better."

"Okay, okay!"

Jodi ran, down the shady alley, feeling like a deer in a meadow. She leaped and jumped and ran, looking for Blane to pop out from under something the way he always seemed to.

AMY SAT LISTLESSLY. Jodi was gone. Would she ever see her again, running, playing, being Jodi? What would she do without Jodi? Jodi always stood between her and the world, it seemed, when she needed her to. In a way it was as if Jodi were the older, yet since they had come with the carnival Jodi was drifting away, and if the talisman were right, Jodi would die.

Amy asked, "Russel? Do you believe in ... ummm ... do you believe the future can be predicted?"

"No, do you?"

"You don't?" Just knowing he didn't made her feel a little better. Yet why had she seen those images? And why had she had the very same image in her nightmare?

"Of course not. If the future could be predicted, seen accurately, that would mean that everything in the world has happened before, and we're just in a rerun, right? Simple creatures with little memory. And you don't believe that, do you? No, this is the first run, Amy. What hasn't happened yet hasn't happened, that's all. You don't believe a future that hasn't happened can be predicted, do you?"

"No, I guess not," she said.

Amy got up and began to clear the table. "She's happy, isn't she? She likes to play with Blane. Jodi always has friends wherever she goes."

"Yeah, she acts happy."

"She won't want to go home to Mama," Amy said. "But then, I don't think Mama wants us anymore."

"You've got a home with me from now on, Amy, both you and Jodi. In fact, I've been planning to discuss this with your mother. I can put you kids in school in Florida this winter, and if you can stand living in this trailer all the time, we'll stay together."

"Really?" Amy cried, delighted, happiness flooding her. She was afraid she was going to start bawling, so she hastily began to wash dishes. She felt really good all of a sudden. "You know, I really don't need Jodi to help me with dishes. She's sloppy. She doesn't dry them good."

"Someday we'll get us an electric dishwasher, what do you say?"

"No, I don't mind washing by hand. It doesn't take that long, and that way I can wash the cabinet, and even the floor. I like the trailer just the way it is. I really like ..." She couldn't say any more. She bowed her head over the soapy water in the tiny sink so that Russel wouldn't see the tears fall.

Maybe Jodi wouldn't die after all, and they would stay with their dad and live happily ever after.

"Hey, ssst."

Jodi looked for Blane and couldn't find him. She knew his voice, and the hissing sound he could make that penetrated her skin like a batch of red ants. She both hated that sound and liked it, because it meant fun coming up soon.

"Where are you?"

For a tantalizing minute there was no answer, then he hissed, "Find me."

She looked beneath the nearest trailer, and saw only Roscoe, tied by his long chain and lying on a mat back in the cool shadows. He thumped his tail.

She looked around the corners of the game tent across the alley from the trailer, then she looked behind the trash can that sat at the corner. Finally she went to the big trash dumpster and tried to pull herself up so that she could look over the side.

She heard giggling.

She looked up, and felt like hitting herself. With all the trees that shaded the alley at this new fairground, she hadn't thought of them as a hiding place. Even though she had used one herself just yesterday.

She began to peer up into the thick, green branches of the nearest tree, and finally she spotted his face, like a Cheshire cat, grinning down at her from around a fat, low limb.

She stamped her foot, but then she started giggling with him. She climbed up and sat beside him on the limb.

Russel opened the grab joint and started the corn popping. He put every-thing out where it was the handiest, the napkins easy to grab, the slick sheets of paper that he wrapped hot dogs in easy to pull free.

Amy came, and he gave her an apron and wrapped one around his own waist.

The gates were opening, and a few marks were straggling in, kids out of school, mothers with little children. He began to box up corn to set aside and have ready to sell. The chili was bubbling gently, and the hot dogs rotating on the spits.

A new day of work was starting, just as if nothing had changed. Yet the scene he looked upon seemed different. The rides were the same: the Tilt-a-whirl, the whip, the merry-go-round, the game tents that were in the center line of the midway were the same, the pokerina—which this town allowed, bingo, bottle pitch, many others on down the line. Yet the people who moved around were like puppets on a stage, their movements somehow jerky and uneven in his eyes, and over it all lay an atmosphere of something invisible but deadly.

For just a few minutes of almost total panic as he stood there looking down the midway, he wanted to leave, to take his two little girls, get in the pickup, and blaze the hell out of there. But then behind him Amy said, "Dad."

The word was like magic. The sunlight brightened, the people became normal. The music and the noise spurred him to move too, to turn, to see that a line of customers stood at both windows and Amy was trying her best to handle them.

"Time to get to work, huh?" he said to his daughter, and went to his small window to take orders.

JODI CRAWLED out from under the flap of the clown-show tent. Izzy and Jade had been really good today, but Jodi was beginning to feel a little like a thief.

She sat in the grass against the side of the tent with Blane, her stomach sore from laughing so hard.

"Maybe if we asked our dads they would let us go in at the door and see the show like other kids."

"What's wrong, didn't you like your spot today?"

"I just don't think it's right to sneak in."

"Let's go to the creek," Blane said, getting to his feet and dusting off his pants.

"I already told you, I can't."

"He'd never know the difference."

"Even if I did, I'd have to just wade, and that wouldn't be fun."

It would be torture, wanting to throw herself all the way into the water and wriggle through it like a fish. It would be torture to stand in the shallows and watch others swim. Of course, if there weren't a lot of people around, maybe she could just swim in her clothes, and then she could hurry and change before anyone saw her, and if Amy or Russel should notice that she had changed, she could say she spilled something on herself. But that would be a lie, and she wasn't into lying very well.

"I said, you can borrow my old trunks."

"I can't. My dad told me he wanted to go down and see the creek himself before I could go."

"Well, when's he going?"

"I don't know. Maybe tomorrow."

"Shucks. We only stay here one week, and then we move on."

"Oh yeah? Where do we go next?"

"I don't know. That's Zulu's business. He's got that all planned before we ever leave Florida in the spring."

"Hey, I get to go to Florida with you," Jodi said, suddenly remembering. "Amy told me so at lunch time, and Russel said it's true."

"You do? How come? Are you going to live with your dad?"

"Yes, if Mama will let us."

"Don't you like your mama?"

She wished he hadn't said that, for a terrible hurt came into her chest and burned like pure fire. She felt an aching longing to see her mother again, and feel her arms warm and secure around her. It had been a long time since she'd been hugged by her mother, though, except for that last day when they'd left on the airplane. Mama had gotten to where she was too busy.

"Hey, let's go in the House of Mirrors again," Blane said.

Jodi looked down the narrow alley between the tent of the clown act and the girlie-show tent. She could hear Zulu shouting on his own platform, and people were walking that way, listening.

"The most amazing mirror maze in the world," Zulu was saying. "Created by a mad genius a century ago. This is the last season for this old House of Mirrors, and then it will be turned over to science to study, to try to discover the mysteries within."

"Did you hear that?" Jodi said. "He's going to give the House of Mirrors to science to study. He said it was created—"

"I know. I heard. A mad genius."

"Is that right?"

"I don't know. I never heard it before. Come on."

"Well ..." If this were the last season the House of Mirrors would be with the show, maybe it would be all right to go back in it again. Especially since they couldn't go to the creek yet. Jodi followed Blane.

"Do just like I do, see?" he hissed back at her. "Don't let anyone see you, or we're dead, see? Watch out, get your head down. Whataya want, get your head shot off?"

They must be playing spy again, so Jodi ducked her head and scooted from tent to tent, and slid along its side looking back to see if any of the marks had noticed them. They were all looking ahead, it seemed, laughing and talking and eating popcorn or cotton candy or candied apples.

Jodi and Blane reached the end of the tent and the corner and looked cautiously up and down the alley. At one trailer several yards down the alley the three little Smithers kids were in their makeshift playpen, and their mother was sitting in a lawn chair reading a magazine. There was a pile of books and magazines on the ground beside her, and a tall glass of something green. She wasn't looking at them either. They had sneaked along without being seen. Except for a cat, which eyed them from a window of a trailer just across the alley. Then it yawned and lay down.

In the trailer next door a little dog, somewhere out of sight, yipped a couple of times.

Blane took an exaggerated look around. "An enemy in the neighborhood. The dog heard it. Hurry, under here."

He dropped to his belly and crawled beneath the House of Mirrors, and Jodi followed him.

About ten feet in from the corner Blane sat up, hunching down to keep his head clear of the floor, and waited for Jodi.

"You ready?" he asked when she reached him.

She looked at the hole in the floor. It was dark, black as a dungeon up in there, and suddenly she wondered about something.

"How come nobody ever noticed that hole in the floor and fixed it?"

"Because this is one of the sections that's closed, that's why."

Blane had a smug, secretive look on his face.

"You made that hole yourself!" Jodi accused, knowing by the look on his face she was right. "How'd you do it?"

"I didn't. And that's a fact. But I'll tell you who did if you'll promise never to tell."

"Cross my heart."

"Okay, listen." Blane leaned forward with his elbows on the ground, and Jodi did as he did. With their faces nose to nose Blane told her, "This kid, Kevin was his name, him and his folks traveled with the carnie last year, see? They worked for Zulu. They weren't concessionaires like my folks and your dad. Well, Kevin said, why don't we make a hole and have part of the House of Mirrors all to ourselves? 'Cause he knew, see, that Zulu had closed off part of it. And besides, we wanted to see what was in there. So he had this hacksaw, a little sharp, pointed saw. Did you ever see one?"

"No."

"You can saw circles or anything, once you've got a little hole to put it in, see? So Kevin and me, we used our knives and made a little, round hole. See, here it is." Blane put his finger in a spot at the corner of the big hole. "Then Kevin sawed the boards out. Just two. Just enough so we could get ahold of it and break it off."

"Did you go in a lot?"

"Sure."

"Where's Kevin now?"

Blane frowned and looked away, under the floor of the House of Mirrors —where, in the midway at the front, they could see the feet of people going in both directions.

"I don't know. I guess he ran away."

"He did?" Jodi said in awe. Running away was such a fearsome and drastic thing to do. Where did kids go when they ran away? "How old was he?"

"He was twelve, going on thirteen."

Jodi shrugged. "Well, yeah, I suppose, if he's twelve he's going on to thirteen."

Blane didn't seem to hear her. "He didn't tell me he was running away. But one day he was just gone, and so his folks left too after a couple of weeks. I don't know if they ever found him. That day he left—he wanted me to go in the House of Mirrors with him. He said he'd found something there, and he wanted to see it some more. But I couldn't. My dad makes me help at one of the games sometimes when my brother can't work, and I had to help."

Blane moved suddenly, his face changing, brightening, getting that sneaky look again that meant he was ready to think up something fun to do.

"Come on, let's go in."

Jodi opened her mouth and then closed it. Blane was already halfway up into the hole, so that he looked as if half of his body grew down out of the floor.

She watched him wriggle upward, and then his legs disappeared too, and there was nothing left but the black hole that had swallowed him.

She didn't want to go in there, she suddenly realized. There was something about those dark, old mirrors, and the way the darkness seemed to stir behind them, opening up worlds she didn't want to see again.

But Blane's head was suddenly looking at her from the hole, so that now he looked like his head was growing down out of the floor like a mushroom. Jodi began to giggle.

Blane frowned.

"What are you waiting for? Come on."

"You look like a mushroom upside down."

"Come on!"

It was a command she couldn't ignore. After all, he was the captain and she was only the private.

Jodi wriggled up through the hole with Blane pulling her.

She stood up in the narrow corridor.

A small bulb in the ceiling a few feet down the corridor was like a star in a cloudy sky. The darkness seemed more complete than she remembered, swelling out of the mirrors like black ghosts, yet the dark mirrors were reflecting—something—movements were within them, subtle movements like the slow swirl of clouds, or of murky water.

"Blane," Jodi whispered, taking his arm in a tight grip. "I don't like it in here."

CHAPTER 16

"Come on, don't be chicken. Let's see what's around the corner. Where is this spooky swamp-looking place you told me about?"

He was starting on, and she had the choice of following or being left alone with the murky mirrors that were too dark even to cast a good reflection of either of them. She could see ahead, as Blane moved along the narrow corridor, a dim reflection of a boy. But somehow it didn't look like Blane. That boy seemed to have darker hair and he was taller.

"Blane," she cried, afraid to raise her voice.

"Come on." He motioned over his shoulder at her, and the next instant he was gone.

"Blane!"

His head came disembodied about a corner, grinning mischievously.

She hurried to catch up.

Her own reflection seemed to be just an added swirl in the dark world beyond the surface of the mirrors. There was no other little girl walking beside her.

"Blane—I saw a boy that wasn't you."

"Huh? Hey, look. You think that part's bad, look at this corridor."

She stepped around the corner. The single light bulb, she now saw, was right on the corner, so that it lighted both corridors, and another that went at right angles to the first. It was like being faced with two roads into a dark and dangerous forest, where huge trunks of trees went off into infinity and beneath them, oozing continually around their thick trunks, a black, brackish water reached toward them, held back only by the glass in the walls.

"This ... Jodi cried in a whisper. "See—it's a swamp. See, Blane?"

"I don't see no swamp—"

Blane stopped, his words cut off suddenly.

He was looking in another direction, and Jodi's gaze followed his.

It was the boy again, the one she had seen walking down the corridor at Blane's side, the reflection that was not Blane's.

"It's him, Blane," she whispered frantically. "It's the boy I saw."

Blane didn't answer. He was staring through the darkness toward the figure that now stood looking back at them. The other boy seemed to be far away, somewhere in the swampland that Jodi could see but Blane could not. The dark ripples of the mirror obscured his face, darkened his skin ...

Maybe it was Blane after all, Jodi thought. But where was her own reflection? She stood in the corridor at Blane's side, her hand on his arm, yet there was no other child with the boy in the mirror.

But maybe the mirror was too dark to reflect her. Maybe ...

Somebody screamed, and then another cry came through the glass walls, and sounds of footsteps.

"It's the marks," Blane said, but his voice sounded strange.

Jodi suddenly remembered the customers. The House of Mirrors was open to the public, and their voices came through into the bad part of the mirror maze, and even the sounds of their footsteps clomped along the floors and sent waves of vibration. And then their laughter came. A girl squealed something that sounded like, "Gross, hideous, weird! I don't look like that!"

"It's a mark," Blane said again.

Jodi knew he was talking about the boy now. Not the people whose cries and voices drifted through the walls. He was talking about the boy that stared at him through the mirrors.

"Can he see us?" Jodi asked.

Blane didn't answer.

The boy in the mirror took a couple of steps forward. He came through the thick tree trunks, the swamp trees that had no tops, no limbs, no leaves, he came through the swirling water as it covered his whole body, and his face became visible.

Jodi drew back in alarm.

The boy's face was twisted in a silent, terrible cry, as if he were in torment and asking them for help.

Blane cried out suddenly, startlingly, "Kevin!"

He walked into the mirrored wall, his hands spread flat against it. With tears streaming down his face he began to pound on the glass, crying over and over, "Kevin, Kevin, Jesus Christ, Kevin, where are you?"

He turned and ran down the corridor, and disappeared into another corner, and as if the reflection were his own after all, it ran too, and disappeared.

"Blane!" Jodi screamed, her cries mingling with the muted cries of the girls and boys somewhere else in the House of Mirrors. She ran after Blane, the boards of the floor creaking beneath her steps, a molding, musty smell growing all around her, rising like old dust.

Blane stood in the other corridor just around the corner, and she ran into him.

He was staring at something ahead.

Jodi looked around him, catching only a glimpse of bright colors in the dreary twilight of the mirrors.

"Jodi," Blane whispered, reaching back and shoving at her with his hand. "There's some—some strange clowns in here. Get out, Jodi. Run."

His voice was low and level, as calm as if he were telling her to go buy a bag of popcorn for them to share, but there was an undertone that frightened Jodi more than anything in her experience.

She started to obey his command, but then froze as she watched the clowns that came out of the darkness ahead.

The cheerfulness of their costumes—the ruffles, the big, fluffy buttons, the funny stockings and shoes, all the frivolities—ended at their necks. The eyes that looked at them out of their hideous faces were slitted and blank and deadly. The clowns were coming single file, one after the other, down the corridor toward them. White-gloved hands were slowly rising, as if pulled by the strings of a puppeteer, and the fingers were curving inward like claws.

Blane's elbow dug into Jodi's ribs. "Run!"

As if she too had become automated, Jodi was moving, turning, reaching for the corner of the glass, pulling herself around, feeling as if her feet were mired in the terrible mud of the swamp.

She tried to run, but the darkness and the swirling mists slowed her, and she found she had taken the wrong turn.

Another of the clowns was at the end of this corridor too, coming toward her, the face knobbed and long, the nose drooping toward the pointed chin like the face of a Halloween witch, and the eyes—the eyes slits of nothing but darkness.

Jodi gasped a silent cry and turned back, and ran into Blane, and his hand closed around her wrist so tightly she was aware of a streak of pain shooting up her arm, but the pain was nothing beneath the fear, the terrible, paralyzing fear of the clowns.

Suddenly Blane was shoving her downward, trying to stop her from running farther on. Instead of telling her to turn, he was holding her back, and shoving her down to the floor with his hand on her head.

Then she saw the hole in the floor.

He was trying to save her, to get her out of this terrible place that was like something deep within the earth, a terrible place of dark mud and endlessness and putrid, decayed things, and death. Death in clowns' costumes.

She was being pushed down through the hole, forced down.

She began to cooperate, and pulled herself down and out into the light and the grass and the world where sunshine and people lived.

She crawled to one side, to leave room for Blane, and sat shaking and trying to get her breath. She began to feel physically sick, and got on her hands and knees and stood with her head in the grass like a dog, her insides heaving.

Then the sickness passed, and she looked back for Blane.

He wasn't there.

Panic surged into her throat, burned her shoulders and her neck.

She crawled back to the hole.

"Blane! Come on out—" her voice was so choked with terror and panic that it was only a squeak.

Where was Blane?

God, oh God.

"Blane …

She was almost physically sick again when she put her hands up into the darkness of the hole. Her body shook with the chills of her terror, but she had to find Blane.

"Blane ..."

Her voice quivered, and the sound was weak even to her own ears.

She pulled herself up into the hole again, and froze there, her hands gripping the rough edges of the hole, her body halfway up into the floor of the House of Mirrors.

The clowns reached back into infinity, it seemed, their reflections going on and on into the murky world of the dark and blighted mirrors, so that Jodi couldn't tell if there were a dozen or two dozen... or only six or seven. They were holding Blane up into the air, raising him above their heads. He struggled, like a small animal caught and held in vicious claws, but he was completely silent as if he had lost all ability to use his voice.

The whole scene was silent.

Jodi was frozen in her position half in the House of Mirrors, and the clowns' movements were silent. Even when they smashed Blane down onto the floor, there was no sound, as if their world were removed from the world of sound. The hideous faces had no emotion. The grotesqueness of their masks remained steady nothingness, and their movements were sudden and jerky like the movements of puppets.

Their curved, clawed-like white gloves, so deceptive, seemed the most frightening of all to Jodi. For it was the gloves that picked Blane up again and again and threw him to the floor, until his body looked in its nonresistance as if it were made of rubber.

Someone was sobbing hysterically. Jodi felt the tears on her cheeks, but only in a half-aware part of her mind. She was no longer able to try to protect herself. She had only one need—to get to Blane and get him away from the clowns.

She crawled into the House and along the floor, so close to the feet of one clown that her arm brushed the oversized shoe. Blane was on the floor, twisted, his arms and legs askew, his eyes bulging from their sockets and oozing blood. His hair was smeared with blood, and the blood ran out of his nose and mouth, his face smashed and red and raw, as if the skin had been ripped from his body.

The clowns were reaching down again, but Jodi, on the floor on her belly, grasped his ankle and began to pull Blane toward the hole. She could hear her own sobs now, but it didn't matter. Sounds were all around, the screaming of the kids in other parts of the mirror maze, voices of many pitches, girls, boys, men, women, a small child crying. Footsteps on the boards of the floor made creaking sounds in the building, and the floor vibrated with their walking. None of it mattered. None of it touched this part of the mirror maze that was closed off, where the clowns were, and where the blood of Blane smeared the floor and ran into the cracks and made the dark and murky water of the swamp turn even darker.

The clowns were reaching down again, but Jodi had pulled Blane away.

They would come for her next. This she knew and accepted, but somehow she had to get Blane through the hole and out into the safety of the saner world.

She pushed at him, she got his legs through, and then his body. His head and arms hung sideways, broken, limp, uncooperative.

"Blane, help me," she begged. He couldn't be dead. He just couldn't be. A few minutes ago he had pushed her out the hole to safety. He could not have died, no, no, no.

By some miracle, suddenly Blane dropped through the hole, leaving behind only the dark trail of his blood.

Just before Jodi put her legs into the hole she looked back at the clowns, expecting now to feel those terrible white gloves picking her up and lifting her high in the air the way they had Blane.

But they were milling about strangely, some of them bent as if looking for something on the floor, others reaching with their curved, white-gloved hands. Milling about aimlessly, undirected, and, Jodi realized in shock, as if they could not see her at all.

She stared, waiting a moment too long, as suddenly, as if they had received a signal, they turned and fell into line, one behind the other, their reflections fading away into the dark, stained mirrors—and they were facing Jodi, looking at her now, and coming toward her.

She moved, hurriedly, and struggled down out of the hole just as the first clown, the one with the white ruffles around his neck and the face of a witch, brushed her arm with the fingers of his glove.

Jodi dropped down into the grass and, crying softly, her chest jerking in total terror and shock, she grasped the shoulders of Blane's shirt and began pulling him through the grass toward the distant front of the House of Mirrors.

Common sense and simple reasoning had left her. She could have reached the alley within ten feet, or the passageway between the clown show-tent of Izzy and Jade and the House of Mirrors in ten or twelve feet. But she pulled Blane toward the front, bumping her head on the joists, crying, moaning like an animal in dreadful pain, because she could see people there—hundreds of feet, walking along the midway.

People ... help for Blane.

The people would help him.

Help him!

She tried to call, but her voice was controlled by the sobs that shook her.

Her first realization that she had come at last out from beneath the House of Mirrors was when someone screamed.

THE CROWD AT FIRST DISPERSED. Girls screamed—one, then another—and a "small child began to cry hysterically. People hurried away in a cluster. The group that had lined up at the ticket booth for the second opening of the House of Mirrors now rushed away, and then stood staring.

Zulu tried to see over their heads. A snake, he figured, had crawled out from under the House. Yet crowds didn't react that way to a snake.

He came down the steps off the platform and shoved his way through the crowd.

In the grass at the edge of the floor Jodi sat, hunched forward, more on her knees and hands, as if she had returned to some previous wild form. On the ground beside her was a bloody bundle of rags.

Then Zulu saw the battered face of the boy.

He ran forward.

Jodi lifted her face to him. Tears were streaming out of her eyes and her chin was quivering and jerking, and her mouth moving, but nothing came out of it but the slobbers that ran from each corner and turned to pink the dark blood on her neck.

She couldn't talk. She could make no sound at all. Even her sobs were silent.

Zulu saw that Blane was beyond help, but quickly he ran his hands over Jodi's neck and chest and back. The blood, he saw, was Blane's. And the trail she had dragged him through was plain, a tunnel through the green grass beneath the floor of the House of Mirrors.

"Get back! Get back!" Zulu shouted, standing, his arms spread. The crowd, which had pushed forward again, now obeyed and moved back. "Someone go call an ambulance and the police! Ken? Whitie? Hurry!"

Russel dabbed mustard on a hot dog, and spooned relish onto another with sauerkraut, and rolled each into the slick paper that would not fall apart in the customers' hands, and slid them out the window. He took the five-dollar bill, made change, and counted it back to the hot-dog buyer. Then he had to turn and grab a couple of drinks for that same customer, and then the kid's date decided she wanted a cotton candy too, so he spun that off and put it through the window.

Amy was busy at the other window, waiting on a line of customers that was half a dozen deep.

It was a busy day, the kind Russel liked. Especially now that he wanted his mind busy, not free to think or feel. Every time he looked up he saw the sign at the front of the tent where Lakisha had worked. All these summers with the carnie he had looked up and seen that sign, and it had given him a thrill and a need that had filled his life. But now, though he tried not to look at it, his eyes just naturally sought it out, down toward the end of the midway, always situated just right for him to see if he looked in the right direction.

As he turned back to get a couple of boxes of popcorn he looked up, and he saw the crowd, moving back this way, moving somehow differently, as if they were hurrying to get out, to get back to the gates.

But this was the late afternoon, night had not even begun, the carnie was just picking up. Peak hours were hours away. Where was the crowd going?

He saw the looks on their faces, and an alarm went off in his brain.

He stood still, holding boxes of popcorn, one in each hand, and watched the crowd.

Something was wrong.

One of the women was openly crying.

A young girl, practically running, had tears in her eyes.

The boys' faces were strained and white, and they kept looking back over their shoulders.

Then Russel could see that a crowd had gathered at the end of the midway, near the House of Mirrors.

He tossed the boxes of corn back into the popcorn machine and began working on the knot that had somehow created itself in his apron tie.

"I'll be back in a few minutes," he told Amy. "Something's going on."

He began to pick up gists of information as he hurried. Words were left hanging in the air as he passed, snatches of sentences that made him begin to run, to hurt his chest with dread and worry.

"My God ... did you ever see anything so terr—"

"So much blood! What happened to that child?"

"Oh Lord, Lordy ... did you see the blood on her?"

And bits and pieces more, and then, as if punctuating all the words, the puzzled cries, the moans of horror and sympathy, there came the sirens of both police and ambulance.

It was a child, Russel knew. A child covered with blood.

Her ...

A female child.

He was running fast by the time he reached the dispersing crowd at the end of the midway. He could hear Zulu's voice, words indistinguishable among all the broken sentences and exclamations coming from the crowd.

He broke through and saw her, Jodi, just as he had feared.

But she was standing, near Zulu, just standing with tears running down her face and into the corners of her open mouth. Blood seemed to have covered her skin from her neck down.

Russel knelt in front of her, took her shoulders in his hands, and looked at her. Then he saw where the blood came from.

The boy lay twisted and battered on the ground, in the grass just at the edge of the underside of the floor of the House of Mirrors. In the same way Lakisha had lain, Blane now lay, but his body was even more battered than hers had been. This child, it seemed, had been brutally beaten to death, and then the beating had continued, on and on, until he was hardly recognizable.

Russel pulled Jodi into his arms and wished he could pull her into himself entirely, to protect her from whatever this was.

He wept against the back of her head as he pressed her face to his shoulder. The sobs started low in his belly and consumed him. For the first time since he was a child he cried hard, holding the yielding child.

"Oh thank God, thank God," he murmured, and knew he shouldn't be saying this, to be expressing his thankfulness that it was not his child who had died.

He heard a scream, and saw that Blane's mother and father had arrived, and Justin was pulling Anna back and holding her from going to her son.

Rudy, their sixteen-year-old son, who helped run the concessions, had run up too, and now simply stood there staring down at the bloody bundle that was his brother Blane. Rudy's face was as white as his shirt.

The medics arrived, and Russel stood up with Jodi in his arms and turned away, carrying her. He told Zulu, "I'm taking her home."

No one tried to stop him.

CHAPTER 17

AMY CLOSED THE WINDOWS OF THE GRAB JOINT AND LOOKED FOR THE KEY TO lock the door. But Russel carried it in his pocket, and had taken it with him.

She didn't know what to do.

She stood outside the grab joint and looked at the empty midway. Most of the people had gone. Police cars had driven into the midway, and an ambulance was down there, the light on top rotating, flashing against the rides, competing with the lights on the rides.

The sun was going down, and shadows were lengthening.

Amy wanted desperately to leave the grab joint and try to find Russel and Jodi, but he had left her in charge.

A young boy came walking across the midway, and she could tell he was coming to her because his eyes were on her. She drew back slightly to stand against the metal wall of the grab joint.

She recognized the boy as one who helped with the concessions. She thought his name was Lanny, but she wasn't sure. He was about seventeen, and he spent his summers working for Zulu and filling in wherever he was needed.

"You're Amy, aren't you?" he said, stopping several feet away.

Amy nodded.

"Your dad said to tell you to just close up and come on home."

"I—I don't have the key."

"That doesn't matter. No one's going to bother it. I'm around. The gates are closed now. The police are all over the place. Again. Worse this time, I think."

Amy wanted to ask if it were Jodi, her little sister, but her tongue felt thick and heavy. She put her hand to her breast and squeezed her pendant between her fingers.

The boy moved away, hurriedly, and began to help close a nearby concession stand. Everywhere along the midway the concessionaires were closing up now, and after closing they drifted away, going down the midway toward the ambulance and the police cars.

Amy moved through the heavy shadows between two tents, feeling more isolated than she ever had in her life.

All sound seemed to have gone from the carnival. The lights flashed silently in all colors, but the music had stopped, the crowd had gone, no one was left except the carnie people and the police.

She was alone now at this end of the midway.

The darkness between the tents seemed deeper than it should have. Then, when she neared the end, she saw that clouds covered the sinking sun and cut off the last rays of light.

Amy began to run, fear crawling at her back, hands reaching for her out of the approaching darkness.

When she reached the step into the trailer she looked back, and in the dark passageway she had just emerged from she caught a glimpse of white, of a ruffle, it seemed, and a glove that was stained with something black. She knew the clowns ... knew them well. She had seen their reflections in her pendant too many times, and she had seen this one and others in the alley, in the dark, usually in the dark. She had seen them enter India's trailer house. But if she told, Russel would know about the talisman she had stolen from the trash can, and he would not like her anymore. He would send her back to her mother and stepfather, where she wasn't wanted, except as a maid.

And they would take away her necklace, her pendant, her jewel.

She hurried on into the lighted front room of the trailer before the clown could follow her out of the passageway.

Jodi sat on the couch, with Russel at her side. She had blood all over her, it seemed. Russel was trying to get her to drink something.

Amy stopped. Unable to move, she stared at Jodi.

In her heart she knew that she had expected Jodi to be dead.

She had seen it in her pendant.

Now all she could do was stand and stare at Jodi, the relief within her too immense to be put into words or actions.

Russel looked up and saw Amy. "Thank God you got here. Did Lan bring you?"

"No, I—I came by myself."

Russel stared at her with a terrible look of fury. "I told him to bring you home."

"That's all right."

Amy's eyes couldn't leave Jodi. She wanted to ask about her, but her voice failed where her sister was concerned. It seemed to work only for the mundane, for herself, for things that didn't matter.

"Amy, why don't you turn the shower on and get it warm? We'll give Jodi a bath."

At that moment, before Amy could move, a man with a white coat and a bag appeared at the doorway. Behind him was a policeman in uniform, a couple of other men in plain clothes, and Zulu.

They stood aside for Zulu to enter first. The man in the white coat reached out to help him up, but Zulu ignored the hand. He grasped the edge of the door and pulled himself up.

"That guy felt he should examine Jodi," Zulu said. "Does she seem to be all right?"

Jodi sat on the couch looking up at the men who entered the room. She had stopped weeping, but she hadn't spoken.

Amy turned quickly away, went into the bathroom for a washcloth. Mama would have washed Jodi's face right away. Mama would want Jodi's face clean.

In the privacy of the bath Amy felt the hard, stone-like qualities of the pendant. She wanted to look into it, to see that now Jodi was safe after all. Russel had been right, nothing could predict a future.

Nothing.

Jodi had blood on her, but she was not dead.

Slowly, Amy pulled the pendant out of her blouse.

The light in the bathroom ceiling glinted into the tiny mirrors and became dozens of other little lights. Amy could see her own face in the pendant, ugly, misshapen. And she could see the curtain that covered the shower stall, and the towels on the towel rack.

And then it seemed dark water was running in the shower, so that Amy almost turned to see. Then the darkness cleared, and there was a tiny body lying all twisted and broken, and covered in blood.

Amy held her breath.

She didn't want to see who it was, but the face was turned toward her, and she recognized the pink sandals and the pink, plaid blouse and solid pink shorts.

Jodi.

As Amy stared in horror at the image of Jodi, broken, bloody, dead, the image suddenly was gone and she was looking at the reflection of her own face grotesquely out of shape, bulging in the center, tapering at chin and forehead to points.

She moved her head, but the image didn't change.

The girl who looked back at her had a misshapen face and eyes that were huge and sunken and widened in abject terror.

The horror that Amy felt increased, because the face was no more a true image of herself than the image of Jodi had been.

Were both of these predictions of the future?

No. Russel, would say no, and she had to believe him. Are we reruns, he had asked her, are we on a rerun of a former life?

No. Her pendant was strange, and she was beginning to be afraid of it, yet she couldn't stop herself from looking into it. Her hand kept going to it as by its own will, and she was compelled to look into the pendant and see the images it wanted to project.

She thought of taking it off and dropping it into the toilet and flushing it down. But she knew she could no more do that than she could stop herself from looking into its ... eyes?

When Amy went back into the front room the doctor was listening to Jodi's heart with his stethoscope. He straightened, and Russel rearranged Jodi's bloody blouse. The blood had dried now, mostly, and looked black in the lights that had been turned on in the trailer.

"You're a strong girl," the doctor said. "You're going to be fine after a good night's rest. But I don't think she should be questioned tonight, gentlemen. I'd leave her alone for awhile. She's had a terrible experience."

Amy sank down onto a chair, no longer able to control the weakness of relief that made her legs feel boneless. Jodi was going to be fine. The pendant had lied to her, once again.

She put her hand against her breast and pressed it to her flesh, so hard she could feel its edges cut into her. She both hated and loved it, but she could never part with it.

JODI COULDN'T THINK. As if her mind had exploded, there seemed to be nothing left of her except the ability to move. Russel and Amy undressed her and put her into the shower. One of them scrubbed her face and stomach ... she thought it was Russel, but she wasn't sure.

Then she was dressed in clean clothes, and this time she was sure it was Russel who dressed her. Amy stood back watching, handing him the things to put on her. He pulled a knitted pajama top down over her head awkwardly, and she finally woke up enough to help him get it off her face before she panicked again.

After that they fed her. Some kind of hot soup that made her stomach feel warm and good, but it was so hard to swallow that she ate only a small amount.

After they put her to bed she could hear the television going, softly, for awhile, then it was shut off.

She didn't sleep. She lay stretched out straight in the bed staring up at the ceiling.

Amy came up to bed, but instead of crawling over her to sleep on the back, she lay down at the front, as if to protect Jodi from falling out of bed. Jodi stirred slightly, wanting to tell Amy to get on her own side of the bed, but it didn't seem worth the effort.

She stared at the ceiling, even after the lights were turned out and the living room was dark.

Out the window by the bunk she could see the high rides of the midway, the Ferris wheel with its one light, and the lower Tilt-a-whirl—and the others, the airplane ride, which also had a single light at the top.

Blane had said that was to keep low-flying planes from hitting them.

Blane had told her a lot of things, taught her a lot about carnival life and the people who worked with the carnival.

But he hadn't known about the House of Mirrors, or the clowns.

He had never known about the clowns.

Jodi frowned into the night and tried to concentrate. There was something about the clowns that she knew ... and couldn't remember. Those terrible, ugly clown faces, and those costumes that were so big and billowy and so colorful. One of the costumes had been pieced from tiny blocks, as if it were some very special quilt ...

She sat up suddenly, and cracked her head against the top of the trailer.

The pain was an electric flash in her brain, but it didn't matter.

She remembered!

She crawled out over Amy, found the ladder, and climbed down. Amy moaned and moved over toward the window, curling with her knees up.

Russel ... she had to tell Russel.

She went down the short, narrow hall to Russel's room, felt her way through the dark to the corner of the bed. She moved upward, guided by the sound of his breathing, and grasped his bare arm.

"Russel! Russel. Daddy "

"Huh!"

He woke and sat up, and at the same time a light at the head of the bed came on. He blinked at Jodi for a second, then he was swinging his legs off the bed and grasping her by the shoulders.

"What's the matter? Are you all right, Jodi? Where's Amy?"

"She's in bed. I'm all right. Russel, I just remembered something."

"What?"

"Where I saw those clowns!"

Russel stared without speaking into her eyes, and then he said with a puzzled frown, "What clowns?"

And she remembered she hadn't told anyone. No one had asked her what had happened, or if they did, she couldn't remember. "The clowns," she said slowly and carefully now, "that killed Blane."

Russel said nothing. He was still holding her shoulders, his eyes glancing from pupil to pupil in her eyes, questioning, wondering without words. He was sitting on the side of his bed wearing only his undershorts, his hairy legs spread, his hairy chest uncovered.

Jodi said, "Maybe you'd better get dressed, Daddy, because we have to go tell Zulu."

Russel didn't question her. He merely got up from the bed and reached for clothes and pulled them on, a shirt of summer knit, and blue jeans. Within a minute he was dressed, and then he took her by the hand and led her back into the living room.

He glanced up at Amy, then turned on a muted lamp at the end of the couch.

"All right, Jodi, I'm ready. Want to talk about it now?"

"Yes. The clowns, Russel, that killed Blane, they're the clowns that India made. The ones I saw in her trailer."

She couldn't tell him all of it. Just trying to go back in memory to the actual killing of Blane made her shake as if an icy wind were blowing over her. But she did tell him about going up into the closed section of the House of Mirrors, and the clowns that came and killed Blane.

"We have to tell Zulu," she said urgently. "He's got to—to ..." She tried to think what he could do with the clown suits, but her mind drew a blank.

197

"Somebody was wearing the costumes, Jodi," he said. "But we will tell Zulu, and we'll have to tell the police."

Jodi felt so relieved that she was suddenly half dead for lack of sleep. Her eyes drooped, her head felt as if it were balanced on a sliver of rubber.

"You need to climb up to bed, Jodi. Damn, I wish I had a telephone in here. Never thought I'd have any use for one. Listen, babe, I'm going to put you to bed, and then I'm going to lock the door and run over."

Russel was frowning deeply, but then the frown disappeared and he looked at her with tender love in his eyes.

Jodi was going to sleep, and she felt him pick her up, but instead of trying to put her into the bunk he simply carried her to his bedroom and put her into his bed.

He pulled the covers gently up over Jodi, and she sank into the restful state of oblivion.

He couldn't leave them alone, not at three o'clock in the morning. It was that time of night the killers attacked Lakisha and India. If he left the girls alone even for a few minutes while he ran to get Zulu or the police, it might be too late.

Nothing would change, he hoped, if he waited until daylight.

Though now, since Blane's death, not even the daylight guaranteed safety.

Tomorrow he was going to get the hell out of here, he was positive of that. He should have gone yesterday, instead of coming here with the carnie. He should have just gone on.

What if it had been Jodi instead of Blane?

The poor boy.

It was a scene he knew he would never forget, and it would haunt him for the rest of his life.

ZULU GOT off his couch at five a.m. and made coffee. He hadn't bothered to go to bed the night before. After the police mostly drifted away, after the body of the child had been taken away, he had wandered around the carnival, his hunting knife strapped to his waist, hanging against his thigh.

It was still there, the tip of the knife hanging well past his knee.

A couple of the big guys had looked askance at him, but he didn't give a damn. He was going to use something to protect himself and his people against that killer.

So far he hadn't been doing a damn bit of good. The scene that had transpired yesterday had played over and over in his mind all night long, even when he put his head back for a catnap.

The little girl, almost unrecognizable with the blood smeared all over her, and her eyes weeping and wild, had suddenly appeared not ten feet from the platform on which he stood, dragging the bloody body of her friend.

What had happened? No one knew.

Of course the little girl hadn't done it.

But she hadn't been able to talk. It was said that the ambulance medics had wanted to take her to the hospital, but her dad had said no. The child had clung to him, and he hadn't wanted to leave the other daughter behind.

Zulu wasn't sure of all that went down during that time—that hour or two following the discovery of the body, following the scene of the one child dragging the other out from beneath the floor of the House of Mirrors.

A knock came now on his door, and he opened it to find a couple of policemen standing on the ground. It was the only time he had looked eye to eye at any of them.

"Mr. Zulumonsque, we have to ask you to come and open up the House of Mirrors. We have found the trail of the children. It leads back to a hole in the floor of the building that only a child could crawl through. We think the murder took place up in the House of Mirrors."

For just a moment Zulu stared at them, trying to make sense of what they were saying. How could it be possible? A hole in the floor?

"The House of Mirrors was open at the time of the murder, gentlemen," Zulu said. "There were customers going through it. If a murder had been committed in there, surely there would be some witnesses?"

But as he spoke his thoughts were going back and picking up the things India had told him about the House of Mirrors, and then he remembered, as if it momentarily had been blocked from his mind—the bad section. None of the customers could have been in there. There was no opening.

Unless—except—the hole the police talked about?

"What hole?" Zulu asked, as he went out the door.

"It looks like someone has sawn a hole under the floor and then broken boards away, for access. Why is it you never noticed it?"

They were walking across the midway. The sky was turning bright rose in the east, and the dawn was coming fast, the shadows lying as long across the midway as if it were twilight and the sun sinking.

"Part of the House is closed to the public," Zulu said. "The mirrors darkened and my partner, India, wanted it closed."

"Why wasn't it just repaired?"

Zulu wondered how much he should tell them. Not much. To embarrass India was beyond comprehension. And they would think her a foolish old woman, with ideas that were more than just a little crazy.

"This murder," said one of the detectives, Zulu didn't know which. They were all beginning to sound and look alike to him. "This murder, you must realize, Mr. Zulumonsque, is the same as the other two back at your former location. So therefore, the murderer is traveling with your circus."

"Carnival," Zulu replied, almost without thinking of the mistake and the correction. "Not necessarily," he added. "It could be someone who is following the carnival."

"Yes, of course, but it doesn't seem likely. Have you noticed any faces that seem to show up no matter where you are?"

"No, not that I can think of."

Even the marks sometimes all looked alike, but it was something he couldn't tell these men. Lately, they had been looking alike. Lately, since India's death, the vitality had gone out of almost everything, even the faces of the customers. They needed the customers, but today it had been hard to open at a new place without India to see the smiles and the shining eyes, all those signs of happiness. He'd had to tell himself over and over that India would have loved it. And perhaps in some way she could still see it. Maybe spirits existed and continued on in a life on a different plane, with the people able to move about and see and feel.

He wanted to believe it were true, but in his heart he just couldn't.

India was dead.

And dead meant that an organism that had lived no longer lived, no longer existed in a sensual way, that she was dead to the world, with no more knowledge of what was happening. She was gone, and some—some bastard had killed her. And he was going to carry his knife until he found that sucker, and then he was going to kill him.

And no law in the country was going to stop him.

He suspected that the police knew what he had in mind, and that was why they looked askance at the knife that was almost as long as his leg.

But it would be done.

The time would come when Zulu would meet the killer, or killers.

CHAPTER 18

THE DAWN WAS ALMOST COMPLETE WHEN ZULU CLIMBED THE STEPS TO THE platform at the front of the House of Mirrors. The light on the House made it seem wet in places, dark and wet, as if wet with the blood of the child, and of Lakisha and India, and the boy who had disappeared here, and India's father, and all the rest who seemed connected to this old House of Mirrors. Perhaps India was right after all and it did date back to Raoell, the magician.

Zulu wondered if anyone alive could give him information on that Raoell geek. As he opened the door to the House of Mirrors, he was trying to remember names of old, retired carnie people who might have heard of him.

Three policemen were on hand to go into the House. On the ground, near the roped-off area where the grass was still dark with blood, stood one uniformed policeman on guard. So far as Zulu knew, he had been standing there all night. The last Zulu had seen of him was past midnight, when Zulu had made his final rounds of the midway. He had wandered, around and around the midway, the alleys, until his legs had hurt so badly he could hardly walk, and then he had gone to his trailer and just sat there.

He was waiting, and someday, some night, he would meet the killer.

But now ... perhaps he had been looking in the wrong place.

There was something about the House, just as India had said.

The policemen went into the House of Mirrors like tourists into a cavern. They walked gingerly, looking up, down, sideways. Zulu walked straight ahead, his eyes on the white line. He could still see the reflections—himself, a squat, little guy, and behind him the dozens of reflections of tall, strong men. Even the strongest of them looked tall in the mirrors.

"The white line," one of them noticed. "What's it for?"

"It's a direct route to the center of the maze and out again," Zulu explained. "I've had some kids come in the past—when I let them in only a few at a time, or one at a time—get lost back in here and not find their way out. I've had to rescue more than one, and so I finally changed my strategy, and now I let only groups in. That way they're not as apt to get lost. But to make sure, I painted the line. It doesn't cover much of the maze, but at least it takes them to the central room."

"Something special about the central room?"

"Yes."

Zulu walked the line, going down a corridor, turning with the line, turning again in another direction, and again, and going down another corridor that was perhaps ten feet long and turning at last to the center room. The simple way to go in. He turned to see the men coming. They were still looking in all directions, but the expressions on their faces seemed to have changed.

Everything had changed. As he looked up now, the light in the ceiling of the central room seemed to reflect on into infinity, and for an instant it seemed he could see a long stairway, with fiery brilliant lights on every step. But a blink later it was gone, and he saw only the sections of mirror that made up the cathedral ceiling, and now the reflections of men who were coming into the room.

"Quite a room," one of them said, looking at the side of the room that lengthened his body grotesquely.

"Yes. As you can see, all the panels in this room make your reflection grotesque in one way or another. And they're all different."

"This is a horror room if I've ever seen one," the tallest of the men said. "I didn't know mirrors could be made like this. What was the object?"

The shorter, heavier man grunted a laugh. "Kids love it. Don't they, Mr. Zulumonsque? I'll bet the kids go wild for it."

"It has always been a popular show, yes."

"You call it a show. Why? Wouldn't it more properly be—uh—just an attraction?"

"I don't know. It was just always called a sideshow." He remembered. The name came from the early days, and he realized now that it must have been coined by Raoell, the magician, when it actually did contain a show.

And he wondered, what kind of show?

He suddenly knew that whatever show it was occurred right here, in this central room.

One of the lawmen spoke up, the shortest, fattest, who seemed to be in charge, even though he wore a suit with no sign of a badge. "The section we want to see, Mr. Zulumonsque, is where we think the murder occurred. Where the hole in the floor is."

Zulu almost told him he needn't pronounce his full name, but the look on the fat man's face stopped him. It was too grim, too impatient, too angry, too suspicious, as if Zulu himself were the main suspect.

Zulu saw the bulge of a gun, a big one, in a shoulder holster. The fat man might not wear a badge out in the open, but the gun wasn't very well hidden when the lawman put his hands on his waist.

"We're dealing with a brutal killer here, Mr. Zulumonsque," the man said. "And we don't have time to waste."

Zulu nodded, stung, wondering if the man thought he had figured otherwise. "I'll have to get the tools to get in there, sir. If you'll wait here, I'll be back."

"Why couldn't we just go with you? Isn't there another way into that area without going through here again?"

Zulu paused. "Yes. I have to dismantle it."

They followed the white line out, and Zulu left them standing near the platform talking among themselves. He found one of the young workers, who today had nothing to do but sit on the railing around the airplane ride, and sent him for Ken.

"Tell Ken to bring a tractor for moving a section of the House. Tell him to put a burr under the saddle."

"Yes, sir!"

Zulu went back and around the House to the left rear corner where more of the lawmen stood, and where, he gathered, the hole under the House must be. He asked, "Is it here?"

They all looked at him, and three of them nodded. Just as at the other location, in the last town, some of the lawmen were from the Sheriff's Department and some from the city police, but he noticed that also there were a couple of big, tall, brown uniforms of the Highway Patrol Department here, with their Stetson-like hats, and there were others who were probably State Police. They were gathering, it seemed, from all over the state for this last murder. He wouldn't have been surprised if some of the men in plain suits or more casual clothes were from the FBI. One murder was bad, but when it became three, it was news. There was, in the midway, one van from a local TV station left over from all the vans from news sources that were here last night, until past midnight. There was one thing he had been glad of—Russel had gotten the little girl, Jodi, out of there and taken her home before the news people had arrived. So there was nothing much said about her.

The police were waiting, though, he knew, and as soon as the sun rose, they'd probably be after her again. Only the doctor had saved her from being pestered with questions yesterday.

Zulu got down into the dew-wet grass and looked beneath the floor. It was dark there. He could see a trail through the grass, but it was a dark trail, as if it were made into the edge of night.

He sat up.

"One of your fellows got a flashlight?"

"We'd rather you stayed out of there, Mr. Zulumonsque. There might be clues."

"Oh yeah, sorry. I was just going to see exactly where the hole is so I'll know what section to move."

Zulu stood up and brushed his pants legs.

"It's exactly ten feet in from the corner, straight in from the corner, to a line going toward the opposite corner."

A confusing description, Zulu thought, but that would mean, if the man were right about the distance, that it would be in the corner section, which would make moving it out easy.

"Each section measures twelve feet wide," Zulu said, just to avoid standing there apart, with nothing to say to any of them. "By twelve long, of course, which makes them ..."

He stopped. What was the object? They could count. Probably better than he could. Each section at the rear was twelve by twelve, which meant the House was thirty-six feet wide. Each section at the front was the same. But the middle sections, while being twelve feet wide, were fifteen feet long, which made the House of Mirrors thirty-six by thirty-nine, or forty by the time a little extra wall was added. And it was filled with narrow corridors that went in all crazy directions—except for the central room, which was fifteen feet by twelve. Big enough for a special show to take place in one end of it, to small audiences of ... Zulu mentally worked it out, frowning at the corner of the gray, unpainted boards of the House. Allow six feet for the show and ... impossible. Somehow, some other part of the House must have been opened up for that show. Another level? The stairway ... he had glimpsed it himself. And the Chief of Police at the last location had seen it. So far as Zulu was concerned that made it real.

Somewhere in that crazy central room there was a staircase leading somewhere, and those disappearances had to do with that staircase.

Zulu made up his mind while he was standing apart from the tall, capable, uniformed men, and the others who came around to the corner, that after the police were through here he was going to take this place apart, mirror by mirror, and find that staircase.

The tractor arrived, putting along the alley, and Zulu motioned for Ken and the boys who came with him to unlatch that corner section from the rest and lift it away.

Ten minutes later the tractor slid the section apart from the rest of the House, leaving a gaping corner open to the light, but the small strip of mirror that was exposed to the light seemed to have drawn into it the permanent dark.

"What's wrong with that glass?" the fat man asked Zulu.

"Some kind of blight, like old mirrors get sometimes," Zulu explained patiently, admitting to none of the feelings that rose suddenly within him. This was the weird section—the most weird section, he should say, since all of it had gotten to seem more weird lately. It was just one third of the area that had been closed to the public.

"Well, I see you kept that part lighted too, didn't you? The guys disconnected wires, didn't they?"

"Yes, each section is fixed to plug into the next, so it's easy to disengage the lighting."

"But wasn't it lighted? I thought I saw a glimpse of something light."

Zulu didn't see how he could have, since the wires were the first thing to come apart, but he said, "Yes, it was lighted. When the lights are on in one part of the House they're on in all parts. Unless it's deliberately unplugged."

"Why?"

The damned nosy cop. Zulu couldn't tell him it was what India wanted. That he himself used to question her reasons. It was not for anyone to question now, especially this cop.

"They're just connected that way," Zulu said. "It's not as though much light was wasted. Each section had about three forty-watt bulbs."

The front sections usually contained sixty watts, sometimes seventy-five, depending on how popular the section was with the marks. But even though he had given in to India—and in no way would he have tried to fool her and leave the lights out—he had put in low-wattage bulbs. Because whoever saw those areas? No one walked there. They were closed off. At least, that was what he had thought.

When the section was moved out a few feet from the rest of the House, Zulu got down on his knees and looked. Sure enough, just a few feet in from the inner corner was a small hole, sawed in places, ripped in others, just large enough for a slender child to go through.

Zulu shuddered. The edges of the hole were dark with blood and something more pale than blood, like loose pieces of flesh. Flies had gathered and were buzzing around the hole. A smell of rotting flesh came through on a wave of air. He controlled an urge to gag.

He stood up.

The grass where the section had stood was mashed down, and there, beneath the place the hole would have been if the section were in place, the grass was dark with blood. Flies had gathered there too. Then a trail went off beneath the rest of the floor, still in place, where Jodi, instead of pulling Blane to the nearest outlet, had pulled him beneath the floor to the front of the building. Nearly thirty feet.

Zulu looked up at the wall of the section. Only one opening, the width of a corridor, was exposed to the world. The House was built so that very few mirrors were ever exposed to daylight. But the mirror that was open to the outside was almost black.

Several of the police were ready to go in, flashlights ready. At first, Zulu thought they were going alone, but before the first man stepped up into the House, the short, fat man with the bulging holster, who seemed all the more in charge the longer Zulu was exposed to them, stood back and said, "Mr. Zulumonsque, would you show us the area above the hole?"

Zulu nodded, but he spread his hands. "I didn't bring a light."

The policeman handed his flashlight to Zulu. It was a small pocket-size, but the light was bright, Zulu saw, when he climbed up into the bad section of the House of Mirrors, the first time he had stood in that corridor for—Lordy, how many years? He had started closing off these rooms back in the forties, a hell of a long time ago. At first, the dark blight had begun in a corridor near the center, and it had spread backward, outward to the left rear corner. To this corner. First. Before it started spreading to the others.

"This was the first to go," he said aloud as he gained a foothold on the floor. Gratefully, no one had offered him assistance. Sometimes, that was the last straw, almost. He didn't appreciate being treated like an invalid or a child, or an imbecile. "This section. It just kept getting bigger and bigger, spreading more and more, until it covered the whole end of the building."

Right behind him the fat man's voice said, "Did you ever get an expert in to tell you what was wrong?"

"No." India didn't want anyone looking at the mirrors, or replacing them. These blighted mirrors were not to be touched. He hadn't understood then, but he understood perhaps a little better now.

"And you just kept hauling the bad sections around?" the man said. "It looks to me like you might as well have kept it open. It's got an interesting pattern to it, even if it is dark. It's almost like swirling water, notice that?"

"Yeah."

But Zulu was looking at the floor. He was following the beam of light the way he had followed the white stripe in the front sections, and he came to the ragged hole, and the dark blotches of blood, and rotting flesh. Flies had gathered here too, and now rose like a cloud, no longer blinded by the dark.

The trail of blood led beyond the hole a couple of feet and ended there, and the blood was all over the place, it seemed, splattered up on each mirror and covering the floor in an area of at least three by eight feet. The width of the corridor.

Solid blood.

"My God," he said and turned his back to it.

He felt vomit rise to his throat. In facing the opening to the outdoors, he saw the other men coming up into the corridor. He wanted to run out, but there was no room.

Another need within him, a more desperate and angry need, was to keep going along this corridor, to go into every corridor of this section, and try to find what had been in here to cause this much blood, to murder that child with the awful viciousness with which it had happened.

"Okay," one of the men said. "It looks to me like that kid was slammed against this floor so hard and so many times that it made this mess—and of course you saw the damage to the child. We didn't need an autopsy to see that." The man pushed past Zulu with a strong flashlight that he swept along the floor past the bloody place. "No blood there, except the splatters. What have we got here?"

"This reminds me of the one time I saw the fall of a guy from a twenty-story building," another man said. "There wasn't this much crap there."

"Mr. Zulumonsque, how could anyone have gotten in here yesterday? Is there any way in except through—the hole?"

"No. Not when the section is in place."

"But you had just moved in the night before. So there's no reason why some nut could not have hidden out here, right? And when the kid climbed up into the hole, he grabbed him. What have we got here?"

"A maniac," someone offered.

Zulu wanted to go past the bloody area and look into the rest of the section, but the man who had stepped in front of him motioned him back.

"We'll have to examine this area, Mr. Zulumonsque. Thanks for showing us up. I guess we won't need you for awhile, but stay close, will you please, and make sure none of your people leave. Not one. We don't want anyone going out of the fairgrounds for so much as a loaf of bread without permission."

Zulu nodded, and made his way out and into the daylight. The smell of blood, that awful, sickening smell, the decaying flesh bits, seemed to be clinging to his clothes. But the sun had risen now, and was casting long, gray shadows from building to tent to trees and beyond, and somewhere in the tops of trees a few birds were trying to sing, but the sounds below had disturbed them. The only outstanding sound now was the throb of the generators from the other side of the midway.

Inside the separated section of the House of Mirrors, the footsteps of the men echoed strangely, sounding as if they were walking in a hollow drum.

Zulu moved over to stand beside Ken. Ken was leaning against his tractor, rolling a cigarette. His muscles bulged, even beneath the shirt he wore. Ken, at one time, had been a wrestler, but had gotten his back hurt and had come to Zulu for a job. He had worked with the carnie for fifteen years now. Zulu trusted him implicitly, just as he trusted all the rest. The lawmen in the towns might think them a bunch of creepy people, strange, like something from outer space, but Zulu knew they were just like himself—people who were slightly displaced in life, for one reason or another—or someone like Russel, who just liked the life.

"Pretty bad, huh?" Ken asked.

"Yeah."

"What do you think they're going to find?"

Zulu thought about it. And his mind swept through all that India had told him, as well as all that had happened since India's death, and the disappearance of the kid who'd wanted a job.

"Nothing," he said. "They're not going to find anything there."

Whatever it was had something to do with that central room and the staircase that was invisible to most people, most of the time.

CHAPTER 19

THE KNOCK CAME ON THE DOOR AT SIX O'CLOCK. THE SUN WAS BARELY UP, BUT Russel had been expecting the knock for the last thirty minutes, ever since it was light enough to see that day was at last dawning. He'd been sitting on his couch since three o'clock, since Jodi had awakened him. And as far as he knew, she was still sleeping soundly. At least she had been thirty minutes ago when he'd last checked on her. In the bunk bed above the couch Amy was sleeping, and not very well, because he had heard her make noises that were almost of nightmare proportions many times. But she hadn't cried out enough for him to try to wake her.

Even now, as he got up to answer the door, he could hear Amy start to whimper again.

There were three men at the door. One, a shorter, heavier man dressed in a brown suit, appeared to be leading the others.

"I'm Captain Reynolds," he said, showing a badge, "with the State Police. I'm here to talk to your child. Is she able to talk yet?"

"She's asleep."

"Could we come in?"

"Sure."

Three of them came in. Names were given, but forgotten almost instantly. Reynolds seemed to be the guy he had to remember anyway. He had met so many lawmen in the past few days that he felt just like he did with the marks—they were all getting to look too much alike. And there were no good-looking girls among them, as there were among the marks, the only faces worth remembering. Only lately, since Lakisha's death, not even the good-looking girls had looked good to him. If any had been around, he hadn't seen them.

"Want coffee?" he asked. "I haven't had a cup yet myself."

"We'd rather you woke your daughter, Mr. Sauer." At that moment Amy cried out in her sleep and threw her hand out, evidently, for something struck the top of the trailer.

All eyes looked upward at the bunk bed.

"Sounds like she's having a nightmare."

"No, that's my oldest daughter, Amy. Jodi is in my bed. She came to me this morning about two or three, and I got up and let her have my bed. I've been sitting on the couch since."

Reynolds had found himself a chair. His legs were too heavy to cross comfortably, so he sat with them spread. His brown suit jacket didn't cover the bulge of his belly. He'd evidently been on the force long enough for his weight not to matter.

"Why did she come to you? Was she in a habit of coming to you in the middle of the night?"

Russel looked into the man's sharp, brown eyes, and decided to make himself a cup of coffee anyway.

"No, you're right. She had remembered something she wanted to tell me."

"Maybe she'd like to get up now and tell us. It was about the murder, I presume?"

"Yes, it was."

"Would you go get her, please?"

They weren't even going to wait until she woke up, Russel thought with rage rising like heat from within him. But then he thought of the parents of the child who was killed. The mother had been taken to a hospital, and the dad had looked as if he would collapse before they got there. He had kept hanging onto that bloody mess that was his son, hanging on and hanging on until they had practically pried him away.

At least Jodi was safe. Waking her from sleep seemed the least they could do to help.

Russel abandoned his coffee cup and went down the hall to the bedroom.

Jodi was twisted in the sheet, one leg out, the other curled in, one arm free. Her face was scrubbed clean, but a speck of blood somehow clung to her hair even though he thought he had given her a thorough shower.

"Jodi? Baby, wake up."

He lifted her, slipping his arms beneath her shoulders and helping her to rise. She blinked at him, and her hands reached out convulsively to grab his shoulders.

"You need to get dressed now, baby. The police are here and wanting to ask you some questions."

Her eyes grew in size, but she only stared at him.

"Nothing is going to happen to you, Jodi. I'll be right with you."

"Are they going to take me to jail?"

"Of course not. Here, get dressed."

He helped her into her clothes as if she were two years old, and in his heart he found himself thinking of her as his baby, someone to be protected from the world, even from the questions of the police, as much as possible.

He led her into the front room, and kept her hand in his. When he sat down he pulled her protectively onto his lap.

"She doesn't know very much of what happened," he explained.

Reynolds gave him a sharp look that suggested he be quiet and not try to put words into her mouth. One of the other men had a small tape recorder, which he turned on.

"Jodi," Reynolds said in a surprisingly gentle voice. "You were with Blane when he was killed?"

Jodi shook her head vigorously and pressed back against her daddy. Russel enclosed her loosely in his arms, patting her, reassuring her that she wasn't alone.

"But you brought him out from under the floor of the House of Mirrors. It looks as though you were in the House with him and dragged him out of the hole in the floor. Is that what happened?"

Jodi began to cry softly, and Russel hugged her to him.

"I know it's important that you hear what she—knows, guys, but you can see this is hard on her."

"We know that," Reynolds said. "But you have to understand, Jodi, and Mr. Sauer, that a little boy has been brutally murdered, the third such murder connected to this carnival. The more we have to go on, the faster we're going to find a suspect. Right now, we have no suspects to speak of, and Jodi either saw the murder occur, or she came upon the boy shortly afterwards. We need to know. You're a big girl, Jodi. You can talk about it, can't you?"

Jodi nodded, and wiped her eyes with her fists. "We went into the House of Mirrors to play," she said. "And it was—it was the clowns that did it. They picked up Blane and threw him on the floor."

The questions began, as if Reynolds were asking about school, and he led her through her experience in the House of Mirrors. And during the process, he turned and told one of the detectives to bring the two clowns and let Jodi see them.

"What are their names?" he said aloud, checking back through his notes, "Izzy and Jade."

Jodi said, "but it wasn't them."

The three men looked at her, waiting.

Jodi swallowed. Her voice had sounded a little hoarse, as if she had been talking for a long time, though her speech had been surprisingly short and to the point. Russel had heard things he hadn't known. The two kids had gone into the House of Mirrors before, and Jodi had seen the dark mirrors and felt afraid. Russel hadn't even known before that a large section of the mirror maze was closed off. She had told about the other little boy, Kevin, the one who had made the hole in the floor, and she had told of Blane seeing him, somewhere behind the mirrors.

Russel felt dismayed at the private lives children lead. Jodi had never mentioned one iota of this to him. He'd had no idea that she and Blane had sneaked into other shows to watch them and that her favorite was the clown show of Izzy and Jade. Did Amy know?

He looked up and saw that Amy was awake, lying quietly in her bed, but looking down upon the people in the front room and listening.

He had a hunch Amy knew nothing of Jodi's experiences either.

Actually, when had either of them taken the time to question Jodi about her daily activities? He had assumed she spent her time in or near the trailer, playing house or whatever little girls played.

"It was ..." Jodi turned her face toward Russel, and her eyes met his in a long, silent, thoughtful gaze. What was she thinking? She had wakened him in the night to tell him the clowns she had seen were the clowns in India's trailer, but now she seemed to be trying to settle something within herself.

Russel kept quiet.

To him the answer was obvious. Someone—several, it seemed—in the carnival, had used the costumes to go into the House of Mirrors, into the closed section, for some reasons of their own. And when they'd found the children there, they'd killed the one they caught.

Yet something was wrong with the scenario. Why would several men work together in disguise to murder a helpless child? A defenseless woman, and a young dancer? Because it would seem that it had only happened that way.

And then he thought of something so obvious he wondered how he had missed it.

"Jodi," he said. "Could it be there was only one clown, and you thought you saw several because of the reflections?"

She still stared at him. Then, thoughtfully, she turned her face away and leaned back against him.

The detective who had gone after the two men, Izzy and Jade, came back with them. They were neither one in costume. Their faces were washed clean, and one of them had a round, pink face with pale, blue eyes and hair and eyebrows that were almost white they were so blond. The other was taller and thinner, with a narrow face and medium coloring. They both looked puzzled and a little scared.

Jodi sat up and stared at them.

"That's not Izzy and Jade!"

Reynolds sighed and looked at the detective impatiently. "They're going to have to be in costume, Smith."

"But ..." Jodi was almost crying again. "Izzy and Jade are good clowns. It wasn't them that were in the House of Mirrors. They were having their show."

"When the little boy was murdered?" Izzy, the tall one said. "We had a house full of customers at that time, sir," he explained patiently, some of the worry leaving his face. "At least fifty or sixty people can testify to that."

The three detectives got up and went outside with the two men Jodi had never seen without costumes and makeup before. Russel himself had seen them without costume only a few times. In makeup, they were jovial and uninhibited. Without makeup, they seemed unsure of themselves and ill at ease. But of course that might have been because of the unsettled state that hovered over the carnival now, the sense of doom, of suspicion that was gathering like a black cloud. Reynolds and the detective with the tape recorder came back into the trailer, and Russel saw the two clowns go along the alley toward their own trailer.

"He's right, of course," Reynolds said. "Jodi, is there anything else you can tell us?"

To Russel's surprise, she shook her head.

"If you remember anything, will you let us know? This is very important, Jodi."

"Yes sir," she agreed.

Russel waited until the other two detectives had followed Izzy and Jade down the alley, and then he said to Jodi, "Why didn't you tell them the costumes you saw were the ones India had made?"

"Because, Daddy ..." She got off his lap and stood looking out the door. "First we have to go tell Zulu that somebody stole India's clowns. And besides, I couldn't see who was in them."

Russel nodded as if he understood, though he didn't follow her reasoning. "All right, let's go."

He looked up at Amy. She had sat up in the bunk bed, forced to lean slightly forward because of the low ceiling.

"Lock the door behind us, Amy, and don't let anyone in. Not anyone. Or do you want to go with us?"

She seemed to cringe back, shaking her head. With Jodi's hand in his, Russel went out the door.

AMY DIDN'T WANT to see the clowns. They were crowding in upon her, it seemed, and she was so afraid. When she looked into her pendant, the clowns were sometimes in the background. And when she dreamed, she saw patterns, mismatched, segmented, patches of color, and sometimes a face, hideous, with empty slits for eyes.

She had never seen the costumes India had made, and she didn't want to see them.

Feeling as if she hadn't rested for a long time, she got out of bed, locked the door, and went into the bathroom to take a shower.

The pendant lay against her chest, on the ripple of bones there that were getting bonier. Where was the rounding that was supposed to happen to her body? She seemed to be getting skinnier and uglier, and the pendant was growing heavier.

She thought of taking it off. She slipped her fingers under the thin, braided silk thread of the necklace and started to slip it over her head, but as she did so she glanced down, and the reflections in the tiny mirrors of the pendant were moving madly, colors changing, red, blue, green, purple, garish, bright, on a background that seemed endless and murky. She didn't want to see into it. She didn't want to know about the world that existed independently in that other realm. She was increasingly terrified of it, as if she, or someone she loved, were being drawn inexorably into it forevermore.

What would happen if she told Russel about the pendant?

But she couldn't.

She didn't want to see the scenes that were being played out in the heart of the pendant, and so instead of taking a shower, she put on her blouse so that the pendant would be covered.

Russel and Jodi found Zulu at the House of Mirrors. He was standing out front, in the sunshine, with some of the men who worked for him, just looking at the house with strange, fierce eyes.

Something had happened to Zulu since India's death, Russel observed. Something inside, and something incredibly fierce and angry. What was on his mind? Russel felt an inner shudder. He looked at the three big, muscled men who stood near Zulu. They were discussing something about the House of Mirrors, and when Jodi's hand tightened on his, Russel saw that the left rear sections had been moved away from the rest.

He didn't have to ask. He knew that was where the murder had occurred.

The men with Zulu, he noticed for the first time, were big enough and strong enough to commit the kind of atrocious murders that had taken place in the past three days and nights. But they were men he had known for several years. Why was he suspecting a man who just the other night he had trusted to escort Amy to the trailer? And the other two—one of whom was called Shorty, Lord only knew why, since he was six feet six, and the other, known as Utah, who also had been a wrestler back when wrestling had been an act with the carnival—were both good old Joes he had drunk beer with in beer joints all over the country. And now he was suspecting them?

He didn't like what was happening to him.

They looked at him as he approached, no sign of their former friendliness apparent on their faces, and he wondered if they in turn suspected him. Perhaps it was getting that way with the carnival people. Each man suspecting another man. And what of the stronger women?

Russel gave himself a mental shake. He only wanted out of here. The atmosphere that had settled over the still carnie was one of darkness, even though the sun was shining, a June Mid-western sun, coming up brightly through a thin layer of pink and gold clouds in the east.

"Could we talk to you, Zulu?" Russel asked.

"Sure."

Zulu moved to one side, then paused and said, "Boys, go ahead and pull the rest of the rear section out from the front. Separate the whole thing, piece by piece. I want to look it over. But take out the bad part first, and wait until I can look at it."

They nodded and moved off to work. On the ropes of a nearby ride several of the younger carnie workers were sitting or leaning, arms folded, nothing to do but wait and watch and talk quietly among themselves. Everyone, so far as Russel knew, had been questioned once again by the police—and probably as before, knew nothing. In the case of Blane's death, probably every one of the carnie workers had alibis.

People had been around them, all during the afternoon, while the murder was being committed. Marks had been in the House of Mirrors, on the other side of the closed glass walls, while the murder was going on.

And that made it all the more chilling, more horrible even, than the night killings. Not only had it seemed worse because of the child, because of the terrible brutality of the killing, the uselessness of it, but because of the fact that it had apparently been done in front of another child.

As if the perpetrators had no fear of exposure.

Why hadn't she told the police what she had told him? He would ask her later, try to get a better answer from her.

"All right," Zulu said, and smiled faintly, the first smile Russel had seen on his lips in several days. Days that seemed centuries. Lifetimes apart. He put out his chubby hand and touched Jodi's hair lightly. "How are you today, little girl?"

"Okay," she said. "Mr. Zulu—I saw who killed Blane."

Zulu's eyes changed expression. The gentleness was gone. "Tell me about it, Jodi," he said. "Tell me."

"We went in the House of Mirrors. I know we weren't supposed to. But while we were in there, Blane saw his friend, Kevin, back in the dark swamp of the mirrors, behind the mirrors, and he ran, trying to reach him, and the clowns came then—"

Zulu interrupted, frowning. "Clowns?"

"Not Izzy and Jade. Izzy and Jade had their show going. And besides, Mr. Zulu, it was the clowns I saw in Miss India's trailer."

She paused, as if to let Zulu comment, but his frown was only growing deeper and his face more fierce.

Jodi continued, "I didn't want the police to know first, because they're India's clowns. And someone took them, and wore them, so that no one would know who they were. And I wanted to tell you first. Because the police would take the costumes away, and India said they were her children, and she wouldn't want them taken away."

Zulu was shaking his head slowly, still staring at Jodi, but, it seemed to Russel, in an absentminded way, as if he were deep in thought.

Russel, surprised, looked at his young daughter.

Her motives probably made sense to her. India's clown costumes must be protected, because they were India's children.

Even he knew how much time India had spent making those elaborate costumes and how important they were to her. And he was touched at Jodi's concern, and it was true the police would probably confiscate them for evidence.

"But Jodi," Russel said. "The police have to know these things. They'd bring the costumes back."

"No, no, they wouldn't. We have to see them first. Zulu—please, Mr. Zulu—we have to look and see, because someone stole them. They're not even there, in India's house, because whoever killed Blane was wearing the costumes."

Zulu nodded as if he had made up his mind. He began to walk fast, his short legs almost running. Jodi trotted alongside him, and Russel gave a delayed start, and followed. Without a word, Zulu dug into keys in his pocket as he went between the tent of the clowns and the koochie-show tent, and into the alley. Jodi ran to keep up with him, and Russel had to walk surprisingly fast. Zulu was almost running.

When they reached India's trailer, Zulu stopped and looked carefully up and down the alley, but the police had gathered down the alley and were milling about in the vicinity of the House of Mirrors, and watching the new sections that were now being pulled out at the rear of the House.

Zulu nodded to himself and unlocked the door. He pulled himself up onto the step that was too high for him to reach easily.

The room was shaded and dark, blinds pulled.

There was a strange, unpleasant odor, as if incense had been burning too long, creating a cloud of strong scents.

Russel stood in the open doorway behind Jodi and Zulu, trying to see in the deep shadows of the room.

Zulu barked an order, as if he were on the midway giving instructions to his men. "Shut the door."

Russel pulled the door shut reluctantly.

Zulu crossed the shadowed room to the end of the couch, where he pulled on the string of the antique lamp. The light it gave out was muted, but sufficient to see the clowns at the end of the room.

Russel felt a lurch in his stomach, something very akin to fear, when the hideous faces were illuminated out of the darkness of the room, their empty eyes seeming somehow not empty at all, but watching ... watching, an evil depth to them that belied the empty spaces in the masks.

He had seen them a few times, on those occasions when he had visited India in her trailer. They had sat and talked on numerous subjects, none of it really important, all of it comforting and at ease, as if India were an aunt or some other close relative. Yet he had known almost nothing about her except that she was the major owner of the carnival and she spent her time making these fantastic clown suits. Suits that were never worn by anyone, so far as he knew.

"They're all here," Zulu was saying. "All seven of them."

He did not seem surprised.

But Jodi was staring horrified at them.

Her mouth hung slightly open, and she pushed back, as far away from them as she could get.

"It was them," she said so softly Russel almost missed her words. "It was them, those clowns—that killed Blane. Look at the blood on their gloves. I saw blood on their gloves."

Russel's eyes were drawn instantly to the gloves that hung at the sides of the seven clowns.

They were as white as if they had been freshly washed.

CHAPTER 20

JODI COULD FEEL THE PRESENCE OF THE CLOWNS AS IF THE WALL BEHIND THEM were the wall of mirrors in which they had been reflected darkly, a part of another world, a world neither Zulu nor Russel had seen. A world neither of them believed in.

But then Zulu said, "Those gloves could easily have been changed. They look new. Whoever wore the suits could have gotten fresh gloves."

She'd love him forever, thought Jodi, looking at Zulu in gratitude. Maybe they didn't doubt her word after all.

"Which one did you see, Jodi?" Russel asked. "Or how many of them?"

"All of them," she said, her voice so low she could hardly hear it herself. She wanted desperately to get out of there, for it was beginning to seem an extension of the mirror maze, and in another minute the clowns would begin to move, and they would kill all of them, Zulu and Russel as well as herself.

She turned her back to them, grasped Russel's hand, and looked up at him. "Daddy, I want to go." Russel picked her up. Her feet hung to his knees and past, but he held her as if she was three years old.

"It's all right, baby, you're safe. They're just empty, old clown suits, that's all."

"India called them her children," Zulu said. "She loved those costumes. They were not just costumes to her. She even had them named. The one on this end she called Sawdust, because he was more like a scarecrow than some scarecrows, she said."

219

Zulu opened the door and pushed it back so that Russel could go out. Russel set Jodi down on the step, and she leaped to the ground, glad to be out of India's haunted house, away from those terrible clown suits.

Zulu, standing close to the door as if he wanted to make sure no one else heard what he was going to say, spoke softly. "You say, Jodi, that you saw all of them in the mirrored house. Could it be that you saw only one or two and their reflections made them seem like six or seven?"

"No. I saw them coming down the hall. And the mirrors are so black in there that they don't hardly make any reflections at all, but they did some, and I remember thinking there were dozens, maybe hundreds of them. But I saw them coming down the aisle between the walls of mirrors, one after the other, and they moved like this." She demonstrated, feeling safe in the sunshine that sparkled through the trees in spots upon her. She lifted her arms slowly, the way they had done, and she curved her fingers slowly into claws. And then her memory took her on to the blood soaking their fingers— or had it? Had their gloves remained white? Even after they had touched the bloodied body of Blane? She began to tremble violently. "And they threw Blane to the floor, and threw him to the floor, and... I knew they were going to kill me too, but I had to get him away from them. And so I pushed him down through the hole, and they acted like they couldn't see or hear me. They kept going around in the aisle of mirrors, and then like someone told them what to do, they saw me, and they almost touched me—that one almost touched me, the one India called Joey."

Russel's arm was around her shoulders. "That's all right, baby, you're safe, and I'm going to keep you that way. Zulu, there's nothing we can do to help. I'm pulling out."

Zulu nodded.

"I'm leaving my grab joint because I don't think my pickup will haul it."

"I'll send you a check for it. We can determine that later, when you send me an address. But Russel, don't say anything to the police about someone using those suits. I'd like to handle this myself."

"I hadn't intended to leave so soon, but I can't keep my kids here, especially now that Jodi has seen the killers and they have seen her. One of them, all of them, might get the idea that she knows who they are."

"I understand that. Have you said anything to the police about these clown costumes being used by the killers?"

"No. Jodi wanted to tell you first."

"Good. I'd like to keep this in the family for the time being. Because you know the police are right about one thing. Whoever it is doing this is part of our bunch. He—they—belong to the carnival."

"But why the hell are they doing it, Zulu? Lakisha? India? Blane, a kid only eleven years old? What connection did those three have?"

"I don't know. I haven't figured that out yet." Zulu reached over and patted Jodi on the head. Once. A hard pat that Jodi understood to mean sympathy, and maybe even a little bit of love.

"I'm going to miss you. When all this is over, come on back and travel with the carnie." He started away, then paused. "Why don't we just get someone to run your grab joint for the rest of the summer, Russ, while you take a vacation. Go to the mountains, or somewhere."

"I thought we'd go home to the farm. You've got my folks' address."

"Yeah, right. Okay, you take the summer on the farm, then join us in Florida for the winter, and next summer we'll travel the country again with the carnie."

Russel nodded.

"Things will be settled and back to old times by then, I promise you," Zulu said grimly.

His face was set, looking square and determined as he went walking off between two tents toward the midway.

It was wishful thinking that things could ever be the same again. For one moment it had seemed possible.

Zulu waved at Andy, who didn't have anything to do lately but sit around on the ropes of the Tilt-a-whirl or wander up and down the midway.

Andy got up eagerly and hurried toward him.

He was a young kid, nineteen or twenty, and still slender, without much bulk in his shoulders. He had a long chin, which he'd kept covered this past year with a beard that was a little too straggly to look good, but his eyes were as pretty as the eyes of a girl, and girls seemed to notice that and pretty much flocked around him. He was bored to death with the midway closed, without the girls of the town and country to come by and flirt with him. Most of the young women who traveled with the carnie were already married and mostly out of his reach. Zulu knew all about him, just as he knew all about all the men he hired, up to a certain point. He didn't know if any of them had prison records, because he had figured it was none of his business up until now. Now he wondered if his practice of never inquiring into the past of the men he hired was a good one. However, he had only carried on a practice set before he became manager. "Let them have their reasons for hiding with us," India used to say when he expressed curiosity about the men he hired on. "They stay a season, or two or three, and then they go on. All we need to know is what kind of men they are when they're with us."

That was why he had begun a sort of human-study program all his own. To determine what kind of men worked for him.

And he would swear on a stack of Bibles that not any one of them was capable of murder.

"Want a job?" he asked Andy.

"Sure do, Zulu. What do you need done?"

"I need someone to board up India's trailer."

Andy looked surprised, but had sense enough not to ask why. "Just the— uh—the door—or the windows too?"

"Windows too. Get someone to help you if you want, and do a damn good job of it, Andy. I want it so tight that no one can get in without a crowbar that will make enough noise to wake the whole damn alley. Okay?"

"Yes, sir. Consider it done."

"I'll be around a little later to check it out."

Zulu walked on down the midway to where the tractor behind the House of Mirrors was still chugging, idling, the men standing there wondering what to do next while the lawmen wandered around looking at the disconnected sections of the mirror maze with stern but puzzled faces.

Only the back three sections had been moved away, just enough to allow room for a man to climb up and enter. The opening on each one was only as wide as a door, each section thoroughly encased in its own wall, although the interior walls were thin, rather than the standard four inches of the outside wall.

Three of the lawmen came to meet Zulu.

"Mr. Zulumonsque, we need to know something that we haven't found an answer to. Are there other entries we haven't found? How could an adult have gotten into that area where the murder was committed? The only opening that we can find was the hole in the floor, and it's no larger than a child can get through, and a quite young child at that."

Zulu shook his head.

"Was there another opening? I understand you had it closed off from the front sections, and I don't see any opening at all at the back of the part that's still in place, that part." He pointed at the two thirds of the House still standing in place on blocks. The parts that had been moved back were on blocks again too, each section sitting just a couple of feet away from its connecting part.

"There was no other entry, sir," Zulu said. And immediately wished he could have thought of something else. Because now, wouldn't they suspect the child, Jodi? "But," he added, "the little girl couldn't have done it."

"No, we're not saying she did. She was much too small to do that kind of damage to a person."

The lawmen turned away, milled about for a moment again, then the big shot from the State Police said to Zulu, "Leave these pieces of house out here where they are. We'll be throwing a rope up around them and we don't want anyone close to them. Someone, somehow got in there."

Zulu nodded again, his eyes on the sections, and the dark doorways that led into them. Just enough light fell into them to glisten on the blackened mirrors and make it look like things were moving behind the mirrors, just as Jodi had said.

"We don't want anyone leaving the fairgrounds either, Mr. Zulumonsque. And we don't want the carnival opening. We have to ask you to stay here until we can find out who's doing these things. I hate to ask you to do that, but we're going to need several days. You have some men here who've served time, did you know that?"

"No, I didn't."

"You don't check up very good on the men you hire, do you?"

"No, I just ask for their real names and Social Security numbers, that's all. A lot of them just stay one season. As long as they don't give us any trouble, we leave it like that."

"And if they cause you trouble? What do you do then?"

"Turn them loose. Tell them to go elsewhere." Tell them to get the hell and gone, Zulu thought, but never bring in the law. And maybe that was one of the reasons the law looked on them with that fishy eye. Suspicions ran deep where carnie people were concerned, it seemed.

"You know, of course, that the killer—or killers—are here among your people?"

"I'm not sure of that at all, sir," Zulu said, and said no more. He had a feeling. More and more he felt as if it had something to do with the House of Mirrors and Raoell, the black magician. No, India hadn't really called him a black magician, had she? She had called him an illusionist.

Zulu had wanted to look the mirror maze over himself, every inch of it, and here the police were blocking him from entering the most important part. He decided to say a few words on Russel's behalf. "The young father,

Russel Sauer?" he said to Reynolds before he could walk away again. "The father of the little girl who dragged the boy out from underneath the House? Well, he'd like to get his daughter to a safer environment. He's got a place to go that might help the child. A farm his folks own up north. Why couldn't you let him go there? You could get in touch with him whenever you—uh—found the clowns?"

"I'm sorry. When had he planned to leave?"

"I don't know." Zulu added. "Soon."

"I'd better get over to see him again."

For crissakes, he'd made it worse instead of better. Zulu walked along beside the lawmen, trying hard to keep up.

"Listen, why keep the little kid here? She's had trauma enough to last her a lifetime. She'll probably have nightmares and will need therapy to help her get over it. Why not let them go? It's not like they're disappearing."

"Nobody leaves this fairground, Mr. Zulumonsque. As soon as we feel we can let her go we'll say so, but she's the only witness we have. Can't you see the importance of that?"

"I can see the danger in that, Reynolds," Zulu said in the rage that lay just under the surface of his outer feelings. Down there in the pit of his stomach, with the pain and the hopelessness and the sorrow. "I can see that whoever killed the boy saw the girl, and knew the girl saw them. Where does that put her?"

"It puts her with guards. We're going to leave a policeman to watch the fairgrounds during the night, Zulu. Don't you worry."

"I'll put my own guards out there, sir," Zulu snapped.

"I don't think you should trust your own guards too far."

Zulu turned away. His rage was building. The men who worked for him were trustworthy, and he knew it if he knew anything in the world. The cop had been wrong when he'd said some of them had records. As far as he knew the one with a record didn't even work for him. Buster Adams had been in jail once for drug possession, but Buster had told him about that. Zulu hadn't checked on him. And Buster didn't work for the carnie. He had his own concession. A dart game, with animal balloons and three walls of stuffed toys to give to the lucky Joe who happened to pierce a balloon.

As long as Buster didn't do so many drugs that it interfered with his behavior on the midway, Zulu had orders from India to let him be.

Zulu stood scratching the back of his head a minute while he calmed down, then he went back into the shady alley to check on India's trailer.

He could hear the hammering, and he found Andy and two more hard at work. Andy had already nailed three boards over the door and was working on the windows. The other two were at each end of the trailer nailing boards on windows there. A small stack of lumber had been brought over from one of the trucks that hauled around spare things occasionally needed by the carnival. None of the activity had attracted the police.

"Put more boards on the door, Andy," Zulu said. "A couple more anyway."

"Yes, sir!"

Zulu stood by and watched two more boards go up. He checked out the windows and found them well secured. No one would be able to get in without being seen. Or heard.

He wandered down the alley, stopping occasionally to talk to people forced into idleness, trying to avoid answering more questions than he felt they had any right to know. He understood their curiosity, their worry, but he couldn't tell them why he was having India's trailer boarded. Whoever had stolen the costumes would know without being told. Whoever had used them as a disguise would have to find something else. Or perhaps the simple act of making sure the costumes were not available would put an end to the killings.

Zulu went back to stand in front of the House of Mirrors and look at it, but nothing came to him, no revelation. Only the feeling that there, not in India's house, was the answer to the killings.

The night fell, at last, after a long day, and lights came on around the midway, and someone turned on the lights on the rides, so they blazed out into the darkening sky as if in memory of happier times, and Zulu let them burn.

He went to his trailer and looked up the number of the oldest carnie veteran he knew. An old man who lived in a home down in Florida, near the wintering park they all lived in. His name was Corcus Lorenzo, and he had owned one of the most popular acts in any carnival, monkeys that rode little bicycles or motorcycles around a pit with sides that were almost perpendicular.

He would have finished his supper now, and be at his peak—if he weren't asleep.

The call went through to the head of the nursing home and was transferred to Corcus's room. The spidery voice answered.

Corcus had told Zulu last winter that he was ninety-seven years old, but his mind was as sharp as the mind of a seventy-year-old, and sharper than some that age. He was one of the lucky ones. He could still walk, still talk, still play cards. He enjoyed his life at the nursing home, though he looked back on his carnie days with nostalgia.

"How are you doing, Corcus?" Zulu asked. "This is Zulu."

"Why, I'm doing just fine. Where are you, Zulu?"

"We're on the road, Corcus, in the Midwest, but we're stuck. Have you been reading about the murders?"

"Oh, yeah. And had it on the television news some too."

"Yeah. We've had a few cameras around, but I think they're barred this time, since midnight or so. I haven't been outside of the gates because I don't want to know. Say, Corcus, I need to ask you about somebody you might have known."

"Yeah, yeah. Who?"

"A magician named Raoell."

"Who?"

His hearing was going, Zulu thought with a sigh of regret. Either that or Corcus didn't know the name. He felt like crossing his fingers and hoping, if it would do any good.

"Raoell. He was the creator of the House of Mirrors that I operate. India called him an illu—"

"Oh, say," Corcus said. "I sure hated to hear about India's death. We are all going to miss her, Zulu."

"Yes, we are."

"She was murdered too, I understand."

"Yes, and she told me about this Raoell, Corcus, and somehow she felt like there was a connection. It seemed that the man disappeared back in the twenties the day her mother was killed."

There was the briefest silence, then Corcus said, "Raoell, the illusionist. Yes, I remember him. I was with that very carnival that year, Zulu. The man somehow wooed away India's mother, but that was a horrible thing too. She was found murdered. They never found the killer."

"Can you tell me anything at all about Raoell and the House of Mirrors?"

"It was called the House of Illusions then, and he had a good show, I was told, though I never went in. I had my own show and was busy. But it was a strange show, and very popular."

"He used clowns, India said, didn't he?"

"Yes, he had clowns—of a sort. I think they were part of the illusions, Zulu, because they never showed up except during a show. He was a very secretive man, very popular with the ladies. He was tall and thin and wore a black cape at all times. His hair was black as coal, and he wore a mustache and one of those sharp, pointed little Vandykes—you know what I mean, the goatee type of beard. He made himself look as mysterious as he could. He wanted India's mother. Somehow, he wooed her away, and she was going to live with him, it seemed, and there was a disagreement between India's father and Raoell ... nobody ever knew what happened. They both disappeared. But the sad thing was the little child, India, found her mother dead in the tent. Raoell was never heard from again, and some of us believed that somehow Jim, India's father, had something to do with his disappearance, and when Raoell found he couldn't have Middy, he killed her. Somehow. There were no explanations that were satisfactory, Zulu."

"Where did this Raoell come from?"

"I don't know. He just showed up with that big mirror maze of his and joined up. It was said the mirror maze was put together somewhere in the mountains in the southeast—Kentucky or Virginia or somewhere, or maybe it was somewhere in Europe. Nobody knew anything about him."

Zulu felt his heart grow heavy. For a while he'd had hopes that Corcus knew something India hadn't been able to remember. But it was sounding as if the illusionist had kept himself an illusion too, to appear and disappear at will.

And the thought of that sent a coldness over Zulu like he had never known before. A fear that was worse than fear, but a deep, deep terror.

India had been right, he suddenly knew. Raoell was still ... alive. Not alive perhaps, in the usual sense, but in existence.

Raoell still existed.

And something had occurred to activate him again. To bring him forth beyond the darkening mirrors of the maze.

What?

Whatever it was had something to do with the arrival of the Sauer girls. Of Jodi and Amy.

What had happened when they arrived that had not happened before?

The answer came to him like a lightning bolt from dark clouds.

The talisman.

CHAPTER 21

THE TALISMAN.

According to India, the talisman had been worn by Raoell, as a part of his costume, or, as she felt, as a part of himself. Then, on that day of the murder of India's mother, and the disappearances of both her father and Raoell, she had seen her papa fighting with Raoell, and he'd had the talisman in his hand.

Presumably it had been fought over and lost.

It had been dropped somewhere in the House of Mirrors, and during the years it was there, in the House, Raoell was quiet, inactive, for some reason Zulu did not yet know. Then what had happened? Russel's two young daughters came, and Jodi had somehow found her way into the House during the early morning hours, and by some quirk of fate, she'd found the talisman.

But Russel had sent her with it to India, and India had seen to it that she threw it into the trash can.

There it was lost again, and probably crushed forever, irretrievably.

Zulu didn't understand, but it looked as though Raoell was in some way brought forth by the removal of the talisman from the House of Mirrors.

Perhaps by losing it he had lost himself, his ability to take human form, and had spent those years looking for it.

Perhaps he was still looking for it, and he had known that Jodi had found it.

Could it be he had sent his clowns after the wrong child? That Blane was caught instead of Jodi?

Why was India's mother killed? Because he could no longer have her for himself? Because she wouldn't come to him after all?

Crazy, crazy. Insane, all of it. What am I thinking of? Zulu wondered.

Yet it made more sense in some terrible, dark way than anything he had heard from the police.

Whatever the strange truth might be, the mystery lay in the House of Illusions, and as soon as he could get in, he was going to find it. He would do as he had planned. He would take it apart now, mirror by mirror, sliver by sliver. He would burn the wood and do whatever he had to do to the mirrors. But he wouldn't stop until he found that—whatever it was—that illusionist, magician, man or devil, who had called himself Raoell.

THE POLICE CORDONED off the entire House of Mirrors. During the later hours of the afternoon, Zulu went to the guard and asked to be allowed to go in.

"I've got some things I need to attend to there," he said—casually, he hoped. "Some cleaning, that kind of thing."

He had been watching the people connected with the law come and go, drifting around the murder site, taking pictures, talking, making notes, fighting the terrible black flies that had swarmed to the blood and the torn, rotting flesh. And he had watched them drift away, car by car, until only a few uniformed guards were left. All through the day and afternoon Zulu had waited, keeping his eye on the House. Although only the left rear section was connected with the murder, the police were puzzled as to how the killer had entered, and that, Zulu supposed, was the reason they had put up a rope around the entire House.

The young police officer looked miserable. Zulu could see he hated to turn down such a request by the owner, but he could see also that he'd had his orders.

"I just can't, Sir," he finally said. "Tomorrow maybe they'll be finished with it. Could you wait until then?"

Zulu put his hands into his pockets, the point of the knife bumping his leg. He hunched his shoulders up and let them fall, then turned away. But he turned back again and asked the young officer if he'd like a cup of coffee.

The man smiled. "I sure wouldn't refuse."

Zulu nodded. "Be right back," he said.

He walked without hurrying back to his trailer. He wanted to get into his

House of Mirrors. Delays were deadly now. Night was coming. Anything could happen.

At least the clown costumes were behind boards as well as under lock and key. They wouldn't be stolen tonight.

Something occurred to him as he made two cups of coffee and put them on a tray. How could Raoell have used more than one costume at a time? He frowned at the wall, and added a couple of doughnuts to the tray, then napkins. The night India had reported a costume stolen, only one of them had been taken. Or was it two? Certainly no more.

How could Raoell, even assuming he were somehow alive, use seven costumes? The mystery of Raoell was too much for the sane mind of man.

Well, Raoell wouldn't be getting any of them tonight.

Zulu contemplated putting a knockout drop in the officer's cup of coffee. That, actually, had been his first thought, the idea behind his offer, but at the last he decided against it. As the young man said, tomorrow the police would probably take the ropes off the front sections and the central room, and that was the part Zulu wanted to see.

Zulu carried the tray back across the midway to the officer, and then stood by chatting as casually as he could while they drank and ate. Zulu watched the sun go down and night fall, and again the boys turned on all the colorful lights of the high rides, and on the street beyond the fairground Zulu could see the lights of cars drifting slowly by, as if their occupants were hoping to find the carnival open.

AMY SLEPT RESTLESSLY, waking just enough to realize that she was dreaming terrible things that she couldn't remember. Her body hurt from holding herself in such small, tight knots, her legs drawn up almost to her chin, her arms tight in against her chest. And the talisman falling to one side and biting into the flesh of her arm or leg. Moaning, she'd wake and turn over and straighten her body, only to fall asleep again and wake soon afterwards drawn into a knot of pain again, with the strange dreams going through her mind like dark, wavy colors and movements that had no meaning that she was capable of deciphering.

Beside her Jodi slept quietly, turned on her side away from Amy, her face out toward the muted lights of the trailer-house front room. From the small bedroom at the rear of the trailer came the comforting snore of Russel.

Amy lay awake listening, hearing the silences that came late in the night.

The lights from the midway glinted through the trees onto the top of the trailer next door.

She closed her eyes, feeling a terrible weariness. She needed rest, good, deep sleep. Please God, take away the dreams.

JODI WOKE to the sound of Amy crying. She sounded as though she were trying to scream, but her voice was choked and gasping, and Jodi knew she was having another of her nightmares.

The pale nightlight in the trailer, and the streaks of light from the midway, lighted Amy's face just enough for Jodi to see the puckered mouth, the jerking chin, the fluttering eyelids that never quite opened.

"Amy, Amy, wake up."

Jodi shook her, reaching around her to grasp her shoulders, but still Amy seemed to be trapped in the torture of her dream. Jodi reached to her arm, the one she had twisted beneath her, and her hand fell on something small and sharp, a teardrop pendant that was attached to a thin, braided necklace. It was lying in the crook of Amy's arm.

The necklace!

"Amy!" Jodi cried.

Amy woke suddenly, stirred, and put her free hand over Jodi's, and the necklace. Amy's eyes looked large and sunken, staring through the meager light into Jodi's face.

She took a long breath, a jagged breath, and let it out slowly. The warmth of it touched Jodi's face.

"Amy," Jodi hissed, keeping her voice down. "That's the necklace that India made me throw away, isn't it?"

It was gripped in Jodi's hand, and she pulled it up, jerking it against the softness of Amy's neck. Amy began fighting her suddenly, rising to an elbow, both hands struggling to pry Jodi's hand off the talisman.

"Don't! Don't, it's mine. I found it. Why should it be thrown away? I found it. It's mine!"

She was beginning to cry, and Jodi drew back in bewilderment, sorrow seeping into every pore of her heart. Amy had gotten the pendant back from Jodi and was cradling it in both hands, cupped, against her heart. Tears streamed down her face and she sobbed, and sobbed.

Jodi put her arms around Amy.

"Don't cry, Amy. Don't cry."

"I found it." Amy wept, her tears smearing against Jodi's cheek. "You threw it away, but I got it out and kept it. What's wrong with that? It was too pretty to throw away."

"But it's not just a pretty necklace, Amy. It's a bad necklace. India said so, and Daddy said she knew."

"It's not bad. It's magic, that's all. Don't tell anyone I've got it, Jodi, please. Please."

Jodi looked into her sister's face undecided, and then she relented. As Amy had said, it was too pretty to throw away.

Jodi said, "Okay, Amy. I won't tell."

Amy hugged Jodi exuberantly. "Oh Jodi, I'll never forget that. I'll do you a favor someday too, I promise."

Jodi shrugged, the way Blane had done all the time. She turned over to her side of the bed, facing away from Amy, but now she had a very bad feeling. A feeling that weighed her down even more. She buried her head beneath her pillow finally, so that she could go to sleep.

ZULU MOVED RESTLESSLY, uneasily, rising from his couch to walk around his office-living room.

It was the time of night nearest death, when even the insects grew quiet, and when guards tended to fall asleep.

He turned out his lights and stood at the window looking out.

The alley was empty. He could hear the steady chug, chug of the generators, but tonight they had an ominous sound.

Shadows beneath the truck beds were black and shifting.

He adjusted the holster of his knife and felt the knife handle. He eased the knife in and out of the holster, and it slid easily, the small leather strap that held it safely in the holster out of his way now.

He opened the door and stood for a moment looking into the night toward the midway. Heavy streaks of shadows were thrown toward his trailer and others nearby, cast by the tents on this side of the midway and the larger rides. Lights gleamed in silence from the top of the Ferris wheel, but they weren't much use in the alleys.

There was no guard. The night was as still as ever a night got.

Zulu stepped quietly out of his door and crossed a shadowed area into the midway. He stood still at the corner of a game tent in the center of the midway, looking in all directions.

After a moment he spotted a guard down by the House of Mirrors, but he was leaning against the corner as if he were asleep on his feet.

Zulu crossed the midway in silence and passed between a couple of tents to the opposite alley. There were more trees here, more darkness.

If any of his own guards walked the alley, Zulu didn't see them.

He moved silently, going from shadow to shadow, looking over his shoulder and into the black spaces, his flashlight face down at his side, ready to turn on at a flick of a movement, his right hand resting on the handle of his knife.

The guards were supposed to be on the alert in the alley, and he caught a glimpse of movement at the far end, just for a second.

He paused, watching, and saw Ken go into a patch of light down at the curve of the alley. He was on his way around, and that should mean all was still and secure, but Zulu couldn't shake the feeling that it wasn't.

Something, somewhere here was wrong.

He lifted his flashlight and shot a spot of light onto India's trailer.

His finger froze on the button of the flashlight.

All the boards had been ripped to one side across the front of the door. They were still hanging by the nails on one end, but the door was open just enough for passage.

Someone had broken in.

Or out.

Zulu began to run.

He climbed up into the trailer, punting with the effort of pushing the boards aside and pulling himself up. The point of the knife nicked his knee, but he didn't pause.

He stood in the cluttered living room and shined his light at the empty wall. It looked as if the room had been stripped, but everything was there just as always, the tasseled lamps, the tapestries, the rugs and knitted throws, everything but the clowns.

All of them were gone.

He whirled to run out again, then remembered another clown costume that India always kept.

Her papa's suit, the suit she had worn the night she was killed.

He'd had it laundered when the police gave it back, and folded it on her bed.

Was it still there?

He hurried down the hall to the bedroom, and saw the folded suit.

The mask of the suit had been hung back onto the stand in the corner of the room and now grinned at him from a stick body.

The good suit, she had called it, the good clown.

On a sudden impulse he tossed his light onto the bed, unfastened his holster, and put the suit on.

It was much too large, but when he fastened the holster back around his waist he gathered enough material under it so that the full bloomer legs wouldn't hinder his movements. He bunched the shirt of the suit down into his pants, and caught a glimpse of himself in India's mirror, a short clown, costume bunched and bulky.

But it was the good clown's suit, and if there was anything there that could help him, he was praying for it now.

Running, leaving the door open behind him, he went out to begin the search for the missing clowns.

AMY LAY with her back to Jodi staring out at the night, the necklace in her fingers. She felt each corner of it, each point, each smooth, tiny face of the sixteen triangles that made it a teardrop.

Jodi wasn't going to tell, that was all that mattered.

No one was going to take away her pretty jewel.

The alley was shadowed, the heavy limbs of the shading trees creating a blackness beneath the lights that angled through from the midway. Someone with a gun, like a shotgun or rifle, slowly walked along the alley, going from shadow to light and back to deep, black shadow. Whoever it was, and she knew it was one of the guards Zulu had told Russel he was going to leave to patrol the midway and alley, went on out of sight down toward the House of Mirrors, where the boy had been killed.

Amy hadn't seen him, and she hadn't wanted to see him.

She was glad all the police cars were gone, except for one or two that were out by the gates. She had seen them before she went to bed. But maybe now they were gone too.

She wished they could move on to another location, somewhere deeper into the mountains maybe, and open the carnival again.

The man was coming back again, she saw, only this time he wore a white collar... .

She jerked alert and stared through the narrow, open window into the empty alley.

Not the guard ... not someone who wore a white collar ... but the clown.

The clown with the ruffle around his neck.

He was standing where she had last seen him, when she had run from him last night. Was it last night? It seemed so long ago.

Between two tents, in the deep darkness there, he stood, and as she stared at him she began to make out the features of his face and of his costume. She could see the billowing, bloomer-like legs of the costume and the big shoes, and she could see the face, the big mouth that curved down and was white instead of red. And gradually she could see the slanted slits of the eyes.

Behind him then she saw another figure, this one with patches of different colors in his costume, and red yarn for his hair. But his face was twisted and terrible, and his eyes were like the eyes of the first, narrow, slanted slits. And they were looking at her, staring at her through the window of her bed. She had a feeling, even as she drew back closer to Jodi, that they could see her far better than she could see them.

Their white-gloved hands raised, slowly, fingers curving. Even across the space of the alley, she could clearly see those white gloves.

Then she saw they were beckoning to her.

They wanted her to follow them.

As she watched, puzzled, afraid, yet drawn to obey, they turned and walked down the alley, keeping to the shadows behind the tents and beneath the trees.

They stopped and looked back at her, and she saw there was another one now, stepped out from a deep, black space between the next two tents, and it too was beckoning.

Very slowly, unable to refuse, Amy quietly got out of bed, going carefully over Jodi so as not to disturb her. She climbed down the ladder and went to the door and let herself out into the night.

The necklace burned against her chest, and she closed it within her hands, both of them, and felt its heat increase to a glowing aliveness as she followed the clowns.

SOMETHING WOKE JODI SUDDENLY, wide awake—a sound, a movement, she didn't know—but she knew before she felt for Amy that her side of the bed was empty. It was still warm, but Amy was gone. Jodi looked down the hall. Had Amy gone to the bathroom? But the bathroom door was open, and there was only darkness in the tiny room.

Jodi crept across the bed to the window and looked out, drawn by a sound, a feeling of something there.

She saw Amy walking slowly down the center of the alley, going from the light into pitch dark beneath the trees, but still the pale and ghostly form was visible to Jodi as Amy went on, almost like a sleepwalker.

Jodi cried out through the window. "Amy? Where're—"

She stopped, chills radiating over her body, her voice freezing in her throat.

Ahead of Amy she glimpsed movement and touches of white. The large ruffle at the neck of the clown, one of the clowns that had killed Blane. She could see the cruel, white mouth, and she saw splashes of color and movements from others as they gathered in the alley ahead of Amy.

She was going straight toward them.

Didn't Amy know they were going to kill her?

Jodi tried to scream, and couldn't. She almost fell out of bed. She started running toward the door, to bring Amy back before it was too late, but then she had presence of mind enough to know she needed help.

She turned and ran down the hall instead to Russel's room. She almost fell on him. Her voice was a squeak, a feeble cry.

"Daddy. Daddy. Amy ... help her."

She ran again, out of the trailer and down the alley toward Amy—only Amy was no longer there.

Amy was gone, and the clowns were gone.

They had blended into the darkness somehow, somewhere.

RUSSEL FELT as if he were moving in slow motion. Jodi had awakened him, leaving him with a sense of panic, that was all. He had no idea where she was. He could remember only that she had said something about Amy. She had cried Amy's name.

Russel pulled his pants on, and ran barefoot into the living room, calling, "Jodi! Amy?"

There was no answer. The front door stood wide open, and the bunk bed was empty.

Russel ran out into the alley, and found that beneath the grass were hidden rocks, just enough to slow him down and make him limp along like a crippled man.

He shouted, "Jodi!"

He saw her then, a pale, little ghost-like figure flitting from shadow to light along the alley.

She was running toward the House of Mirrors.

Lights came on in the trailer next door, but Russel passed it by without stopping. He ran for Jodi, as fast as he could, cursing himself for coming out without his shoes. But there wasn't time to go back.

Ahead of him Jodi disappeared into darkness.

And there was no sign of Amy.

SHE HADN'T SEEN Amy again. Jodi ran into the dark tunnels between the tents, and out again into the brightly lighted midway. She called once, but her voice was too terrified to make enough sound to reach any ear, so she didn't try to call again.

Where had Amy gone?

And then she knew.

It was all so logical, in some kind of mad way.

Amy had been following the clowns, and the clowns belonged, somehow, in the House of Mirrors. The first time she had seen them they were in the House of Mirrors, looking for something. And she had found the necklace, and India had said it was evil and made her throw it away.

But Amy had taken it, and now the clowns knew she had taken it.

They were taking Amy to the House of Mirrors because she had the necklace.

Jodi ran down the midway, and just as she reached the platform of the girlie-show tent, two platforms away, Amy came out of the shadows and went up the steps to the front door of the House of Mirrors.

The door opened, and Amy went in.

Jodi screamed, her voice bursting from her in volume. "Amy! No! No!"

But the door closed behind Amy.

Jodi ran up the steps and tried to open the door, but it was locked.

CHAPTER 22

JODI POUNDED ON THE DOOR AND SCREAMED, HER VOICE RISING AND FALLING IN a cry that from a distance could not be distinguished from the scream of an animal. Her terror, her fear for Amy, now combined with her memory of the killing of Blane, with her memory too of the dangers of the clowns, of the strangeness in the House of Mirrors, brought her to primal terror, and so her scream went on and on.

It brought the guards running.

And from the area near India's trailer Zulu came, his legs hurting from the added weight of the costume that whipped around his body.

Just for an instance he visualized the spectacle he was—the dwarf in the large clown suit, bunched and gathered beneath his belt, pushed into the tops of his shoes, flapping loosely at his elbows. And just for an instance he wondered at his stupidity for putting it on. But it was too late now. He dared not take the time to rip it off.

With the knife now in his hand, the empty holster beating against his right knee, he ran, out of the alley where India's trailer was, while the scream quivered in the air and the generators kept on chugging and throbbing as if nothing at all were different from any other time. He ran, into the brightly lighted midway.

He saw the little girl across the midway, on the porch of the House of Mirrors, pounding on the door.

He saw two uniformed guards running toward her, and he saw his own guards, men he had equipped with guns and other weapons hidden on their person, coming—from all directions, it seemed, the men were running—toward the child on the porch.

From down the midway came Russel, his face a white blur as he ran as if something were wrong with his feet. He was wearing jeans, but only a thin, sleeveless undershirt otherwise, though the night had turned cold, with a breeze down from the north.

As Zulu ran toward the little girl beating on the door of the House of Mirrors, she suddenly turned away, her voice silenced, and ran down the steps and around the side of the building, successfully dodging the hand of a policeman who reached out to grab her.

She ran out of sight into the darkness at the back of the House of Mirrors, and as if he could read her mind, Zulu knew where she was going.

There was an opening at the back, where the other sections had been pulled away from the front. Just one narrow opening, hardly wide enough for a child, where the closure hadn't been fully completed because it fitted up against a wall in the bad sections of the mirror maze.

She was going in, and only God—or perhaps the devil—knew why.

Zulu adjusted the heavy handle of the knife in his hand, arranging it to throw. With his free hand he reached into his pocket for the key to the front door of the House of Mirrors.

Whatever was destined to happen in the mirror maze was happening now, he realized.

The waiting was over.

The meeting with Raoell was imminent.

And Zulu was going to win.

In the dark she found the crevice that she had to turn sideways to get into. She hadn't known for sure if there were a doorway back here, but she had seen the doorways into the bad part of the mirror maze, and she knew, she prayed, there was a way in.

She had to save her sister.

She climbed up and into the corridor.

A bulb burned in the ceiling about fifteen feet away, at the end of the aisle between mirrors, and other passageways branched off from it.

The little girl in pajamas was reflected in a hundred places, it seemed, and she paused, but she had been here before, and she knew if she put her hands out and felt the glass she would be guided. She wouldn't be walking into walls of glass doors that weren't there.

When she reached the end of the first corridor, she stopped for a heartbeat, her breath held, to listen.

Faintly she could hear the sounds of men's voices, but they were outside.

"Amy!"

Her cry came back to her in echoes, one after the other, as if she were faced with a multitude of caverns.

Amy, Amy, Amy ...

Then she thought she heard Amy answer, and she hesitated again, but the sound was not repeated.

She was faced with four different ways to go. To turn right would take her closer to the wall, the outside wall, so she discarded it quickly, and to go straight ahead would take her toward the front right corner.

If she turned left, and then took the angle to the right, it would take her, hopefully, toward the center.

The center, the room that was crazy, the place she had first seen the clowns. They would be there, those clowns, for they were leading Amy to the center of the maze.

Because of the necklace, they were leading her to ...

Panic boiled into her chest and throat.

But there was no use calling again. Amy would not answer. She had been hypnotized. She didn't know what she was doing.

"Oh, Amy," Jodi cried beneath her breath, and began to run down the passage that she felt would lead her to the central room. With her hands out to touch the glass, she turned when the passage turned, trying to remember never to turn back.

She became confused. Everywhere she looked the light of the ceiling was reflected, and the little girl in the pajamas with the blond hair loose on her shoulders like Alice in Wonderland, only this wasn't Wonderland, this was ... a nether world, where gods like Hades ruled ... a world of crazy mirrors where children were lost and never found, a dark world of swirling waters and black tree trunks and clowns with terrible faces. It wanted Amy, this world, Amy and the necklace. It was the necklace that had caused it all. And Jodi had found the necklace, and it was because of her that this world wanted her sister—because she had the bad necklace.

She had to stop Amy from going into this world.

"Amy!" she screamed again, and the echoes replied, Amy, Amy ...

"Where are you, Amy?"

She was crying, and this bad world waved and undulated beyond her tears.

She stopped long enough to see if Amy would answer, but she heard only the shouts of the men and the pounding of their footsteps as they entered at the front door.

She could hear Zulu shouting, "Branch out! Go that way! Close in on the central room!"

So Zulu knew too.

Jodi ran again, turning inward, always inward, discarding the corridors that seemed they would lead her to the outer edge of the maze, or to the front or back.

The corridors became shorter, and she knew she was closer to the center, and the mirrors became, oddly, brighter, more reflecting, with more worlds and brighter lights, and the lights began to look like colored strobe lights, whirling somewhere, and the heat was building.

She could feel a terrible, smothering heat.

She could hardly get her breath as she turned another corner.

The huge, dark, winged creature came out of the mirrored ceiling, swooping down at Jodi's head. She ducked, but in silence, her fear an internal force that no longer gave voice. She could hear its wings beating in a hot, stale air as it swept past her, and she could hear it turn and come back.

She crouched, flattening herself on the floor with her arms over her head, and she felt the hot swish of its passing and the stench of its smell, and then it flew on, into the infinity of the mirror world ahead. She lifted her face and watched it fly away, and it was like something out of prehistory, when winged creatures were beginning to fly the skies, back before the world changed.

The bitter gall of fear was in her throat and weakening her limbs, but she had to rise and find Amy.

She was close to the central room now, she knew. The thing with wings lived only near the central room.

She got to her feet and ran again, her hand out to the right to guide herself.

There was another corner, then suddenly she was in a large arena of distorted images, of mirrors that wobbled and twisted and turned, as if they were alive. The ceiling rose to a peak of thousands of slivers of glass, and Jodi was reminded of the necklace. It was built like the necklace.

But there was something she hadn't seen before.

A stairway. It rose from the other side of the enormous-looking room, the room with the endlessness, with no walls, only the distortions, and it too was made of glass that reflected. Almost invisible, it rose straight up into the peak of the cathedral ceiling.

Amy was standing at the foot of the stairs looking up.

And going ahead of her up the stairs was one of the clowns, while at the top, or what seemed like it should be the top, sat the winged, dark creature, its small, shrunken human head drooped between the shoulders of wings, black, rough wings that reached folded down to the human-like feet that curled around a mirrored perch.

The creature seemed to be hundreds of steps upward, and Amy began to climb.

"No," Jodi screamed. "Amy, please, don't! Amy! Amy!"

Amy paused, turned, and looked down at Jodi.

Jodi rushed forward, her hands out reaching for Amy, to pull her back, to drag her away if only she could reach her.

Jodi came forcefully up against a wall of glass.

It knocked her back, and when she rose, she saw that Amy had turned away and was again climbing the stairway, her face raised toward the creature at the top.

Jodi began trying to feel her way around this deception, this sheet of glass that was not a mirror.

Then she saw the clowns.

They were coming at her from all directions. The clown with the full white ruffle around his neck, with the painted white mouth that looked as if it hid needle-sharp fangs, was reaching toward her with his curved hands, the white gloves that suddenly were no longer white but stained red with the blood of Blane.

The other clowns, the scarecrow clown, the Rube clown, the witches' faces, the horrible faces that India had bought in stores that sold horror masks, were closing in. And the empty slits of the eyes stared at Jodi as they came toward her, and she was surrounded.

Forced now to try to save herself, she fought for a way out.

She felt the iron strength of the white, blood-stained gloves lift her into the air as if she weighed no more than a feather.

She gave one last, tortured scream.

At the sound of her voice Amy turned.

ZULU FOLLOWED THE WHITE LINE, his eyes on the line, knowing that if he raised his head he could be confused. As confused as the other men who were trying to find their way through the maze toward the central room.

Toward the room where the clown shows had taken place over half a century ago.

He heard Jodi crying out for Amy, and then he heard a silence, and it chilled him more than the calls.

Then came her scream, and he knew if he didn't hurry it would be her last cry in this world, for it was a wordless scream of desperation, the kind of scream that no man or animal could fail to interpret.

The line ended in the central room.

But in amazement at what he saw, Zulu stopped. For just an instant he stopped and looked at the changed room.

There were no longer any boundaries. The distortion of the mirrors went away into infinity, and the lights had changed. Instead of one light, there were thousands, it seemed, all colors, probing the endlessness of this space with their blazing eyes, yet within it was a darkness, a shadowy quality, and a heat that rushed at Zulu and almost knocked him back.

He had entered hell itself, he thought, the only thought that entered his head as the scene in front of him played itself into his mind.

A thousand clowns, it seemed, distorted, horrible, had lifted a child, one child, that in the walls looked limp and dead, her limbs twisted and broken, but the child in the clowns' hands was so far still alive. They were holding her over their heads, while beyond, Amy was climbing an endless stairway, and glittering in her hand, as if it were an offering, was a tiny jewel of mirrors, created to match the cathedral ceiling of this room.

She was offering the talisman to a creature perched on a glass rung far up the staircase. She was walking upward as if drawn inexorably into the world ahead.

The clowns moved, suddenly, unexpectedly, and the small body of Jodi was slammed to the floor.

Several other men had entered the central room, and they stood as if turned to glass themselves, staring, and the silence was as endless as the walls except for the one series of sounds.

Her bones broke, her head, against the floor, split open, her skin was split from her body. Her blood squirted and ran, small rivers carrying the last of her heartbeats.

Zulu heard these sounds.

As if they were magnified in the horror of the distorted world.

He even heard the bursting of her heart.

He screamed a scream of fury, and he raised the knife and threw it, and it went through the mask of the clown India had called Joey. The mask split open and lay in two slices, one hanging on one side of the ruffled neck and the other hanging askew down the back.

There was nothing within the mask.

Zulu pushed through the clowns and grabbed up the long-bladed knife and began slashing at them, while their hands tore like talons through his clothes and into his skin. With blood streaming down his body in tiny rivulets, with his cries reduced to grunts, he slashed at the clowns, tearing costumes and masks to shreds, empty pieces of material that finally fell inert.

The costumes lay empty on the floor, surrounding the bloody body of Jodi like strange, silky, dead flowers thrown upon a grave.

Zulu turned.

He looked upward to where the other child slowly, woodenly turned, and began climbing the mirrored staircase again. She was about three fourths of the way up, and the creature at the top was leaning forward, its wings beginning to lift out from its body, its shriveled, human-like face reaching toward the necklace the girl held out in her hand.

With a roar of fury and terror Zulu began climbing the staircase he had never known for certain was there at all. He put a foot up and found the step a normal height, and the strain on his legs was an effort of pain.

He cried out, "No! Amy! No!"

God only knew if she heard, because she kept on going, and she was within four steps of the top, then three.

Zulu climbed up, his body struggling with the steps that seemed to grow higher and more difficult. He screamed at the child again, using needed breath, and she paused.

If she would only step downward again, come toward him, but she stood still. Then her head was lifting again in response to a low call, toward the black, winged creature at the top.

Although he was close, Zulu's legs refused to climb, to reach toward heights that demanded too much of his legs. The pain raced shooting up into his body, and he fumbled for support. No banisters here on these nearly invisible stairs, no way to pull himself upward.

"Amy, come back," he cried.

She was moving upward again, slowly, one more step.

The winged horror was beginning to lift itself from the perch, reaching toward her, its humanoid beak opening, ready to take the necklace.

Then Zulu saw she was holding it out with both hands, the braided silk spread open. She was going to put it around the creature's neck.

What would happen then?

Would Raoell's power explode into being and overcome them all?

Zulu had no breath for again screaming out at Amy to withdraw. With all his efforts put into one single surge of energy, with the shredded material of the good clown suit he wore gripped in his hand, he gained a needed ounce of strength and scrambled another step nearer, nearer again to Amy.

Just before she was ready to drop the necklace over the tiny, naked, obscene head, Zulu reached her.

With his left arm he grabbed the necklace, jerking her backwards and shoving her down the mirrored stairs. And from his right hand he threw the knife at the winged thing at the top of the stairs.

The creature rose, an unearthly cry pouring from an open mouth, the wings tattered with stubby, feather-like quills, a breath of fetid heat rushing down at Zulu as the knife found its mark.

As Zulu's hand closed on the necklace, his fingers crushing the teardrop talisman, the knife fell clattering. The beast had disappeared somewhere into the top of the mirrored world.

The creature screamed a final, horrible, haunting cry that tore at the senses of all who heard, then its voice trailed to silence.

When Zulu turned and looked down the staircase was gone—and he was falling, falling ...

EPILOGUE

RUSSEL DROVE.

His pickup rattled and shook as the odometer turned over to 100 thousand miles.

He had been driving for three months, stopping here or there, he never knew where, one town or another, it didn't matter.

Still, he had not and could never drive away from the hell in his mind.

Jodi was dead. She was buried in a small cemetery up in South Dakota where others of his family lay. His ex-wife hadn't objected to letting her be there.

The only good part was that Amy had gone home to her mother, welcomed, loved.

Zulu had saved her from a fate only God—or the devil—knew. But Zulu had given his own life in the saving.

Others, the boys, India's father, the creator of the House himself—Raoell, all were still missing.

The law officers had torn the House of Mirrors apart. Every glass, every panel of mirror in the House had been crushed, but first each panel had been subjected to scientific examination, and nowhere was any one of those mirrors different from any ordinary mirror in any house, the mirror over the dresser or at the end of the hall, or the mirrors that people look into in shops when they try on clothes.

The mirrors were no different.

Even the stained mirrors in the maze that had been closed off turned out only to have an aging quality that antique mirrors get, a—he didn't remember the scientific explanation that had been given.

The house was made of mirrors, that was all.

And there was no explanation of how the clown costumes had moved with such strength, and murdered with such viciousness.

The necklace, the talisman, was gone now. Zulu had crushed it, and the broken glass shards had been discarded.

There was nothing left of it now but the silk thread.

It had been wrapped around Zulu's fingers.

So Russel drove.

And he thought constantly of the two little girls, and the years of their lives that he had missed.

Always he thought of that.

Even as he tried to understand the rest—no, he had given up on understanding any of the rest—still he thought of the years of their lives that he could never recover.

Ken, Zulu's head man, had given the silk thread to Russel.

It was all he had left.

OTHER NOVELS BY RUBY JEAN

1974 The House that Samael Built
1974 Seventh All Hallows' Eve
1974 House at River's Bend
1975 The Girl Who Didn't Die
1978 Child of Satan's House
1978 Satan's Sister
1978 Dark Angel
1982 Hear the Children Cry
1982 Such a Good Baby
1983 The Lake
1983 MaMa
1985 Home Sweet Home
1985 Best Friends
1986 Wait and See
1987 Annabelle
1987 Chain Letter
1988 Smoke
1988 House of Illusions
1988 Jump Rope
1989 Pendulum
1989 Death Stone

1990 Vampire Child
1990 Lost and Found
1990 Victoria
1991 Celia
1991 Baby Dolly
1992 The Reckoning
1993 The Living Evil
1994 The Haunting
1995 Night Thunder
Pending Bear Hollow Charlie
Pending Cry of the Soul
Pending Pride of Bella Terra
Pending Animal Backtalk